PRAISE FOR
STAR TREK TITAN: TAKING WING
BY MICHAEL A. MARTIN AND ANDY MANGELS

"Martin and Mangels wisely know how to balance the character introductions and byplay against a well-written story . . . [and] how to balance the action with the character moments. . . . *Taking Wing* is a great first novel in the new *Titan* series. . . . It's a solid tale rich with character exploration and action, and its follow-up installments should be just as exciting. Sit back and enjoy!"
—Bill Williams, trekweb.com

"*Taking Wing* is full of surprises. Thoroughly engaging from beginning to end, the story satisfies on every level. . . . It is always very rewarding when a book you've been anticipating lives up to expectations. It's even better when the book exceeds them. *Star Trek Titan: Taking Wing* is a superb debut for an original new series."
—Jackie Bundy, treknation.com

"Based on this first novel, I can't wait for the follow-up."
—Kilian Melloy, wigglefish.com

STAR TREK
TITAN™

THE RED KING
ANDY MANGELS
AND MICHAEL A. MARTIN

Based upon STAR TREK® and
STAR TREK: THE NEXT GENERATION®
created by Gene Roddenberry

POCKET BOOKS
New York   London   Toronto   Sydney   Starbase 185

An *Original* Publication of POCKET BOOKS

 POCKET BOOKS, a division of Simon & Schuster, Inc.
1230 Avenue of the Americas, New York, NY 10020

This book is a work of fiction. Names, characters, places and incidents are products of the authors' imaginations or are used fictitiously. Any resemblance to actual events or locales or persons, living or dead, is entirely coincidental.

ISBN-13: 978-0-7434-9628-5
ISBN-10:   0-7434-9628-0

This Pocket Books paperback edition October 2005

10 9 8 7 6 5 4 3 2 1

POCKET and colophon are registered trademarks of Simon & Schuster, Inc.

Cover art by Cliff Nielsen
Cover design by John Vairo, Jr.

Manufactured in the United States of America

For information regarding special discounts for bulk purchases, please contact Simon & Schuster Special Sales at 1-800-456-6798 or business@simonandschuster.com.

While working on this book,
I had the opportunity to serve my local community
in fundraising and leadership arenas.
Many people gave me immense support,
and I dedicate this book to Marc Hoffman,
Steve Suss, Jerry Dahlke, and Rick Watkins & Les Lewis.
Gentlemen and friends,
may your ships always sail true.
—A.M.

This is for: my wife, Jenny,
whose patience during the writing of this volume
deserves special recognition here;
and the space visionaries at NASA,
the Jet Propulsion Laboratory,
and the European Space Agency
who this very year successfully landed
the Huygens probe on Saturn's moon Titan,
thereby providing humanity's first glimpse of the surface
of our eponymous starship's mysterious namesake.
—M.A.M.

If seeds in the black Earth can turn into such beautiful roses, what might not the heart of man become in its long journey towards the stars?

—G. K. CHESTERTON (1874–1936)

Penetrating so many secrets, we cease to believe in the unknowable. But there it is, nevertheless, calmly licking its chops.

—H. L. MENCKEN (1880–1956)

"He's dreaming now," said Tweedledee: "and what do you think he's dreaming about?"

Alice said "Nobody can guess that."

"Why, about *you!*" Tweedledee exclaimed, clapping his hands triumphantly. "And if he left off dreaming about you, where do you suppose you'd be?"

"Where I am now, of course," said Alice.

"Not *you!*" Tweedledee retorted contemptuously. "You'd be nowhere. Why, you're only a sort of thing in his dream!"

"If that there King was to wake," added Tweedledum, "you'd go out—bang!—just like a candle!"

"I shouldn't!" Alice exclaimed indignantly. "Besides, if *I'm* only a sort of thing in his dream, what are *you*, I should like to know?"

—LEWIS CARROLL, AKA CHARLES LUTWIDGE DODGSON
(1832–1898), *Through the Looking-Glass and What Alice Found There*

ACKNOWLEDGMENTS

The authors owe an enormous debt of gratitude to: John Logan, Rick Berman, and Brent Spiner, whose collaborations on the story and screenplay for *Star Trek Nemesis* not only gave Will Riker his much-deserved fourth pip, as well as command of the good ship *Titan*, but also allowed us to pen the untold tale of the Riker-Troi honeymoon in Keith R. A. DeCandido's recently released *Tales from the Captain's Table* anthology; Jeff Mariotte, whose *Deny Thy Father* chronicled an important chapter in Riker family history; John Vornholt, Dayton Ward & Kevin Dilmore, Robert Greenberger, David Mack, and Keith R. A. DeCandido, the authors of the *A Time To* series of novels, whose collective work so adroitly teed up *Titan*'s maiden voyage; fellow *Titan* author Christopher L. Bennett for critical insight and sfnal inspiration; Diane Duane, whose novel *The Wounded Sky* introduced the concept of de Sitter space to the (literary) *Star Trek* universe more than two decades ago; Jeri Taylor, whose novels *Mosaic* and *Pathways* provided some valuable insights into Tuvok's past; Chris Cooper, who wrote the *Star Trek: Star Fleet Academy* series (Marvel Comics, 1996–1998), which chronicled the early career of Lieutenant Pava Ek'Noor (sh')Aqabaa; legendary TOS scenarist Dorothy Fontana, who midwifed a little bundle of joy named L. J. Akaar (in the TOS episode "Friday's Child"); the inimitable band leader Dominic James "Nick" La Rocca (1889–1961), whose Original Dixieland Jass (Jazz) Band did much to popularize Captain Riker's musical instrument of choice, and served as the namesake for one of *Titan*'s auxiliary vessels; the many fans who told us how much they enjoyed *Taking Wing* while the follow-on volume that now rests in your hands was still largely incomplete; and Marco Palmieri, who believed we were up to the task of launching Captain William T. Riker's first permanent command, who always immeasurably improves every manuscript he touches, and who never fails to make us look like geniuses.

CHAPTER ONE

SMALL MAGELLANIC CLOUD, 7 JANUARY 2380 (AULD GREG AERTH CALENDAR)

"**B**ehold," Frane said, unable to keep a slight tremor of awe out of his voice. *Or is it fear?* he wondered in some deep, shrouded corner of his soul.

But the vista that stretched before the assembled Seekers After Penance took Frane to a place far beyond fear. It was the most beautiful and terrible sight he had ever beheld. Effulgent tendrils of energy reached across millions of klomters of trackless emptiness toward the battered transport craft, like the probing fingers of some great, grasping hand.

Frane heard Nozomi gasp as she cowered behind him, as though the image threatened to reach straight through the cramped vessel's viewer and grab her.

"Have faith," Frane said. As a Neyel who had forsworn his own people's conquest-hardened traditions to live among society's slaves and outcasts, he knew well that faith was often the only thing that sustained him. To comfort Nozomi, he took one of her hands even as her graceful forked tail gently entwined with his. He gently disengaged from the female Neyel after noticing that one of her feet was grasping his leg hard enough to whiten the gray flesh beneath his loose pilgrim's robe.

"I'm keeping station here," said Lofi, the female Sturr who was handling the helm as well as the sensor station. Because she belonged to a race of multipartite colony creatures—one of the first local peoples, in fact, to be conquered by the ancestral Neyel after their arrival centuries ago in M'jallanish space—Lofi was able to separate several of her rounded thoracic segments briefly in order to perform disparate simultaneous tasks. Looking toward Lofi, Frane considered how this ability had made the Sturr species so useful to the earliest, most expansion-bent generations of precursor Neyel, the eldest Oh-Neyel Takers who spread throughout the M'jallan region to build the Neyel Hegemony on the backs of dozens of conquered slave races.

Will my people ever expiate the shame of those sinful days? Frane wondered. He feared he already knew the answer.

Eager to chase those dark thoughts away, Frane turned his gaze back toward the great, slowly coruscating starburst of energy that filled the screen before him. He saw that the image was holding the attention of everyone else in the narrow, dimly lit control room.

"Can't we approach it more closely?" g'Ishea said, cuddling up against Fasaryl, her mate. Members of an indigenous species that had been displaced—and then largely slaughtered—to make room for the shining Neyel capital of Mechulak City and the other great metrosprawls of the Neyel Coreworld, g'Ishea and Fasaryl had never known a time when their kind had been free to graze unhindered. Frane could only wonder what it was like to live as a forced laborer on what had once been a bucolic paradise, toiling endlessly beneath the Neyel lash and the lidless eye of Holy Vangar, the Stone Skyworld that had orbited their planet since the times of the First Conquests. How would it be, he wondered, to live that way for a dozen generations without any hope of freedom?

Frane cast a questioning glance at Lofi—or rather at the globular, leathery portion of Lofi to which her primary sensory cluster was attached.

"I would advise not getting any nearer to it than this," Lofi responded, an overtone of fear coming through the vocoder that rendered her guttural native utterances into Neyel-intelligible speech. "That phenomenon is throwing off spatial distortions like nothing I've ever seen before. I can't guarantee this ship will hold together if I let us drift any closer to them."

"Disappointing," Frane said, though he wasn't completely certain that he meant it.

"I'm more than happy to keep my distance," said Nozomi in a quavering voice. Her tail was wrapping nervously around Frane's waist again. He brushed the prehensile appendage aside with his own.

Frane turned toward her, prepared to offer a waspish observation about her tiresome, almost theatrical displays of faintheartedness. Why couldn't she keep her fears to herself, as he did?

"Why has this appeared?" Fasaryl said, pointing the opposable digits of one of his front hooves toward the tendrils of energy displayed on the screen.

"You know why, beloved," g'Ishea said, worrying her dewlap with her wide, rough tongue. "Because the Sleeper has at last begun to awaken." Though g'Ishea's low voice sounded calm, the gurgling noise emanating from her multiple digestive organs told Frane otherwise.

"So everyone keeps saying," Fasaryl said, clearly unsatisfied with the obvious answer.

Since the puzzling energetic phenomenon had abruptly appeared several weeks earlier, just pars'x from the very Coreworld itself, the Neyel intelligentsia had offered countless theories to account for it, as had the clergy, both on the cultural fringe and in the mainstream. To some it was a rare instance of interspatial slippage between adjoining regions of subspace. To others it was merely the beginning of yet another iteration of the cycle of cosmic death and rebirth, a phase that would take the universe billions more years to pass through entirely. To others it was merely a localized natural disaster, a thing of rare beauty and thankfully even rarer violence.

Frane knew that some saw the vast, multihued energy eruption as a cause for fearful rejoicing, because it had destroyed but a single Neyel-settled world.

So far, he thought.

Or was the expansive, colorful energy bloom, as those of a more secular bent had suggested, merely a temporary reopening of one of the long-neglected spatial rifts through which the Devilships of the Tholians had launched their savage attacks some ten generations back?

Frane felt certain he knew the true answer to the mystery. The real nature of the thing on the screen. And he knew that the other Seekers After Penance, the natives who had traveled with him to the ragged edge of this lovely, savage manifestation, shared his certainty deep down, regardless of their fears and doubts of the moment. Their own peoples, after all, had compiled the stories, had told and retold them for uncounted thousands of planetary cycles.

This blaze of unimaginable forces was nothing less

than the Sleeper of M'jallanish legend, stirring at last from His aeons-long slumbers. And Frane was here to witness it.

Maybe we haven't come merely to watch *the Awakening,* he told himself, almost overwhelmed at the purity and audacity of his purpose now that he was finally able to stare directly down the maw of the Infinite. *Perhaps we have come to help bring it about.*

So that the Neyel, Frane's own people, might atone for the many crimes they had committed against virtually every sentient species they'd met in M'jallanish space—at least before Aidan Burgess had come all the way from Auld Aerth and tried to show the Neyel the gross error of their ways.

The Seekers After Penance revered Federation Ambassador Burgess, and it was their devoir to complete what she had begun: to continue teaching the entire Neyel race the lessons of peace to which the long-dead, martyred diplomat had introduced them. Even if the aim of those lessons—atonement—cost the lives of everyone who had participated in the Neyel Conquests. Even if their heirs who perpetuated those injustices even now, knowingly or not, had to suffer—along with native peoples too weak-willed to have even tried to oppose their conquerors.

"Is it true, Frane?" Fasaryl asked. "Is it true that every world in the M'jallan Cloud will vanish when the Sleeper finally comes fully awake?"

Frane nodded. "So say the legends of the His'lant. And those of the Sturr. And the tales of your ancient Oghen forebears as well."

"The His'lant Taletellers say that the Sleeper dreams all the worlds in the Cloud," said Nozomi. "And when the Sleeper awakens—"

"The dream ends," Frane said, finishing her thought. *Along with every evil act our people have ever perpetrated against those worlds.*

Fasaryl shrugged his thick, bovine shoulders. "Or so say the stories. We won't know until and unless it happens."

"We already know that the Sleeper stirs," said g'Ishea, nodding toward the colorful energy pinwheel that now lay just a few hundred thousand klomters before them. "And that stirring has already wiped out at least one whole world. After Newaerth's disappearance, I need no further convincing."

Frane nodded grimly. The truth of g'Ishea's words was undeniable. Newaerth was no more, having vanished cataclysmically along with its entire planetary system, within days of the initial appearance of the colorful spatial distortions—a beautiful blue world, settled only a century after the arrival of the ancestral Neyel in the Lesser M'jallan Cloud, extinguished by the stirrings of the Sleeper.

"Perhaps the Sleeper will spare us if we conduct the propitiation rituals," Nozomi said in a quiet, frightened voice.

Unlike Nozomi, Frane had no realistic expectations of being spared whatever divine wrath was about to engulf the entire region. Nor did he believe himself particularly worthy of any such mercies. But he was ready and willing to undertake the meditative ritual, if only on behalf of his companions, whose faith in the efficacy of the ancient native rites clearly exceeded his own. After all, why should his fellow travelers face summary death when it was *his* forebears, not theirs, who had truly earned the ire of the cosmos?

While still tending to the ship's instruments, Lofi detached one of her scaly, rainbow-colored thoracic segments. Its multijointed arms and sensory clusters immediately set about arranging the ritual materials on the deck before the viewer. Scuttling to and fro with purposeful deftness, she covered about a square metrik with a precise arrangement of colorful soils from the Sturr homeworld, mixing them with several large droplets of her own viscous body fluids, secreted directly from glands hidden beneath the arms of her independently operating body segment.

Frane lowered his head, his eyeshutters closing out the vaguely disturbing ritual as Fasaryl began to make a gentle lowing sound. His song chilled the base of Frane's spine; he knew that the archaic words Fasaryl sang were far older than the Neyel's most ancient ancestors from Auld Aerth.

Fasaryl reached the end of the ritual utterances within the space of a few dozen heartbeats, as though in anticipation of something momentous. Frane glanced upward, opening his eyeshutters enough to see the energy tendrils that remained displayed on the screen. The image was unchanged. The Oghen repeated the words again, and Lofi's artificial voice joined in, forming an oddly tinny counterpoint to Fasaryl's mournful, bass-laden chant.

The image on the screen continued its slow, stately pirouette, stubbornly constant. *What was I expecting?* Frane thought, chuckling quietly to himself. *Was the Sleeper supposed to answer our prayers? Did I really expect Him to come fully awake right at this moment and promise to save us from the destruction that's coming down upon us?*

There would be no engraved invitations to watch the apocalypse from some safe cosmic balcony. When the Sleeper finally awoke, when its mystical dreams no longer served to sustain the very existence of M'jallanish space,

Frane expected to wink out of existence along with everything else within at least a hundred pars'x—just as the ancient His'lant physicist-priests had foretold.

An alarm whooped loudly at that moment, startling Frane out of his doleful reverie. Nozomi jumped high at the sound, her tail and bare feet instinctively grabbing purchase on one of the control room's ceiling-mounted gangways.

"Frane!" said Lofi, an unusual urgency underlying her customarily even, synthetic voice. "I am detecting several ships, closing rapidly on the energy cloud. They are headed straight for us."

A knot of apprehension began to form in Frane's stomach. "What kind of ships?"

"Neyel military, cylindrical configuration. They're warning us to stand down, and to prepare to be teleported aboard their flagship." Lofi turned an eyestalk directly toward him. "They're asking for you specifically, Frane."

The knot in Frane's belly suddenly tightened like an ancient slavecatcher's noose. He could think of only one military officer who would have asked for him by name.

"Bring the male Neyel prisoner directly to me," Drech'tor Gherran said, his eyes remaining fixed upon the strange phenomenon that covered his main control room's central viewer. He glanced away from the coruscating cloud, looking down at the bracelet of exotic shells and stones and fabric that adorned his left wrist.

"And the woman?" replied Harn, his ever-efficient helmrunner and subaltern. If Harn had noticed how distracted Gherran was feeling at the moment, he betrayed no sign of it.

"Leave her in confinement with the indigies," Gherran

said, gently caressing the bracelet with the spade-shaped tip of his tail.

Harn looked slightly askance at Gherran's order, but dutifully moved to the communications panel on the opposite side of the control room, where he began carrying out his instructions. Crisply and efficiently, as ever.

Moments later, a pair of black-uniformed Neyel security officers exited the lift tube, a slight, robed figure herded between them, his hands bound behind his back. The guards looked confused at having been told to bring their charge to the ship's sensitive control room.

The prisoner seemed far too calm for someone in such a vulnerable position. But that came as no surprise to Gherran.

"Release his bindings," Gherran said. "Then leave us."

"Sir?" said the senior guard, his eyeshutters opening and closing rapidly in surprise.

"Do it!"

The guards hastened to comply, and seconds later had withdrawn from the control room. The handful of instrumentation officers present watched discreetly as the prisoner stepped toward Gherran, rubbing his just-freed wrists as he moved.

"Are you going to interrogate me here, Drech'tor Gherran, right in front of everyone?" the prisoner said in what the drech'tor recognized as a mocking tone. He gestured toward Harn and the other members of the control room crew. Each of them immediately looked away, conspicuously busying themselves at their various consoles.

Gherran pointed toward a hatchway located equidistant between the lift tube and the head. "In my prep chamber. *Now.*"

The prisoner shrugged and did as he was told. After the hatch had closed, ensuring their privacy, the robed detainee turned toward him, the hard gray skin of his mouth turning up slightly at the corners. "Hello, Father," he said, an insufferable irony suffusing his words.

"What do you think you're doing out here, Frane?" Gherran said, struggling to keep his son from seeing how angry he was. He doubted he was succeeding even a little.

"Perhaps I should ask you the same question, Father."

Gherran sighed, shaking his head. "You know perfectly well that the Hegemony Navy can't permit interlopers to approach the . . . phenomenon."

"Why, Father? Are you afraid we're going to rouse the Sleeper further?"

Gherran snorted, his tail switching involuntarily behind him. "Nonsense. There's no Sleeper, Frane. Only ridiculous native legends, kept alive by the fantasy-prone offspring of slaves. And enabled by gullible, bleeding-heart Neyel trash like you."

"How can you be so certain that the Sleeper's dreams aren't *really* all that keeps M'jallanish space intact, Father? Do you have a better explanation for what happened to Newaerth?"

Gherran decided he wasn't going to let himself be baited. "Why are you traveling with those smelly cattle, and the rest of those alien *kaffir*, Frane?"

Frane was finally beginning to look rattled, which Gherran found gratifying. "We Neyel are the aliens here, Father. And those '*kaffir*' are my friends."

"Then you have made a very poor choice of friends," Gherran said with a long-suffering sigh. Certainly, he wasn't proud of the excesses of the earliest generations of Neyel. Their tradition of treating native species roughly— a habit developed during the years immediately following their accidental exile from Auld Aerth, when their day-to-day survival had been uncertain in the extreme—hadn't really begun to soften until the days of Ambassador Burgess, more than eighty Oghencycles ago.

"What are you planning to do with my friends, Father?"

Gherran offered his son what he hoped was a beneficent smile. "Once our patrol is done, they will be turned over to the civilian authorities on Oghen. The vessel in which we found you all has been reported stolen. If your friends were involved in the theft, they will be punished accordingly."

Now Frane looked truly distraught; piracy, after all, was punished in the most severe and irrevocable fashion possible. "Let them go. I'm the one at fault. I'm the one who stole that ship."

"We shall see in due course, my son," Gherran said, his eyes once again straying to the bracelet wrapped around his left wrist. The bracelet had been in the family for eight generations prior to his own, handed down from Gran Vil'ja, who had received it directly from Federation Ambassador Burgess herself. Every tiny stone and shell and bone and gem and fiber woven into the bracelet's cloth-and-metal frame represented a story added by each successive generation that had held it. The bracelet itself was an unbroken tapestry that reached all the way back to the far distant Great Pinwheel of Milkyway—and the un-reachable orb of Auld Aerth itself.

Gherran saw that his son, too, was eyeing the bracelet. "I must be a great disappointment to you, Father," Frane said quietly. "Who will you appoint to carry the story bracelet forward into future generations?"

Gherran felt righteous indignation rising within him. "I thought that your bizarre death cult didn't believe in future generations."

Frane shrugged. "Look beyond the hull of this vessel.

Whether or not there will be a future doesn't appear to be up to us at the moment." He looked significantly at the bracelet. "Perhaps you should send our family heirloom somewhere safer than this place."

Gherran raised his wrist, brandishing the bracelet as though it were a weapon. "Do not mock tradition, Frane. Someone in our lineage must eventually get the bracelet back to Auld Aerth, as Gran Vil'ja and Burgess Herself intended. You know that, at least as well as you know the silly precepts of your sleeping *kaffir* god."

"I suppose we each have always embraced myths of our own choosing, Father," Frane said, smiling. "Mother always said that you and I were very much alike in that regard."

Gherran felt his teeth bare themselves involuntarily. He knew that the death of Lijean, Frane's mother, had devastated both of them equally. Though more than half a decade had passed since the shock of her suicide, Lijean's absence remained both an unhealed wound and a cause for mutual blame. Even now, her death remained a weapon that both of them still used against one another from time to time.

"How dare you—"

The ship lurched violently, its abrupt movement punctuated by the sharp cry of an alarm klaxon. Harn's strident yet controlled voice blared across the intraship circuit. *"Tactical alert! Drech'tor Gherran to the control room!"*

Frane had never before seen his father move so quickly. Gherran used his tail and all four of his opposable-digited hands to vault across his desk and bound through the hatchway back into the control room. Not quite as physically robust as his father—he lacked Gherran's extensive military conditioning—Frane followed more slowly, though he moved as quickly as he could.

Frane could see that his father had all but forgotten about him as he queried the members of his crew, each of whom worked at least one console with a fervid intensity. *No surprise that he's ignoring me,* Frane thought. *Duty always did take precedence over family, even when there weren't any emergencies to deal with.* Not for the first time, he wondered if Mother had taken her own life out of sheer neglect and loneliness.

The great cylindrical vessel rocked again beneath Frane's bare feet, prompting him to turn to face the wide viewer that filled the forward portion of the control room.

The energy bloom was . . . *changing.*

"Report!" Gherran shouted to his crew as the room shuddered yet again.

"We're being subjected to intense gravimetric waves, Drech'tor," said the young male officer seated at the nearest console. The tip of his tail was assisting his hands as he hastily entered commands. "They're coming from deep within the phenomenon."

"Ship's status?" Gherran queried.

"Our energy screens are compromised and failing, Drech'tor."

The tendrils of multihued energy shown on the viewer were becoming more agitated and twisted, gnarled like the native scrub vegetation of the Coreworld of Oghen.

Frane allowed a fatalistic smile to cross his face. *Perhaps the Sleeper truly* is *awakening at last.*

He knew that if such was indeed the case, then his own petty family squabbles, as well as the suffering of every species the Neyel race had conquered over the past several centuries, would soon be rendered moot.

Is today the day when it all finally comes to pass, as the prophets of the ancient M'jallan races foretold?

"Hail the fleet, Subaltern," Gherran said. "We're withdrawing to a safer distance. I want to put another million klomters between us and the phenomenon."

But before the subaltern could finish carrying out his orders, Frane noticed something else on the screen. Several dark, swooping shapes were approaching.

Unlike Father's fleet, however, they seemed to be approaching from *inside* the now-roiling energy bloom.

"Drech'tor!" shouted another junior officer, this one a young female. "A number of ships are closing on our position—and their source is the energy phenomenon itself." She shook her head in disbelief.

Gherran was facing the screen. Though his face was a grim, gray mask, he could not keep the surprise out of his voice. "That's not possible."

Frane felt equally surprised. Watching the approaching ships, he supposed his father was recalling old tales of the Tholian Devilships that had preyed on Neyel vessels many decades ago, before Ambassador Burgess had crafted a peace arrangement with them, before both sides had agreed to allow the interspatial fissures that had connected their two distant realms to close from simple disuse.

"How many ships approach us?" the drech'tor wanted to know.

"Several dozen, Drech'tor," the subaltern said. "And I have detected directed-energy weapons signatures."

A raptor's smile cracked Gherran's military impassivity as he cast a brief glance at Frane. "So. We face no sleeping god here, do we? We are up against a new wave of invaders. The Devilships of old." To his subaltern, he barked, "Level one tactical alert. Make challenge as we fall back. And charge all weapons batteries. Be ready to fire on my command."

"No response to our challenges, Drech'tor," said another junior officer a few moments later, her voice hard and businesslike.

As the alien ships grew swiftly larger on the screen, Frane's initial impression of them became ever stronger. With their sleek, winged shapes and iridescent gray-green hulls, they truly *did* resemble nothing so much as a flock of predatory birds on the hunt. And they were bearing down on Gherran's ships, flying in a wedge-shaped formation that implied a merciless sense of purpose. Frane couldn't help but admire their grace and coordination as they moved as one, as though guided by a single, resolutely determined mind.

"They don't look like any Devilships I ever saw," Frane said to no one in particular, and no one replied. Neither he nor his father had been alive during the Devil Wars that Burgess had ended, but they had both seen pictures from that era.

Each of the alien ships' forward weapons tubes now emanated a menacing emerald glow. As the interlopers drew closer, Frane could see several small but agile Neyel destroyers approaching them on a gently curving intercept course. At Gherran's direction, the forward tubes of the Neyel ships released a lethal braid of bright red particle beams and a fusillade of armored projectiles.

The initial Neyel salvo seemed to have little effect on its targets, whose own glowing weapons ports responded by unleashing powerful streams of directed energy. The alien vessels' armaments blazed as brightly as the heart of a star, forcing Frane to look away momentarily, despite the viewer's light-filtering system.

A sidelong glance moments later confirmed the worst: the aliens were tearing through Gherran's ships as though they were defenseless. Within moments, three destroyers had flared up in roughly spherical, roseate eruptions of fire, vessel and crew alike vaporized in an instant commingling of molecular fire and hard vacuum.

As Gherran rattled his terse, precise orders to his own control room staff, the foremost of the alien ships loosed their weapons for a second salvo, their formation passing by without so much as pausing, as though their opposition was unworthy of the invaders' valuable time. A loud BOOM! shook the control room, as though the vessel it drove had just collided with an asteroid. The deck lurched perhaps forty-five degrees before the inertial compensators set things more or less right. Frane instinctively grabbed a nearby railing, which glowed in the suddenly dimmed lighting. His tail wrapped tightly about one of the railing posts as an added measure of security.

The ship rocked yet again, ringing like some great duranium bell as a console exploded nearby, singeing Frane's hair and causing his eyeslits to slam shut involuntarily. Fierce heat scorched him, even through his hardened Neyel skin.

When he opened his eyes, he saw clouds of acrid-smelling coolant hissing into the smoky air as various crew members busied themselves putting out fires all around the control room, while simultaneously running the ship's defensive and offensive systems. On the viewer, another pair of Neyel ships tore themselves apart, their extensive battle wounds finally yielding terminal conflagrations.

Coughing, his stinging eyes watering, Frane noticed a pair of bodies sprawled beside the wreckage of the exploded console, both in the unmistakably awkward postures of death.

One of the corpses belonged to his father.

Not knowing what else to do, Frane knelt beside Gherran, feeling for his carotid artery. His father, the man who had sired and then abandoned him and his mother in favor of his endless duties to a corrupt and belligerent Hegemony, now lay lifeless on the soot-smeared deck. He took one of Gherran's still, gray hands.

And noticed the bracelet.

Without knowing why he was doing it, Frane took the bracelet and slipped it into a pocket in his robe. He was, after all, his father's son. And that meant he was next in line to take possession of the bracelet, whether future generations were fated to be or not. *If the Sleeper wakes and wipes us all from existence, then this will all be moot anyway,* he thought, not certain whether the act of taking the bracelet represented faith or its repudiation. Perhaps that, too, didn't matter.

Frane noticed only then that his father's subaltern—Harn, was it?—was shouting at him, his words only barely comprehensible over the blare of klaxons, the beating of Frane's own heart, and a surreal sense of time-dilated confusion.

"—said we have to get everyone to the evacuation capsules now!" Harn was saying, apparently annoyed at having to repeat himself. "We're about to vent our ceeteematter. Our Efti'el drive will go critical in mennets."

One of Frane's hands was still in his robe pocket, where he worried the beads and stones of the bracelet with quaking fingers. He could see the viewer, which displayed the aft sections of the dwindling alien ships; they were flying on into the space that lay beyond the stirring Sleeper, apparently uninterested in all the death they had so casually dealt. As the strange vessels receded into the distance, like a pack of hunters with sated appetites, their formation remained as perfect as the moment they had first appeared. It made Frane think of encounters with deadly, implacable forces of nature, like the Sleeper itself—encounters which were apparently survivable, at least sometimes.

But he knew he'd received only a momentary reprieve at best.

"You have to evacuate my friends," Frane shouted to the subaltern, momentarily putting aside his anticipation of the end of the world.

CHAPTER TWO

U.S.S. TITAN, STARDATE 57024.0

"There's been no mistake, Captain," Lieutenant Melora Pazlar called with an incredulous shake of her head. Her fine, pale blond hair swayed like the fronds of a shallow-water Betazoid oskoid as she floated unfettered amidst a holographic simulation of the Small Magellanic Cloud, calling attention to the microgravity that prevailed within the stellar cartography lab's broad, parabola-shaped expanse. It was an environment to which Pazlar—the lone Elaysian in *Titan*'s varied 350-member crew—was uniquely adapted, and which she insisted be maintained within the lab whenever she was present, which was most of the time.

Gripping his control padd, William Riker also drifted in freefall, a few meters away from the gentle one-sixth g that prevailed on the lab's central observation platform. He relished the rare feeling of freedom, of unrestrained, uninhibited flight among these simulacra of the stars that lay beyond *Titan*'s hull. This was a sensation alien to his ordinary experience, and he found it exhilarating. He noted that Pazlar wore only a standard duty uniform, without the antigrav exo-suit that permitted her to function in the ship's standard one-g sections. It struck him then that the lieutenant, a humanoid whose species had completely adapted to microgravity—"ordinary" one-g environments caused Elaysians excruciating pain and made antigrav technology indispensable to them in such conditions— must feel far more liberated by weightlessness than he could ever imagine.

Silhouetted against the numberless hosts of stars, as well as wide lanes of bright gas and coal-black dust, Pazlar moved with the nimble grace of a desert bird, drifting down toward the observation platform, where the other officers in attendance had gathered. As Pazlar descended, Riker saw in her eyes the verdict he was hoping most not to receive. He entered a command into his padd, and the room's network of directed forcefields responded by moving him gently toward the platform until he felt the tug of lunar gravity beneath his boots. "It turns out that our initial guesstimate was completely on target," the stellar cartographer said, hovering just out of the reach of the platform's artificial gravity. "Unfortunately."

In response to Pazlar's padd manipulations, the mass of stars on the screen abruptly receded thousands of parsecs into the intergalactic void, as though viewed from the portals of a ship capable of virtually instantaneous travel, regardless of distance. The stellar cartography lab's viewpoint had changed to a long, wide-angle view that showed the vast stellar formation from a vantage point far above its galactic north pole, with the periphery of the Milky Way looming deep in the background.

Riker had had no doubt that the readings and measurements taken by his Bajoran senior science officer, Jaza Najem—and repeated several times over the past several, emergency-filled hours—were indeed accurate, much as he would have preferred otherwise. He knew that Jaza would have asked Chaka, *Titan*'s arthropod-like Pak'shree computer specialist, to subject the initial cartographic findings to the most rigorous computer analysis regimes possible. And Dr. Cethente, a tentacled, exoskeletal Syrath with an uncommon grasp of spatial relationships, would certainly have examined all the astrophysical details very closely as well. There was simply no refuting the conclusions reached about *Titan*'s abruptly altered whereabouts.

The captain looked around the room toward the three others who had accompanied him down to stellar cartography. Fleet Admiral Leonard James Akaar wore his customary impassive expression. His iron-gray mane, which was usually pulled back into a single, tidy ponytail, trailed behind him, unfurling to shoulder length. A meter to Akaar's left, Commander Tuvok stood attentively; he was still serving as *Titan*'s temporary security chief and tactical officer while Ranul Keru lay comatose in sickbay. The Vulcan's brow was only slightly furrowed, though Riker couldn't tell whether or not this was because of Pazlar's report or something else entirely.

For much of the past day, Riker thought he had noticed a fair amount of mutual discomfort in both Akaar and Tuvok, both of whom seemed to be carefully avoiding making eye contact with one another even now. Before they had left Romulan space, Akaar had confided to Riker that a decades-old personal conflict had interrupted a close friendship between these two men, a relationship that had begun during their service together aboard Hikaru Sulu's *Excelsior* more than eighty years ago. Although the admiral hadn't revealed the specific circumstances behind this falling-out, he had given Riker the impression that both men were now prepared to let bygones be bygones;

Akaar had, after all, been eager to rescue Tuvok from Vikr'l Prison, and Tuvok had shown Akaar a Vulcan's typically reserved gratitude during their subsequent reunion aboard *Titan*.

But now, judging by the apparent unease between them, Riker was no longer so sure that they had set aside their old differences. *Maybe being married to a veteran counselor is just making me hypersensitive to body language,* he thought. *But I think I could cut the tension between those two with a* bat'leth.

"So *Titan* really *has* been tossed clear out of the galaxy," said Commander Christine Vale, *Titan*'s ever-efficient executive officer.

"The stellar-cartographic records don't lie," Pazlar said, spreading her delicate hands in a helpless gesture. She had come to a full stop along the same plane the platform occupied, though she remained a good two meters beyond the effects of its artificial gravity. "And neither do the multiple sensor-scans Jaza and Dakal did in every bandwidth all the way from subspace radio to X-rays. According to the relative locations of every pulsar detectable from here to the Milky Way's Orion Arm, we've just been thrown two hundred and ten thousand light-years from our previous position in Romulan space."

"Into a completely different galaxy," Vale said, clearly still trying to get her mind around the idea.

"We're actually well inside one of the relatively small, irregular satellite galaxies that orbits our own," Pazlar said as she entered another series of manual commands into her padd. "Elaysian astronomers refer to it as the Minor Outlier. But the more familiar Federation designation is the Small Magellanic Cloud."

The stars and nebulae and dust lanes of the Small Magellanic Cloud abruptly vanished, replaced by a much tighter view of the same place—specifically, the precise portion of the Cloud in which *Titan* was now located. The lab was filled with a holographic image of the spatial rift that had brought *Titan* here.

The multicolored, tightly braided tendrils of energy covered hundreds of thousands of kilometers of space. *Titan* had withdrawn to a position nearly seventy-five thousand klicks from what Jaza had judged to be the anomaly's event horizon. Riker had taken this precaution both to protect *Titan* from inadvertently being caught up again in the rift's embrace, and to get far enough away from the interference generated by its energetic discharges to enable the ship's sensor nets to obtain some usable scans of the thing's mysterious interior.

So far, however, the phenomenon was doing a very good job of maintaining its secrets. Riker was thankful at least that it had apparently begun to settle down during the four hours since *Titan* had been flung unceremoniously from the energy cloud's depths. The starship's bumpy passage had evidently caused considerable disruption to the phenomenon itself, judging from the initial virulence of its energy output compared to its current relatively quiet condition.

Staring up at the image, Vale sighed. "Okay. I can accept that we're here because I *have* to accept it. What I still don't understand is exactly *how* it happened."

"Evidently the spatial disturbance we were helping Commander Donatra investigate within the Romulan Empire," Tuvok said, "has the capacity to link widely distant regions of space."

"Like the stable artificial wormhole that connects the Bajor sector to the Gamma Quadrant," Akaar said.

Pazlar nodded. "It's a similar phenomenon. But also different."

"Different how?" said Riker.

"Well, in spite of the strange energetic readings the phenomenon is still giving off even now, we haven't picked up even the faintest trace of the verteron particles associated with the Bajoran wormhole. If this thing really *were* a stable artificial wormhole, it would have verterons, as Dr. Bralik might say, 'coming out the wazoo.' "

Riker cracked a small, fleeting smile at that; judging from the few brief encounters he'd already had with Bralik—and from the bits of shipboard scuttlebutt he'd overheard in the mess—he could easily imagine the ship's often salty Ferengi geologist using that very turn of phrase.

"So if it's not quite a stable wormhole, then what is it?" Vale wanted to know.

"Perhaps it is an interspatial fissure of the same type that drew *Excelsior* here eight decades ago," Tuvok ventured, casting a glance at Akaar, who nodded solemnly.

Riker considered that for a moment. He had to concede that Tuvok, a veteran of the *U.S.S. Voyager* during its seven-year Delta Quadrant sojourn, knew at least as much as he did about being hurled instantly to remote parts of the universe. So, for that matter, did Akaar, who had served alongside the Vulcan eighty years ago on *Excelsior,* the last Federation starship to visit these parts, under circumstances rather similar to those that had swept *Titan* here.

Nevertheless, he found something bothersome about Tuvok's "interspatial fissure" notion.

"I thought *Excelsior* was in the vicinity of the Tholian Assembly when it entered the rift that took it here," Riker said, recalling the decades-old reports he had reviewed shortly after *Titan*'s arrival here. He pointed up at the vast energy bloom that now filled over half of the lab's volume.

"The other end of this thing is located inside Romulan space, over three-hundred light-years away from the rift *Excelsior* encountered. It seems like quite a coincidence for two spatial rifts located so far away from each other to end up in the same place."

"Not really," Pazlar said as she typed another series of instructions into her control unit. "Not if you take into account the multidimensional interspatial topology of this part of the universe."

A complex schematic diagram replaced the image of the energy anomaly. To Riker's untrained eye it looked for all the world like a collection of thick blue pipes running into and around each other in an arrangement so busy and complex that it might have given the ancient Earth artist M. C. Escher a headache.

"What, precisely, are we looking at, Lieutenant?" Tuvok asked Pazlar, raising an eyebrow.

"A little something that Jaza, Cethente, and I spent the last two hours putting together while the computer was verifying our initial scans. It's a map of the subspace topology of a volume of space that encompasses both the Small Magellanic Cloud and most of the Alpha and Beta Quadrants of the Milky Way Galaxy. The mathematics are complex."

"No kidding," Vale said, punctuating her observation with a low whistle. "Makes me glad I never opted for the sciences track at Starfleet Academy."

Riker was growing impatient to get at the meaning of the cryptic diagram that loomed overhead. "Can you get to the point of this, Lieutenant?" he asked, gesturing toward the bizarre tubular agglomeration.

Pazlar nodded. "Certainly, Captain. The reason that two widely spaced interspatial fissures in our galaxy both ended up here, is—as near as we can tell so far—because the

Small Magellanic Cloud seems to be 'downhill' from almost every location in the Milky Way. Interspatially speaking, of course."

"Logical," said Tuvok.

Akaar nodded. "I agree."

Riker let out a low whistle of his own, wondering whether his senior science officer and stellar cartographer had just invented a mathematical proof of the nonexistence of coincidence—or if they had instead proved that coincidence itself amounted to a previously undiscovered fundamental force of nature.

"Captain, what about Donatra and her ship?" Vale asked. "The *Valdore* was only a few kilometers away from us when we were drawn into this . . . 'Great Bloom,' or whatever the hell that thing out there is. Is it possible that the Romulans were thrown here as well?"

"That's hard to say," Pazlar said. "Jaza and Dakal are still scanning for any sign of the *Valdore,* or the fleet Donatra believes she lost inside the energy rift. So far, no one has turned up so much as a scrap of debris. Either Donatra's ships all somehow managed to escape being sent here, or else the phenomenon is still generating too much interference for us to completely trust our sensor readings."

Riker hated to think that Donatra, who not only had been instrumental in the defeat of the mad Praetor Shinzon weeks ago, but had also just helped him hammer out a tenuous peace between the rival political factions in contention over control of the Romulan Star Empire, might have been killed by the same energy phenomenon that had displaced *Titan.* He also knew that until the fate of Donatra and her lost fleet was definitively understood, any attempt to return home via the rift would pose an unacceptably high risk.

"Stay on it," he told Pazlar. "I don't have any intention

of remaining out here indefinitely. We're going to get *Titan* back to the other side of that rift. But we need to make an accurate assessment of our chances of re-crossing it in one piece before we can seriously think about going back in there."

"That's Jaza's top priority," Pazlar said, sounding somber. "As well as mine, and everybody else in astro-sciences."

Silence filled the room for the next several moments, until Riker broke it. "Well, until that's worked out, we ought to spend some time considering the locals: specifi-cally, the Neyel."

" 'Locals' is perhaps not the most accurate way to de-scribe the Neyel, Captain," Akaar said. "Have you taken the time yet to read *Excelsior*'s official reports about them?"

Riker nodded. "I have, Admiral. But apart from Mr. Tuvok's original astrometric observations and Dr. Chapel's medical and biological reports, they didn't take long to read. In fact, they left me with a lot more questions than an-swers. So I'm going to have to rely on your prior experience with the Neyel." He trained his gaze on Tuvok next. "And yours as well, Commander."

Both Akaar and Tuvok nodded, but didn't look at one another.

Vale shook her head, looking embarrassed. "With the repairs I've been coordinating and all the other emergen-cies I've had to deal with since *Titan* got dumped here, I'm afraid I still know next to nothing about these Neyel— other than the fact that they're supposed to be a long-lost offshoot of terrestrial humans."

"One might accurately describe them that way," Tuvok said. "Despite their alien outward appearance, the Neyel were—*are*—entirely human at the genetic level."

"According to *Excelsior*'s reports," Riker said, "the

Neyel were the descendants of the scientists and engineers who worked aboard one of Earth's early L-5 colonies."

"One of the hollow-asteroid spacehabs that Zefram Cochrane's team used to develop his prototype warp drive?" Vale asked.

"The same," Riker said. "The Vanguard colony had been thought destroyed in an accident during a warp-field test several years before First Contact. Instead, its imploding warp fields sent it on a very long voyage. Of course, no one on Earth knew that at the time."

"The Neyel had been cut off from Earth for nearly two and a half centuries when *Excelsior* first encountered them," Tuvok said. "However, they had already evolved into a form that bore almost no outward resemblance to the mainstream branch of humanity that went on to participate in the founding of the Federation."

"But how can that be?" Vale said. "How could they have evolved such a fundamentally different physical form in such a short time?"

"Genetic engineering," Riker said.

Akaar nodded. "Apparently born of rather urgent necessity."

"Amazing," Vale said, her eyes widening. "You'd think their ancestors would have remembered the lessons of the Eugenics Wars at least as well as we do. I mean, those times had to still be within the living memories of at least some of the Neyel's ancestors when they left Earth."

At least for those who'd managed to survived the nuclear strikes and bioweapons attacks of the Third World War, Riker thought. He would never forget the devastation that had still been evident on his home planet only a decade after the outbreak of that horrible conflict, having seen it up close during the *Enterprise*'s mission to stop a Borg attack on twenty-first-century Earth.

"Do not judge them too harshly, Commander," Akaar said to Vale. "From what little we were able to glean from their history, the progenitors of the Neyel found basic survival to be an extreme challenge after they were cut off from your homeworld."

Tuvok nodded. "Indeed. Had they not used gene manipulation—to add microgravity-adapted grasping tails and feet to their phenotypes, for example, or to increase their resistance to hard radiation or accelerate their maturity to reproductive age—they might have died out more or less immediately, or at least been rendered sterile."

"Right after we first arrived here, you said something that struck me as fairly ominous, Commander Tuvok," Vale said. "You compared the Neyel to the Romulans. Since we might find ourselves stuck here in Neyel territory for at least a little while, I hope you were just being melodramatic."

"Vulcans are never 'melodramatic,' Commander," Tuvok said, tipping his head in what might have been either curiosity or umbrage. "We found the Neyel to be highly aggressive, ethnocentric, territorial, and paranoid in the extreme."

"That's understandable, considering the lousy hand they were dealt," Riker said. "Their ancestors were a relative handful of humans who were suddenly forced to live on their own in a totally unexplored universe, dependent on an L-5 habitat that wasn't designed to be completely self-sufficient. Yet they left the Sol system years before Archer did—hell, before *Cochrane* did—and settled a huge swath of space that no other human would visit for centuries. Along the way, they must have faced all sorts of dangers no human had ever seen before."

Riker wondered momentarily what *he* would have done in their place. Though the forebears of the Neyel had been presumed killed, they had survived and persevered, utterly isolated from the relentless march of human history. And while they had been preoccupied first with survival, and later with conquest and empire-building, the main branch of mankind back on Earth had progressed from its early post-thermonuclear-war phase to the creation of a grand interstellar democracy that would eventually span more than one hundred and fifty worlds.

One branch had yielded an idealistic Federation, born of cooperation. And apparently another branch had instead created a hegemonic empire, forged in the fires of conquest.

But Riker knew that Earth's upward social evolution had by no means been inevitable. Only a few years before the destructive Romulan-Earth War of the twenty-second century, and the subsequent coalescence of the Federation, first contact with the Xindi had cost millions of human lives. The Xindi attack on Earth had spawned the xenophobic Terra Prime movement, and might very well have placed human culture on precisely the same distrustful, aggressive trajectory that Neyel civilization had evidently taken.

And the Neyel path was never set in stone either, Riker thought. *Their empire grew out of the decisions they made both as individuals and as a society. And those decisions would have created consequences of their own as time went on.*

That idea brought to mind a salient question.

Turning toward Akaar, he said, *"Excelsior's* reports said nothing about follow-up Federation contact with the Neyel after 2298."

Akaar nodded. "That is because no such contact has occurred."

Riker smiled, relishing the prospect of gently correcting the admiral whose presence had made *Titan*'s maiden voyage so much more difficult than he had anticipated.

"That isn't entirely true, Admiral. A good deal of human-Neyel contact may have gone on for some time after 2298."

A look of comprehension dawned in the large Capellan's dark eyes. "Burgess."

Tuvok again raised an eyebrow, then nodded. "Indeed."

"Who or what is Burgess?" Vale asked.

"Aidan Burgess was a Federation special envoy whom *Excelsior* ferried to a diplomatic meeting with the Tholians," Tuvok explained. "She ended up settling a war between the Tholians and the Neyel, using rather unorthodox means."

Akaar nodded. "Means that included appropriating one of *Excelsior*'s shuttlecraft and taking it on a one-way journey through the rift that linked Tholian space with the region in which we now find ourselves."

"I can only think of one reason any human diplomat might do something that extreme, Admiral," Vale said. "This Federation envoy must have planned to live among the Neyel and teach them how their human cousins deal with their problems without A: wiping each other out or, B: trying to conquer the known universe. Am I right?"

"Essentially," Akaar said. "Or so we have hoped all these years."

Vale offered the admiral a thin smile. "So how did the ambassador's plan work out?"

Akaar answered with a mirthless smile of his own. "We are the first Starfleet personnel since the time of *Excelsior*'s encounter with the Neyel who may have the opportunity to answer to that question."

Riker's combadge chose that precise moment to chirp. *"Engineering to Captain Riker."*

"Go ahead . . . Dr. Ra-Havreii," the captain said after tapping the badge. He had almost used the name of Commander Ledrah, *Titan*'s recently deceased original chief engineer, and hoped that no one had noticed his near-lapse.

"The repairs and replacements of the burned-out bridge stations are all nearly complete, Captain. And the shield generators will all be back on line within the next three hours. All other systems are already working within acceptable norms, though I believe we can still improve engine performance a great deal."

"I'm glad to hear it, Commander," Riker said. *Titan*'s new Efrosian chief engineer would take some getting used to, but not because Riker had any real concerns about the man's competency. Xin Ra-Havreii had, after all, been *Titan*'s principal designer at Starfleet's Utopia Planitia Fleet Yards, and therefore knew the vessel's every specification better than any other living sentient being did.

"The damage control teams have already put right the new hull breach deck five sustained during our passage through the anomaly, Captain," Ra-Havreii continued, reminding Riker once more of the recent battle over Romulus, which had not only placed the Efrosian in charge of *Titan*'s engine room, but had also left Lieutenant Commander Keru, *Titan*'s tactical officer and security chief, critically injured. During that skirmish, the deck in question had taken a fair amount of damage; although the engineering teams had sealed that breach within hours of the battle, *Titan*'s abrupt transit to this region of space had evidently stressed those same weakened portions of the hull beyond their tolerances yet again.

"A lot of the repairs still don't look very pretty," Ra-Havreii went on. *"But in a few hours I expect* Titan *to be essentially 'ship shape' once again."*

"Good work, Commander. And thank you. Riker out."

His errant recollection of the death of *Titan*'s first chief engineer reminded him that he had another duty to perform, and that it had to be tended to very soon. The timing of this sad task was dictated not by a duty roster or a Starfleet regulation, but rather by certain strict cultural requirements of the planet Tiburon, the homeworld of the late Lieutenant Commander Nidani Ledrah, who had perished horribly during the recent skirmish between Romulan and Reman forces.

According to Tiburon funerary custom, the deceased had to be formally eulogized and interred no later than one thirty-two-hour Tiburoni day following the onset of death. Very soon, that time would be up.

As if on cue, Riker's combadge chirped yet again. This time, the subdued voice of his wife, Diplomatic Officer Deanna Troi, issued from the small gold chevron on his chest.

"Will. It's almost time."

"Understood, Deanna. Thanks."

After Deanna signed off, Riker regarded Vale, Pazlar, Tuvok, and Akaar, all of whom wore dour expressions and drifted in weightless silence.

Riker gestured toward the weird energy phenomenon that still loomed high overhead, all but filling the stellar cartography lab. "Let's revisit all of this a bit later. After the memorial service."

Lieutenant Commander Nidani Ledrah was about to embark on her final voyage.

CHAPTER THREE

His dewclaws clicking on the uncarpeted portions of the deck as he made his way through sickbay, Dr. Shenti Yisec Eres Ree was feeling the weight of fatigue. Because of their carnivore heritage, Pahkwa-thanh tended toward relatively brief bursts of activity following their feedings, punctuated by several hours of dormancy. But in pursuing his medical duties—namely, dealing with all the major and minor injuries caused by both the skirmish at Romulus and *Titan*'s rough crossing into what was evidently a distant region of space—Ree had been awake and active continuously for nearly three duty shifts. His eyelids were nictitating more often than usual, but he had not yet been able to secure sufficient time away from sickbay to get any significant quantity of food or rest.

And eat and rest he would. But not before he had finished making his rounds. Looking across the main sickbay area, Ree saw Nurse Ogawa and Nurse Kershu, the three-armed Edosian, both of whom were attending to *Titan*'s

Reman guest. All three turned their heads toward Ree as he approached.

"Doctor," said Mekrikuk, nodding in greeting. The Reman, a political prisoner who had been rescued from Vikr'l Prison along with Tuvok, was sitting on the edge of the biobed. He was no longer under restraints, as Commander Troi had recommended, contrary to Ree's ever-cautious instincts. Ree had to admit, though, that Troi's assessment of Mekrikuk had been correct; he had caused no trouble whatsoever, merely engaging the medical staff in conversation and asking innumerable questions. Though Mekrikuk's massive, heavily muscled form was wrapped in a blue hospital gown, the roadmap of old scars that covered his chest—doubtless the legacy of past battles, some fought against the Dominion, others in opposition to his Romulan rulers—remained starkly visible.

"It occurs to me that I have yet to thank you properly for saving my life," Mekrikuk said in a surprisingly gentle tenor voice.

Removing his medical tricorder from his belt, Ree displayed his formidable array of teeth. "Nonsense, Mr. Mekrikuk. My first responsibility is the preservation of life." He ran a brief scan, comparing the results to the readings he saw displayed over the biobed. Fixing his gaze back upon his patient, he said, "I must say, you have remarkable recuperative powers."

Mekrikuk smiled, revealing his own sharp dentition. "That may be the only reason I have endured these many years, Doctor. When do you think I might be released from your infirmary?"

Ree resumed looking at his tricorder. "A few days at most." *And what then?* he thought, recalling that Mekrikuk had already made a formal request for political asylum so as not to be returned to captivity at the hands of the

Romulans. He knew that the captain would have to hold a hearing, whenever circumstances permitted. But since there was no place to drop Mekrikuk off afterward, would the Reman become a permanent passenger aboard *Titan*? Or a member of the crew?

Ree was thankful then that such matters fell outside his purview.

Bidding his patient a polite farewell, Ree crossed sick-bay to one of the other biobed alcoves. He noticed that Ogawa had fallen into step beside him as Ranul Keru's pale, still form came into view. Lieutenant T'Lirin, a female Vulcan security officer, sat ramrod-straight in a chair at Keru's bedside. Though her facial expression was as impassive as that of any Vulcan, Ree got the impression that she was holding a personal grief vigil for her fallen superior officer.

T'Lirin nodded a silent acknowledgment at Ree and Ogawa as they approached Keru's side. The Vulcan woman then quietly withdrew.

"Is there any good news on Commander Keru?" Ree asked Ogawa quietly, even though he could see the biobed readings—all of which indicated coma—as well as she could.

Ogawa frowned and shook her head. "I'm sorry, Doctor. There's been no change."

Ree nodded sadly, reminding himself that Keru's condition had at least not declined any further. There was no reason to despair, at least not yet. The tall, bearded Trill breathed shallowly, as though he was merely asleep. The facial contusions and scrapes he had received during the battle over Romulus were healing, but Ree could see that underneath his eyelids, Keru's eyes were motionless.

Not sleeping. Elsewhere.

Backing out of the biobed alcove, Ree headed toward the isolation room. Along the way, he passed the biobed of Lieutenant Feren Denken, the Matalinian security officer who had lost his right arm during the raid on Vikr'l Prison. Denken was sleeping, and Ree saw the man's bandaged stump lying atop the blanket. Denken had made it known that his culture's philosophical beliefs forbade him from accepting any kind of artificial body part, meaning that for all intents and purposes, his career in security was likely over. Ree knew that it wasn't his place to question such decisions, even if he didn't understand or agree with them. *Of course, Denken's injury would be far easier for* me *to endure,* he thought. *Pahkwa-thanh limbs regenerate on their own.*

Leaving Ogawa to tend to the comatose Trill, Ree moved on toward the OB/GYN room. Although Pahkwa-thanh biology supported no human-compatible pathogens, he nevertheless donned a sterile gown before entering the chamber's bio-isolation field. He saw Axel Bolaji, the father of the premature infant Dr. Onnta had delivered some thirty hours earlier, dozing in a chair to the right of the biobed. Shuttle pilot Olivia Bolaji was sitting up on the biobed, gazing into the mobile incubator unit in which her tiny, dark-skinned child lay sleeping.

As alien as humans and humanoids were to him, Ree had no trouble recognizing the fatigue etched in her dark brown face—as well as the anxiety that creased her forehead.

Olivia offered him a tired smile. "Hello, Doctor." She trained her gaze back on the tiny, still form contained within the plasteel barrier. "How is my son?"

Ree paused to examine the readouts attached to the incubator. For such a premature child—his birth had occurred approximately seventeen weeks early—the youngling already seemed to be thriving beyond Ree's conservative expectations.

"You appear to have little cause for worry, Ensign. In fact, in a few weeks' time, you may even be able to begin administering little Totyarguil's feedings yourself."

"Alyssa has already shown me how to work the feeding tube."

"You misunderstand me, Ensign. I was referring to mammalian autotrophic feeding." Ever since he had first read about it as a young pre-Healer, the strangeness of this uniquely mammalian trait had always utterly fascinated him.

The ensign blinked several times, apparently confused by his terminology. "You're talking about breast-feeding."

"Of course," Ree said, dipping his head forward rapidly and repeatedly in what he had learned was an affirmative gesture. "It's really the best thing for him, nutritionally and emotionally. I would greatly appreciate being permitted to observe, once you begin—I am contemplating writing a paper on the practice for one of the medical journals on my homeworld."

Her response took a moment to arrive, but sounded cheerful enough when it finally did. "Oh. Good. Great. Well, we can discuss that later."

Ree chuckled in appreciation. "I would be particularly interested in witnessing your mammalian feeding behaviors once the little carnivore's teeth begin coming in."

As he spoke, Ree took a medical tricorder from its place on a nearby shelf and scanned the child more thoroughly than the incubator's sensors could manage. The readings scrolled down the screen, but he had to refresh it and read them again; his eyes were becoming dry and tired.

"I've confirmed that his biosigns are strong indeed," Ree said. "With the exception of size and weight variances attributable to his premature birth. Totyarguil seems to be responding well to the lung- and skin-tissue stimulation treatments Dr. Onnta has been administering."

Olivia's face beamed with happiness. "Thank you, Doctor. Axel will be relieved to hear that as well."

Ree pointed one of his long, clawed fingers over to the sleeping conn officer. He regarded the man's blissfully closed eyes with a faint sense of envy. "I suggest you let him rest now and give him the good news later."

He turned to leave, and then turned back. "Dr. Onnta will be in to check in on you in a few hours. I must go get some rest of my own." *After paying my respects to Commander Ledrah.*

As Olivia waved to him quietly, Ree turned again to leave. He fully intended to sleep soon, but first he had to get some food. He wasn't entirely joking when he had told Captain Riker recently that the sight of small mammals tended to make him hungry. In another context, on his home planet, a warm-blooded creature about the size of Totyarguil Bolaji would have made for a nice predormancy interval snack.

It's probably best that I keep that to myself, though, Ree thought, wishing his patients well, and dreading the sad ceremony that was to come.

Every detail must be perfect.

K'chak'!'op turned her head segment upside down, and used one of the six tentacles that protruded from the right side of her head to tap the instrument panel. They left a slightly moist smudge behind on the display.

The holodeck shimmered into life, and a placid scene

from the world of Tiburon took form. Nidani Ledrah had hailed from the north quadrant, a land that was in a perpetual twilight for half the Tiburoni year due to the planet's extreme axial tilt. According to K'chak'!'op's research, the area was largely devoid of modern technology and large cities; its tribes lived in small, independent settlements. The native Tiburon did not mix with the Suliban settlers or the Vanoben, who had arrived more recently.

K'chak'!'op clicked her mouth pincers together several times, vocally reminding herself that the caves nearby would have featured rust-colored rocks, not the dusty orange ones that she had just programmed. Her tentacles moved fluidly as she altered the scene.

Her four eyes swiveled independently, looking for other flaws. Some of the others had offered to help her to program the tableau—much about Tiburon was missing from the main computer's files—but Melora Pazlar was otherwise occupied at present and K'chak'!'op didn't trust the male engineers. She understood that most alien species had evolved differently than the Pak'shree, but some prejudices were hard to let go.

Pak'shree were born neuter, became male at puberty, and transitioned to female at full maturity. Males were only concerned with fighting for the right to reproduction with the older, fertile adult females. K'chak'!'op had always struggled to take males of any species seriously and to trust their abilities; she would never admit it to anyone, but even Captain Riker worried her at times.

K'chak'!'op moved down the knoll, feeling the gray, featherlike grass brushing pleasurably against her six legs. She had enough time to take in the beauty of her program before the others arrived. Once they did, she would retreat to one of the caves. She would rather have stayed in her nest, away from the rest of the crew—most of whom seemed small and awkward to her—but the captain had requested that everyone who wasn't on shift attend.

Besides, Ledrah was one of the few people aboard *Titan* that K'chak'!'op had actually cared for. And now she was gone, too.

In the last minutes before the others arrived, K'chak'!'op began to stridulate her mouthparts and wave her tentacles, lifting her front segment up vertically until it had nearly reached its full three-meter length.

Then, she sang a song of loss to her departed friend.

Riker cleared his throat and stepped to the dais, which was flanked by Admiral Akaar and Commander Tuvok, both looking appropriately somber and dignified in their dress uniforms. Riker felt the cool wind moving through his own dress jacket, though the goose bumps on his skin weren't the result of the ambient temperature.

Assembled in front of him before the pristine backdrop of a Tiburonian hillside was the majority of the crew of *Titan*. Only about a hundred were working on ship repairs, maintenance, systems monitoring, or other tasks. The other two-hundred and fifty or so had gathered here.

It was an awesome sight, regardless of the reason it had come to be. Here, all at once, he could see the wide array of people and species that he commanded. Although bipedal humanoids comprised a significant proportion of his crew, the number and variegation of nonhumans was high, especially among the science and technical officers.

Dr. Cethente stood next to Cadet Orilly Malar, the Irriol exobiologist. Cethente reminded Riker of a tall, delicate tribal carving he had seen during his childhood in Valdez, the Syrath astrophysicist's spindly, arachnid legs seeming absurdly fragile, while the quadrupedal Malar was solid-looking and armored. Next to them were Dr. Bralik, the Ferengi geologist, and Kekil, the Chelon biologist. Nearby stood Dr. Ree and Dr. Ra-Havreii; the former was as stock-still as an exhibit in a natural-history museum, while the latter, eyes downcast, seemed unaware of the swelling crowd behind him.

Riker scanned further and saw so many others with so much diversity reflected in their bodies, their experiences, and their personalities. Whether Skorr or Vulcan, Cardassian or human, Arkenite or S'ti'ach, each of them brought something utterly unique to *Titan*.

"We are gathered here today to honor our friend and comrade, Lieutenant Commander Nidani Ostiquin Ledrah," Riker said, projecting his deep voice toward the back of the room. He knew he was echoing the words that Captain Picard had said at Tasha Yar's memorial service so long ago; the words that countless captains had likely said in countless services across countless years.

"The landscape around you reflects the home of Nidani, where she was born thirty-two years ago. Most from her tribe were antitechnological, preferring instead to live a simpler life, relying upon the land. But Nidani had different dreams. She wanted to explore the skies above her.

"She eventually enrolled at Starfleet Academy and achieved her dream. Graduating with honors, she accepted a post as an engineer on the *U.S.S. Zapata,* where she was stationed for five years. Assignments to the *U.S.S. Hathaway* and the *Lakota* followed, before she requested to join the crew of *Titan.* She told me once she'd fallen in love with the *Luna*-class design, and adored the idea of a crew as varied as ours."

Standing in the front row, Ra-Havreii suddenly looked up at him, his eyes filled with pain. Almost immediately, the new chief engineer set his gaze downward again.

Riker resumed: "Some of you are billeted in special customized quarters designed by Nidani and her engineering team. You no doubt got to know her as a funny and friendly woman who truly cared about your well-being." Riker knew that Chaka, the insectile Pak'shree computer specialist, was likely observing the ceremony from one of the simulated hillside caves; her den, Ensign Aili Lavena's water-filled accommodations, and Melora Pazlar's vertical micro-g quarters were some of the more impressive feats of Ledrah's ingenuity.

"As we face the future aboard *Titan,* this crew has been robbed of further interaction with Nidani. And yet, her influence, her spirit, remains everywhere within these bulkheads. The place she strove to make a home for all of us is infused with her dedication, her passion, and her love.

"For those who wish to partake, Nidani will now become a part of us as well."

He gestured to Vale, who stepped forward with an elaborately decorated container. Everyone on the ship had been notified of this Tiburon funereal custom, and he expected that most would choose *not* to participate. Ledrah had been cremated within six hours of her death, and her ashes had been pulverized to a fine dust. Still, despite the fact that the ashes were sterile, he doubted many of the crew would actually choose to ingest their comrade, though it was the highest honor one could pay a fallen Tiburon.

Riker glanced at Deanna, then accepted a tiny vial which Vale had removed from the container. Removing its stopper, he lifted it toward the twilight sky.

"*Jancarik terme ikkos preen,* Nidani Ostiquin Ledrah," he said, in Tiburoni. "You live within us forever, Nidani Ostiquin Ledrah," he repeated in Standard.

Then, he poured the tiny amount of powder out of the

vial and onto his tongue. It was flavorless. He held it there for a moment, and swallowed.

Deanna stepped forward next, taking a vial from Vale, and hoisting it aloft.

Through eyes that brimmed with tears, Riker saw others—many others—from the crew begin to step forward behind his wife. He saw that Ra-Havreii, looking haggard and haunted, was the first in line. Even Chaka was exiting one of the caves to take a place in the queue.

He closed his eyes and wondered how many other such ceremonies he would have to preside over in the coming years, as *Titan* continued its voyages.

And as the voices of his crew washed over him, calling to the memory of Ledrah, he held fast to the hope that occasions such as this would be few and far between.

As she entered the quarters she shared with her husband, Deanna Troi immediately noticed that the lights were low. Will's dress tunic lay on the table, but she didn't pick it up.

Imzadi? She reached out with her mind, not hearing anything from the other rooms.

"In here, Deanna," Will said, his low voice coming from the bathroom.

She turned the corner and looked in at him. He was leaning on the washbasin, staring into the mirror. He had changed into his regular duty tunic, but hadn't closed the front of it yet.

"Are you all right, Will?"

He continued staring into the mirror. "Yeah. I just prepared a message for Nidani's family. When we get back to Federation space, I'll send it."

She felt a pang of guilt. "I haven't been here for you

much since the attack," Troi said, stepping into the smaller room and reaching out her hand to brush Will's ear.

He smiled wanly. "It's not your fault. The crew needs you *and* it needs me. Duty comes first, especially during a crisis."

But duty can always be tempered with the love we share, Troi thought, joining her mind to her husband's. *If we take the time do so.*

He didn't respond at first, but slowly closed his eyes. Finally, he turned toward her.

"A few weeks ago, when we were in the stellar cartography lab, I told you that this ship was our chance to recover some of the wonder we lost over the last decade serving on the *Enterprise.* Our chance to explore what lay beyond. And yet, our first mission is filled with warring Romulans and Remans, space battles, a prison break, and death. What's changed?"

Troi turned her head and looked at Will's reflection in the mirror, training her dark eyes on his. "I won't deny your feelings—and my feelings as well—of disappointment that *Titan*'s launch will be forever remembered because of what happened over the last week. But show me a starship that hasn't been drawn into some kind of conflict, or run into some unforeseen impacts when dealing with new lives and new civilizations, or had to deal with bizarre consequences when faced with spatial anomalies . . . and I'll show you a starship that only exists in some Academy textbook.

"Here we are in uncharted space, about to encounter gods only know what or who. This is the very definition of *Titan*'s mission. We may be about to reconnect with humanity's long-lost offshoot. We may save lives or be forced into battle to save our own. We'll learn and grow along the way, and more importantly, we'll *explore*. You and I and this crew with all its unique differences.

"We'll explore, *together*."

Riker straightened his posture and turned, enfolding Troi into his arms. She felt his beard atop her head, smelled the scent that he gave off when he was worried. But his embrace was strong, and she returned it.

I love you, Imzadi, he thought.

And I love you, Will.

Troi knew that their embrace would end. Duty would call. But for now, their fragment of the universe was utterly at peace.

Darkness.

Warmth.

Fear.

Concern.

Love.

Near silence, except for the noises and things at the edges of consciousness that threatened to wake him.

He wanted to sleep like this forever. But he feared that the red in which he floated would not permit it.

CHAPTER FOUR

STARDATE 26795.2 (18 OCTOBER 2349)

"When have you known Flenrol ever to give up searching for anything?" Captain Akaar asked, grinning. "He is the most anal-retentive Bolian I have ever encountered. Perhaps that is why he makes such an excellent XO."

Tuvok moved a hand across his brow, wiping the sweat away. "I do not believe that even he will be able to find us here, Captain. Our communicators are inhibited by the local geomagnetism. Additionally, this system is littered with four-hundred and thirty-six other satellite planetoids, each of which contains a sufficiently metallic core to generate magnetic fields capable of confusing the Wyoming's sensors. Logic dictates that in the time it will take Commander Flenrol to find us, we will have perished either from the heat or from thirst and starvation."

"I enjoy the way you always manage to find the bright side in every crisis situation, Tuvok," Akaar said, grinning. "It is what makes you the best possible company when roasting to death on a Neltedian planetoid."

It had been four days since they had last been inside the shuttlecraft Auraciem. *The small vessel had become Akaar's favorite during the weeks since Starfleet Command had promoted him from exec and acting captain to the permanent commander of the U.S.S. Wyoming following the untimely death of its longtime CO, the volatile Captain Karl Broadnax.*

Akaar and Tuvok had embarked on what was actually supposed to have been a fairly routine mission of exploration into the Neltedian system—until an unexpected and unusually intense solar flare had fried the Auraciem's *shields, her propulsion and guidance systems, and had bled away most of her power.*

After flying the dying shuttle into the relative protection of one of the planetoid's powerful magnetic fields, Tuvok had barely managed to get enough power to the transporters in time to beam them out of the shuttle before it crashed. Then, what should have been half a day's trek across the unknown world's barren wastes became a torturous four-day climb through the ravines and crevices of the sunbaked sphere. Though the sere, pitiless environment was technically M-Class—which Tuvok had called remarkable, considering the planetoid's relatively small size—the plant life here was clearly being sustained by resources located far underground; the spire-like trees had somehow managed to contribute enough oxygen and nitrogen to make the arid atmosphere barely breathable, but evidently did not support any large fauna. And they seemed to provide precious little protection against the system's roiling, merciless sun. Worse yet, the hard, rocky ground made whatever subterranean water the trees were using effectively inaccessible, especially since the planetoid's geomagnetism had evidently cooked their one hand phaser.

By the time they finally reached the wreckage of the

shuttle, both men were dehydrated, sunburned, and very nearly in a state of hallucination. Akaar was amazed and thankful to discover that several of the shuttle's aft compartments had been relatively unharmed by the crash, giving them some emergency supplies, two sheltering tents, and a small amount of water and foodstuffs.

Despite his obvious hunger, Tuvok had offered his portion to Akaar, but Akaar would have none of it. He finally had to order Tuvok to eat before the often-maddening Vulcan would ingest any sustenance other than sips of water.

Now, with some small measure of food and fluid in his large frame, Akaar felt fatigue gripping him. "I will try to sleep until nightfall," he said, gesturing toward his shelter.

"Sir, you must be aware that this planetoid is tidally locked to the second planet in the system. Therefore there is no night on this—" Tuvok stopped, apparently realizing from Akaar's weary grin that the captain was engaging in a small jest.

"I will be in my own tent, meditating," Tuvok said finally.

Akaar watched his friend turn away, and then entered the relative cool of the tent—relative in that it wasn't plus-sixty-five degrees Celsius as it was under the outside sun.

Perhaps during our time here, my old friend will finally learn the value of humor, *he thought as he lay down on the remnants of upholstery they had salvaged from one of the shuttle chairs that hadn't been too badly burned.*

It seemed an impossible task. But so, too, had escaping from the plunging shuttle.

DAY 6—STARDATE 26798.9 (19 OCTOBER 2349)

In the state of eiihu, experienced only by Vulcans during deep meditation, Tuvok didn't exactly dream of his family and his past, though he imagined that the visions he saw and interacted with were probably not unlike the dreams experienced by other species. It was here that he best remembered the flawless beauty of T'Pel, his wife of forty-five years. He cherished the memory of her dancing in the graceful korl'na that her mother had made for her, and that she had worn for him when they both had experienced their first throes of Pon farr.

He remembered, too, his five-year-old daughter Asil and his three older sons, Sek, Varik, and Eliath. He recalled the somber way each of them had stared at him as he taught them the fundamental principles of Vulcan cthia that he had learned so painstakingly throughout his life. Unlike fathers of other Vulcan children, however, he had access to knowledge that came from far past the mountains of L-Langon, or even the ancient, bloodstone-covered halls of ShiKahr. He had experienced the galaxy beyond for nine years, first as a cadet at Starfleet Academy, then as a junior science officer aboard the U.S.S. Excelsior.

But he had left that ship—and Starfleet—dissatisfied with the perplexingly emotional manner in which Captain Sulu and the other humans he encountered had made their decisions.

Still, his five years aboard Excelsior had given him a wealth of stories and wonders to share with his children. And it had also been enough to bring him two close friends—friends with whom he had become at least as intimate as any he had ever acquired back home on Vulcan—in the deposed Capellan teer Leonard James Akaar and the Halkan outcast, Lojur. After Tuvok had resigned his Starfleet commission in 2298, Lojur had come to Vulcan with him in the hopes of learning to control his decidedly un-Halkan propensity for violence; restless and *frustrated after half a Vulcan year, the Halkan had returned to Starfleet to seek his answers.*

The absence of constant interaction with either of his outworld friends, to Tuvok's great surprise, gave him the greatest sense of loss he had ever experienced.

Tuvok had not been able to explain to his wife and children why he had chosen to return to Starfleet earlier this year; he wasn't even certain he could explain it to himself. Perhaps it had been his nigh-mystical desert encounter with the a'kweth—the Underlier, or repository of all knowledge, from Vulcan's most ancient myths—or perhaps it was simply a gradual accumulation of what humans sometimes called "wanderlust." Whatever the reason, it almost seemed that a part of his very katra had gone missing while he had been home on Vulcan, and that it only rejoined him when he journeyed into space.

He had been reinstated to Starfleet as an ensign, and was given minor assignments, until an old friend asked for Tuvok to transfer to his ship; Akaar was now the first officer of the U.S.S. Wyoming, and had urged his captain to take on Tuvok as a member of his crew.

While the posting seemed a blessing at first, Tuvok soon grew to disapprove of Commander Akaar's superior officer, the abrasive and confrontational Captain Karl Broadnax. At least Captain Sulu had allowed Tuvok to speak his mind when he found particular actions or commands to be illogical; Broadnax had practically cashiered him back out of Starfleet the first time that Tuvok had dared question one of his decisions.

Thus it was that Tuvok was "loaned" for a brief time to the U.S.S. Stargazer, under the command of Captain Jean-Luc Picard. He might have asked to return to that ship, had not Broadnax made a particularly egregious error in judgment and allowed his temper to get the better of him in a ramshackle bar on Farius Prime. Even though complete Starfleet and civilian investigations were undertaken, no one had ever determined precisely which local underworld denizen—or which gang of lowlifes, judging from the condition of the remains—had ended the captain's contentious existence.

After Akaar was promoted to captain of the Wyoming, he had requested that Tuvok remain aboard as his science officer. Although Tuvok knew that Akaar tried not to show any overt favoritism to his old friend—which Tuvok assumed explained why Akaar had not promoted him beyond the rank of ensign—Tuvok still felt little camaraderie with his other crewmates. Rather than dwell on their illogical and delusional jealousies, he pushed himself harder and focused his energies more than ever before on his work. He even began an exhaustive study of battle tactics and security protocols on the side.

But most of the tactical skills he had learned in the short time since coming back aboard the Wyoming were useless here, on Planetoid 437. There was nothing to defend against, other than the heat, the thirst, and the hunger. There were no animals or sentient aliens or anything living other than the imposing trees that were spiked into the cracked and otherwise barren ground.

A hot breeze pushed through the shelter, momentarily stirring Tuvok from his meditative trance and his memories. Rather than let it bring him completely out of his contemplative state, he incorporated the feeling into his mind, matching it to recollections of his second trip into the desert as a child, when he had run away from home after his pet sehlat, Wari, had been killed. Inconsolable when his parents told him that Wari did not have a katra, he had embarked on the ritual of tal'oth, making his way over the desiccated wasteland of Vulcan's Forge, and across the jagged mountains that marked its eastern boundary.

The winds that pushed against him during that trip were just as broiling and powerful as those here now. The difference was that then he'd had a mission to purge himself of emotion, to feel nothing except dispassionate, irrefutable logic. He had returned after four months away from home, having realized that goal, if only temporarily.

Now, however, he had no objective save basic survival. And of somehow keeping his captain—his friend—alive as well.

But no matter how he tried to distract his mind with memories and ruminations, Tuvok knew that his chances of success were almost nonexistent.

And yet some suppressed part of his consciousness was being warmed in an entirely different way . . . by the dim yet still-visible light of hope.

DAY 9——STARDATE 26806.7 (22 OCTOBER 2349)

Tuvok heard Akaar's scream, but he couldn't tell immediately where the sound had come from. He pushed at the rocks around him, glad that the baked sandstone was crumbling and loose rather than hard and impacted. That was probably the only reason he had been able to dig his way out of the avalanche of rocks that had covered him after the ground had collapsed beneath them both. The only way Tuvok had been able to distinguish up from down was by feeling the rocks sliding downward as he pushed them away.

Desperate because of their nearly depleted supplies, he and Akaar had embarked on an attempt to find water and *sustenance earlier that day. They found a crevasse only four feet across, but which went down for at least a hundred meters or more. Perhaps more importantly, one of the planetoid's curious trees grew near the edge of it, and they could see what appeared to be parts of its root system further down, near a ledge.*

Wedging themselves against the side, they had climbed down, inch by agonizing inch, toward the ledge. Akaar had reached it first, and had begun scooping soil away from the roots, which appeared to be oddly brittle and unyielding. The soil was clumpy and slightly damp, however, indicative of the presence of underground moisture.

Tuvok had just moved onto the ledge when the lip of it crumbled way, sending him tumbling down into the ravine. He wasn't sure how far he had fallen, but he knew that the plug of soil and debris that supported him now was likely just a temporary clog; he needed to get out of there, immediately.

Moving as little as possible, even though the dusty air made him want to cough and vomit, he felt for the sides of the crevasse, then pushed against both sides, his feet on one and his hands on the other. He rolled his body around so that he was facing downward, allowing the debris that was still tumbling down—and that which had already collected on his body—to fall away into the planetoid's interior. Slowly, he began making the climb back up to the surface, his undernourished muscles screaming in agony.

He heard Akaar bellow again, from above him, though he couldn't tell if his cry was intended to find Tuvok, or to express pain.

"I am here, Captain," he called out with as much volume as his desiccated throat could manage, although through the dust that caked his mouth he wasn't certain if

he could have been heard two meters away, much less the twenty meters he estimated that he had fallen.

Eventually, he crawled his way back up to what was left of the ledge. There he saw Akaar, whose face was contorted in pain.

"Captain, we need to return to higher ground. It isn't safe for us down here."

Akaar grimaced. "You will have to help me, Tuvok." *He held out his hands, one clutching the other, and then opened them. A bleeding gash had been torn through his right hand, showing tendon and bone. And a large volume of bright red blood.*

"How did this happen?"

Akaar looked back over toward the recessed area and the portion of the exposed root system. Tuvok saw blood spattered on several of the roots.

"They are just as sharp and unyielding down here as the trees are up there," *Akaar said, his voice tremulous with pain.* "I grabbed for one when the ledge gave way and ended up running my hand completely through."

Tuvok felt his muscles aching and trembling as he held himself taut. "I will help you get back to the top, Captain. We will climb out together. You must hold onto my torso as best you can."

"You cannot support both my weight and your own," *Akaar said, protesting.* "We will both fall to our deaths."

Tuvok took a sterner tone than he normally did with anyone other than recalcitrant children. "Leonard, Vulcans possess much greater strength than do most other humanoids—even Capellans. I will be able to get us back to the surface. But time spent arguing is a waste of my admittedly depleted energies."

Akaar nodded, either persuaded by Tuvok's logic or

unable to argue further because of his pain. Gingerly, he reached out and wrapped his thick arms around Tuvok's midsection. Tuvok felt him jockeying with his hands, probably to have his good hand hold the wrist of the injured one.

"Are you prepared?" Tuvok asked, trying to keep his croaking voice steady.

"As prepared as I can ever be," Akaar said.

Tuvok began to climb, immediately feeling the larger man's weight as it trebled his own. He concentrated on breathing deeply, attempting to channel every erg of energy in his body into his arms and legs. He moved one arm up, then the other, then a leg. A fourth movement, and he felt the entire weight of Akaar on him; his captain was free of the ledge.

As he began the excruciating climb back to the surface, Tuvok attempted to clear his mind of everything save his goal. The more overheated his body became, the closer he knew he was to the top.

As he climbed, his mind wandered. He felt as though his body was becoming heavier, as though whatever internal gravimetric aberrations allowed this improbably small worldlet to maintain a Class-M atmosphere—a superdense core? he wondered—had chosen him and Akaar for special torment. It was as if the planetoid itself wanted to draw them both downward to their deaths.

Foolish. Illogical.

He began to imagine instead that he was back at the outskirts of Vulcan's Forge, intent on completing the time-honored tal'oth *survival ritual.*

His mind raced, despite all of his mental disciplines. By the seventh time he had replayed the entire tal'oth *rite in his mind, he saw the bright light above, and knew that they had almost reached the top.*

And the desolation that lay above. In which they would both surely die.

DAY 12—STARDATE 26815.4 (25 OCTOBER 2349)

As closely as Akaar could estimate, they had been on the planetoid for nearly twelve standard days. Twelve standard days of nightless, sunbaked hell, *the Capellan thought.*

Their rations were exhausted save for a final liter or so of water, and there had been no sign of rescue. When he was lucid and not feverish from the injury to his hand, Akaar admired the calm that Tuvok exuded. The Vulcan still seemed to disbelieve that they would ever be found, but at least he had stopped arguing the point with his superior officer.

Mostly, they sat as immobile as possible in their shelters, emerging only every now and then to speak to each other briefly, lest the heat and fatigue overtake them. By now, Akaar knew every detail about Tuvok's life that the Vulcan was willing to share. And Akaar had shared his own long backlog of personal memories of his lifelong off-world exile with his mother, the Regent Eleen.

As they watched each other gradually withering and dying, they came to know one another better than most friends ever could or ever would. But that knowledge had prompted Akaar to make a difficult decision.

Tuvok was refusing to drink much of the water, deferring to Akaar, whose injury, the ensign felt, gave him priority for the precious liquid. And yet, of the two of them, Akaar felt Tuvok had more to offer the universe should he survive than did he. The Vulcan had a wife, and children, and a longer lifespan to share with them. Akaar had only his mother, the woman who, acting through friendly

Capellan intermediaries, was endlessly building his tomb on their homeworld; it was not a sign that she wanted him to die, but rather a monument to remind everyone concerned that, deposed or not, he was the rightful high teer of the Ten Tribes of Capella.

As Tuvok slept, Akaar put his plan into motion. He had saved some scraps of fabric from the shuttle's wreckage, as well as a razor-sharp shard of splintered duraplast. Now, he opened the dressing on his hand, wincing at the pain. Picking a particularly bruised area, he drove the shard in far enough to draw blood.

Holding a large scrap of fabric steady, he began to write his vriloxince, the last testament he would leave behind. He wrote to his mother, to Keel and his confederates who had conspired to keep him from the teership, to those he had served with in Starfleet, to those he had captained, and to those for whom he held a special place of friendship in his heart. He explained that his final act of w'lash'nogot was not the action of a coward, but rather a way for him to allow Tuvok to survive for a few days more, under the assumption that help would arrive in time to save his friend.

He had already explained w'lash'nogot to Tuvok in one of their many conversations about death and the afterlife. The ritual suicide was one of the most holy of the Capellan customs, reserved as the highest honor one could perform for another; to die for one's loved one or friend was a sacrifice beyond words, the ultimate expression of love and loyalty. Tuvok had listened intently then, but did not comment, nor offer any stories of comparable Vulcan rituals.

The Capellan concept of afterlife was different than that of any other culture that Akaar had ever encountered. Rather than believing that their souls or spirits or memories would live on, the Capellans believed that the emotions *they felt upon death would live on. Thus, those who died filled with rage would fuel the anger that the living might feel for decades to come. Those at peace or in love would bring happiness for generations past them. The actual memory of the dead person and his or her life were the reasons that so many monuments to the dead existed on their world; they were the only tangible markers that someone who was no more had ever been.*

Akaar finished his note, then exited his tent, squinting into the bright, eternal light. He could hear Tuvok's labored breathing inside the shelter, a sure sign that even his great strength was declining quickly. He placed the note, and the remaining water, near the opening of Tuvok's tent.

Returning to his own shelter, Akaar sat, cleared his mind, and slowed his breathing. He closed his eyes and began moving his lips in a silent chant as old as the High Teers of antiquity. He could feel the pace of his heartbeat slowing as the ritual took him steadily downward in a deathward spiral. Soon, death would be irrevocable. This would all be over, and all pain and deprivation would be behind him forever. He opened his eyes for a moment and noted that his vision had already begun to gray around the edges.

With a little luck, his friend and colleague could stretch what resources remained after his passing, thus ensuring Tuvok's survival—at least until such time as rescue finally arrived. Within minutes, he would be gone, and his emotions, his love and loyalty and courage, would be released into the universe. He prayed that it would strengthen his friend as much as their residual food and water would.

He opened his eyes again. The sunlight brightening his shelter was steadily dimming, and he viewed the interior of his tent as though through a narrow tube.

He focused on the memories of joy he held, of his mother, his crew, his friends.

On courage.

After Ledrah's memorial, Tuvok had filed out of the holodeck with the rest of the crew, then retired to his quarters for quiet, but ultimately fruitless, meditation, ending as it had in an onslaught of memory, all of which he recognized—but not all of which was his.

He rose from the mat on the floor, snuffed the candles he had left burning, and brought the lights up to half-illumination.

He hadn't thought about the crash-landing in the Neltedian system—the incident that had essentially ended his friendship with Akaar—for years. At least, not until after he had seen his old friend and colleague again in *Titan*'s transporter room right after the escape from Vikr'l Prison.

Following that surprising reunion, Tuvok had begun to think that Akaar had finally put his old resentments behind him. Now, however, Tuvok understood that his apparent initial rapprochement with the admiral had merely been the result of the exigent circumstances arising from Tuvok's hair's-breadth rescue.

Why am I having such vivid recollections of the Neltedian planetoid? he wondered as he began exchanging his black robe for a standard duty uniform. Perhaps the reason was merely Akaar's presence aboard *Titan*.

Or maybe it is because Akaar, too, is plagued by those memories. Thanks to the unexpectedly strong telepathic bond he and Mekrikuk had forged during their imprisonment together, Tuvok was inclined at least to see this as a possibility.

And, perhaps, to consider that the time might have come to bury the past, once and for all.

"Computer, where is Admiral Akaar?"

Approximately four minutes later, Tuvok stood in a nearly empty corridor on deck five. He touched the controls to the door chime.

"Come," answered a deep voice from the keypad on the wall.

The door hissed open and Admiral Leonard James Akaar stood in the open doorway. Gone was the dress uniform tunic he had worn hours earlier at Ledrah's memorial service, but the sleep-rumpled red uniform shirt he still wore, opened at the sternum, as well as the dark pigmentation surrounding Akaar's eyes, testified to the restless night his old friend had spent thus far, and the troubled state of his psyche.

"Commander," Akaar said. "The hour is late."

"But perhaps it is not too late for either of us, Admiral," Tuvok answered. "We need to talk."

Akaar smiled thinly but without any evident humor. "Then perhaps you had better come inside." He stepped back from the doorway and gestured toward the interior of the wide VIP quarters he occupied.

"Sit. Be comfortable," Akaar said, taking a seat on a sofa after the door had closed, ensuring their privacy.

Tuvok took a seat near the far wall. "It is time for us to set our differences aside."

Akaar regarded him impassively for several moments before replying. "Why now, Commander? Do you anticipate that we will be forced to share one another's company for an extended period?"

"Given some of my previous experiences," Tuvok said, raising an eyebrow. "I must acknowledge that as a distinct possibility."

The huge Capellan chuckled, a great rumbling sound that reminded Tuvok of better times. "It must be getting tiresome for you, constantly being catapulted thousands of light-years from Federation space."

"That is something of an understatement," Tuvok admitted drily. "After three such events, I have begun to wonder if my presence aboard a starship should be considered a warning to its crew." His former friend's laughter gave Tuvok hope that their old enmities might finally be laid to rest.

A look of something that resembled sadness crossed Akaar's weathered features. "I tried to save your life, Tuvok."

"And I will always appreciate that, Leonard."

Akaar's eyes narrowed. "Can you explain how denying a Capellan warrior his honorable death constitutes 'appreciation'?"

Tuvok had rehearsed this conversation for years. Despite that, he found it difficult to govern his rising anger. "Perhaps. If you can explain how ritual suicide is an action befitting a Starfleet captain."

Akaar rose, his eyes blazing as they had just before Tuvok's abrupt transfer off the *Wyoming* all those years ago. The rapprochement the Vulcan had hoped for had suddenly become as remote as his home planet. "Leave now," the Capellan said. "While you still can."

Tuvok slowly rose. With as much dignity as he could muster, he nodded, turned, and withdrew back into the corridor.

DAY 12—STARDATE 26815.4 (25 OCTOBER 2349)

Tuvok pounded his hands onto the chest of his captain with as much force as he could muster, then pulled the other man's mouth open and breathed into the Capellan's still, supine body yet again.

He didn't know how long it had been since Akaar had attempted suicide, since Tuvok had awakened only a minute earlier, and had found the note outside his tent.

Akaar's skin was cold, and he had no pulse, but Tuvok continued breathing into him, willing his old friend back to life. How could this have happened? There were no apparent physical causes; Akaar's body bore no mark save those this planetoid had already inflicted upon them both.

Another minute passed. How long has it been now? *Another ten breaths, another five chest compressions.*

And nothing.

Tuvok put his arm behind his friend's neck and pulled his rag-clad torso up to him, cradling him close. Acting on equal parts desperation and instinct, he extended the fingers of his left hand and placed them against Akaar's temple.

He spoke directly into the essence of his dying friend. My mind to your mind. *Deliberately constructed barriers lay in his way. Tuvok's will crashed right through them, though he knew that the intensely private Akaar would not approve of the intrusion. Tuvok did not care; he would not permit Akaar to die if there was anything he could do to prevent it.*

Tuvok's will encountered that of Akaar, which sat in the center of a cyclone of honor, love, and loyalty. Tuvok realized then why his friend's imminent death had left no phys-

ical marks on him: it had come as a result of some form of self-induced biofeedback. A ritual, psionic suicide?

He also saw that the proximity of death had blunted Akaar's usual ferocious determination to carry out his decisions. Akaar's fading consciousness drifted aimlessly, spiraling ever downward toward final oblivion. Therefore the Capellan was unable to put up a fight when Tuvok's mind reached out, gasping Akaar, straining to drag him back from the abyss the way a drowning man might be pulled out of Vulcan's Eastern Sea.

The mind-meld abruptly dissolved, and Tuvok found himself sprawled across the hard ground beneath Akaar's tent. He turned his head and saw that Akaar lay beside him, utterly still.

Failure. I have failed to save my friend. And he killed himself because of *me.*

Despite every bit of Vulcan training he'd had, and every iota of power he had used to block his emotions, Tuvok was overcome. His bellow to the sky was followed by tears of shock, of shame, and of sacrifice.

Then came the anger.

Tuvok turned his back on Akaar's body, stood, and exited the shelter.

Another wail passed his lips unbidden, and the loss poured down his cheeks. But as his anguish echoed across the desert landscape, he heard something behind him.

A cough.

Then another.

Whirling, he tore open Akaar's tent and saw his dead friend raise his hand to his throat, his motions shaky and tentative.

Tuvok knelt beside him, his grief turned to a smile that he would never have recognized on his own face.

"Leonard?"

Slowly, Akaar opened his eyes. They were intensely bloodshot, and this gave his glare a strange, ruddy cast.

Minutes later—or was it hours?—Akaar finally spoke.

"Why did you stop me?" It was barely more than a whisper.

"Because it wasn't your time to die," Tuvok said.

"I had decided that it was."

"You were wrong," Tuvok said. "They will find us. We will be rescued. We will have many years to continue our friendship."

Akaar stared at him in silence, blinking once, then twice, then a third time.

"No," he said, finally. "You disrupted the w'lash'no-got. You have dishonored me. You have betrayed our friendship."

Akaar turned on his side, away from Tuvok. The Vulcan sat still, unable to respond.

Though he wanted to, Tuvok would not leave Akaar's side for the next day. No matter the cost to their friendship or himself, he would not allow his captain to die.

A short time later, a shuttlecraft from the Wyoming *landed on the planetoid. Rescue had arrived. Finally.*

But aboard the shuttle, and in the Wyoming's *sickbay, and later still, Tuvok felt the chasm between himself and Akaar growing ever wider. The captain would only speak to him when duty required it.*

During the ship's next starbase visit a week later, Tuvok learned that he was being unceremoniously transferred off the Wyoming. *His trajectory would not intersect again with Akaar's for another three decades.*

Until Titan *brought them together again.*

CHAPTER FIVE

Donatra heard the voice, but only barely, as though it was coming from a considerable distance. She felt as though she were floating at the bottom of a well, her eyes swaddled in a heavy blanket of darkness.

Death, she thought. *This is death, come for me at last.*

But the fire that lanced her side, the stubborn remnant of the wounds she had received during her recent struggles against the hated false praetor Tal'Aura, argued eloquently that she was anything but dead. The blackness that surrounded her slowly morphed into a deep red. She became cognizant that she still possessed eyes, though she had to expend an extraordinary amount of effort just to force them open.

"Commander!" shouted Seketh, the young female decurion who crouched over her. Seketh's voice sounded far more shrill than it had ever sounded before.

The remainder of her senses beginning to return to her, Donatra felt the hard deckplates beneath her back. Heat from a smoldering duty station across the room warmed the back of her neck. Ozone stung her nostrils, helping her focus her energies. Emergency lighting cast bizarre shadows across the bridge of the warbird *Valdore*. The broad central viewscreen, which dominated the forward section of the wide, semicircular chamber, displayed a violent hailstorm of static.

"Report," Donatra said, her throat feeling as rough as ancient granite as she pushed herself up into a sitting position. Seketh hastened to take her arm, helping her rise to her feet.

"Most of the ship's systems are functioning only marginally, if at all. All propulsion will be down for at least an entire *eisae,* and we have hull breaches on B and C decks. Damage control teams have already been dispatched. Reports of injuries are coming in from all over the ship, six of them critical. There have been three deaths, including Subcommander T'Kraith."

Akhh! Donatra thought as she surveyed the details of the systems report, which were scrolling upward on the nearby operations console. *My first officer, gone. Still more death during my watch.* She thought she remembered having seen something rush toward the ship from the center of Shinzon's Folly, the mysterious energy cloud that was already becoming known throughout the Empire as the Great Bloom. What had the Bloom—the remnant of Shinzon's dreaded, and thankfully exploded, thalaron weapon—done to the *Valdore*? It seemed to Donatra that the vindictive shade of the dead praetor was still taking the lives of her crew, if only indirectly. And that didn't even take into account whatever had happened to the rest of the fleet.

She found that completely unacceptable. "What exactly happened to us?" she asked Seketh.

"Something hit us, Commander."

Now vividly recalling the moment of impact, Donatra frowned at the decurion. "Obviously. Were we fired upon?"

"We can't rule it out, Commander," Seketh said. "But if it was weapons fire, it wasn't like anything I've ever seen before."

Moving shakily, Donatra headed toward the command chair, which was mounted atop a riser in the bridge's center. She took her seat in silence, wondering if one of Governor Khegh's warships might have cloaked itself, then followed the *Valdore* and *Titan* to the Bloom. Had the Klingons then launched a sneak attack while her attention had been occupied by the Great Bloom, and the missing fleet she sought to recover from its maw? She seriously doubted that *Titan*'s commander, whom she had aided in the battle to bring down Praetor Shinzon, would have employed such treachery.

The Klingons, however, were another matter entirely.

But hadn't whatever struck the *Valdore* come from *inside* the Great Bloom? Her best recollection told her that this was so.

Still, her gut warned her that she still needed to stay alert for cloaked Klingons. Khegh's skillful ascension to the governorship of a Klingon-Reman protectorate in Romulan space made it clear to her now that the Klingon officer's blustering churlishness was but a tactic calculated to make him easy to underestimate. Tal'Aura might have fallen for the ruse, but Donatra was determined not to be so foolish.

Liravek, a male centurion with somewhat more experience than Seketh, approached Donatra from one of the bridge's few undamaged consoles. "I can find no trace of the residual energy particles characteristic of weapons fire anywhere on the *Valdore*'s hull."

Donatra's frown deepened. "Then what has happened to us?"

Liravek shrugged almost imperceptibly, his composure far more strained than Donatra had ever seen it. "We appear to have been caught in a natural energy discharge of some kind."

"Originating where?" Donatra asked, though she was becoming certain that she already knew the answer.

Liravek nodded toward the main viewer, whose static had finally cleared enough to reveal an image that was simultaneously familiar and strange. "From somewhere inside the spatial rift."

Donatra looked toward the multicolored, fiercely beautiful image of what amounted to a gigantic rent in the fabric of space. The florid, grasping hands of the Great Bloom, the fell thing created by dead Shinzon's overweening ambition, had evidently turned its fury upon the *Valdore,* just as she had suspected—and just as it had apparently already done to the fleet she had so carefully hidden just inside the energy cloud's coruscating periphery. As a result, the several dozen warbirds that she and Commander Suran had painstakingly assembled had vanished without a trace. She was now more determined than ever to locate and recover those vessels, and their loyal Romulan crews.

She wondered: How had Captain Riker's vessel weathered the Bloom's wrath? Had *Titan* been drawn here as well?

"Scan the rift and the region surrounding it as carefully as you can for other ships, Centurion Liravek," she said, her eyes fixed upon the viewer as though her stare alone might tease out the phenomenon's secrets.

As Centurion Liravek, Decurion Seketh, Centurion T'Relek, and a pair of junior technicians made haste to carry out this order, a chime sounded on the arm of Donatra's command chair, indicating an incoming message.

"Infirmary to bridge," said Dr. Venora, the *Valdore*'s chief medical officer. *"We're being swamped with injuries down here, Commander. What happened up there?"*

In spite of herself, Donatra smiled slightly at Venora's overly gruff tone. Nobody else aboard the *Valdore* would dare to speak to her in this manner. Except, perhaps, for Commander Suran, with whom Donatra had served under the command of her murdered lover, Admiral Braeg.

Suran, with whom Donatra had uneasily shared control of the Romulan Star Empire's combined military forces during the many weeks that had passed since Shinzon's death.

Suran, she thought. *Why isn't he on the bridge?*

"I'll inform you fully once we've found a definitive answer to that question, Doctor."

A pause. *"All right. But I'm quite sure that Commander Suran won't be satisfied with that. Once he regains consciousness, that is."*

Donatra needed a moment to process this news. Suran's expertise had been quite useful to her on a number of occasions, so she had no wish to see him die. However, there were also times when he had proved to be a real impediment to the plans she had made to expand the military faction's influence and resource base. If he were to die in service to the Empire, Donatra would lose the value of Suran's not inconsiderable experience.

But there would be far fewer challenges to her decisions, in that event.

Like my decision to hide the fleet within the periphery of the Great Bloom? asked a small, accusatory voice in a still back corner of Donatra's mind.

"What is Suran's prognosis, Doctor?" she said, forcibly pushing her self-recriminations aside.

"His injuries are superficial, Commander. A concussion and some cuts. It would have taken far worse to keep him out of action for long."

Relief and disappointment wrestled within her breast in equal measure. How long would it be before Suran was back on the bridge, reminding her that she had placed the security of the Empire in grave peril by losing the fleet?

"Then I will hope for a speedy recovery, Doctor. Keep me advised. Bridge out."

Donatra rose from her chair, her old wounds aching slightly as she moved toward Centurion T'Relek's duty station. He was staring intently into a small, console-mounted monitor, and the perplexed expression on his weathered, angular face had drawn her attention.

"What is it, Centurion? Have you found any sign of our fleet? Or of *Titan*?"

T'Relek turned his dark eyes on her. "The Bloom's energy emissions are interfering greatly with our sensors, Commander. So the readings we're getting are inconclusive. Even the subspace bands are jammed."

"Then we must increase our distance from the Bloom until we've cleared the interference it is generating."

"Yes, Commander. It will be so as soon as the propulsion systems are repaired. But there's something else."

She noticed that his look of perplexity had deepened. "What is it?"

"The constellation of Khellian the Hunter has vanished. As have Dhael the Raptor and Ravsam the Sisters."

Donatra looked over T'Relek's shoulder so that she, too, could study the starfield that his scans, such as they were, had compiled thus far.

She saw then that it was a completely unfamiliar stellar

arrangement, as though the stars had suddenly been re-set, tossed instantly into a new random pattern, like the dice some deity might roll in a cosmic game of Trayatik.

"This has to be a sensor error of some sort, Commander," T'Relek said.

Donatra felt her throat suddenly go dry. A horrible, plummeting sensation was developing in her belly. She recalled a report filed a decade ago by Commander T'Reth, who had captained the Imperial Warbird *Draco* when a temporary spatial rift had instantly displaced it by over a dozen parsecs. Had something like that just happened to the *Valdore*?

"Dispatch a full complement of sensor drones," Donatra ordered. "Use ordinary EM transmissions for telemetry if you cannot overcome the Bloom's subspace interference. We cannot afford to wait for functional engines to determine what has become of our ships, *Titan,* and any Klingon vessels that might have quietly followed us to the Bloom."

And I must know exactly what has happened to the stars.

It had taken several *veraku,* a goodly portion of a Romulan day in fact, to receive and analyze the data the drones had collected and transmitted to the still-crippled warbird *Valdore.* During that time, Donatra had kept some of her bridge crew busy scanning the depths of the Bloom to the very limits of the ship's sensor acuity, despite the energy cloud's persistent—and uniformly successful—efforts to withhold its secrets.

She had ordered the uninjured members of her science and stellar navigation staff to keep their eyes and instruments turned outward, toward the brilliant scattering of unfamiliar stars that lay far beyond the Great Bloom in every direction.

Now she almost regretted the alacrity with which her people had discovered the answer to her most salient question: *Where are we?*

"There is no mistake, Commander," Liravek said with an almost resigned calm. "The *Valdore* is no longer located in Romulan space, or anywhere near Romulan space."

"But how can that be?" Suran said, almost growling as he stabbed a thick finger toward the majestic energy cloud displayed on the main bridge viewer. Then he adjusted the bandage that swathed his thick brow; he was no doubt still in considerable pain from the fall he had taken when the Great Bloom had lashed out at the *Valdore* the previous day. "The spatial rift is obviously still there. And we all know that the Great Bloom is positioned well inside Romulan space."

Donatra glanced toward Dr. Venora, who stood beside an unoccupied diagnostic console, her lined face framed by her shoulder-length, gray-streaked hair as she kept a watchful medical eye trained squarely on Suran. Donatra closed her own eyes briefly, choosing not to respond to Suran's remark. He had, after all, regained consciousness only a little while ago, immediately after which time he had bullied Dr. Venora into releasing him earlier than was probably wise.

"The Great Bloom apparently has the capacity to displace objects across vast interstellar distances, Commander," Centurion Liravek said. "Or even inter*galactic* distances. The Bloom we see now is merely the other side of a spatial rift that extends all the way out here."

"And just *where* is *here?*" Suran asked, sounding ever more frustrated.

"Well inside the small satellite galaxy known on our maps as Enhaire."

Suran shook his head, which made him wince in pain. "That's impossible, Centurion. No ship has ever traveled so far out of the galaxy."

"Perhaps not before today," Donatra said. "It's possible that we're the first." *And there's always a first time for everything.*

She wondered then whether the other ships of the fleet were here as well. But if that were so, then where were they?

A sensor alarm suddenly whooped on Decurion Seketh's console, whose touch-sensitive surfaces were alight with frantic brightness.

The Valdore *may be among the first to get out this far,* Donatra thought as she strode toward Seketh's station. *But perhaps she isn't the only one to have made this voyage* today.

"What have you found, Decurion?" Donatra asked.

Seketh's eyes grew wide. "At least one large vessel, and what appear to be several small metallic objects."

"Debris?"

"Negative, Commander. They read as pressurized, and there appear to be intermittently detectable life signs coming from within each of them."

"Escape pods, then."

"I believe so, Commander."

Donatra nodded. "Are there any life signs on the large vessel?"

"Apparently, Commander, though it is difficult to be certain because of the sensor interference created by the Great Bloom."

"Can the ship and the pods be recovered?" Donatra asked.

"Possibly," Seketh said. "Though the power cost and the strain on ship's systems will be excessive. The escape pods and the other ship are drifting in opposite directions, nearly a thousand *k'vahru* deeper inside the periphery of the Bloom than our current position. And they all appear to be spiraling dangerously close to the rift's event horizon. Unless the Bloom's energy discharges are fooling our sensors."

"What is the ship's configuration?" Donatra asked, only now allowing herself to hope that she stood a real chance of conferring with Captain Riker about a mutual problem.

The decurion studied her readings for a moment longer, then looked up again, her eyes widening further. "It's *Klingon!"*

"Tactical alert!" shouted Donatra.

Whatever punishment the *Valdore* had suffered during its passage through the Great Bloom, the Klingon warship she now approached had clearly experienced far, far worse. It had been in no condition to put up a fight when the *Valdore* tractored her, along with the nearby quartet of escape pods, away from the immediate vicinity of the Bloom's hazardous event horizon. The Klingon vessel, which belonged to the large, heavily armed and armored *Vor'cha* class, apparently no longer possessed even the capacity to be coaxed into a deliberate, self-immolating warp core breach to prevent her from being captured by Romulan personnel. Because the larger vessel was so much more damaged than any of the escape pods, Donatra made rescue operations on the former a higher priority than of the latter.

Donatra studied the battered, broken Klingon ship, beyond which drifted four tiny, dented and scorched escape pods. She marveled that anyone aboard the Klingon vessel had survived its countless hull breaches, even as a pair of its officers materialized on the warbird's primary transporter stage before her, Suran, Dr. Venora, and a heavily armed Romulan security team.

"I am Commander Donatra," Donatra said, stepping toward her two guests a moment after they had finished materializing. "You are aboard the Imperial Warbird *Valdore.*"

The taller of the pair of Klingon figures who now stood on the transporter stage was a fierce-looking male whose thick, rough-textured forehead bore an angry wound that oozed a viscous lavender fluid. His heavily mailed though distressed leather uniform bore the rank insignia of a ship's captain in the Klingon Defense Force. Beside him stood an equally imposing if slightly smaller female, who appeared relatively uninjured and whose uniform markings identified her as a lieutenant. Their sharp, snaggly teeth reminded Donatra of the summer during her childhood she had spent tending *thraiin* on her uncle's *waith* farm. What she recalled most about that experience was that *thraiin* were vicious, smelly, and thoroughly repugnant creatures, however succulent their flesh might taste.

Animals, Donatra thought as she eyed the Klingons, feeling the profound, visceral revulsion she always experienced when in the presence of these people. Unlike *thraiin,* Klingons lacked even the single redeeming characteristic of being edible—or so she had been told. *How could we have allowed the likes of* these *to establish a beachhead in Romulan space?*

The male Klingon puffed up his chest in an apparent effort to compensate for the shabby condition of his uniform. "I am Captain Tchev, master of the *I.K.S. Dugh,*" he said, gesturing toward the female beside him. "My second officer, Lieutenant Dekri." Coldly eyeing the armed guards who now flanked him and his third in command, Tchev added, "And we would appear to be your prisoners."

Donatra smiled mirthlessly. "I thought our respective empires were allies now, Captain. You are our guests."

"That was during the war," Tchev sniffed. "How many of the rest of my crew now number among your 'guests'?"

"Besides yourself and your second officer," Donatra said with studied calmness, "we have identified thirty-four other surviving personnel on your vessel, which we have taken in tow." *At considerable cost,* she added silently, regretting the huge drain the salvage operation was placing on the *Valdore*'s power resources. "We are in the process of bringing your people aboard this vessel, for their own safety."

"And what, exactly, do you intend to do with them?"

"All of your personnel will be well accommodated," Donatra said, nodding. It had been relatively easy to convert one of the *Valdore*'s empty cargo bays into an impromptu detention area nearly as secure as the ship's brig.

"And I will ensure that they will receive whatever medical care they need," Dr. Venora told the Klingon captain, prompting Donatra to raise an eyebrow slightly in the physician's direction. Venora, who had been practicing medicine aboard Imperial military vessels for nearly a century, frequently did not see fit to seek her considerably younger commander's leave before speaking her mind. It was a trait that Donatra found both invaluable and annoying.

Dekri hawked and spat a noxious, yellowish mass onto the transporter stage. "None of our crew will ever allow a Romulan *bachHa'* to lay hands upon them. They would take their own lives before accepting such a soiling."

"Good," Suran said, staring with evident disgust at the spittle-dabbed transporter. "That would greatly simplify matters for us. Would they prefer to commit suicide here, or back aboard your wreck of a ship?"

Venora scowled at him. "Is that any way to talk to our wartime allies, Commander?"

"A great deal has happened since the Dominion War, Doctor, just as our esteemed Captain Tchev has suggested," Suran said, evidently disgusted by the good doctor's naïveté.

"Why did you follow us to the energy cloud?" Donatra asked Tchev, cutting off the exchange between her colleagues.

"We will tell you nothing, Romulan *taHqeq*," Tchev growled, displaying his brown, uneven teeth.

"Perhaps not willingly," Suran said. "However, we could always acquaint you with our mind probes."

"I have been trained to withstand the highest settings on a Klingon mind-sifter," Tchev replied, raising his chin contemptuously. "Your interrogations hold no fear for me."

Glaring at Suran, Dekri bared a phalanx of sharp, crooked teeth that looked every bit as unattractive as Tchev's. "I doubt you would dare to try it. Not with a Reman-Klingon alliance poised in the skies above your Empire's capital city."

Suran appeared unruffled by Dekri's threat. "Perhaps you haven't noticed yet, but we're a long way from Romulus at the moment."

Donatra was growing impatient with Suran's sparring with the Klingons. "It doesn't matter, Suran. It's perfectly obvious why the Klingons are here. Governor Khegh must have observed the *Valdore* flying from the vicinity of Romulus to the Great Bloom, with *Titan* at her side. He would have been remiss not to have dispatched a cloaked vessel in an attempt to discover the reason behind this joint voyage."

Donatra met Tchev's stare, which gave away little other than a Klingon's characteristic belligerence. But that, in itself, told her that the Klingons were very likely still completely in the dark about why the *Valdore* and *Titan* had quietly left the vicinity of Romulus together. *Were it otherwise, would Tchev not boast of his knowledge?* Donatra seriously doubted that neither Tchev nor Dekri were aware of the Romulan fleet that the Great Bloom had unexpectedly swallowed the previous day.

"Regardless," Donatra continued, "we will now commence rescuing the personnel aboard your escape pods."

Tchev tipped his head, frowning. "What are you talking about, Romulan *petaQ?*"

"Excuse me?" Donatra said, carefully blanking her face so as not to register surprise.

"We launched no escape pods," Dekri said, her bulbous head lofted haughtily. Donatra decided she didn't much care for the lieutenant's stare, which she now noticed was drifting away from her face and moving down her torso in an appraising, almost lascivious manner.

Revolted, Donatra turned to face the decurion who was in charge of operating the transporter console. "Have you obtained a transporter lock on the personnel contained in those escape pods?"

"Yes, Commander."

Donatra turned back to Tchev. She fixed him with a hard stare as she continued addressing the decurion. "Scan the life-forms within. Are they Klingon?"

"No, Commander," the junior officer said, surprise evident in his tone.

"Do you recognize the species?"

"Not all of them, Commander. One pod contains several biosignatures that I've never seen before. But all the rest of the life signs . . ." He trailed off momentarily as he tapped commands into his console, as if double-checking a result that couldn't possibly be correct.

"Well?" Suran demanded, scowling. "Do you recognize any of the rest?"

The decurion looked up from his instruments, his pale features presenting a study in incredulity. "They're *human*, Commander."

Frane grasped the bracelet nearly hard enough to crush some of its more ancient stones. To avoid doing just that, he carefully wrapped the bracelet around his left wrist, the way his father had worn it.

Quaking in fear as she pressed up against him, Nozomi established a similarly viselike grip on Frane's other hand, while her tail wrapped around his waist almost tightly enough to cut off his air. The Oghen pairbond, g'Ishea and Fasaryl, as well as the sensory portions of Lofi, the multi-partite Sturr, crowded behind him in an effort to see what he was seeing. The five of them were all that remained of the Seekers After Penance.

Gazing through the small, round window of the evacuation capsule, Frane watched with mounting horror as the graceful, predatory-looking ship made its slow, menacing approach. Though the vessel had taken a fair amount of exterior damage, its appearance was unmistakable.

It was definitely the same type of ship that had comprised the flotilla that wiped out his father's military vessels scarcely an Oghenturn earlier.

"So they've come back to finish us off," Fasaryl said, his multiple stomachs gurgling loudly in evident terror.

"Be quiet," Frane said. "And please try to keep your innards under control." He had been in close quarters with the Oghen pair for too long, and could tell that he was growing irritable because of it. Immediately regretting his brusqueness, he turned toward the cowlike creatures and continued speaking in milder tones. "The other ships attacked from a much greater distance. This one appears to be only a handful of klomters away."

"And they have other concerns as well," Lofi said, one of her sensory stalks crossing over Frane's shoulder and bobbing close to the glass. "They appear to be towing another ship."

"How can you tell?" Frane said, squinting into the blackness. Lacking Lofi's extraordinarily sensitive vision, he thought he'd have to take her word for it.

Then he saw it: a hole among the stars, a slowly moving region of blackness that obscured the tendrils of energy visible within the ragged edges of the Sleeper. A shape that resembled a large vessel of some sort. It evidently lacked the power even for running lights, and had a swooping, tapered shape similar to the profile of the vessel that was apparently towing it.

"They attacked before," Fasaryl said. "They'll attack again."

"We don't know that," Frane said, though he had to admit he felt every bit as frightened as the Oghen.

Then Fasaryl vanished in a shimmer of light, followed immediately by Lofi, who shrieked in pain at being teleported away in pieces, since her multipartite body had not been gathered into a single unit when the aliens' teleportation beam found her. Frane heard g'Ishea lowing in panic, her hooves clattering frantically against the capsule's floor as she, too, vanished.

Before he could utter a single word of comfort to the terrified Nozomi, the shimmering light returned, claiming them both.

The next several hours were a blur of terror for Frane. He recalled little, except that he had been separated from the other Seekers After Penance, and had been permitted neither to see nor to speak with Nozomi. They had been taken by sallow-skinned men and women who resembled nothing more than the marauding, green-blooded elves from out of the centuries-old legends of the People of Oh-Neyel. His captors had confiscated almost every bodily adornment from him, including his pilgrim's robe and underclothing, and had struck him when he'd tried to prevent them from snatching away the ancient story bracelet he had removed—had it been only yesterday?—from his father's corpse. After taking even that, they had drugged him, as best as he could recall through his current state of befuddlement, and had shouted at him repeatedly in a tongue he couldn't understand.

At some point they had evidently shaved his gray scalp, and a gray-haired, pointed-eared woman with an oddly kind face had attached slender cables to his skull. She spoke several unintelligible commands into a handheld control device.

Red, raging red pain followed, during which he screamed and pleaded and babbled and cried and laughed like a lunatic. He had been a Seeker After Penance, and now he had found a surfeit of it. A black pit of unconsciousness opened next, and he fell gratefully into it, tumbling end over end over end into oblivion.

Then he slept. He dreamed that the Sleeper had at last

come fully awake, sweeping away the alien ships, the evacuation capsules.

And every planet his people had ever colonized, exploited, and ruined.

After an eternity, he came awake in a pool of cold sweat, suddenly disappointed that the Sleeper had *not* risen to relieve his misery once and for all. The kind-faced elf woman he had seen earlier was staring beneficently down at him. She spoke to him in an almost gentle voice.

To his enormous surprise, he understood her words this time.

Standing beside Dr. Venora, Donatra watched the sleeping alien patient through the infirmary's one-way transparisteel window. The strange semihumanoid creature, now dressed in a short-sleeved, open-necked infirmary smock, lay unconscious on one of the treatment beds, a rumpled white sheet draped over flesh that looked as gray as that of a Cardassian, and nearly as tough as that of a Nasat.

"You're sure you've overcome the language barrier?"

Venora nodded, a rueful expression on her lined face. Donatra knew that she avoided using coercion on her patients whenever possible. But the doctor had bowed to the necessity of expediting the information-gathering process. And the missing fleet *had* to be found, after all.

"The sessions with the mind-probes greatly accelerated the work of our translation matrix," Venora said, glancing down at the padd in her hand. "It might have taken an entire *eisae* otherwise merely to parse his language. We seem to have managed it in just a couple of *veraku,* possibly because it appears to contain certain elements of Federation Standard."

Donatra's eyes widened at this surprising revelation, and she nodded an acknowledgment. "Well done, Doctor. I wonder how the language of the Federation managed to spread so far from its source."

"I imagine that must have happened the same way their human biosigns got out here." Venora offered her superior a small, lopsided grin. "But since human migrations aren't my area of expertise, Commander, I'll concentrate instead on matters of medicine and physiology. The biomonitors show that he's regaining consciousness. You may speak with him now. His name is Frane. So far, I've had time to learn little else."

"Thank you, Doctor." Donatra said, then strode toward the infirmary door. Venora followed her to the patient's bedside, as did a pair of armed guards.

Donatra looked at the recumbent figure on the infirmary bed; the sheet draped over it did not obscure the rough gray hide, the opposable thumbs on its feet, nor the long, thick-thewed tail that dangled limply onto the deck-plating.

"This creature is an Earth human?" Donatra asked quietly, leaning toward the doctor.

"Genetically, though obviously not in phenotype," Venora said in a near-whisper. "This individual appears to possess a number of adaptations to long periods of micro-gravity, with traits that resemble those of arboreal pri-mates."

"I've never seen any other humans with such traits."

"Nor have I, Commander. But there's no reason these creatures could not have evolved from baseline human stock, just as we split off from our Vulcan forebears, mil-lennia ago."

Donatra stared in growing wonderment at the slumber-ing alien. "An Earth human."

Venora leaned over her patient, studying him with evident concern. "As counterintuitive as that may be, that is the essential truth of it," she said quietly. "This creature's genes, or at least most of them, originated on Earth."

The alien's stiff, shutter-like eyelids slowly opened then, revealing dark, extremely alert eyes. Those deep brown orbs showed fear at first, until they lit upon Venora, whose presence appeared to calm him, at least somewhat. The doctor had evidently built up at least some degree of trust with the alien already.

"Not . . . not of Aerth," the creature said, sitting up in a tentative, cautious manner. The guards stood by attentively only a few paces away, obviously ready to vaporize the alien at the first sign of trouble. The alien's eyes fell upon Donatra and narrowed with obvious distaste.

"Who are you?"

"I am Commander Donatra, of the Romulan Imperial Warbird *Valdore,* which you are aboard," Donatra said, trying to sound both authoritative and nonthreatening.

He nodded. "You want something of me."

"Only the answers to a few questions."

"I cannot prevent you from asking them, Commander."

"You've already told us that you're not an Earth human," Donatra said. That made sense, considering how very far away Earth was from this extremely remote region of space. "So what exactly *are* you, Mr. Frane?"

The creature, this Frane, tilted its head in evident puzzlement.

"What do your people call themselves?" Venora said, by way of clarification.

"We are called Neyel." Looking at Venora, Frane added, "Where are the others who accompanied me in the evacuation capsule?"

"We found a total of four of your escape pods . . . evacuation capsules," Donatra said.

"Four?" Frane appeared surprised, but Donatra couldn't tell if that was because he had expected more or fewer of the pods to have survived whatever disaster had precipitated their launch.

"Three of the pods contained members of your species, all of whom are apparently uniformed members of your people's military. You were found in the last one, along with a female . . . Neyel. And three aliens of species we have never encountered before."

The creature sat more fully upright, moving quickly enough to provoke the guards, who raised their weapons in a gesture of unambiguous warning.

"Easy," Venora said, clearly speaking to the guards as much as to Frane.

Frane remained sitting up in the bed, utterly still and rigid as a statue. The only movement Donatra could see in him was contained in the sound of his voice. And in the play of emotions behind his eyes.

"Where are they? Nozomi and g'Ishea and Fasaryl and Lofi. What have you done with—"

Donatra spread her hands and interrupted him. "Those who shared the pod with you are safe. They are elsewhere aboard this vessel."

Frane met Donatra's gaze directly. "I wish to see them."

"You shall. But I need to get a few more answers from you first."

The Neyel only glared at her in stony silence.

Donatra didn't need Venora's training in psychology to see that Frane was becoming oppositional. She knew that if he was to be spared the very real risk of permanent brain damage from truly invasive mind scans, then she had better do more than simply intimidate him. She had to win his confidence.

She reached into a pouch on the lower front of her uniform jacket and withdrew a short loop of fabric, into which countless stones, shells, bones, and gems had been sewn. She held it up so that the Neyel could see it clearly.

"You were wearing this when you were brought aboard. It seemed to be very important to you." Indeed, he had fought like a wild rainjungle *zdonek* to keep it.

She handed him the object in silence. It lay in his open palm and he regarded it in what might have been silent reverence.

"Your remote ancestors were obviously Earth humans," she said, disturbing the deep quiet that had descended upon the infirmary. "How did they get out into this region of space?"

Frane shrugged, still staring at the small loop of fabric in his left hand. "No one knows for certain. Many records were lost during and after the Great Sundering, centuries ago."

The term "Sundering" took Donatra somewhat aback. Romulans often used this very same term to refer to their own people's millennia-past separation from their Vulcan ancestors. It made sense. After all, if Vulcans could beget Romulans, then why couldn't humans have begat the Neyel?

"So how did *you* get out here?" Frane asked, tilting his head slightly.

"The Great Bloom evidently brought us here," she said. In response to the blank stare that greeted this revelation, she added, "The large energy cloud from which we retrieved you and your people."

Frane's eyes widened slightly, though he maintained his composure well. "The Sleeper brought you here then."

Donatra sighed; whatever this "sleeper" was, she had no desire to receive a lecture on interstellar mythology. At least not now.

"Why were you and your people in evacuation capsules?" she asked, trying her best to keep the military steel out of her voice. Her fleet, after all, remained missing, its fate unknown.

Frane replied after a lengthy pause. "We were forced to abandon our ship. Surely you were able to divine that for yourselves. Or learn that from one of the ship's officers."

Donatra shook her head. "You're the first Neyel we've succeeded in communicating with so far."

"Ah," Frane said, a look of understanding crossing his strangely immobile, gray features. "You must have assumed I would be easier to coerce than the military officers would be. My father always underestimated me in much the same way."

I had better tread very carefully here, Donatra thought, wondering why the Neyel military had been transporting civilians. *Were they mission specialists? Or perhaps prisoners?*

Aloud, she said, "Civilians often have a . . . less rigid perspective in situations such as these."

Frane's hard lips curved upward ironically. "And they may also be less likely to die from a brainbleed if you were to apply those mental scanners of yours to some purpose other than basic language acquisition."

He's no simpleton, this one, Donatra thought. *I mustn't make the mistake of underestimating him.*

"I have no desire to test that proposition, Mr. Frane," she said aloud, smiling as compassionate a smile as she could muster. In truth, she had no wish to inflict harm on this creature, or on the other civilian Neyel—the female—that they had rescued. Indeed, Donatra had decided to make communicating with Frane a priority because the female had seemed far too frail and terrified to withstand interrogation. And the three unknown sentients that had also shared Frane's escape pod were simply *too* alien for even shallow mind-probing to yield any predictable outcome.

Frane slumped back onto the bed in apparent resignation. Donatra wondered if he had decided to cooperate in order to safeguard his female.

"What do you want to know?" he said, sighing.

"Why, exactly, you abandoned your ship, Mr. Frane."

"We were attacked."

"By whom?" Donatra asked. Once again, she was growing impatient, though she continued doing her utmost to conceal that fact.

"By other ships that emerged from the Sleeper and have since disappeared into the space of the Neyel Hegemony."

Donatra's throat suddenly went dry. "Other ships. What did these other ships look like?"

"They were large warships. Long, tapering vessels that greatly resemble this one, unless I'm very much mistaken. I saw dozens of them. Their attack was brief, but devastating."

Donatra's heart thudded in her side, feeling like a singularity drive going rapidly into overload. *My fleet. My fleet* is *here, somewhere in this gods-forsaken corner of space.*

But why would her people have used her ships to mount such a senseless attack, and then flee ever deeper into the unknown?

Then, even as Donatra began to frame that question, the infirmary was plunged into stygian darkness.

CHAPTER SIX

The baleful green dullness of the *Valdore*'s emergency lighting kicked in a moment later. Making her way carefully through the dim illumination, Donatra crossed to the comm panel mounted on the nearest wall.

"Bridge! Report!"

Centurion Liravek's crisp, businesslike voice replied. *"Attempting to take the Klingon vessel in tow has evidently overtaxed our primary power circuits, Commander. Even at the very low-power impulse speeds available to us. We owe it to the effects of the Great Bloom."*

"Are we clear of it?"

"Negative, Commander. The rift's random subspace effects will probably stop and reverse our drift sometime over the next several veraku. Even at our current distance from the event horizon, we are still well within the Bloom's strongest zone of subspace interference."

So sending a distress signal would be an exercise in futility, Donatra thought glumly. *Even if we had a function-*

ing comm system. She had begun hoping that the appearance of her fleet in Neyel space meant that there was at least *some* chance that Riker and his Starfleet vessel had made it here intact as well. But without a fully operational communications system or sensors, there was no way to tell.

"How soon can we effect repairs and resume a course away from the Bloom and its interference zone?"

Liravek paused briefly before responding, which was unusual for him. *"Commander, we've vented so much coolant due to the power-circuit failures, that I'm not even certain engine repair is even possible without access to spacedock facilities."*

Donatra looked back toward her Neyel "guest." Frane hadn't moved from where he lay on the infirmary bed, apparently in a well-advised effort not to alarm his two armed guards—both of whom had maintained their poise as well as a tight grip on their weapons.

The sight of the still-prone Neyel—whose presence here had resulted entirely from a chance encounter with something that lay beyond the *Valdore*'s battered hull—suddenly gave Donatra an idea.

Perhaps I should continue looking beyond my vessel for solutions to its problems.

"Thank you, Centurion," she said aloud. "I'll be on the bridge shortly to go over our options. Donatra out." She thumbed the comm circuit closed.

Dr. Venora approached, the diminished lighting accentuating the deep lines and hollows of her wise, patrician face. "Well, Commander. What now?"

Donatra offered a lopsided smile. "I'll let you know as soon as I've entirely figured it out." Turning toward the guards, she instructed them to return Venora's patient to his quarters—albeit under close watch—as soon as the doctor declared it safe to do so. Then she turned on her heel and exited into the dimly lit corridor.

"So you need my help, Commander," Tchev said. He sat across the table from Donatra, where the faint lighting did little to obscure his snaggly brown teeth. "And rather desperately, too, I gather. Delightful." His voice dripped with a liberal mixture of sarcasm and smugness.

Donatra wanted to get out of her chair and kick those vile teeth straight down his throat. Instead, she contented herself with silently grinding her own molars. *Why did I permit Venora to persuade me to grant these Klingon animals the dignity of guest quarters? They deserve nothing more than to be penned like the beasts they are.*

Of course, each of those guest quarters was being guarded very carefully by the *Valdore*'s vigilant security officers. And Donatra had made no effort to conceal that fact from the Klingons, who would doubtless have tried to move against the *Valdore*'s crew had their confinement depended upon the ship's currently de-powered security forcefields. Further, granting them the status of untrustworthy guests, rather than prisoners, at least kept them from attempting ritual suicide, as their sense of honor demanded.

Leaning forward across the table, she said. "You would appear to have little choice other than to cooperate with us, Captain Tchev. Otherwise, both the *Dugh* and the *Valdore* will slowly spiral into the center of the spatial rift. My staff is all but certain this would destroy both our vessels." *Or what's left of them,* she amended in silence.

He grinned as he leaned back in his chair, hooking his thumbs in his ornate metal baldric. "And that frightens you." It was not a question.

Of course *it frightens me,* she thought, wondering yet again how such pathological people had been able to build and maintain their civilization, such as it was, for so many centuries. *Akhh, who but an imbecilic* dha'rudh *would not fear and seek to avoid an entirely unnecessary and completely avoidable death?*

"The strain of rescuing your vessel in our current damaged state has cost us most of our power couplings and virtually all of an already-depleted coolant supply, Captain."

He made a single "tsk" sound and glowered from beneath his heavy brow. "A shame."

Donatra mustered every iota of determination she possessed to keep her tone calm and even. "We cannot hope to safely maintain our singularity drive without additional coolant supplies. And our scans show that your ship still has large quantities of the materials we need in order to get under way."

Tchev leaned forward, planting his elbows on the table. His unfriendly grin broadened further. "So why tell me? Why not simply board the *Dugh* and take what you need?"

Donatra felt her anger nearing its boiling point. "Because I wouldn't know in advance where all the booby traps are, Captain."

He looked impressed, though his insufferable grin remained. "You surprise me, Commander. Not that I didn't expect you to beg for my assistance. However, I had assumed you would insist on discovering our antipersonnel countermeasures the hard way."

She stood. "That's still an option, Captain. If both gentle persuasion and our mind-scanning equipment prove ineffective, that is. But in that event, I think I would have to insist that you and your people walk the rest of the way home from here."

Tchev's grin collapsed into a more appropriately businesslike expression. After all, there had to be *some* rational limits to the innate Klingon propensity for empty bluster.

"Very well, Commander Donatra," said Tchev, a gratifying growl thrumming beneath his words. "Only a fool fights in a burning house. And only an idiotic *Duy'* would meekly allow that house to burn down around his head."

Frane was relieved to discover that the almost lightless cabin to which the guards had escorted him contained all four of his fellow Seekers After Penance. Though each of them appeared justifiably apprehensive, none appeared to have suffered any serious injuries. Even the multipartite Lofi seemed to have all but completely recovered from the shock of having been teleported piecemeal from the evacuation capsule.

He was surprised, however, when the guards returned within a few hours to escort him away yet again. At least they had let him recover and don his pilgrim's robe. And they had made no attempt to take the story bracelet from him again. Still apprehensive that the guards might change their minds about that, he kept the bracelet out of sight, tucked into the front pocket of his robe where he could feel its stones and shells and beads whenever he felt the need. For some reason, it reassured him, as though its very presence could somehow keep him safe. Of course, that notion hadn't worked very well for his father.

Soon Frane was even more nonplussed to discover himself being escorted into what could only be the main control room of this vast ship of war. Commander Donatra was seated in the raised, thronelike chair at the brightly lit room's center, while at least half a dozen dark-haired, pale-skinned elves—*Romulans,* he corrected himself—busied themselves at various duty stations. The wide viewer that dominated the front of the chamber displayed a broad, brilliant image of the energy tendrils that made up the mysterious substance of the Sleeper.

Donatra turned her seat toward him, perhaps alerted to his entrance by her sensitive-looking pointed ears. "Ah, Mr. Frane. Welcome to my bridge."

He nodded to her, hoping she would regard the gesture as a courteous one. "Thank you. It's very impressive." His tail switched behind him involuntarily, until he forced it to remain still.

"Yes, it is that. And thanks to the cooperation of our Klingon . . . friends, our propulsion system and tractor beam are once again operational."

"Klingon?" Frane asked, as unfamiliar with the word as he had been with the term 'Romulan' until very recently.

"Our . . . *other* guests, Mr. Frane. You must have seen their ship from your escape pod. You'll likely meet them soon enough. By working in tandem with the Klingons we should have both of our ships under way and clear of the disturbances created by the spatial rift."

"Again, impressive. But why have you brought me up here?"

Donatra smiled, though the expression looked more predatory than amicable on her saturnine features. "You're very direct, Mr. Frane."

"There's little time to waste," he said, nodding toward the image on the viewer.

Frane noticed that the Romulan woman's mien had darkened. "Why? Do you know something we don't about the Great B1—about the phenomenon out there?"

"We call it the Sleeper."

"Why?"

Frane squeezed the bracelet between his fingers, imagining that he could draw strength from it. "Because its dreams mold reality itself, at least here in Neyel space. And its infrequent awakenings *end* those dreams, causing whole worlds to vanish as though they were nothing but errant thoughts to begin with. Or so say the ancient stories of the Indigenous Races."

"Ah. I see." She appeared to relax then, obviously having dismissed the wisdom of the ancients as mere myth and folklore.

And perhaps that is all it ever really was. After all, very few modern Neyel—and certainly *no* Neyel ancestor of which Frane was aware—had ever taken such tales seriously. The Oh-Neyel People whose earliest struggles and conquests had built the Neyel Hegemony had had time for aught but survival.

But the native peoples the Neyel had conquered over the centuries had known the truth, perhaps from the time that intelligent life had first emerged here, billions of Oghenturns before the Neyel or the human species that sired them had come into being. The long-vanished His'lant, among other races, had understood the true nature of the Sleeper, and may even have been tied to it somehow, perhaps more intimately than any species dreamed by it.

If the His'lant legends are merely stories, then why did Newaerth and its entire system vanish when the Sleeper first began to stir? Frane thought. *Why did a billion Neyel and their subjects disappear into oblivion like a dream?*

"Why do you need me here?" Frane asked.

"It's quite simple, Mr. Frane. Until we find a way to return home, we're going to need a knowledgeable guide to help us find our way around in this region of space."

"Congratulations, Mr. Frane. You've just been hired into the service of the Romulan Star Empire."

Though he was grateful still to be alive—a fact he knew he owed to Commander Donatra—something in her smile made him recall the cold-bloodedness he had often seen in the eyes of his late father. This was all that kept him from questioning her directly about what might have motivated a fleet of warships—craft that so resembled Donatra's own vessel—to make an unprovoked attack on a Neyel military flotilla.

Clutching again at the beads and stones of the story bracelet in his pocket, Frane suddenly found himself wishing that the Sleeper would come fully awake sooner rather than later.

CHAPTER SEVEN

"You're frowning at it again."

Christine Vale shook herself out of her reverie, and turned to see Deanna Troi smiling at her.

Troi gestured at the blank space on the bulkhead next to *Titan*'s main bridge turbolift. "The missing dedication plaque. We're going to have to settle on an epigram for it soon, or else I'm going to have to give you and Will a serious talking to." She grinned mischievously.

Vale smiled back. "I've just never been on a ship since its initial launch before, so it's weird for me. All the other ships I've served on—the *Den-sxl,* the *O'Keefe,* the *Enterprise*—had all been up and running for years by the time I came on board. Whenever I was on the bridge of any of them, I always looked to the plaque as a sort of touchstone."

"I know what you mean," Troi said. "When the saucer section of the *Enterprise*-D crashed on Veridian III, one of the first things I made sure we rescued from the wreckage was the plaque. Even though we could have made a new one—it's not the physical plaque that's so important, but the message it's inscribed with—leaving it behind would have felt like abandoning a family member."

Vale nodded, and turned to look back at the bridge. Riker was studying readings with Jaza Najem at the primary science station, and the other bridge personnel were busy at their various posts. She didn't even remember how or why she had walked over to stare at the blank spot on the bulkhead; she'd simply done it.

"Will's told me some of the mottoes you've been bandying back and forth," Troi said. "He's even half-seriously offered to put up a suggestion box on the bridge for crew input. It's good that you've been tempering some of his wilder ideas."

Vale snorted. "I've told him at least five times now that *'It don't mean a thing if it ain't got that swing'* is not an acceptable motto, but he keeps coming back to it."

"You know," Troi said, "almost all the options I've heard from both of you are very Earthcentric. Why aren't you considering the words of some nonhuman philosophers?"

Vale was about to protest that they *had* looked at non-human aphorisms, until she realized that Deanna was mostly correct; the vast majority of their choices had been from ancient Earth writers, artists, and leaders.

"I'm a little embarrassed to admit that you're right, Deanna," Vale said, her voice low. "And with the crew on *this* ship, of all the ships in Starfleet, the motto should be from some non-Terran culture."

Troi nodded. "If you'd like some suggestions, I've found some of Kahless's proverbs quite eloquent, as well as a few of the Ferengi Rules of Acquisition, the Andorian speeches of Thalisar and the poetry of Shran, not to mention the philosophical writings of a few dozen Vulcans through the last two millennia. I even read a slim tome on Horta mysticism recently."

Vale's eyes widened with surprise. "Horta mysticism? What kind of read was that?"

Troi turned to walk away, offering her answer over her shoulder.

"A little rocky in places."

Vale groaned and shook her head. She'd walked right into that one. Nevertheless, Troi had effectively lightened her mood, which, Vale knew, was precisely the counselor's intent. This evening's memorial service aside, the crew was already operating under extremely high stress levels. Repairs on the ship from the Romulan-Reman conflict were still ongoing, as were the attempts to reconfigure many of their systems to keep them operable in such close proximity to the thalaron-generated rift that had whisked *Titan* all the way to the Small Magellanic Cloud. Or Neyel space, as many members of the crew were calling it now.

She wondered how long it would be before they actually *met* one of the Neyel, and if the Neyel had continued to evolve past what old Starfleet records had shown them to be eighty years ago.

Riker tugged at his beard absentmindedly, studying the numbers and graphics that scrolled down both sides of the main viewscreen.

He didn't like to give up, but they'd been scanning for other vessels for almost a day now, and they hadn't found any yet. The interspatial anomaly was still interfering with the ship's sensors, and they'd found no trace of the *Valdore* or any of the rest of the missing Romulan fleet that Donatra had sought when she had requested *Titan*'s assistance near the phenomenon she called "the Great Bloom."

"Ensign Lavena, let's put another five hundred kilometers between us and the anomaly," he said, "Mr. Dakal, continue scanning for other vessels. Maybe our sensors will be more effective once we're out of range of the worst of its subspace interference."

He turned to his right, where his executive officer sat. Vale looked up at him expectantly, lifting her gaze from the chair-mounted padd console on which she had been studying various readings.

"The bridge is yours, Commander," Riker said. "I'll be in my ready room. Call me when you have some good news."

As he strode toward the doors of his sanctum, he hoped that his final phrase had sounded optimistic enough. *Not "if" there's good news. "When."*

He felt a familiar presence.

It was a warm red splashed across the dark canvas of his consciousness.

Other colors had been there before, but he subsumed them.

Turned them dark.

Pushed them away.

Solitude was comforting.

But the red splashed, again and again.

STARDATE 57026.9

Returning to the bridge after the recent accidental collision with the Reman ship had been a bit of an embarrassment to Aili Lavena. After all, the shielded face mask of her hydration suit had cracked when she'd been flung from her chair and onto the bridge deckplates. The resultant rupture hadn't caused her any permanent harm, though the Selkie conn officer had been forced to spend almost her entire subsequent shift recuperating, first in sickbay, and later in her own water-filled quarters. Even now, the twin gill-crests that ran along her cranium ached slightly, though they steadily continued to heal.

The particular suit she wore now didn't fit her quite as well as the damaged one had, and she found herself unconsciously fidgeting as she sat at her station. She hoped the others hadn't noticed. Instinctively, she was aware that the loud sloshing sounds that her self-contained liquid environment made all around her as she moved were virtually inaudible even to those nearest to her. Still, the noises made her a bit uncomfortable and more than a little self-conscious at being the only water-breather living and working aboard *Titan*.

Quit gretzing, Aili, she thought, gently scolding herself. *You wanted a bridge job, you got a bridge job. If you're unhappy, go be a* sepkinalorian, *like your fourteen siblings.* She shuddered. That job was mind-numbing, and she suspected she'd rather be a meal for Dr. Ree than return to Pacifica and its expectations of mundanity.

Seated at her immediate right, Cadet Zurin Dakal scowled down at the screen of his ops control panel.

"What is it, Zurin?" Lavena asked.

"I'm getting some strange readings here. *Really* strange."

Lavena tapped her own console, and the screen before her filled with a myriad of numbers and sine-rhythms. She studied them for a moment, then turned back toward the center of the bridge.

"Commander Vale, Commander Jaza, we've found something highly unusual."

Vale cocked an eyebrow. "On screen."

Two smaller images opened to the starboard side of the forward viewscreen. One was nearly black, the other was filled with the same scrolling coordinates and other information that both Lavena and Dakal had just seen.

"Analysis?" Vale asked, and Lavena saw both the haggard-looking Vulcan, Tuvok, and the Bajoran science officer, Jaza Najem, running diagnostics at nearby science stations.

Jaza didn't look up as he spoke over his shoulder. "Commander, I'm finding widespread spatial instabilities throughout this region. Entire sectors of the Small Magellanic Cloud are being affected to varying degrees."

"Affected in what way?" Vale asked.

"The black portion of the screen shows a segment of space that should have something there. But there's nothing there. No stars, no planets, no gases, no debris, no energy fields, no readings whatsoever. It's a complete void. I can't even find any sign of virtual particles popping in and out of existence. That shouldn't happen even in the emptiest parts of intergalactic space."

"How can that be? If it's a void, wouldn't whatever surrounds it be rushing in to fill it?"

Jaza waggled his hand from side to side. "Yes and no. But nothing's coming into or out of this void."

Lavena half-expected Vale to tell her to chart a course closer to that sector of space; many starship captains would have done just that. She was relieved then, to hear the ship's first officer instead tell her to pull back.

"One interspatial anomaly at a time for this crew," Vale said, half under her breath. She tapped her combadge.

"Bridge to Captain Riker."

The captain's voice issued immediately from the tiny speaker. *"Go ahead."*

"You're needed on the bridge, sir."

As the doors to the ready room slid open, Lavena turned back to the conn, studiously avoiding making eye contact with the captain. She hadn't had much direct interaction with him since she had first come aboard weeks ago. Given their checkered—if brief—history together, it was probably better that way.

After Vale and Jaza had finished briefing the captain on what they had learned so far, Tuvok turned to address all the bridge officers at once. "This 'void,' for want of a better term, has been reordered on an elementary particle level. Put simply, nearly half a cubic parsec of space containing what *was* has been replaced—by utter nothingness."

"Which is pretty much the definition of a 'void,' " Dakal said quietly. Lavena supposed that she wasn't the only one who heard him, however, since her aquatically adapted hearing wasn't particularly acute in the bridge's prevailing M-Class environment. She also wasn't sure what had triggered the sarcastic timbre of Dakal's voice. Did the cadet have some personal issue with the commander, or was he simply living up to his people's reputation for arrogance? She decided she would have to let time determine the answer to that question.

"What do those readings there mean?" Riker asked, pointing to another window-inset image that had been opened on the forward viewscreen's port side.

"That's an analysis of several other points we've been scanning throughout this portion of the Small Magellanic Cloud," Jaza said. "Some of them are showing unusual activity. Whether this is also being caused by whatever created the void is unclear."

"So, essentially we have a huge volume of local space that has been erased from existence," Riker said.

"Except for the empty space itself, yes, that's correct, sir," Jaza said.

Riker nodded. "And we also have widespread spatial instabilities that are threatening other local regions."

"Apparently, sir," Jaza said. "I can't explain it just yet. Not without resorting to the metaphysical, that is."

"This pocket of the universe doesn't seem terribly friendly to starship crews or other living things," Vale said wryly.

Though Lavena found Dakal a bit difficult to understand, she decided then that Vale and Jaza were anything but. Noting how close together the two of them were standing at the main science station, and how often that seemed to happen, she wondered how anyone else could have failed to notice it.

Lavena's peripheral vision was drawn to a light on Dakal's ops panel, which had just started blinking rapidly. Before either Dakal or Lavena could say anything, Tuvok spoke up again from tactical.

"Captain, we're receiving a hail. It's from the *Valdore*."

Jaza turned in his chair, looking over his shoulder toward the bridge's center, where the two most senior officers present were now seated.

"She's exiting the rift's main zone of subspace interference, Captain. And long-range scans show that she's not alone," he said, his dark eyes suddenly widening.

"There's a *Klingon* vessel with her."

CHAPTER EIGHT

"It's good to see you again, Commander Donatra," Riker said, meaning every word. After everything he'd witnessed since being catapulted into this region of space, he was keenly aware that both he and his Romulan counterpart were lucky to be alive.

Donatra stepped down from the stage in *Titan*'s transporter room one, while the three others who had materialized alongside her—two Klingons and a gray-skinned humanoid of a type Riker recognized immediately, but had never before encountered in the flesh—remained standing on the pads.

"Likewise, Captain," Donatra said, a hint of a smile playing at her lips. She nodded curtly to him, a gesture of courtesy among Romulans, an acknowledgment between individuals of equal status, such as ship commanders. "We have a great deal to discuss."

"Indeed we do, Commander," said Deanna Troi, who was standing attentively at Riker's side. "Welcome aboard." Turning to face the trio that had yet to step down from the transporter stage, she added, "All of you."

Riker recognized the two standoffish Klingons instantly. Shortly before fate had thrown them all into this remote region of space, he, Christine Vale, and Ranul Keru had shared a meal with both of them aboard General Khegh's flagship, the *I.K.S. Vaj*.

"Captain Tchev. Lieutenant Dekri," Riker said, taking a step toward the dais. "Welcome aboard *Titan*. It seems we'll all be working together."

The Klingons acknowledged his greeting with simultaneous salutes—right fists to left breasts—then stepped down onto the deck. "I look forward to it, Captain," Tchev said, casting a momentary derisive glance in Donatra's direction, as did Dekri.

The Romulan commander either failed to notice this or didn't care.

Satisfied for now that Donatra and the Klingons were already well past the point where they might come to blows—and, even if they weren't, the unobtrusive yet watchful presence of Commander Tuvok near the doorway would certainly act as a deterrant—Riker turned his attention toward the tall, robed, gray-skinned creature who had remained in place on the stage. The being's scalp was nearly hairless, and looked as though it had been shaved in haste; it was beardless, adding to its overall impression of youth. But its flesh seemed somehow hardened, bringing to mind both leather and tree bark. Its dark, thick-lidded eyes were taking in the room attentively but apprehensively. The restless tail whipping back and forth behind it underscored the being's obvious uncertainty.

Now thoroughly familiar with *Excelsior*'s eighty-year-old reports, Riker had immediately recognized this individual as a Neyel. A male, probably an adult, though definitely on the younger side. The same young Neyel who had numbered among the few survivors of an apparent attack by Donatra's missing fleet, according to the Romulan commander's earlier communication.

"Welcome aboard," Riker said, extending his right hand toward the extremely alien-looking creature. He had to remind himself that this person—whose bare feet were essentially a second set of hands, and whose spade-tipped tail moved in a way that suggested it was capable of reaching and grabbing as either of Riker's own arms—was more like himself than any of the more familiar aliens in the room.

The Neyel regarded him in silence for a seeming eternity, prompting Riker to wonder whether the Neyel-specific universal translator program that Jaza had adapted from *Excelsior*'s records had somehow failed to function. Except for the restless twitching of his tail, the creature remained stock-still.

"Be careful, Will. He's terribly nervous," Deanna said quietly, but quite unnecessarily; Riker recognized fear when he saw it.

Tchev chortled, then glowered at Donatra. "A consequence, no doubt, of Romulan hospitality."

Riker noticed then that the Neyel was studiously avoiding looking in Donatra's direction. He also saw something he hadn't seen before: a pattern of subtle lines running along the creature's shorn right temple, barely visible beneath the thin layer of black fuzz that covered his gray scalp.

Surgical incisions? Riker wondered.

His arm still outstretched toward the Neyel, Riker glanced toward the Romulan commander, who met his gaze momentarily before abruptly breaking eye contact.

Riker frowned. What had Donatra done to this being?

Turning back toward the Neyel, he noticed that the creature's hands were stuffed defensively into the front pockets of his robe. Tuvok was no doubt keeping a weather eye on him for any sign that he might be preparing to draw a weapon.

"Welcome aboard," Riker repeated, moving slightly closer to the Neyel. "I am Captain William T. Riker of the Federation starship *Titan*." He gestured in Deanna's direction. "This is Deanna Troi, my diplomatic officer."

"Federation," the Neyel said. "You are from Aerth?"

Riker nodded, recognizing the name of his homeworld in spite of the odd pronunciation. And now he knew that the universal translator was indeed working properly. Trying a warm smile, he said, "Born and raised there, in a place called Valdez, Alaska."

The Neyel seemed to roll the place name over in his mind several times before replying in a surprisingly pleasant, sonorous voice. "Alaska. The revered Burgess left behind stories about Alaska. Beautiful, but cold."

Federation Ambassador Aidan Burgess, Riker thought. He smiled, wondering if the storied diplomat had ever actually visited the land that had once been called the last frontier. "It's definitely both of those. And I hope to see it again someday." He offered the Neyel his hand in the traditional human greeting.

"Frane. My name is Frane." The Neyel withdrew a pair of gray hands from the pockets of his robe, and with one of them he clasped Riker's proffered hand, enclosing it in a grip that was firm yet surprisingly gentle for someone who presented such a hard, almost armored exterior.

Riker looked with wonder into the creature's dark, still-frightened, and unmistakably human eyes.

"Captain Riker," Donatra said, interrupting the captain's momentary reverie. "We have a great deal to discuss. I suggest we waste no time pooling our knowledge of this place, and of the circumstances behind our arrival."

Disengaging from Frane, Riker turned to face Donatra. "I agree completely. Commander Troi has already prepared a room where we can do just that."

Smiling, Deanna made a *follow-me* gesture as she moved toward the doorway, where Tuvok was standing vigil. "Our science team should already be waiting for us."

Deck one's forward observation lounge presented a spectacular view of the spatial rift's slowly drifting, multicolored energy tendrils. Troi had asked Will to have the lounge area cleared of all unnecessary personnel specifically for this joint briefing, and he had immediately understood the need to do exactly that. It wouldn't do, after all, to allow anything unexpected to damage the fragile bond of trust they were trying to build to the still-apprehensive Frane.

Or to slow down the increasingly urgent scientific agenda of Science Officer Jaza, who stood anxiously at the head of the long conference table.

Two other key members of *Titan*'s science staff were already present and seated—or otherwise positioned—at the table near Jaza: Melora Pazlar, the head of stellar cartography, and Dr. Se'al Cethente Qas, *Titan*'s senior astrophysicist. Clad in her gravity-canceling exoframe, Pazlar nestled comfortably into a chair, her garlanic wood walking stick leaned up against the table. Dr. Cethente, whose Syrath physiognomy precluded "sitting" in the conventional sense, was poised opposite from her near the head of the table; chairless, Cethente stood on his four intricately articulated legs.

Taking a seat beside Cethente, Troi watched as Will

and Christine Vale took seats across from one another. Tuvok and Akaar did likewise, all the while seeming to go to great lengths to avoid looking directly at one another; the pair of Klingons and Donatra staked out positions at opposite ends of this same side of the table. Only two chairs, both located on Will's side of the table, remained empty.

Still standing, Troi turned back toward the doorway, where Frane stood quietly, under the watchful eyes of Lieutenants Hutchinson and Sortollo. The two security officers, assigned by Tuvok to chaperone Frane, were discreetly hanging back from their charge, though they were clearly on the alert for any sudden moves on the Neyel's part. But Troi sensed no aggression whatsoever coming from Frane; the Neyel merely seemed to be experiencing apprehension, though not nearly as intensely as he had a few minutes earlier in the transporter room.

The low conversational buzz in the room began to subside after Will rose from his chair, signaling that the ad hoc briefing should now come to order. Troi quickly crossed to Frane and favored him with her most disarming smile. He didn't resist as she took one of his arms and gently led him toward the two unoccupied seats located near Will. Frane quietly took the chair nearest the bulkhead, where he paused to look at a pair of chess sets—one three-dimensional, the other set up in the far more ancient, traditional flat arrangement—that adorned a corner recreation table. Sensing the Neyel's clear recognition of the flat board and its array of ornate game pieces, Troi wondered what other commonalities Frane's people shared with his human cousins.

Such as myself, she thought, pondering how closely related the Neyel's forebears might be to the ancestors of her own human father.

"We've already learned a lot about the phenomenon that brought all of our ships here," Will said, quickly gaining the undivided attention of everyone in the room. "Just as I'm sure you have, Commander Donatra. Captain Tchev. And if we're to stand any chance of getting home, we're all going to have to share everything we know."

"Agreed," Donatra said. "Now that the *Valdore*'s comm system is up and running again—and with both our vessels out of the worst of the subspace interference zone surrounding the Bloom—my crew has begun transmitting its data to *Titan*."

"Thank you, Commander," Will said, nodding. Gesturing toward the science specialists, Will made quick introductions, then turned the floor over to Jaza.

Troi noted a certain tension in the room, as curiosity about the happenstance that had brought everyone to this distant place was neatly balanced by anxiety over whether those very circumstances might successfully be run in reverse. She sensed that everyone who had come through the rift was worried, at least to some extent, that returning home might not be an option.

"First of all," Jaza said, still standing at the head of the table, "we've discovered that there's a lot more at stake here than just getting home."

"For you, perhaps," Tchev said. "We have no interest in this region of space, other than expediting our departure from it."

"I agree," Donatra said. Troi sensed her surprise at hearing herself utter this phrase in the context of an accidental collaboration with Klingons. "My first concern is locating my . . . misplaced ships, and returning them and their crews safely to Romulan space."

Troi felt Donatra's anguished sense of loss, and saw her hard gaze settle briefly on the two Klingons who had accompanied her here. Off of the veiled-yet-surprised reactions of Tchev and Dekri, Troi gathered that this was the first time Donatra had admitted to having lost her fleet in the Klingons' presence. But Frane reacted with only a small degree of startlement, as though Donatra had merely confirmed his own strong suspicion.

Of course, Donatra must have realized that she wouldn't be able to conceal this doubtless embarrassing fact from any of them for very much longer.

"Of course, Commander," Will said to Donatra in soothing tones. "*Titan*'s sensor are fully engaged in the search, now that we've cleared most of the disturbances coming from the rift."

Donatra inclined her head forward toward him, her dark eyes momentarily refulgent with gratitude. "Thank you, Captain."

Jaza's emotional state, in stark contrast to Donatra's, seemed nearly as serene as ever, though it covered an undercurrent of great urgency. "I wouldn't be so quick to dismiss the importance of this place," the Bajoran science officer said, obviously speaking primarily to both Donatra and the Klingons. "The spatial rift out there seems to be having some extremely strange effects on local space."

"What sort of 'strange effects'?" Dekri asked in surly fashion.

While Jaza seemed to be gathering his thoughts, Norellis stepped into the conversational breach. "Simply put, space itself here has begun coming apart."

Donatra's eyebrows rose, and she radiated equal parts incredulity and incomprehension. " 'Coming apart'?"

"More precisely, large volumes of space are in danger of being . . . permanently displaced," Jaza said.

Tchev bared his snaggly teeth. "Displaced by what?"

Jaza leaned forward and touched a control on a keypad

that was built flush into the tabletop. A meter-wide model of the spatial anomaly obligingly appeared nearly a meter above the conference table, the image overlaid by a latticework of fine, distorted grid lines that reminded Troi of twisted nets woven by ancient Betazoid oskoid fisherfolk.

"By what appears to be another universe," Jaza said. "An emergent universe, which is even now in the process of forming. A protouniverse, if you prefer. The process could complete itself in a matter of weeks, or perhaps even days. And if this happens while we're still anywhere near the rift . . ." He trailed off, obviously aware that finishing that particular sentence was unnecessary.

Dekri looked askance at the spatial rift's holographic image, then fixed a skeptical eye on Jaza. "You have evidence of this?"

Only now did Troi sense a disturbance in the tranquillity of Jaza's emotional surface. The senior science officer nodded, a look of sorrow darkening his features. "Definitive evidence. Unfortunately."

In response to Jaza's next quick manual command, the image of the spatial rift vanished, to be replaced by a computer-rendered schematic of a blue, Earthlike world.

"This is the sort of evidence I hope never to encounter again," Jaza continued. "The world you see before you has endured for perhaps five billion years since its formation by the ordinary processes of stellar and planetary evolution. Until recently."

"What are you saying?" Donatra asked.

Jaza looked haunted. "Simply that this world, its primary star, and every other object in its system from the size of a planet all the way down to dust grains has . . . *disappeared*. We believe the protouniverse that's now emerging from the spatial rift has something to do with the phenomenon."

Although Troi already knew this much, like all the *Titan* personnel present, a hush again descended on the room as Donatra and the Klingons processed Jaza's revelation.

"Newaerth," Frane said. Troi realized then that he was familiar with the arrangement of oceans and coastlines of this world.

"Our guest," Donatra said, nodding toward Frane by way of explanation, "would also have us believe that the Great Bloom—the spatial rift—caused a world and its entire system to vanish mere weeks ago. We have trained the *Valdore*'s long-range sensors on the coordinates Frane provided for this system. Other than a few stray subatomic particles, there's no evidence that anything at all ever existed there."

"So where did this image come from?" Tchev asked, gesturing at the blue holographic planet.

His huge hands folded primly on the table before him, Akaar chose that moment to speak. "Mr. Jaza and Lieutenant Pazlar have accessed the long-range mapping data gathered eighty years ago by *Excelsior*." He pointed toward the slowly turning blue sphere that hovered over the table. "This image was obtained then. Since that time, this world and its system have indeed disappeared. You may review *Excelsior*'s detailed survey logs at your leisure." Seated beside him, Akaar's former *Excelsior* shipmate Tuvok nodded quietly, though his coal-dark eyes remained focused straight ahead.

Donatra shrugged. "Even if we were to accept this incredible story at face value, it would provide us with only one thing: yet another good reason to hasten our departure for Romulan space."

Troi had to admit that the Romulan commander had just made an excellent point.

"If we understood the mechanics of emerging pro-touniverses better, I'd say you were right," Dr. Cethente said, his synthetic, wind-chime-like voice slightly startling *Titan*'s guests, but only for a moment. *"But we don't currently understand this process very well at all. The damage this protouniverse will cause as it fully forms will no doubt be widespread."*

"Again, a damned good reason to get out of here," Dekri said. *"Now."*

Cethente chuckled, a sound like winter icicles falling from the poinciana trees at Lake Cataria. *"And that might also be a fine way to spread that damage back to Romulan space."*

"And perhaps far beyond," Jaza said.

"How can you possibly know that?" Tchev said, jabbing a thick finger toward the Bajoran. "You don't witness the births of these so-called 'protouniverses' every day."

"No," Jaza said, his patient, level tone calming everyone somewhat. "But Starfleet personnel accidentally brought a very similar phenomenon into the Bajor sector from the Gamma Quadrant about ten years ago. That protouniverse threatened to destroy both Deep Space 9 and the Celestial Temp—" He caught himself, and paused for a moment before continuing. "—the Bajoran wormhole, until DS9's crew safely relocated the phenomenon."

Dekri threw her hands in the air. "Why don't we simply do something like that? Transplant this thing. Hook on a couple of tractor beams and drag it back to wherever it came from in the first place."

"I'm afraid this particular protouniverse is already at far too advanced a stage of development for that approach to work," Jaza said, shaking his head sadly. "If we were to attempt to move it with a tractor beam, we might well accelerate its spread. Or create another chaotic energy inter-action just like the one that brought us all here in the first place."

"What if we had more power?" Will asked. "Say, the amount of power that could be generated by all of Com-mander Donatra's missing ships?"

"That would give us considerably more options," Jaza said. "With a couple of dozen warp fields operating in tan-dem, we might be able to coax the protouniverse back across the rift and into the same extradimensional space where it formed in the first place."

"But we don't even know where my ships are," said Donatra. "We might or might not recover them. So unless it would somehow jeopardize our ability to use the rift to return home, we may well have no option other than sim-ply destroying this thing."

"Good answer," Tchev grunted. Troi surmised that the Klingon captain took personally the severe damage the rift had inflicted on his ship, and that he wasn't above taking a bit of revenge. "A brace of *Titan*'s quantum torpedoes ought to be ideally suited to the task."

Jaza and Pazlar exchanged worried glances, and the Bajoran then busied himself by restoring the holographic image of the colorful spatial rift, its bright energy tendrils slowly rotating in the space above the center of the confer-ence table in place of the defunct planet.

"Maybe, or maybe not," Jaza said. Troi noticed that his emotional aura was growing increasingly jangled as he appeared to consider the risks of poking and prodding the phenomenon. "The truth is, we don't know what effect de-stroying an emerging protouniverse would have on the rift itself. Or on the space that contains our ships, for that mat-ter. Or even on the space on the Romulan Empire side of the rift. I have to agree with Dr. Cethente—we can't do anything that might risk taking this thing's destructive potential back home with us."

"To say nothing of the risk of getting us all vaporized because we've gone off half-cocked," Pazlar added. "We've already seen the damage the rift's chaotic energy discharges can do to nearby ships." Troi heard grumbling coming from Tchev, whose ship and crew had already learned that lesson the hard way, as Pazlar continued. "We need more information before we can do much of anything."

Vale caught Donatra's eye. "Speaking of more information, Commander Donatra, I'm curious to hear what your crew has learned about our current, ah, situation. And yours, Captain Tchev."

"We've had little opportunity to do scientific research here," Dekri said acerbically. "Our ship was incapacitated almost immediately."

Donatra shook her head. "I'm afraid we've uncovered very little data of concrete value either, at least so far." She turned toward Will and grew more serious. "Other than our scanner readings, which we've already transmitted to your staff, everything we've learned so far about the Bloom—about the spatial rift, rather—has been rather . . . metaphysical in nature."

Jaza looked surprised, and Troi could tell that his curiosity was roused. "Metaphysical?"

Donatra turned and fixed her gaze squarely upon *Titan*'s sole Neyel guest. "Mr. Frane?"

Frane, who had been studying a tall, red chess piece he had apparently picked up from one of the nearby game boards, returned Donatra's stare warily, his hooded eyes large.

Setting the piece on the tabletop before him, he looked

around the diversely populated room, clearly still over-whelmed by so much alien contact in such a short span of time. Though Troi sensed that her proximity to him was having a calming effect, being called upon to speak was bringing to the fore all of the young man's intense feelings of trepidation and vulnerability.

His moment of indecision having passed, Frane rose, apparently taking his cue from Jaza, who had remained standing as he oversaw the briefing.

To Jaza, Frane said, "You claim that this . . . spatial rift is giving birth to a new universe."

The Bajoran smiled, but shook his head slowly. "Not precisely. Our best hypothesis is that a new universe is emerging from outside the boundaries of this universe—from the same 'ocean' of de Sitter space on which our own universe 'floats,' so to speak."

"De Sitter space?" Donatra asked as the Klingons exchanged blank glances.

"De Sitter space is a meta-etheric medium. A sort of 'overspace' that contains this universe, as well as count-less others," Cethente said in clear, crystalline tones. *"Federation scientists have named it after the Terran physicist who first hypothesized its existence several cen-turies ago. At any rate, the rift has become an entry point for a newly formed universe, one that will soon displace a significant volume of* this *universe as the emerging pro-touniverse expands and develops."*

"New universe form in this manner all the time, by the way," Jaza added. "They're a little bit like bubbles that form in water. They come into being somewhere virtually every nanosecond, expanding countless orders of magni-tude as they develop. As they grow, these 'baby universes' sometimes pass through portions of *our* universe, or other universes, depending on a given universe's particular interactions with de Sitter space. An interspatial rift like the one that brought us here represents such a passing interaction."

"It's hard to believe," Tchev observed, looking at Donatra. "Your mad praetor's thalaron weapon creates a spatial rift in Romulan space, which just happens to toss our three ships here, along with a new universe, only a few weeks later. That sounds like quite a coincidence."

Cethente chimed in, as it were. *"Not really, Captain Tchev. Not when you consider the subspace topology of this region of our universe in relation to many others. Neyel space is 'downhill' from our respective origin points, as well as in relation to many other spatial regions in this universe. It appears that this region of our universe lies 'downhill' from the perspective of de Sitter space as well. So the 'baby universe' out there has simply 'rolled downhill' toward us on its way toward being born."*

Frane, once again gripping the red chess piece, seemed to consider all of this for a protracted moment, then shrugged. "That isn't so," he said at length.

Jaza's curiosity was obviously becoming piqued even further. "Excuse me?"

"You say we are witnessing the birth of something new. But uncounted millennia of local legend contradicts this."

Troi felt Frane freeze as he noticed that the room had again fallen silent—and that everyone's eyes were suddenly upon him, her own included.

"Go ahead, Mr. Frane," Troi said.

The Neyel took a deep breath and again set the chess piece down on the table before him. Though Troi perceived that Frane was still nervous, her encouragement had obviously bolstered the younger man's confidence.

"The rift is not introducing anything new to Neyel space. It merely heralds the long-prophesied return of something unimaginably ancient. Something that may be older than the universe itself. It is the Sleeper, at last awakening."

Will's eyebrows rose. "The Sleeper?"

"Apparently a deity in which many of the races indigenous to this region believe," Donatra said. "This 'Sleeper' is said to slumber for billions of years, waking only periodically."

Frane, still standing, nodded. "And when It wakes, It ceases to dream. But all the worlds that surround it are part of that dream. Like Newaerth, the first world to vanish as the Sleeper begins stirring from its long ages of slumber."

Vale's eyes grew huge. "Are you suggesting that this galaxy and everything in it is just a part of this ancient god's dream?"

"Yes," Frane said, nodding. "And when the dream ceases . . ." He trailed off meaningfully.

Despite Frane's unscientific claims, no one in the room was smiling. Troi realized that everyone present was thinking of the planet that the young Neyel had called Newaerth. The disappearance of Newaerth and its entire system was essentially beyond dispute now. Had some cosmic Sleeper inadvertently destroyed it, simply by rolling over during its fitful slumbers? Would that casual destruction spread farther and wider once the mysterious entity came more fully awake?

Troi recalled a very old story from Earth that her father had told her when she was a little girl. For centuries, the Hindus had believed in a deity known as Brahma, upon whom the existence of the entire universe depended. To Brahma, a day and a night lasted more than eight billion years, far longer than either Betazed or Earth had existed. During Brahma's periods of sleep, he would dream into existence the entire universe—which would be destroyed each "morning," setting off the next iteration in an infinite cycle of cosmic death and rebirth.

That story had both frightened and fascinated her on some primal level, perhaps because she was half-human. *Maybe it's no wonder,* Troi thought, *that a similar belief would be attractive to others who have Terran blood in their veins.*

"Ridiculous," Tchev spat, glaring at Frane. "Mere superstition."

Donatra chuckled. "That's a curious observation, coming from one whose people bash each other with ceremonial stun sticks and worship statues of dead warriors."

Tchev rose, his leather-gloved fists bunched on the table. *"PetaQ!"*

Will, still seated, moved not a millimeter. "Let's all settle down, folks," he said, smiling like a kindly innkeeper. "We all have better things to do than snipe at one other."

"Agreed," Donatra said, apparently both unfazed and unchastened.

"You're not actually giving any credence to this . . . aboriginal fantasy, are you, Riker?" Tchev said, gesticulating in wild frustration.

"I'm simply trying to learn everything I can, Captain," Will replied. "Even ancient legends might shed some light on our current situation."

"Nonsense," said Donatra.

Jaza cleared his throat, signaling that he was still in charge of the scientific end of the meeting—and perhaps also betraying his Bajoran reticence about dismissing fervidly held religious beliefs out of hand. Tchev reluctantly sat, and everyone else who had risen immediately followed suit.

"I'm sure we can all agree that now is not the time for a metaphysical debate," Jaza said. "We need to consider the facts before us calmly, and arrive at a solution to this problem."

"What we need," Tchev said, stabbing a finger at the holographic display, "is to destroy this 'protouniverse.' Once we've finally figured out how to get ourselves home, of course."

"Again, I have to concur," Donatra said, a sour expression on her face.

"That would seem to be our most prudent course," Akaar said.

"I'm not a big fan of the wholesale destruction of entire universes," Will said, sounding the same note of caution that was already coming through loud and clear to Troi's conscience. "Even one that's apparently still in an embryonic form. But with so much at stake, I agree that we may find that we have no better choice."

Troi detected a sudden, extreme change in the emotional timbre of the scientific team. Jaza and Pazlar were again glancing uneasily at one other, and even Cethente's usually placid aura seemed to grow almost turbulent. The uncomfortable silence that ensued spoke volumes.

"Gentlemen?" Will prompted.

Jaza cleared his throat. "Captain, I would have agreed with you, if only reluctantly."

" 'Would have'?"

"Yes. Until we compared the energy signatures and thermodynamic readings of this protouniverse with the one DS9's crew discovered a decade ago. They're substantially similar."

"Meaning?" Vale asked.

"Meaning that this new universe," Jaza paused to nod in Frane's direction, "or this awakening Sleeper, if you prefer, is already showing signs of life."

"And intelligence," Pazlar added quietly.

Troi's mouth fell open involuntarily at this entirely un-expected revelation. This was undoubtedly the reason the members of the science team had just experienced such emotional discomfiture. It was obviously far too recent a discovery to have made it into any of the already-distributed reports and summaries.

The room erupted in a gabble of raised voices, as every-one present radiated varying intensities of incredulity. Will, to his credit, displayed a healthy undercurrent of wonder that made her smile in spite of her own shocked reaction.

Troi noted that one of the strongest disbelieving reac-tions was coming from Vale. "*This* continuum was al-ready almost ten billion years old before the first signs of life appeared on Earth," she said.

"Or Qo'noS," Tchev said, nodding in agreement.

"So how could any life, intelligent or not, appear so quickly in such a young universe?" Vale concluded.

Cethente spoke up. *"Time flows at varying rates in dif-ferent universes, Commander. The equivalent of many bil-lions of years may have already passed within the confines of this protouniverse."*

"The Sleeper emerges from his slumbers only after billions-year-long intervals," Frane said, delivering this pronouncement in the same matter-of-fact manner that Jaza or Cethente might make a scientific report.

"So what are you saying?" Vale asked, facing the sci-ence team. "That this . . . baby universe is giving off some-thing that looks like brainwave patterns?"

"Not exactly," Jaza said. "But there are other easily-recognizable signs of emergent life, and these generally converge with intelligence. Highly organized replication patterns that occur far more frequently than nonliving processes could possibly account for. Nonrandom energy generation and consumption curves. Vast pockets of accumulating negative entropy, as well as numerous other extreme and sustained environmental disequilibriums, similar to those we can detect at galactic distances, in such things as the spectra of M-Class planets. So far as we know, those sorts of environments cannot come into being except via biological processes."

Troi offered a tentative nod, granting at least part of Jaza's point. "But we've founds lots of blue planets where microbes and plants are the crown of creation. The biological processes that create M-Class environments don't necessarily imply the existence of intelligence."

"No, but we've turned up other patterns that do," Cethente said. *"For instance, we've detected complex, highly organized, orderly releases of power. Not to mention significant, otherwise unexplainable releases of neuromagnetic energy."*

Jaza nodded. "Taken together, these readings look a lot like the ones taken ten years ago aboard DS9. And just like that incident, it's a safe bet that *this* protouniverse has already developed at least some sort of awareness."

"He is awakening," Frane said. "The Sleeper rises. Soon, His dreams will cease. Along with all the corrupt works and sins of my people."

And maybe along with the entire Small Magellanic Cloud as well, Troi thought, shuddering as she picked up a momentary burst of fear-tinged exultation from Frane. Did some part of him really want such a catastrophe to come about? The notion caused her an intense sensation of revulsion, which struggled mightily against the compassion she automatically felt for all such troubled souls. She breathed a quiet prayer of thanks to the Old Gods of Betazed that the latter might remain stronger than the former.

"The Red King," Vale said, her light brown eyes fixed

on the chess piece that Frane had set back upon the tabletop.

"What?" Troi asked before she even realized she was speaking.

"From Lewis Carroll. *Through the Looking-Glass.* The Red King dreamed all the characters that appeared in the book, from the Tweedle boys to Alice herself. But if the Red King were ever to wake up . . ." She trailed off, just as Frane had done.

Frane raised the red chess piece toward Vale, as though in salute. Troi realized only then that the piece was indeed the king. And that the Neyel had comprehended Vale's literary allusion.

"The Sleeper," the Neyel said. "You understand."

"I suggest you save your literary symposium for another time, Commander Vale," Tchev said with a low snarl.

"Agreed," Will said, glancing significantly at his first officer, who acknowledged his mild rebuke with a silent nod.

"Does it really matter whether this is an exotic physics phenomenon, or the Sleeper coming awake, or some creative dreamer out of ancient Terran literature?" Jaza asked. "No matter how we look at it, the potential result is the same: destruction on an almost unimaginable scale."

"Also, we appear to be unable—and some of us are almost certainly unwilling—to simply *kill* this 'Red King,' " Donatra said, her dark, intense gaze locking with Will's. The Klingons cast expectant looks at *Titan*'s captain, and Troi sensed her husband's increasing desperation over the prospect of finding a morally defensible course of action.

Will's combadge chirped perhaps half a second later.

"Bridge to Captain Riker," it said, speaking in the precisely enunciated voice of Zurin Dakal.

"Please excuse me," Will said, then stood and tapped his combadge. "Go ahead, Cadet."

"I think I have good news, sir. The long-range sensor nets have picked up dozens of bogies, apparently flying in formation at high warp. They are on an outbound trajectory from a G-type star system located less than five light-years from our present position."

"Configuration?"

"Exact configuration isn't determinable at this range, Captain. But the warp signature readings are consistent with those of Romulan singularity drives."

Donatra rose, her dour face suddenly flushed green with emotion. Her voice, however, scarcely rose above a whisper.

"My fleet."

Troi saw that Jaza was quickly entering commands into his tabletop console controls. He then consulted the display of a padd he was carrying. "I'm tapping directly into the main science station," he said.

Whatever he saw in the padd's tiny screen was making him scowl in perplexity. His Bajoran nasal striations seemed to spread upward vertically across his brown forehead until they nearly reached his hairline.

"Are we sufficiently clear of the rift's interference to hail them?" Will asked the cadet.

"I think so, sir."

"Then do it, Cadet."

"Aye, Cap—"

"Belay that, Cadet!" Jaza shouted, prompting every head in the room to swivel in his direction. Surprise filled the room as quickly as a wildfire fed by pure oxygen.

"Captain?" Dakal said, his own confusion evident even over the tiny combadge speaker.

Troi knew that the usually reserved senior science officer would never have countermanded one of the captain's orders without an extremely good reason. But what was it?

"Stand by, Cadet," Will said. To Jaza, he said, "Well, Commander?"

Still scowling at his padd, Jaza said, "I'm seeing a peculiar oscillation in the warp signatures of those ships."

Without any prompting, Pazlar and Cethente began consulting padds of their own. Though the expression on the Syrath's exoskeletal "face" remained as unreadable as ever, both he and his Elaysian colleague shone with the same feeling of shocked recognition Troi was sensing in Jaza.

"Peculiar in what way?" Donatra asked. "Are those my ships or not?"

Jaza nodded slowly. "They're Romulan ships, all right. But their warp signatures seem to have been slightly modified, at least in comparison with that of the *Valdore*."

"Modified how?" Will said.

Jaza paused to tap another set of commands into his padd, and then into his tabletop console. In the space above the table, a jagged network of red and blue lines superimposed themselves over the image of the spatial rift.

"These are the same entropic patterns that argued in favor of extant intelligence within the protouniverse," Jaza said, and touched yet another tabletop control.

Then the image of the rift morphed into that of a sleek *Mogai*-class Romulan warbird. The colorful overlay of jagged lines remained in place.

"And these are the oscillations I noticed in the Romulan warp fields."

"They're the same," Donatra said. "But what does that mean?"

A bizarre notion occurred to Troi then. Through the link she shared with Will, she knew with certainty that he had tumbled to it as well.

"The Sleeper must have taken control of those vessels," Frane said, articulating Troi's flash of insight, though he was obviously seeing reality through the prism of local mythology. "The ships are its arms and legs now. Perhaps they will be used to help cleanse M'jallanish space of our people's sins. Maybe that was why those ships attacked my father's military fleet the moment we saw them emerge from the Sleeper's embrace."

"So our Red King is . . . *sleepwalking?*" Vale said, shaking her head.

"Apparently. For now, anyway," Will said. Then he frowned. "But if some sentient force living in that protouniverse really has taken control of Donatra's fleet, then why didn't it grab the *Valdore,* too? Or *Titan?*"

"It may be nothing more than random chance," Cethente said. *"Perhaps the same element of chaos that determined how much damage each of our ships would sustain during their passage from Romulan space."*

"Or perhaps this . . . Sleeper finds something uniquely attractive about large conglomerations of Romulan warp fields," Jaza said with a speculative shrug. "After all, Romulan warp drives are based on artificial singularities, whose physics superficially resemble that of emergent protouniverses. A large concentration of such singularity-driven warp fields coming into sudden close proximity might have gotten the entity's attention in a way that our three vessels simply couldn't."

Will's blue eyes widened. "So you're saying that the Romulan fleet is . . . *possessed,* Mr. Jaza?"

"Well, I'm not claiming that the *Kosst Amojan* is running riot in the Small Magellanic Cloud, sir. But for want of a more scientific term than 'possession,' yes."

Donatra looked as though she were about to become physically ill. Clearly she lacked any better explanation for her fleet's bizarre behavior. And she was just as obviously in anguish about the fate of her crews; if some inscrutable alien intellect had indeed seized control of her fleet, all of the personnel aboard those vessels might well already be dead.

Will touched his combadge again. "Chief Bolaji."

"Bolaji here," said the conn officer.

"Plot an intercept course, Chief. We'll leave at my signal, best speed. I want to drop out of warp just outside the Romulan fleet's sensor range and stay inconspicuous. If they *do* detect us, I want them to think we're nothing more than a sensor shadow."

"Aye, sir. Are you expecting combat?"

"I sure as hell hope not, Chief. Riker out."

"Aye, Captain. Bolaji out."

Troi saw Will and Tuvok exchange a silent look and equally silent nods. Then the Vulcan tactical officer rose and quietly exited the room. *Must be checking on the weapons systems,* she thought. *Just in case.*

Donatra turned to face Will. "I must return to the *Valdore* to confer with Commander Suran. We will depart when *Titan* does, and follow a parallel course."

"That's exactly what I was going to suggest," Will said, nodding. "Your warp signature will make it easier to pass ourselves off as a sensor shadow if your fleet manages to detect our approach."

Tchev stood, as did Dekri. "We will return to the *Dugh,*" said the Klingon captain. "As will the rest of our crew. My people will not participate in this . . . *targ* hunt."

"Your vessel is so much wreckage," Donatra said. "She would only slow us down. You might consider abandoning her."

Dekri sneered openly at Donatra. "We will not leave her to the tender mercies of whatever scavengers frequent these parts. We will make such repairs as we can before attempting to re-cross the rift."

"It wouldn't be a bad idea to post the *Dugh* near the rift while *Titan* and *Valdore* go hunting," Vale said. "Somebody ought to keep an eye on it close up. And watch for more escape pods from the Neyel ships."

Tchev nodded to Will. "We will remain vigilant until you return, Captain. Or until we complete sufficient repairs to attempt a return voyage through the rift."

"All right," Will said. "Make sure they have a working subspace transmitter, Mr. Vale. And whatever other assistance they might require." He turned to Donatra again. "If you have no objections, Commander . . ."

Donatra shrugged. "What is the human expression? 'It's their funeral.' If they wish to hasten theirs by attempting to cross the rift unassisted, then it is none of my concern." Troi sensed eager anticipation of the Klingons' departure lurking beneath the commander's calculated display of indifference. Donatra clearly cared not a bit whether or not the Klingons survived their captain's perhaps reckless decision.

Frane rose as well then, the red chess piece clutched so tightly in his hand that Troi thought it might shatter. His pleading gaze was solely for Will.

"I wish to remain aboard *Titan*. And I want all the other survivors from the Neyel fleet brought here as well. There are only about twenty of us."

Will looked toward Donatra, who merely responded with another "suit yourself" shrug. He crossed to the

Neyel then and took the large gray hand he offered in a firm clasp.

"My diplomatic officer will issue guest quarters for your people, Mr. Frane," Will said. Troi made a mental note to confer with Tuvok about security issues as she set up accommodations for *Titan*'s new guests.

Frane's stiff features smoothed into a grateful smile. Troi experienced a sensation of something akin to joy, a feeling that made her think of long-overdue family reunions.

Disengaging his hand from the Neyel's, Will crossed back to Donatra. "It's going to take several hours to reach the fleet's current position. It might be a whole day before we actually catch up to them."

"I'll make sure we're on the lookout for Neyel military patrols along the way," Vale said.

"Good," Will said, nodding. "According to *Excelsior*'s reports, they weren't a very trusting bunch."

"And after we catch up to the Romulan ships, what then?" Vale wanted to know.

The room fell silent yet again. A cloud of uncertainty permeated the observation lounge. Still, Troi could sense Will's faith that he would find an appropriate course of action, that a better explanation than "possession" could be found for the behavior of Donatra's fleet. *Titan,* the *Valdore,* and the *Dugh* were going to need the help of those ships and their crews if they were to stand any real chance of getting home in one piece.

And Troi knew that the clock was ticking relentlessly toward the time when even the combined power of Donatra's fleet wouldn't be enough to save them.

CHAPTER NINE

"Please, come in, Admiral," Deanna Troi said, looking up at the towering, snow-haired man who stood in the doorway of her office.

"I understand that you requested to see me, Commander?" Admiral Akaar ducked slightly as he entered the room. He remained standing, not quite at full attention, but remained straight enough to be more than a little imposing. "What can I help you with?"

Troi stood from behind her desk and gestured toward the plush turquoise settee near the one wall that was lined with crowded bookcases. "Please, sit, Admiral."

Akaar regarded her with a silent stare for a moment, then moved to the couch and sat. "Should I assume I am here for a professional visit, Counselor? Are you sensing that I require therapy?"

Troi smiled as she sat down on a nearby matching chaise longue. "Professional, yes. Therapy, no. I wanted to get some more background on the Neyel."

"Then I suggest you speak to Frane. Or perhaps one of our other Neyel guests."

"I've already done that, Admiral. And the captain and I have both learned quite a bit about the Neyel that way— and the non-Neyel aliens who accompanied Frane— despite the reticence I sensed from several of our guests after they learned about my Betazoid talents."

"And what new insights have you gleaned?"

"Well, for one, the non-Neyel aliens we brought aboard are all members of races the Neyel Hegemony treats as second-class citizens."

"Former slaves?" Akaar said.

"Evidently. I'm glad the Neyel seem to have done away with slavery as an institution, but they have a long way to go in terms of establishing equality."

Akaar offered her a small smile. "No one knows better than I that such things take time, Counselor." Troi knew that he had to be talking about his homeworld of Capella IV, which would no doubt enter the Federation some-day—though probably not during the admiral's life-time.

Troi nodded sadly. "I have also learned that the Neyel people's pride in their self-reliance seems to be quite ingrained. It explains their continued insistence that they don't need outside help to deal with the current crisis."

Akaar nodded soberly. "That is not surprising. The ear-liest generations of Neyel overcame almost unimaginable adversities merely to survive. And those adversities made them understandably distrustful of outsiders."

"Yes, it's certainly understandable. But their 'go it alone' attitude might be working counter to the survival of their species now."

"I agree. How may I help?"

"I want to try to get a better sense of who these people *are*, Admiral, based on what we know about who they *were*. Fortunately for me, I have two primary sources to consult: Commander Tuvok and yourself."

Although Akaar's face remained impassive, Troi sensed a flare-up of intense emotion being restrained when she mentioned the Vulcan tactical officer's name.

"What can I tell you that was not already in my report, or in Captain Sulu's?" Akaar asked. "Remember that it *has* been eighty years since I last set eyes on a Neyel. I do not enjoy admitting that I am growing old, Counselor. Yet here I am, eight decades older, more stubborn, and—some would say—none the wiser." His smile returned. "What do you wish to know?"

She was tempted to ask Akaar who might have any reason to question his wisdom, now that he and her husband finally seemed to have worked out the differences that had brought them into conflict during the recent diplomatic mission to Romulus. Then she considered the tension she had been sensing lately in both the admiral and his old *Excelsior* crewmate Tuvok whenever circumstances forced the two men into close proximity; she realized that she had answered her own question.

Putting those ruminations aside, she said, "I'm trying to get a sense of just how much these people and their culture may have changed over the past eight decades."

"Because of the influence of Ambassador Burgess."

Troi nodded. "Exactly."

"I have noted that Mr. Frane speaks with a definite Federation Standard accent that the Neyel did not possess eighty years ago," Akaar said. "Doubtless a result of the time Burgess spent among his people."

"She was definitely influential. I've learned that Burgess died about two decades after beginning her work on the Neyel homeworld."

Akaar looked intrigued. "I was not aware of this. How did the ambassador die?"

"By violence. It was a political assassination."

Akaar nodded sadly, and his gaze took on a faraway aspect. "It is the fate of all too many peacemakers and great shapers of history, I am afraid." Troi couldn't be sure, but she imagined he was thinking of his own father, who had been assassinated by political rivals shortly before Akaar's birth.

"That's unfortunately true," she said. "Burgess clearly represented the prospect of hope to many, but also stirred up the fears of others in Neyel society. She became a martyr to those who wanted to look forward, and a dangerous, justly slain villain to those who couldn't or wouldn't let go of the past."

"A war of ideas. So your next question must be: which idea seems to be prevailing now?"

Troi nodded. "And it's a difficult question to answer accurately under our current circumstances."

"I suppose a Neyel military detachment, a pair of Neyel cultists, and a handful of aliens from species we have never encountered before does not qualify as a representative sampling of Neyel society."

"Exactly, Admiral. But what I can't learn from the present I might learn by studying the past. Can you remember anything else that might be significant about the Neyel of 2298 that isn't in *Excelsior*'s mission logs?"

"I do not believe so. But I will certainly contact you if I recall any other pertinent details not reflected in the reports."

Troi nodded. "Thank you, Admiral. Perhaps Commander Tuvok might be able to give me some additional insight," she said, thinking out loud.

Akaar squinted, leaning forward before answering. Troi suddenly became keenly aware of how much larger than her he was.

"The commander had less direct contact with the Neyel than I did. Although in his uniquely Vulcan way, I imagine that he feels that he has a deeper insight into them than the rest of us do. But I sincerely doubt it. Commander Tuvok is not the expert on humanoid behavior that he often pretends to be."

Troi stopped herself from raising an eyebrow at Akaar's remark, and at the now-familiar emotional tension she sensed in him. "Is there some conflict between you and Commander Tuvok that you wish to disc—"

"No." Interrupting her, Akaar stood, tugging at his uniform tunic as he rose. "Whatever passed between Tuvok and myself in the past belongs precisely where it is—in the past. Now, if you will excuse me, other duties require my attention."

Troi stood and extended her hand, trying to radiate all the calm she could muster. "I'm sorry if I brought up a sensitive subject, Admiral. Thank you for your time."

He turned to leave without taking her hand, and the door slid open in front of him. Before he crossed its threshold he turned back toward her.

"I regret that I could not be of more help with your questions about the Neyel, Commander. And I *sincerely* hope I never discover that this interview was actually an attempt by Riker's senior counselor to dig into my past relationship with *Titan*'s current tactical officer. If that were to be the case, I would consider that a gross violation of trust. Please see to it that I *never* discover any such thing, Commander."

The azure-colored door whisked closed after Akaar stepped out into the corridor, and Troi quietly considered the admiral's stern warning.

Well, that *certainly didn't end well, did it?* she thought, chastising herself.

Suddenly, she wasn't quite so keen on calling in Tuvok to chat about the past.

CHAPTER TEN

"All right. So poker's not your game," Riker said, pushing his deck of cards and two piles of chips to the left side of the table.

He watched as the young Neyel eyed the gaming accouterments with undisguised suspicion. "We are a conservative people. Games of chance have never held much appeal for us. Chess, however, was one of the games that our Oh-Neyel ancestors deemed worthy of preserving."

"I suppose survival is as much a game of skill as it is a game of chance," Riker said.

Frane nodded. "Exactly."

When Frane had asked to be taken aboard *Titan*, Riker had exulted, as though the Neyel had just formally applied for repatriation to mainline humanity. But now he was beginning to wonder whether Frane's request had been motivated more by a desire to get away from his Romulan hosts' "hospitality" than by a need to rejoin his terrestrial cousins.

I guess this is where I learn how much diplomatic expertise I picked up on Romulus, he thought wryly, feeling entirely inadequate as a stand-in for Deanna.

"Let's try chess, then," Riker said, rising. He crossed the mess hall, stepping past the Blue Table, where Cadet Torvig Bu-kar-nguv sat in quiet conversation with Melora Pazlar and Zurin Dakal. The one-meter-tall Torvig's multijointed bionic arms were swiftly arranging piles of colorful foodstuffs into something that resembled a sandwich; this skillful multitasking apparently distracted none of the fur-covered, ostrich-like engineering trainee's attention from whatever doubtless highly technical topic was presently being mooted about the table.

From the corner table just beyond, Riker retrieved a flat, two-dee chessboard. Moments later he had set it on the table between himself and Frane, opened it, and laid out the pieces randomly next to the board.

Riker smiled, he hoped ingratiatingly, toward his prospective opponent. "Choose a color, Mr. Frane."

Frane eyed him speculatively for a long moment. "Red," he said finally.

"That puts you in charge of the Red King, then."

The Neyel appeared somewhat startled by this, then quickly settled into a task with which he was obviously familiar. He sat silently as his large but surprisingly dexterous hands moved rapidly, arranging the red pieces on his side of the board into two neat ranks. He began with the king and queen, then moved outward toward the board's edges with his bishops, knights, and rooks, all of which soon stood behind a protective stockade of pawns. All the while, Riker studied the intricate braid of colored beads, shells, and fine chains he noticed adorning the Neyel's right wrist.

Riker took his time setting up his white pieces, allow-ing his languid movements to stretch out the silence that ruled the table. "You and your friends have been aboard *Titan* for almost a whole day. I'm surprised you're still being so quiet."

Frane shrugged, staring at the red pieces before him over steepled fingers. "What is there to say?"

Riker returned the shrug. "I suppose I just expected you to be more talkative than the other Neyel we brought on board. Particularly the ones in uniform." *And a "thanks for the rescue" might have been nice, too,* he thought.

"They all no doubt believe they are your prisoners."

"I've asked Commander Troi to assure them other-wise."

"She has," Frane said, nodding. "Repeatedly. And I don't doubt that she, at least, sincerely means us all well."

Riker eyed the board, its sixty-four spaces pregnant with unrealized possibilities. True, chess had never seized his imagination in quite the way poker had, but the ancient game nevertheless satisfied a need for tactical one-up-manship in ways that made even fast-paced strategema tournaments pale in comparison.

Deciding that caution wasn't likely to increase his op-ponent's garrulousness, Riker decided it was best to get his "light brigade" of bishops, knights, and rooks ready for a skirmish as quickly as possible. He picked up the knight on his left and set it down again at c3.

"She told me she's shown you our comparative genetic profiles, too," Riker said.

"Yesterday," Frane said evenly. "You, your first officer, your head nurse, her son, some of your bridge crew—even Commander Troi herself—all possess genes that origi-nated on Auld Aerth, just as we Neyel do."

Riker took this as an encouraging sign. Still, the Neyel seemed to have all his shields up, and at maximum intensity. "So what's the problem? Why do I still get the feeling that you don't trust us much more than you do the Romulans?"

Frane mirrored Riker's move, then turned his head, apparently to look at the variegated group of perhaps a dozen or so *Titan* crew members that was present. To his right, Riker glimpsed Lieutenant Kekil, the large, pale green Chelon biologist, chatting with the golden brown-scaled, quadrupedal exobiology trainee Orilly Malar. Dr. Onnta, the gold-skinned Balosneean physician, crossed the room toward one of the replicators.

"Imprisoned by the Romulans, imprisoned by you," Frane said. "What's the difference?"

Riker leaned forward and got his other knight into play, setting it down on f3. "You're not saying you want to go back aboard the *Valdore,* are you?"

Once again, Frane mirrored Riker's move. "No," he said, a vague smile playing against his hard, gray lips. The thin—and, according to Dr. Ree, very recent—scar that ran along his shorn temple flushed a dark, angry red. Human blood, and human emotion.

"Frane, if you and your friends really were prisoners here—"

"I would not describe all of them as my 'friends,' Captain Riker," Frane said, interrupting. "Other than my Nozomi, all the other Neyel you recovered are soldiers who once answered to my late father. I believe I recognized Subaltern Harn among them."

This piqued Riker's interest; in a few seconds, he'd just learned more about *Titan*'s other Neyel guests than he had since they first came aboard.

"This Harn is in charge now?" Riker asked.

"He's probably the ranking officer, now that my father has gone to his reward."

Riker nodded, understanding at once that he'd struck a filial nerve. It was a sensitivity that he could easily relate to. "Friends or not, if the lot of you really *were* our prisoners, then don't you think we'd have made a serious effort to . . . break you before now?"

Frane and Riker exchanged their next several moves in silence, each player getting his pawns into motion just enough to enable the bishops to join the fray with the knights.

"Aren't your counselors really nothing more than alternative, more-devious-than-usual interrogators, Captain?"

"Our counselors are an important means of maintaining the emotional health of Starfleet crews on long voyages. They've been indispensable aboard our vessels for nearly half a century now." Riker couldn't help but wonder whether the sainted Aidan Burgess would have succeeded in stranding herself in Magellanic space in her crusade to reform Neyel culture had a competent counselor been present aboard *Excelsior,* just to keep an eye on her.

"So says Commander Troi. Maybe she's even right about that. But . . ." the Neyel trailed off.

"But?" Riker captured one of Frane's pawns, and the Neyel responded in kind during his turn.

"But your chief counselor belongs to a telepathic species," Frane said.

Frane's misgivings didn't surprise Riker in the least. "You really have been studying up on us, haven't you?" he asked, impressed by the younger man's initiative. Although none of the Neyel appeared to be able to read Federation Standard, the universal translator was able to translate any of the texts stored in *Titan*'s computers into Neyel-intelligible audio.

"You did give us unlimited access to your Federation historical records, Captain. Did I misunderstand something?"

"Only partly. It's true, Betazoids are telepathic. But Commander Troi is only half-Betazoid. Her telepathy isn't as well-developed as other members of her kind. She's primarily an empath."

"Meaning she reads emotions rather than thoughts?"

"Mostly."

"Somehow I find that even more disquieting."

"If you'd be more comfortable dealing with one of *Titan*'s other counselors, there's Huilan—"

Frane shook his head. "Bizarre creature. I can remember playing with something that resembled him when I was small."

"All right. Maybe you should schedule a session with Counselor Haaj. He's a Tellarite, and one thing nobody's *ever* accused him of being is overly cuddly."

In the turns that followed, Riker lost a bishop and another pawn, then took down one of Frane's knights. Frane castled, moving his king toward the right-hand side of his board.

All the while, the young Neyel kept glancing uneasily over his shoulder toward the various crew members who were using other areas of the room, eating, conversing, or strolling to or from either the food service areas or the wall-mounted replicator units.

"Something's still bothering you," Riker said, pausing in mid-move. "And I don't think it has anything to do with our counseling staff."

Frane turned back to face Riker. "No. It had more to do with the many . . . nonhumans I see aboard this ship."

Riker's eyebrows rose, then he reminded himself that the Neyel *Excelsior*'s reports had described had been nothing if not xenophobic and paranoid. Discovering that Frane perhaps shared those characteristics should have come as no surprise. Still, the thought came as something of a disappointment, considering the close relationship between humans and Neyel.

"Are you referring to any particular member of the crew?"

"At the moment . . . yes," Frane said, and nodded toward a table located near the exit. Admiral Akaar sat at the table, quietly sipping a hot beverage that might have been tea. He was looking over his mug directly at Frane.

"His eyes," the Neyel said, almost inaudibly. "So dark and cold and judgmental. He reminds me of my father."

Riker suppressed a smile. *Welcome to the club,* he thought, recalling those all-too-infrequent occasions when his own father, the late Kyle Riker, had been present for mealtime staring contests of this very kind.

Riker suddenly felt a much greater degree of emotional rapport with Frane than he had since the Neyel had first asked him for permission to stay aboard *Titan.*

"I could go over there and ask him not to stare," Riker said quietly, leaning forward conspiratorially.

Frane started at that, apparently having taken the suggestion more seriously than Riker had intended it.

"I was kidding," Riker said, taking one of Frane's rooks. Somehow, he hadn't expected Frane to play the game so inattentively. "Whatever's bothering you, I can tell there's more going on than simple rudeness from Starfleet's admiralty."

Frane appeared to realize all at once that it was again his turn to move. His knight took the bishop with which Riker had captured the red rook. "You're right. It's not just your admiral."

"What, then?"

"It's . . . your entire crew."

That blunt declaration brought Riker up short. "I'm quite proud of this crew, Mr. Frane. It's the most diverse group of sentients currently serving in the entire fleet."

"I don't doubt that for an instant. But . . ."

Riker sighed, his impatience getting the better of him. "But?"

Frane cleared his throat and started over. "You keep assuring me that your intentions are benign. Yet you've acquired slaves from just about every world across your galaxy."

Riker was glad he wasn't drinking anything at that moment; he almost certainly would have sprayed a generous amount across the chessboard and into Frane's lap. *"Slaves?"*

"You run this ship and command her crew, don't you?"

"Titan is under my command, yes."

"And you're a human. Commander Vale, your first officer, is also a human. Commander Troi, your diplomatic officer—whom I'm given to understand is also your wife—is half-human, and certainly looks human enough to pass for one, as does that staring admiral—"

Nettled, Riker interrupted. "What are you saying?"

"Only that this 'diverse' crew of which you are so proud answers to a small group of powerful humans—or else to beings who so resemble humans that no one can tell the difference. Just as most of the elder species of M'jallanish space answer to a relative handful of their Neyel overlords."

Riker watched in stunned silence as a cold-eyed Frane moved the red queen, placing Riker's white king in check. The Neyel began absently playing with the bracelet on his wrist as he continued looking down at the board.

"You obviously missed a lot of the nuances of our historical database," the captain said at length. "Our Federation is based on mutual cooperation. Not conquest."

Frane looked up at him. "Then why do humans seem to be at the top of all of the Federation's most significant hierarchies?"

Riker castled, buying himself a move or two. "The Federation Council has always had equal representation, Frane, and a good number of nonhuman presidents. Bolians, Grazerites, Andorians, Efrosians—"

"But a human sits in that office presently. Correct? And humans have held it more often than any other single species."

Riker found that he was back in check yet again. "Humans are a big constituency in the Federation, Neyel racial guilt notwithstanding. So, yes, garden-variety humans are bound to get into the Palais de la Concorde from time to time. But that doesn't make us conquerors. I admit that humans have assumed a large role in running the Federation. It's a heavy burden of responsibility, but it's one we share freely with many other species. Humans also assume our fair share of the risks involved in maintaining and defending the Federation. But the Federation is a big place, and we don't see ourselves as having—or deserving—a dominant position in it."

Frane looked impressed, if not altogether convinced. "What about that large, white-skinned fellow I saw when I visited your doctor in sickbay?"

"You mean Mekrikuk. He's a Reman—they're recent wartime allies from outside the Federation—and he came aboard temporarily just before the . . . accident that brought us here."

"Ah. I noticed that he seems to be confined to your infirmary, even though very little appears to be wrong with him. Is his enslavement justified by his being from 'outside the Federation'?"

Riker sighed, unused to such cynicism, particularly from someone of Frane's tender years. "Mekrikuk is no slave, Frane. At least, not since we freed him from those who *had* enslaved him and his people. At the moment, Dr. Ree is still keeping him under observation. But I won't lie to you—Mekrikuk does present us with certain . . . security concerns."

Riker felt uncomfortable being reminded that he wasn't going to be able to keep Mekrikuk detained this way forever. Once he was well enough that Ree felt he could discharge him, the Reman would have to be declared either friend or foe, bound for either guest quarters or a security cell. And Mekrikuk himself had complicated matters greatly by having made a formal request for political asylum.

Riker was also beginning to feel discomfiture about something else: the notion that some of the prejudices Frane was projecting onto him might, even in some small way, be real. He considered the initial revulsion he'd felt when Deanna had introduced him to Dr. Ree. And Frane's trenchant observation that despite *Titan*'s highly variegated crew, humans dominated the ship's command hierarchy. *Am I really as species-blind as I've always given myself credit for being? When I chose Chris to be my exec, was it really because I thought she was the best candidate? Or was it because I thought I might relate better to a human first officer?*

It suddenly became very important to Riker to end this particular debate. "Let me ask you something, Frane: Should I assume the aliens we found with you in your escape pod are *your* slaves, just because of your people's history as slavers?"

"But they *were* slaves of my people, in reality if not in legal fact. At least, that's very much how it seemed before we came together in common brotherhood as the Seekers After Penance."

"Ah. Your pilgrimage to wake up the Sleeper. And to punish the Neyel for being slavers, as well as everyone else around here for having allowed the Neyel to enslave them."

Frane gave a rueful nod, his eyes haunted. He looked as though he was ready to bolt. Riker decided that now might be a good time to change the subject.

"That's an interesting bracelet," he said, looking down at Frane's gray wrist. The Neyel's tail suddenly rose behind him, going rigid as his other hand pulled the sleeve of his robe down to cover up the bracelet. Obviously, it meant a great deal to him.

Riker tried to make his tone of voice as soothing as possible. "Relax, Mr. Frane. Remember, you're among friends."

Frane reached forward and moved one of his rooks. "Checkmate. Thank you for the game." He stood. "Please excuse me, Captain. I wish to be with Nozomi and the others, to meditate." And with that, he headed for the exit. Riker watched the Neyel's retreating back long enough to see Lieutenant Hutchinson from security discreetly following.

Riker continued sitting, and stared dolefully at the board and its scattered game pieces as though he were surveying an ancient killing field.

"How'd it go?" said a gentle voice from across the table.

Riker looked up and saw that his wife had somehow taken Frane's place without his having noticed.

"I think this is the last time I'll try working your side of the street, Counselor."

"That bad?" she asked, extracting his right hand from the wreckage of battle and holding it between both of her own.

"Let's just say he's got 'daddy abandonment issues' that make mine pale by comparison."

Deanna, with whom he had been sharing every fact he'd been able to tease out of Frane to date, fixed him with a look of mock surprise. "No. Do you suppose he's auditioning you as a replacement for his own late, emotionally distant father?"

"Very funny, Counselor. You really think I'm 'emotionally distant'?"

"Not at all," she said, squeezing his hand. "But the relationship Frane had with his father strikes me as very similar to the one you had with yours. Maybe he's picked up on that, and therefore sees you as a kindred spirit."

Riker shrugged. "There's a lot more going on with him than father-figure issues, though. He's also carrying around at least a couple of centuries worth of collective racial guilt on his shoulders."

"That much was fairly clear to me from the beginning," she said, nodding. "My impression is that 'slavemaster guilt' attitudes such as Frane's are fairly common among Neyel of his generation. His reverence for the native religious tradition of the Sleeper may even be part of a growing Neyel countercultural movement. And another thing about Frane is even clearer to me now as well."

"What's that?"

"I already knew that he doesn't want to talk to me because he perceives me as untrustworthy because of my empathic talents. But what I didn't realize until now is just how much he genuinely seems to like you. I think he trusts you on some very fundamental level. Or at least he wants to, if he could only let himself do it."

Riker chuckled. "He could have fooled me."

"You're just hearing his own self-hatred and fear talking. As well as his deep contempt for his people's past excesses."

"Why do you think he trusts me?"

"I've overheard bits of some of your conversations about your relationships with your respective fathers, and I've sensed that you're right about his issues in that regard. You've definitely got that in common."

"Wonderful."

"It might not be much, Will, but at least it's *something*. Besides, he knows that humans and Neyel are related, and I think he's drawn to you because of that as well."

"So what should I do?"

"Keep after him, but go gently."

He chuckled quietly. "Isn't 'gently' more your department than mine?"

"Don't sell yourself short, Will. Remember, Frane isn't as apprehensive of you as he is of me and my staff. That makes you the best chance he has of successfully rejoining humanity. And maybe the best hope his entire people have of successfully finishing what Ambassador Burgess started eighty years ago when she began trying to teach the Neyel how to live without war and exploitation."

"To think that humanity's relationship with the Neyel might all come down to whether or not I start giving Frane trombone lessons . . ." he said, trailing off.

"That might not be a bad idea," she said, nodding.

Riker thought that Deanna's assessment of his importance might be more than a little grandiose. Then he considered the dozen-plus Neyel soldiers who were even now sitting in uncommunicative silence in their guest quarters aboard *Titan*. So far none of them had shared anything of themselves beyond their names, ranks, and the local equivalent of serial numbers.

Maybe Frane really is *the best shot the Federation will ever get at making a successful re-contact with the Neyel,* he thought, wishing, as always, for broader shoulders whenever such a crushing load of responsibility seemed determined to settle onto them.

"He's obviously projecting his people's historic motivations onto us," Deanna continued. "As well as his own related personal feelings of guilt. It's certainly understandable, considering his cultural baggage. The Neyel have spent the last few centuries building a star-spanning, hegemonic empire across the backs of whole worlds of indigenous slaves. It's probably difficult for Frane to imagine that our own Federation could have come about in any other way."

Riker nodded, though he had to suppress an inward shudder. *There but for the grace of blind luck and even blinder gods go we,* he thought.

"How did your own Neyel-related fishing expedition go this morning?" Riker said, content that there was little else to say at the moment about Frane.

Deanna turned in her chair, apparently to make certain that her subjects weren't eavesdropping. She faced him again a moment later, and spoke very quietly. "I'm not sure yet. The only thing I *am* sure of is that Akaar and Tuvok still have some unresolved issue between them, though both refuse to discuss it."

"Do you sense it might be anything I need to worry

about?" Riker asked. What he didn't need now were distractions stemming from old interpersonal conflicts.

Deanna shrugged. "That'll have to be up to them." She gave him a wry smile. "Remember, Will, I'm an empath, not a precog."

His combadge chirped, interrupting the discussion. *"Vale to Captain Riker."*

"Riker here. Go ahead, Christine."

"You wanted hourly reports on the chase, Captain. Titan *and* Valdore *are still slowly closing on the Romulan fleet. We'll be within transporter range inside of two hours. And none of the ships are showing any sign of having noticed us yet."*

Very strange. "Any challenges yet from Neyel military vessels?"

"No, sir. And Jaza has been scanning constantly. He even found a way to increase sensor net acuity by cannibalizing and replicating some of the circuitry from those Tal Shiar listening devices we picked up back in Ki Baratan, in the Romulan Senate chambers. We've detected a few warp profiles, but no Neyel ships have expressed any real interest in us, and they've made no active scans."

That struck Riker as even stranger, given the Neyel's historic penchant for paranoia and aggression. Perhaps the sainted Ambassador Burgess had done her peacemaking job here a mite *too* well.

"Any change in the fleet's warp field oscillations?"

"Negative. They're still displaying the same electronic 'thumbprint' as the Red King."

Riker exchanged a significant glance with Deanna, and he knew at once that her thoughts were mirroring his own. *The intelligence that's evolving inside our restless new protouniverse really* has *gone . . . sleepwalking.*

"There's something else, Captain," said another businesslike voice. This one belonged to Jaza. *"I've just completed some new long-range scans on the G-eight star system that lay along the fleet's heading when we first detected their warp signatures yesterday. The fleet has passed through the system, and the primary star has been . . . disrupted."*

"Disrupted how?"

Magnetospheric distortions are kicking up huge flares and prominences, some stretching nearly fifty million kilometers from the photosphere.

Riker blanched, as did Deanna. Neither of them were astrophysics specialists, but they both knew that such huge solar events in either the Sol or Betazed systems would be considered unparalleled catastrophes. Starfleet would respond with nothing short of planetwide evacuations.

"Inhabited planets?"

"Local stellar cartographic data is incomplete. But if there were any typical M-Class worlds in that system, there certainly aren't any there now."

Riker felt his body slacken, and his chair shifted backward to take up the suddenly dead weight. Somehow, after an indeterminate and indeterminable amount of time, he straightened and found his voice.

"Was this another spatial effect created by the protouniverse?"

"Not directly, sir, according to my latest scans. The star seems to be responding directly to subspatial distortions consistent with the deliberate activation of multiple tandem warp fields in extremely close proximity to the star's photosphere."

"You're saying . . . Donatra's fleet caused this *on purpose?*" said Deanna, her jaw hanging open.

"We won't know their intentions for sure until we talk to them, Commander," Jaza said. *"But that's certainly how things look from the bridge."*

Or maybe the Red King likes to play with matches in its sleep, Riker thought.

"What about the rift's ongoing general effects on the composition of local space?" he asked aloud. "Any changes?"

"The general integrity of normal space is still deteriorating steadily along predicted and measurable curves. No surprises reported by listening post Dugh, *for whatever that's worth. Bottom line: I still expect that within a few weeks at the outside, most of the systems located within two parsecs of the rift will be blotted from existence, violently. Just as Lieutenant Pazlar's initial holographic models predicted."*

"It's trying to clear out a space it can grow into," Deanna said, her tone a mix of sobriety and horror. "And take over."

Unless we somehow nudge this "Sleeper" back down into a deeper sleep, Riker thought. *Or persuade it to finish waking up someplace else, someplace very far from here.*

He was suddenly and uncomfortably reminded of his own ancestors, who had "cleared" an entire continent on Earth, heedless of the fact that it was already occupied.

"Keep closing the distance between us and Donatra's fleet," Riker said. "And keep me informed. Riker out."

He saw that Deanna was regarding him in silence. "And once we catch up to it?"

He gave her what he hoped was a reassuring smile. "We board one of Donatra's ships and try to . . . persuade this thing to start making nice."

"Are you sure it's safe to assume that it *wants* to make nice?"

He allowed his smile to fall as he began absently placing the toppled, captured chess pieces back on the board before him. "As our esteemed Capellan admiral might say, I'm going into this with open hearts and hands.

"But also with phasers locked and loaded."

CHAPTER ELEVEN

*R*ed.

Lost in a ruby sea and embraced by silence, he gradually became aware of tiny noises, mechanical sounds that whispered and sluiced along, steady yet hidden. The red had finished its violent churning and had finally calmed, steadied itself into tranquil crimson stillness near the top of the stein.

Keru recoiled from the bloodwine, wondering what had possessed him to order the vile drink, suspecting Bishop-Walker of pulling a prank on him. He scanned the vast room for the bartender, but Titan's *mess hall was dark and conspicuously empty at the moment. Almost.*

"Aren't you done yet?"

Keru turned. His companion wasn't looking at him, but rather reclined in his chair, his crossed feet resting atop the corner of the table, opposite Keru, his nose buried as usual in that odd human book he never seemed to tire of reading. Keru looked at his face, recognized the sapphire eyes, the strong jaw, the rumpled-but-stern smile, and found that he couldn't answer at first. His throat felt dry and parched, his tongue swollen. "What did you say?" Keru whispered finally.

Sean finally met his eyes. "I said, aren't you done yet?" he repeated with a chuckle. "It seems like you've been contemplating that drink forever, and I really want to hear about your new ship."

A wave of anxiety slammed into Keru. "I didn't order any damn bloodwine."

"Oh, I beg to differ," Sean laughed. "Personally, I dunno how you can stand it. Too bitter."

Keru's anxiety mixed with confusion. "Sean," he breathed. "What are we doing here? We're supposed to be back on the Enterprise."

Sean's expression turned to one of disappointment. "Oh, come on," he complained, snapping closed his copy of Peter and Wendy *and tossing it onto the table as he sat up and leaned toward Keru. "You're kidding me, right? You have this new ship, this new life, and you're still clinging to the past? Whoa, who the hell is that?"*

Keru turned. In the shadows, Dr. Ree walked past their table, dragging the corpse of an enormous targ *behind him. Keru winced. The stench of the Klingon animal was stifling, but Sean seemed unaffected by the smell; his eyes were merely alight with awe at the sight of Ree.*

"That's the CMO," Keru said dismissively. "Look, we don't have to stay here."

Sean ignored him. "What is he, a Pahkwa-thanh? I've never seen one in the flesh before. There's, what, less than a hundred of them in Starfleet?"

"Something like that," Keru said. "Can we leave now?"

"Okay," Sean said amiably as he refocused on Keru. "Where can we go next? What's Titan's *engine room like?*

Do you think Captain Riker would mind if I visited the bridge? I'd love to see what the conn—"

"No!" Keru snapped. "Sean, look, I . . ." He faltered, trying to re-form his emotions into words. "I just want us to go back home."

Sean tilted his head to one side. "You are home, Ranul. I'm just visiting."

"No, I mean our home, back on—"

"Knock it off," Sean said. "Honestly Ranul, I knew you could be a stick in the mud at times, but you've graduated to becoming an honest-to-goodness killjoy, you know that? What's the matter with you?"

Keru's hand closed tightly around the stein. He looked back down into his drink, the choking scent of it at once unbearable and irresistible.

"It's the damn bloodwine," he rasped. "I can't get the taste out of my mouth. It's poisoning me."

Silence had settled between them. Finally Sean agreed with him. "Yeah," he said quietly, his voice sounding sad for the first time. "Yeah, I'm afraid it is."

Keru met his eyes, felt tears streaming from his own. "Am I dying?"

Sean shrugged and gave him a lopsided smile. "Let's just say you aren't exactly living."

Keru reached out, tried to take Sean's hand, but his old love was beyond his reach. The realization crushed him. "Why'd you come here?"

"Honestly? Maybe just to kick you in the ass." Sean's eyes brightened. "How am I doing so far?"

Keru laughed in spite of himself. "Up to your usual standards, I think."

"Let's just assume you meant that as a compliment and move on, shall we?"

Keru's laugh turned bitter. "Move on to where?"

"I need to get going, Ranul. And you have a life to get back to."

Keru hesitated. "I just wish . . ."

"Yes?"

"I just wish we had more time."

Sean's eyebrows drew together. "Was the time we had really so terrible?"

"What? You know that isn't what I meant," Keru protested.

"Hey, you're the one from the culture that reveres memories above all else. What am I supposed to think when you make choices like this?" Sean gestured at the bloodwine between them. "Because this doesn't honor what we had together."

Keru shut his eyes and bit into his lip. With a deep breath, he said, "I'm not sure I can do this without you, Sean."

"Then let me be sure of it for both of us."

Keru looked at his drink again. With deliberate effort, he relaxed his grip on the stein, and pushed it away from him.

"There's the big lug I know and love," Sean said approvingly.

"Oh, shut the hell up," Keru laughed. Then, after a moment he whispered, "I miss you."

"I know," said Sean. "But that's okay." He grinned and started to walk away. Keru's heart ached to watch him go, but then he saw that Sean had left his treasured book behind.

"Hey, Sean," Keru called.

Sean turned back one last time.

Keru smiled. "Have an awfully big adventure."

Sean Hawk winked at him, and the darkness melted away.

CHAPTER TWELVE

"Do you think this will really work, Captain Riker?" Donatra asked, her saturnine face glowering out across *Titan*'s bridge from the main viewer.

Seated in the command chair, Riker saw that her gaze seemed to linger for a moment on Frane, who was standing quietly near the turbolift in the raised aft area of the bridge. She no doubt was looking askance at his lax security, though to Riker the Neyel's presence was merely a gesture meant to convince Frane that *Titan*'s multispecies crew was indeed a product of cooperation rather than conquest.

"I think a lot of that depends on just how good this artificial intelligence of yours turns out to be, Commander," Riker said, crossing his legs.

"Don't discount the expertise of your own people, Captain. They stopped a civil war on Romulus, which is no small feat. So I have to imagine that they'll be more than up to the task of handling a simple case

*of—what is it you humans call it?—'demonic posses-
sion.' "*

Riker smiled gently at that, realizing that she was attempting to lighten the mood with a bit of gallows humor.
"Is your team in position, Commander?"

"We're standing ready."

Riker rose and cast a nod toward an attentive Cadet
Dakal, who was watching him from the forward ops console. Looking back up toward Donatra, he said, "I'm
headed for the transporter room now. My ops officer will
coordinate the precise beam-in time with your crew."

"Then we'll see you shortly, Captain. Donatra out."
The image of the Romulan commander vanished, replaced by a velvet-black starscape. Several dozen of the
fixed stars that were now visible, however, weren't stars at
all. They were moving slowly, in an almost languid drift
against the fixed backdrop of infinite night.

Warships, flying in formation, nearly thirty-thousand
kilometers distant. Romulan vessels, *D'deridex-* and
Mogai- class all. And all of them were no doubt heavily
armed.

Riker gave silent thanks that none of the errant vessels
seemed as yet to have noticed their pursuers.

He turned to face Vale, who was staring at the tiny blips
displayed on the screen, no doubt preoccupied by
thoughts very similar to his own. "You have the bridge,
Commander," Riker said. "I'll be leading our away team
myself."

She frowned as she fixed him with a level gaze. "Respectfully, Captain, you're too valuable to place yourself
at risk."

Tuvok stepped forward from the aft tactical station. "I
must agree, sir."

Riker looked toward Deanna, who was seated in her

customary position to the immediate right of his command chair. Though she was gazing up at him with an expectant expression, she said nothing.

"Objections noted," Riker said. "But this situation is too critical for me to keep it at arm's length. If we should fail, it won't make a hell of a lot of difference whether I'm out taking the point or back here aboard *Titan*."

Besides, Deanna said to him silently, in a wordless speech that shimmered along the mental-emotional link they shared, *you can't just chicken out in front of Donatra, can you?*

Well, I suppose there is *that,* he thought back, knowing all too well how useless denial was when pitted against Deanna's empathy.

His eyes once again locked with Vale's, he said, "I'll tell you the same thing I told Commander Keru when he called me from his sickbay bed to try to talk me out of leading this mission. You see, I made a solemn promise to our former CO."

"Excuse me?" Vale said, brushing a stray wisp of auburn hair back behind her ear.

"Captain Picard anticipated that my new first officer might be . . . overly nervous about my possibly stepping into harm's way—and might even try to stop me from doing it from time to time."

She nodded gravely. "Just like I'm sure you used to do with him. Sir."

"I have no idea what you're talking about, Commander," he said with a lopsided grin.

Vale sighed, obviously realizing she'd get precisely nowhere pursuing this particular tack. "And may I ask you what, exactly, you promised Captain Picard?"

"That I'd politely ignore you on occasions like this." Looking toward Tuvok at tactical and Jaza at the main science console, he said, "Commander Tuvok, Lieutenant Commander Jaza, you're both with me. Christine, you're in charge until I get back." Then he turned and strode toward the turbolift, entering it just ahead of the other two officers.

As Riker had expected, Deanna followed the group inside, wordlessly scolding him. Riker turned and exchanged a quick glance with Frane, who had remained standing vigil on the bridge; once again, Frane was unconsciously worrying the bracelet on his wrist, but with the kind of reverence usually reserved for religious medallions or revered family heirlooms. And as the turbolift doors closed, Riker saw something in the Neyel's dark, hooded eyes that resembled admiration.

But that might have been wishful thinking.

"The transporter is solidly locked on the coordinates provided by Commander Donatra," said Lieutenant Radowski, who stood behind the main transporter room's wide, curving control console. "Romulan shield nutation, modulation, and frequency data are all programmed exactly as specified. But environmental readings at the beam-in site are still dodgy."

Though Radowski was speaking in low tones, Troi had sensed from the moment she'd entered the room that the young man was far more nervous than usual. And who could blame him? He was about to deliver *Titan*'s captain into a situation that might well prove to be lethal. Especially if the shields of the target Romulan ship somehow turned out to be less permeable than expected, even with the shield data Donatra had provided. And if that turned out to be the case, then the away team could find its atoms scattered over millions of cubic kilometers of Magellanic space in a fraction of a second.

Don't even think *that,* Troi told herself as she pushed down the torrent of refulgent anxieties that streamed not only from Radowski, but also from the taciturn Admiral Akaar and *Titan's* uncharacteristically somber new chief engineer, Dr. Ra-Havreii. The latter two senior officers—both clearly uneasy about having to allow subordinates to step into harm's way—flanked Radowski behind the transporter console. They watched in silence as the away team members, all of them now outfitted in environmental suits, double-checked the status of their phasers, comm circuits, and tricorders before making their way up onto the round transporter stage.

After Tuvok and Lieutenant Rriarr, a Caitian security officer, took up protective positions on either side of the captain, Troi strode to the last empty pad, between a not-quite-so-serene-as-usual Science Officer Jaza and a palpably jumpy Ensign Crandall from engineering. The latter winced as he set his toolkit down at his feet with a too-loud clatter.

Will favored the away team with a backward glance and a reassuring grin that Troi could tell buoyed everyone, at least a little. "Sounds like everyone is ready."

From beside the console, Akaar nodded with great solemnity as he touched his combadge. "Akaar to bridge."

"Vale here."

"The away team is prepared for transport, Commander. Are Donatra's people still in position?"

"They've just signaled again that they are."

"Confirmed," Radowski said, glancing at his board, where a new stream of data had apparently just begun scrolling. "Preparing for coordinated transport in twenty seconds."

"Good work, Lieutenant. And Will?"

"Go ahead, Christine."

"Godspeed. But if I even think *you might try to leave me in permanent command of* Titan, *I'm coming after you. Sir."*

Will's grin expanded, in obvious appreciation of his exec's penchant for dark humor. "So noted. I'll try to be home in time for dinner. Mr. Radowski, energize."

Radowski executed Will's order, and to Troi's eyes, *Titan*'s transporter room dissolved. She wondered if the temporary state of nonexistence through which she was passing in any way resembled what the Sleeper experienced during his long journey toward wakefulness.

IMPERIAL WARBIRD *RA'KHOI*

His breath sounding a bit too loud inside his helmet, Riker found himself standing in a broad alcove lit with a subdued, greenish light. He wondered if the beam-in had taken significantly longer than usual, or if his imagination had merely decided to work a double shift. He assumed the former, since it wasn't every day that one beamed straight through a *D'deridex*-class warbird's formidable deflector shield envelope, and with Romulan cooperation no less. Looking around, he saw that the other members of the away team were positioned just as he'd expected. Tuvok and Rriarr had their weapons drawn—also just as he'd expected.

"Captain Riker," said the familiar voice of Donatra, which echoed slightly in the high-ceilinged chamber. Ensign Crandall responded with a startled yip, nearly tripped over his toolbox, then settled into an embarrassed silence.

Riker turned toward the voice that had called to him, as did the rest of his party.

"Welcome aboard the Imperial Warbird *Ra'khoi*," Donatra said. She stood at the front of a group of four Romulan officers, including herself. Like the *Titan* team, she and her staff were dressed in pressure suits and helmets, the livid orange-amber of the Romulan garments presenting a sharp contrast to the stark Starfleet white. The quartet stood in a rough circle, evidently having just beamed over from the *Valdore*.

Jaza, Tuvok, and a pair of Donatra's people ran some quick scans and within moments determined that the room—an alcove adjacent to the main engineering section—was utterly empty. Riker and Donatra then exchanged quick introductions of their respective teams. Seketh and Daehla, both of whom were running scanners, were apparently youngish women, a decurion and a sciences specialist respectively, while Liravek was an imperious male centurion of perhaps early middle age.

"Life readings?" Riker asked.

"The entire crew complement seems to be alive, but unconscious," Daehla said.

"Comatose is a more apt word, I should think," Seketh said, consulting her own scanner.

"What could cause such a thing?" Centurion Liravek asked sharply, as though interrogating a group of recalcitrant prisoners. Riker was beginning not to like him very much.

When it became clear that neither Seketh nor Daehla had a ready answer, Jaza spoke up. "This . . . entity that's controlling the fleet's computer systems seems to have altered the environmental control system. I'm picking up high concentrations of anesthezine in the air supply, which didn't show up on our sensor scans, probably because of interference caused by the shields. If we hadn't taken the precaution of putting on environmental suits . . ." The Bajoran trailed off significantly.

"So you're saying that our . . . 'Red King' just wanted to nudge the crew out of its way," Crandall asked.

Still consulting his tricorder, Jaza nodded. "I'd wager it probably did the very same thing on every ship in the fleet. Our long-range scanners must have missed it because of distance and spatial distortions."

"The intelligence that hijacked this fleet can lay waste to entire stars and planets," Riker said. "But it left the crews relatively unharmed. That doesn't make any sense."

Jaza shrugged. "Well, we're positing that our Sleeper has somehow subverted the computers of the entire fleet network, except the *Valdore,* which wasn't present at the time of the takeover. Perhaps the entity ran afoul of some sort of personnel-protection fail-safe subroutine in the Romulan *rokhelh* software. Something like Asimov's Laws."

Riker nodded. The fact that the emerging intelligence that had seized control of Donatra's fleet hadn't simply killed the crews outright argued in favor of that idea. *But it's wiped out at least one inhabited world so far, whether intentionally or not,* he reminded himself again.

He turned toward Donatra and noted the relieved expression he saw through the faceplate of her helmet. "I am grateful not to have found my crews dead, whatever the reason."

Riker nodded. "We need to access this ship's computer system," he said, keenly aware that the Red King's current beneficence might not last. "Now."

Donatra nodded back, then immediately took the point, leading the group across a corridor and into an adjacent chamber, a room lined with consoles, monitor screens, and holotanks. A pair of uniformed figures lay across a bank of consoles, their bodies sprawled in deathlike postures. Donatra and Liravek paused beside them long enough to confirm that they were merely unconscious, like the rest of the crew.

With a gauntleted right hand, Riker tapped the external communicator key located near his suit's neck ring. "Riker to *Titan*."

"Vale here, Captain. What's the away team's status?"

"We've arrived safely, as has Commander Donatra's team. What's the condition of our Sleeper?"

"Still yawning and stretching, but apparently only very slowly. Pazlar, Norellis, and Cethente have been continuously monitoring the correlated ongoing breakdown of local space. They've found no acceleration in the protouniverse's spatial displacement rate—at least not yet. But that also means the effect's not slowing down any, either. Another two weeks, three tops, and . . . pfffft. We'll want to be very far away from here when that happens."

Am I capable of doing that? Riker thought as he considered his exec's report. *Cutting and running just on the off chance I* might *manage to save my ship and crew, and get them home? Or do I do my damnedest to head this thing off, and maybe save billions of lives, regardless of what happens to* Titan? After all, in helping to defeat Shinzon, he had been at least partially responsible for opening up the spatial rift that may have ultimately drawn the protouniverse here.

But all he could do at the moment was to cling to the hope that he wouldn't have to face the answers to his own questions head-on.

Aloud, he said, "We're about to attempt to gain control of the Romulan fleet's computer network. I'll check in with you again once that's done, Commander. Riker out."

Crandall carefully set his toolbox on a chair before one of the computer consoles, then uncovered an access panel.

He then opened the toolbox and began carefully arranging his instruments on the oilcloth-lined interior of its lid.

"It seems . . . I don't know, wrong somehow, to just wipe this Sleeper off the computer network," the junior engineer said as he worked. "I feel almost like I'm helping to kill somebody."

"In a way, you are," Donatra said in matter-of-fact tones. "But what of it? We routinely patrol our computers for signs of our *rokhelh* artificial intelligences developing self-awareness. Whenever we detect such signs, we purge the affected systems."

"We don't have a lot of alternatives," Riker said by way of encouragement to Crandall as Daehla began pulling her own small instruments and several hair-thin, glowing cables from a compact kit she carried on her hip.

"But why can't we at least . . . *talk* to it first?" Crandall wanted to know.

Riker thought that was an excellent question. He cast a quick interrogative glance at Deanna.

Though her smile was gentle, her reply carried a therapist's firm *it's-time-to-face-reality* tone. "Besides the fact that we have virtually no common frame of reference with it, Mr. Crandall? Don't forget, we're talking about an anentropic pattern of inferred sentience that arrived here from an entirely alien, non-Euclidean universe whose physical laws in no way resemble our own."

Riker's eyes widened involuntarily. "Couldn't have said it better myself."

Crandall looked chastened. "Oh. I suppose when you put it that way . . ."

Deanna offered the engineer a smile that shone through her helmet's faceplate. "Your instinct is a good one, Ensign. But it could take decades or even centuries just for us to get this creature's attention. A little like Micromegas."

"Who?" said Crandall, pausing in confusion.

"Maybe six centuries ago, Voltaire, a writer from your home planet, told the story of Micromegas, a gigantic being from another world. He was so huge that it was just about impossible for him to see Earth people as living things worth communicating with. And *he* encountered other beings that were at least that large compared to *him.*"

Noting Donatra's impatient glare, Riker placed a reassuring hand on Crandall's shoulder. "Try not to worry about it *too* much, Ensign. Talking to our sleepwalking intelligence—or least to the computers it's hijacked—is the *rokhelh* software's job, not ours."

Riker watched in anxious silence as Crandall and Daehla each carefully hooked up their cables and handheld control units, working in tandem to create a pair of seamless interfaces with the warbird's central computer, and thereby the entire fleet network. Though the entire operation had taken perhaps three minutes so far, Riker was uncomfortably aware of the passage of time. He couldn't help but wonder what this so-called Red King might do if it were to discover what their plan was before they actually managed to carry it out.

"Actually, what you said a moment ago was only half right, sir," Crandall said, as he confirmed his final connections with his engineering tricorder. Riker saw his face flush with color as he apparently realized how insolent he had sounded.

"Easy, Ensign," Riker said. "I've never claimed to know everything. Why don't you enlighten me?"

Crandall sputtered and hawed for a moment, studiously avoiding looking at Riker as he resumed his work. "Yes, sir. What I meant was just that the *rokhelh* software we're installing now will replace the resident *rokhelh* software that our Red King apparently corrupted, then resume that program's task of talking to the network. And Chaka's new algorithm will let the new *rokhelh* know precisely what we expect it to do."

"Let's just hope the *rokhelh* will see its way clear to following the new instructions we're feeding it," Jaza said. "From my previous experiences with artificial intelligences, they're sometimes a rather independent lot."

Riker couldn't help but think of those few occasions when Data had malfunctioned, had been technologically manipulated, or had been impersonated by his predecessor, Lore; he couldn't help but sympathize with Jaza's apprehension.

As Crandall and Daehla began uploading software into the control panels of their respective interface units, Riker turned toward Donatra, who displayed a disapproving scowl.

"You seem to know a great deal about Romulan technology," she said in a mildly accusing tone. "Hardware and software both."

Riker nodded. "And it appears to be coming in handy just now."

"Agreed. But how did you acquire this knowledge?"

He offered her what he assumed she would see as a slightly guilty-looking smile. "About seven years ago, the *Enterprise*'s second officer came into extremely close contact with one of your empire's AI security programs."

A look of understanding crossed Donatra's face. "Ah. The late android, Data. He must have uploaded a good deal of *rokhelh* program code during that encounter."

"A pretty fair portion, as it turned out," Riker said. "Enough to enable one of *Titan*'s computer specialists to reverse-engineer most of the rest."

"Since our arrival here in Neyel space?" Donatra said. "I'm impressed."

"Don't be *too* impressed," Deanna said. "It isn't as though Crewman Chaka whipped up this entire program today. Fortunately for us, she's been studying the *Enterprise's rokhelh* encounter as a sort of 'pet project' ever since she first entered Starfleet."

Riker turned to his wife and grinned. "Looks like we may have lucked out this time."

No sooner had he uttered those words than he found himself wishing, absurdly, for a stout piece of wood to knock on.

U.S.S. TITAN

Mekrikuk was startled out of a deep slumber. Suddenly aware, once again, of his surroundings—*Titan*'s sickbay, where he had remained confined ever since his rescue from the Vikr'l Prison on Romulus—the sensation that had awakened him persisted.

Something had reached out for him, had touched his mind. At first, he wasn't quite sure what it was. Then he closed his eyes. And the image came to him, very clearly.

Ships. Dozens of Romulan warbirds, as "seen" by one another's external sensors, he supposed. All of them being driven by a single, unified intellect. An intellect whose thoughts were somehow obscured and jumbled, as though by a thick blanket of sleep.

That mind was now lashing out in extreme distress. Curiosity warred with caution, and won a narrow victory. Very carefully, Mekrikuk opened his mind, hoping to learn more about this unknown thoughtforce.

Then he screamed.

IMPERIAL WARBIRD *RA'KHOI*

"There," Daehla said as she turned away from the console to address Donatra. "I've confirmed that both the *rokhelh* and its guidance program have been uploaded into the system. Both are actively engaging the alien programming that's taken hold."

Riker felt a surge of happy anticipation, but he carefully reined it in. Anything might still happen. "How long will it be before we know if—"

"Done, sir," Crandall said with a grin, his gaze rising from the display on his tricorder. "Or near enough to done. The neuromagnetic signatures the entity had imposed on the network are already dwindling as the *rokhelh* forces them into the background and into secondary and tertiary systems."

Studying the displays on her own instruments, Daehla nodded in agreement. "Confirmed. The alien programming is being shunted out of primary core systems."

"Great work," Riker said, exchanging triumphant smiles with Donatra as he reached for his combadge.

U.S.S. TITAN

Keru lay in one of the sickbay biobeds, reclining against a pile of pillows as he sipped from a glass of cool water. He was as restless as he had been at any other time in his life. Dr. Ree had kept him in sickbay for observation ever since he'd regained consciousness a couple of hours earlier. Of course, he couldn't blame Ree for his caution; Keru's chest remained bandaged, despite multiple surgeries and dermal regenerations, thanks to the all but mortal wounds he had sustained during *Titan*'s skirmishes in Romulan space.

He was grateful that Ree and Ogawa had brought him up to speed on most everything that had happened over the past several days, including the death of Chief Engineer Ledrah, the birth of the Bolajis' child, *Titan*'s unexpected relocation to the Small Magellanic Cloud, and the disappearance of Commander Donatra's hidden fleet, which had evidently been spirited away by some sort of emergent life-force.

I spend a few days on the disabled list, and the whole damn universe spins down into utter chaos, he'd thought more than once, though he knew all the while that such self-centered notions were completely preposterous.

He was also frustrated in that he had been able to learn precious little about what was going on presently. All he knew for certain was that his captain was off the ship— against Keru's recommendation—leading a boarding party onto one of Donatra's vessels. His captain was in danger right this minute, as was Commander Tuvok, the man who was currently filling in for Keru as *Titan*'s tactical officer and security chief.

And Keru knew he wouldn't be able to do a damned thing to help either of them.

Keru hadn't forgotten that he had been prepared to leave Tuvok behind on Romulus during the Vikr'l rescue after that operation had begun coming apart at the seams. And although he had merely been following both regulations and the mission profile that day, he still hadn't quite been able to forgive himself.

You'd better get the captain back aboard in one piece, Mr. Tuvok, he thought. *And yourself as well. Otherwise you and I are going to have* words.

A piercing shriek interrupted his reverie, causing him

to send most of the contents of his glass splashing onto the bed and the deck beneath it.

Despite the pain that lanced through his chest, he swung his bare feet to the floor, discarding his suddenly emptied glass as he turned toward the source of the sound.

In the opposite corner of the sickbay lay Mekrikuk, the hulking Reman whom he'd helped rescue from Vikr'l Prison. Every muscle and tendon in the Reman's large, chalk-white frame seemed to strain as a scream of pure fright issued from some primal place deep within him.

Keru moved unsteadily in Mekrikuk's direction, though he saw that Ree and Ogawa were already converging on the Reman's biobed. Mekrikuk had already stopped screaming, though his eyes remained huge and terror-stricken.

"Tell your captain he must stop what he's doing!" Mekrikuk said in a surprisingly mellifluous tenor voice. "Now!"

"Maybe he's hallucinating," Ogawa said as she prepared a hypospray with a prestidigitator's speed. "He could be having some sort of drug reaction."

Or maybe not. Some Remans are pretty damned strong telepaths, Keru thought, stumbling slightly before righting himself against one of the biobeds. The time he'd spent on Trill, tending the telepathic symbionts who dwelled in Mak'ala's deep, aqueous caverns, had taught him never to dismiss any being's apparent telepathic impressions completely out of hand.

Keru watched as the head nurse slapped the hypo into the doctor's outstretched claws. Ree quickly placed the device against Mekrikuk's battle-scarred neck. The hypo's contents instantly hissed home and the Reman went slackly unconscious a moment later.

Keru noticed then that Ogawa was glowering at him,

though in a good-natured manner. He was, after all, Noah's adoptive "uncle," a member of her chosen family because of their shared history of pain and loss. "You need to get back into bed, mister. Or do I have to have you restrained?"

Keru offered her a weak smile and lofted his large hands in a gesture of surrender. Then he noticed a slight draft coming from the air circulation system, and realized only now that his sickbay gown had left his aft section entirely unshielded.

"All right, Alyssa. I'll go quietly. But I need to call the bridge first." *And some pants might be nice, too,* he thought.

Seated in the command chair on *Titan*'s bridge, Christine Vale watched the constellation of viewscreen blips that constituted Donatra's runaway fleet and felt vaguely uneasy. Occasionally she glanced at the main science station, from which Jaza was conspicuously absent.

Belay that thought, Vale. The bridge is no place for infatuations, she told herself. Then she paused for an instant to consider Riker and Troi, whose relationship had gone about as far past infatuation as imaginably possible. *On the other hand, I ought to be able to get away with marrying him.*

Looking away from Jaza's console, which was now occupied by Lieutenant Eviku, Vale noted that Frane had remained standing beside the turbolift. He watched the screen, as still and silent as a gargoyle. Admiral Akaar, who had come up from the main transporter room a few minutes earlier, also stood nearby, apparently keeping an eye on Frane as much as on the viewscreen. Frane, for his part, seemed to be studiously avoiding the Capellan's piercing basilisk stare.

"Riker to Titan."

Will Riker's voice, though filtered through her combadge, sounded calm and businesslike, which reassured her somewhat. But *only* somewhat. Her faint sense of dread persisted.

"Vale here. Go ahead, Captain."

"We're making excellent progress here. We should have manual control over the entire fleet in just a few minutes. The entity inhabiting the computers knocked everyone unconscious with anesthezine gas. We're reinitiating all environmental and life-support protocols right now, to blow every deck of every ship clear of the stuff. I'll advise you as soon as the operation's complete."

The captain signed off, and Vale slumped back slightly into the chair, sighing in relief and simultaneously blowing a stray hank of her fine auburn hair away from her face.

Dakal turned from the forward ops station and fixed her with a puzzled stare. "Commander, I'm picking up some pretty strange readings."

Vale rose and glanced at the Cardassian cadet's console. She wasn't quite sure what to make of it, until she glanced to the starboard science station, where Eviku was obviously studying the very same readings.

"This is not good, Commander," Eviku said, the Arkenite's seashell ears twitching on either side of his elongated head.

Titan rocked, forcing everyone on the bridge to grab at chairs, railings, or consoles until the inertial dampers compensated, leveling things out a second or so later. It felt as though the ship had been struck very hard by something large and blunt. But Vale had seen the data on Dakal's console, so she knew that no such thing had occurred.

She also knew that what had apparently just *really* happened might turn out to be infinitely *worse*.

"Yellow alert, Mr. Dakal. Raise shields."

"Aye, sir," Dakal said. "But I haven't quite figured out yet what hit us."

Vale breathed a pungent Klingon oath under her breath. "Open a channel to the capt—"

"Keru to Vale." As Dakal complied with her order, she tapped her combadge. "Vale here. It's good to hear your voice, Ranul, but this isn't a good—"

"Chris, you need to know something. Our Reman guest has just given us a strange warning. He said that Captain Riker has to stop his current operation aboard that Romulan ship."

"That sounds a bit vague," Vale said, scowling slightly. As worried as she was, she didn't care much for "mystical portents," at least not outside the pages of old horror novels. "Did he offer you any specific reason?"

"Afraid not. And he's unconscious now, so I can't follow up. But suppose he picked up some sort of telepathic flash of something horrible happening that nobody else has noticed just yet?"

A telepathic alarm from our Red King? Vale thought, well aware that she had rarely been steered wrong by Ranul's hunches, which he never offered lightly. And she also had to admit that Mekrikuk's admonition completely squared with her own misgivings—and with the readings that were even now scrolling across Dakal's and Eviku's consoles. Not to mention whatever force had just slammed into *Titan. There's obviously something more going on here than simple senior officer jitters.*

"Thanks, Ranul," Vale said. "I'm going to check this out."

Vale's combadge chirped yet again, followed by the synthetic voice of Dr. Cethente. *"I believe we may have a serious problem, Commander."*

"Looks that way," Vale said. "Any ideas on explaining it?" She turned her gaze back toward an inset display on the main viewscreen's port side, where data from the science station was scrolling upward. She glanced in Eviku's direction and saw that the xenobiologist was looking at her expectantly, as were Frane, Akaar, Dakal, Lavena, Dr. Ra-Havreii—who had evidently stepped out of the turbolift a few moments ago—and the rest of the bridge crew.

"It appears," said Eviku, speaking very slowly and carefully, "that space itself has begun to . . . *buckle* locally. And the effect is accelerating."

"Cethente?" Vale said.

"Lieutenant Eviku is correct, in my opinion."

Vale felt her heart begin to race. Though she had never worked with Cethente prior to *Titan*'s maiden voyage, she was well acquainted with his reputation. His scientific analyses were only very rarely wrong, even when given off the cuff. *And he doesn't even* have *cuffs.* She forced herself to breathe slowly and evenly, calming herself.

"Meaning?" Vale asked.

"Meaning that the rate at which our 'Sleeper' is apparently rearranging space has abruptly begun to accelerate. It may increase by about an order of magnitude. Perhaps more."

"And the cause?"

"I can't prove it conclusively, Commander, but it has to be related to our efforts to force the entity to relinquish its control over those Romulan ships out there. Forcing this emerging intelligence from the Romulan computer systems pushed a substantial part of it back into the very space its emergence has been affecting ever since its initial arrival here. The accelerated breakdown of space appears to be strongest in the immediate vicinity of the Romulan fleet.

And the effect is spreading at many times the speed of light, propagating directly through the subspace medium."

Swell, Vale thought. To Eviku, she said, "What's in its immediate path?"

"Stellar cartography shows an inhabited system directly in the path of the disruptions," Eviku said. "It's less than two parsecs from our current position. At the rate the effect is spreading, the entire system will be devastated. By the time the effect reaches its peak—I'd give it between seven to ten standard days—it'll be as though this whole star system never even existed."

"That is the system of the Coreworld," Frane said, stepping forward several paces. Akaar regarded him the way a herpetologist might study a deadly serpent. "A planet called Oghen."

"Oghen?" Vale asked, blinking rapidly as she turned her chair so that she faced the Neyel, whose tail switched uneasily from side to side behind him.

"Oghen is home to nearly two billion sentients," Frane said. "It's the homeworld of the Neyel Hegemony."

And it's maybe a week away from being completely erased from existence, Vale thought, her heart dropping into a sudden freefall. *Maybe along with every other inhabited world in Magellanic space, and perhaps even farther off than that.*

And she couldn't think of a single damned thing she could do about it. Except one.

"Dakal, get me the captain and Commander Jaza. *Now.*"

Chapter Thirteen

"We've recovered our fleet, Donatra, and with minimal loss of life," Commander Suran said quietly, though an audible edge of irritation tinged his voice. His head remained bandaged, as it had been since just after the *Valdore*'s rather bumpy arrival in Neyel space. "The fleet is operational, fully crewed, and ready to move out.

"So why in the name of Karatek's bones are we lingering here while space itself is disintegrating all around us?"

Donatra watched her colleague carefully, noting the vehement, almost fearful urgency in his manner. The last time the usually reserved Suran had seemed so agitated had been immediately after his discovery that the Great Bloom had swallowed their hidden fleet. *And now that we've recovered that fleet, he wants to take no further chances.*

She looked around the *Valdore*'s busy bridge, which had become even busier during the few *siuren* that had elapsed since Donatra's and Riker's boarding parties had departed from the *Ra'khoi*.

"That's an excellent question, Suran," Donatra said as her eyes lit on Decurion Seketh, who stood beside one of the operations consoles. "I trust you can explain more concisely than I can, Decurion."

The young woman looked slightly frazzled to be put on the spot in front of both of the fleet's flag officers so soon after the mission aboard the *Ra'khoi,* but she quickly recovered herself. "I would advise against trying to move the fleet out of the region for at least the next half-*eisae*," Seketh said.

"Why?" Suran wanted to know, scowling.

"Because of the growing spatial instabilities that have been appearing all around us during the past several *dierhu,* Commander."

Suran's scowl deepened. "So we avoid them."

"Yes, sir. Of course. But unless we allow the computers enough time to model the phenomenon precisely, some of our ships are bound to suffer severe damage from subspace shearing effects. If we try to leave the vicinity without the ability to adjust our warp fields instantaneously to accommodate the ongoing spatial changes, we could lose singularity containment on half our ships."

"Or maybe all of them," Donatra said. Though she had never been one to jump at shadows, she had never fancied herself a wild-eyed optimist. Not when it came to the safety of her ships and crews.

Suran acquiesced, but still seemed impatient. "I see. Well, I don't want us to stay here a single *siure* longer than absolutely necessary."

"I agree," Donatra said, quietly wondering what would happen when and if she and Suran could no longer achieve a meeting of the minds with such apparent ease. *We can't exactly pull rank on each other, after all,* she thought. *Far easier to pull our disruptors, or our Honor Blades.*

"Captain Riker is hailing us, Commander," Seketh said, interrupting Donatra's brown study. She wondered whether the young decurion was addressing her or Suran.

"Put him on visual," Donatra said quietly, then faced the bridge's central viewer while Seketh complied.

A look of intense concern radiating from his blue eyes, Riker started in without preamble. *"Commander, we have to discuss what's begun happening to the space around our ships."*

In spite of herself, Donatra felt a surge of hope bloom within her. "Have you discovered why the breakdown of local space has begun accelerating?" Despite her hopes, she feared she already knew the answer.

Riker nodded, his expression remaining grave. *"My people are of the opinion that* we're *responsible. My crew and yours."*

"How?" she asked quietly, already all but certain that her question was unnecessary.

"When we forced the growing protouniverse's emerging intelligence out of your fleet's computer network, it had to go somewhere else. So once it was effectively locked out of your ships, it began 'reordering' local space at an even faster rate than before."

"In other words, this 'Sleeper' deity the natives worship is awakening even faster than your briefing data had indicated."

"That's one way of looking at it. But that's not all. The accelerated spatial breakdown will utterly wipe out the central homeworld of the Neyel people within ten Earth days. Titan and your fleet can get there within about two days, though, to assist with their planetary evacuation—"

"You can't be serious!" Suran said, almost bellowing.

Riker's eyes flashed like twin glaciers beneath a sunrise. *"I'm deadly serious, Commander. We're directly responsible for what's happening now. Your people, as well as ours."*

"Perhaps. But what can we hope to accomplish other than throwing all of *our* lives away—along with this doomed planet?"

"I don't intend to turn my back on people that our actions placed in danger," Riker said, beginning to reveal an anger that Donatra didn't doubt could easily match that of Suran.

Still, she had to favor Suran's hard pragmatism over Riker's softer optimism. "How many live on the Neyel homeworld, Captain?" Donatra asked.

"About two billion."

Her eyes grew wide. "Two *billion?"*

Riker soldiered on as though he hadn't noticed her incredulous reaction. *"And our Neyel guest tells us that their spacefaring capabilities have diminished quite a bit over the past several decades, as they've slowly learned to put aside the worst of their imperial ambitions."*

Donatra shook her head in disbelief. The Federation peacemaker, this Burgess she had read about, had evidently weakened these once-puissant Neyel to the point of utter helplessness. And Federation idealism seemed to have given Riker delusions of omnipotence.

"Suran is right, Captain," she said. "We couldn't hope to save more than a tiny fraction of the Neyel population anyway, even if we were to use every ship in my . . ." She paused to glance at Suran before amending her declaration. ". . . in our fleet for the purpose."

"I know that Romulan military officers are fond of paying tribute to the idea of honor by displaying ceremonial

swords," Riker said. *"I hope you're not telling me those Honor Blades of yours are entirely for show."*

As Riker's insult sank in, Donatra's upper lip trembled in an involuntary display of rage. The scars that laced her side became livid, singing a silent aria of old pain and anger. "Take care with your words, Captain. I respect you. But there are limits even to that."

But Riker wasn't deterred in the least. *"Is it honorable to simply* abandon *an entire world that you've helped place in jeopardy?"*

"Of course not, Riker. But do you seriously expect to save billions of people?"

"Truthfully, I don't know what *I expect, Commander. But I don't expect to sit back and do nothing. Not when I'm partially responsible for what's happening."*

"This is absurd," Suran said. "As soon as our own crews deem it safe, we're taking our fleet back to the Great Bloom, which we will then use to return to Romulan space as quickly as possible—before this entire sector truly *is* erased from existence."

"We'll still have time enough to do that," Riker said, his tone now almost pleading rather than accusing. *"After we've rescued as many Neyel as we can."*

"Perhaps," Donatra said, shaking her head yet again. "But perhaps not. The evacuation you propose could easily take more time than we have left to us. And if this entire region of space completely 'reboots' itself before we re-enter the Bloom, the entire endeavor will have been in vain. *Titan,* the *Valdore,* and the rest of the fleet will all be wiped from existence."

"I know it's risky. But I'm prepared to take the risk to correct our error. Alone, if necessary."

Despite her lingering anger over his harangue, Donatra

couldn't help but admire this human's dogged courage. For a fleeting moment, it shamed her.

"Of *course* you're willing to risk everything on behalf of these people, Captain," Suran said. "They're members of your own species, after all. Despite outward appearances, you have much in common with them."

Riker's azure eyes blazed. "*As do you, Suran.*"

"Start making sense, human," Suran said, mirroring Donatra's own confusion.

"*Yes, the Neyel* are *an offshoot of my own species. Just as Romulans are descended from the Vulcan people.*"

"So?" Suran said.

"*So Vulcan and the rest of the Federation very recently averted what could have been a terrible bloodletting on your homeworld. I'm merely asking you to return the favor—by assisting people who are probably no less vulnerable than your ancestors who made that first crossing from Vulcan to Romulus.*"

Donatra thought of the ancient blood relationship between Vulcan and Romulan, and between human and Neyel. And she considered the wide panoply of other, nonhuman species that also served aboard *Titan*. As well as Riker's apparently perfect sense of assurance that all of those variegated nonhuman/non-Neyel personnel would do whatever was required to save even a relative handful of entirely unrelated strangers from certain death.

Shame returned then, seizing her heart in an unyielding grip. Riker, after all, as Captain Picard's first officer during the Shinzon affair, had all but become one of her comrades-in-arms. She couldn't deny that the crews of the *Valdore* and the *Enterprise* both owed one another their lives. And Riker had just helped her regain control of an enormously important military asset—her fleet.

But she and Suran both had a responsibility to safe-guard that fleet, and the thousands of Romulan military personnel it carried.

She saw that her duty was clear. And hated herself, and her ingrained priorities.

"I'm sorry, Captain," she said. "I must decline."

U.S.S. TITAN

Flanked by Deanna Troi and Christine Vale, Riker slumped backward into his command chair a split-second after the alien starfield of Neyel space replaced the images of Donatra and Suran.

Seated at his right, Vale issued a weary-sounding sigh. "That's it, then. We're on our own."

"Looks that way," Riker said.

"*Titan* is going to assist at Oghen, with or without the Romulans," Deanna said. She wasn't asking a question.

Riker nodded to her. "Seems to me we don't have any other legitimate option. Even if the ship is placed at risk."

"It would be nice to have the official sanction of the Neyel government, though," Vale said.

"I'm still working on that," Deanna said. "The fact that the Neyel civil and military authorities seem to be too busy with crisis management to even talk to us argues that we ought to help them, with or without permission."

"I just wonder how the crew will take this," Vale said.

Deanna tipped her head, considering Vale's question. "They're a good crew. They'll adapt." Her dark eyes locked with Riker's, and she offered him a gentle smile. "They'll be frightened, of course. But they have faith in you, Will. They'll follow wherever you lead."

No pressure, Riker thought.

He turned his seat until he faced the aft portion of the bridge. Akaar and Frane regarded him from the railed upper section, where they loomed over him like monuments.

"You've both been fairly quiet since I came back aboard," Riker said.

"If you were expecting me to second-guess you, Captain, I fear I must disappoint you," Akaar said. "The risks are yours to take."

"Your life will be at risk as well, Admiral," Riker said. "Along with mine and everybody else aboard *Titan.*"

Akaar's shoulders rotated in a slow shrug. His dark eyes twinkled beneath his pale, lined brow. "All of our lives would be at risk, even if we were to attempt to recross the anomaly and return home right now. I was born amid risk, Captain. As one of my namesakes once said, 'risk is our business.' "

Riker's eyes lit next upon the taciturn Neyel. "And you, Mr. Frane?"

Frane's arms were folded, drawing the sleeves of his robe up so that the bracelet he had earlier seemed so reticent about displaying was clearly visible. His leathery face assayed a very slight smile. "I wish danger upon no one, Captain. But if you expect me to object to anyone's effort to save my birthworld, I'm afraid I must disappoint you."

"I was starting to think you really were rooting for the Sleeper," Riker said.

The Neyel tipped his head inquisitively. " 'Rooting'?"

"Hoping that the Sleeper would wake up and erase your people from the universe."

Frane nodded. "So I was. Once, at any rate, when I had less hope than I do now. Perhaps I misjudged myself somewhat. Just as I misjudged you as a slaver."

Riker replied with a narrow smile of his own. Here was a young man whose cultural alienation and nihilism had led him to implore his adopted deity to punish his own people with nonexistence. Now that actual destruction—whether from divine retribution or cosmic happenstance—was en route, Frane had evidently had a change of heart. Not only that, he felt he had a reason for hope; Riker could only hope that it wasn't a sadly misguided hope.

It occurred to Riker that Frane's transformation had to bode well for any effort at human-Neyel rapprochement. *Assuming that the Neyel people somehow manage to survive this,* he thought as he turned back to face the main viewscreen.

"For what it's worth," Deanna said, "Commander Donatra is highly conflicted about having abandoned us."

Riker scowled. "Not conflicted enough." He leaned forward toward the ops console, behind which Cadet Dakal was seated. "Are the sensor nets fully integrated with Cethente's spatial breakdown models?"

"Yes, sir," Dakal said. "We're only one ship, and we're equipped with a more refined sensor network than the Romulans have. I'd expect their fleet to take a bit longer than we did to figure out how to navigate the local spatial instabilities safely."

So they can't just bolt straight back for the anomaly and a quick ticket home, at least not right away, Riker thought. The notion provided cold comfort.

He turned toward the flight control console, which Ensign Lavena was studying intently, her hydration suit gurgling slightly as she moved her sheathed hands to work the controls.

"Best speed to Oghen, Ensign," Riker said to the Pacifican conn officer. Then he turned back toward Dakal.

"And keep trying to raise the civil authorities on Oghen via subspace radio. I want to make sure they fully understand what's coming their way."

"Aye, sir," the Cardassian said as he set to work.

I suppose we'll have to figure out how the hell we're going to save a whole planet on the way there.

CHAPTER FOURTEEN

Soon it will be time, Donatra told herself yet again.

Seated at the forward operations console, Centurion Liravek studied a set of readouts, then rose and faced Donatra with a perfect salute, the inside of his right fist touching his sternum directly between the lungs. "Sensors and warp-field governance *rokhelhu* are coordinated fleetwide, Commander Donatra. All units report they are presently in readiness to move out."

"Outstanding," Donatra said, her voice steady though she was beside herself with unease. She watched impassively as Liravek returned to his seat and resumed working his console.

Standing beside the bridge's centrally located command chair, Donatra turned toward Suran, who stood a short distance away, eyeing the starfield on the viewscreen with evident impatience. Intermittent flashes of deep, bloody green and furious orange flared across portions of the interstellar blackness, each small conflagration revealing nearby loci of intense spatial disruption caused by the protouniverse whose influence the boarding parties had just chased from the fleet's computer network. *Our own handiwork,* she thought grimly, considering once again how she and Riker had unwittingly accelerated the process that threatened the lives of so many, across such an enormous volume of space.

And we prepare to flee it, along with the craven Klingons. There was no honor to be found in this. None at all.

A small green light on the arm of Donatra's command chair began flashing silently. She stepped toward the chair and toggled it off. *Thank you, Dr. Venora,* she thought, satisfied that no one else had noticed.

"Then let's get these ships underway," Suran told the centurion. "The Empire needs the fleet's protection, especially now that the Klingons have a beachhead on the Two Worlds. We can't afford to wait around here any longer than we have to."

"You're right, Suran. We must act," Donatra said, her eyes lingering on the bandages that still swathed Suran's head.

Suran noticed her stare and scowled. "What? Why are you looking at me like that?"

"Are you sure you're feeling well, Suran?"

Suran's scowled deepened. "I'm fine."

Donatra assayed her most serious *I'm-terribly-concerned-about-you* expression. "You've gone as pale as a Reman, Commander."

"Nonsense."

"Dr. Venora wasn't very happy when you checked yourself out of the infirmary."

"Venora's *never* very happy," Suran said with a grim laugh.

Donatra nodded toward the centurion. "Take over up here, Liravek. Get the fleet under way."

Liravek rose again from his seat and again saluted smartly, though his countenance betrayed a look of growing confusion. Was he becoming suspicious? "At once, Commander Donatra."

She turned and strode toward the lift doors. "I need to speak with you, Suran. Alone."

Stepping into the lift, Donatra saw the thunderclouds gathering behind her colleague's bandaged brow. He stepped into the lift with her.

"Infirmary," she said once the doors had closed.

"I haven't the time for this," he said. Turning his face toward the ceiling, he said, "Computer, halt lift."

But the lift continued. "I have overridden the lift's voice-command protocols, Suran."

"Why?" Suran asked, the suspicion in his voice now plainly evident. "Do you believe me somehow unfit for duty, Donatra?"

"That depends upon what you decide to do next. How long has it been since you last visited Dr. Venora?"

"You know I've been a bit busy since my release from the infirmary, Donatra."

"You released *yourself*," Donatra reminded him yet again. "Now that we have recovered the fleet and have gotten it under way, I insist that you make some time to visit the good doctor. Now."

"*I* will decide if and when I visit the infirmary, Commander."

Donatra reached quietly into her tunic pouch. She sighed, truly regretting what she had to do next. "I'm afraid I must insist."

Suran froze as his eyes lit on the small disruptor unit in

her right hand, which she leveled straight at his lungs. At that moment, he truly did look as pale as any Reman.

"This is tantamount to mutiny, Donatra!"

She made a brushing-away gesture with her left hand. "Nonsense. Unless you mean to imply that I'm your subordinate. We are equals in rank, Commander."

Suran seemed to ignore the point. "You can't fire that without setting off every security alarm on the ship." But he remained still, clearly not willing to test his assertion. After all, if she had tampered with the lift command protocols, how could he count on the security alarms?

Donatra allowed her left hand to fall to her side, where it moved toward a second pocket on her tunic.

The lift settled to a stop, and the doors whisked open, revealing Dr. Venora standing near the threshold. No one else was visible in the corridor beyond, which led directly to the infirmary entrance. That, Donatra knew, was a detail that Venora had arranged.

"So you're in on this, too, Doctor," Suran said, turning toward the *Valdore*'s chief medical officer. He moved into a defensive crouch, as though daring Venora to attack him.

Never, ever turn your back on me, Suran, Donatra thought, removing the hypo from her left tunic pocket. Striking with the speed of a *jhimn* adder, she emptied its contents into Suran's neck.

Suran turned toward her, eyes blazing, before sagging insensate toward the deck. Donatra caught his limp form on its way down, hoisting him up and draping one flaccid arm across her back. Venora picked up and pocketed Donatra's hypo and disruptor, then assisted Donatra and Suran out of the lift, down the empty corridor, and into the infirmary, where several officers, all injured during the *Valdore*'s passage through the Great Bloom, still lay recuperating. Moments later the unconscious Suran lay safely on one of the infirmary beds, Venora standing over him and verifying that his vital signs were strong and stable. Two nearby patients, a man and a woman—Donatra had noticed that both wore the insignia of enlisted uhlans—watched in silent surprise.

"Commander Suran's injuries were evidently worse than we had believed," Donatra said before crossing to a wall-mounted comm unit.

She jabbed the activation button with her thumb. "Bridge, this is Commander Donatra."

"Acknowledged, Commander," came Liravek's crisp response.

"Patch me into the fleet, Centurion. There's been a change of plans."

U.S.S. TITAN

"I've finally got one of Oghen's senior civil authorities on subspace channels, Captain," announced Lieutenant Rager, who sounded both relieved and tired.

Troi felt the same way. It had taken hours to reach anyone with any apparent decision-making authority in the Neyel Hegemony's power structure, such was the chaos that seemed already to be taking hold on the central Neyel world. From the disjointed gabble of communications *Titan* had already intercepted, the planet seemed to be in the grip of a steadily growing global natural disaster.

"On the screen, Lieutenant," Vale said from the seat at Will's right.

A hard-looking gray Neyel with dark, close-cropped hair filled most of the screen a moment later. Troi didn't realize it was a female Neyel until she began to speak. *"I am Defense Subdrech'tor Hiam, outworlder."*

Will rose, standing in front of his command chair as a sign of respect. "I am Captain William T. Riker of the Federation Starship *Titan*."

"I have received your earlier transmissions, Captain."

"Then you understand the seriousness of the danger you face."

The Neyel official neatly sidestepped the question. *"Explain your presence in our space. Are you responsible for what is happening on the Coreworld?"*

"No, we are not, Subdrech'tor," Will said, though his emotional aura gave the lie to his words. For a variety of reasons, Will evidently felt very much responsible for the rift and what it threatened to do to this reason of space. After all, the rift might never have opened in the first place but for the battle two months ago between Shinzon and the crew of the *Enterprise*.

Hiam's shuttered eyes widened in apparent recognition. *" 'Federation.' First one of your representatives comes among us bearing sweet words. Then you avenge her death by visiting destruction upon us."*

This woman is clearly not one of her people's pro-Burgess progressive thinkers, Troi thought sadly.

"You must evacuate your world's people, Subdrech'tor. We are here to help you."

"Help us? The Neyel people have always been more than capable of helping themselves."

However true this assertion might have been in the past, Troi knew that the subdrech'tor couldn't back it up now. The disasters being caused by the subspace distortions were evidently causing so much havoc that the Neyel military hadn't been able to send even a single ship to challenge *Titan* as she continued to make best speed for Oghen.

"Subdrech'tor, whatever anomalies are plaguing your world right now will only intensify over the coming days. My staff believes you will have to take steps to evacuate your homeworld. We offer you whatever assistance we can provide."

Hiam paused, apparently thinking the matter through. She was too far away, of course, for Troi to get a true empathic "read" on her. Nevertheless, it wasn't hard to conclude that Hiam was a canny tactician with a flexible outlook; whether her primary concern was saving as many lives as possible, or how heroic she might make herself appear after the crisis, was an open question.

In the end, it didn't really matter. *"All right, Captain Riker. Bring your ship to Oghen, for whatever good it will do. You can hardly make matters worse than they already are."* And with that, she signed off, her stern visage replaced by the star-speckled vista of the Small Magellanic Cloud.

Will sat back in his chair, his mind a study in stress and tension, as were his shoulders.

Vale had noticed this as well. "Captain, you look like you have the weight of the world on your shoulders right now," she said.

He offered up a wan smile. "That's because I do, Chris."

"We're still a few hours away from Oghen, Will," said Troi. "I recommend you use them to relax a little bit." *We need you sharp,* Imzadi. *Not tired and distracted.*

At first, he stared back at Troi as though she had just said something unutterably ridiculous. Then his expression softened as he acknowledged the wisdom of the suggestion.

Will rose from the center seat and nodded to Vale. "Take over for me up here, Commander. I'll be down in the mess if anyone needs me," he said, and then headed for the turbolift.

"So when was the last time you returned to Oghen?" Riker asked as his adversary studied the chessboard between them. As usual, Frane had selected the red pieces, though Riker wasn't certain if this signified anything meaningful.

The Neyel raised his dark eyes from the farrago of red and white chess pieces arrayed before him, and stared into the middle distance of the sparsely populated mess hall as he appeared to consider Riker's question with great care.

"Five or six oghencycles," Frane said at length. "Years, in your Federation parlance. It was the last time I saw my father. Before his ship picked me up near the Riftmouth, that is, when the Romulans came . . ." He trailed off.

Riker nodded, beginning to understand Frane's ambivalence about the world of his birth. "Your friends in the Seekers After Penance must have been keeping you pretty busy during that time."

He glanced briefly toward one of the room's far corners, where the four other individuals who had shared Frane's escape pod—including a young Neyel woman and a member of a local species whose multijointed body parts possessed the remarkable ability to separate and operate independently—were seated. Ever since coming aboard, the other members of Frane's Sleeper-worshipping sect had largely kept to themselves, evidently as suspicious of *Titan*'s crew as they had been of the authorities from the Neyel Hegemony. Their initial encounter with Dr. Ree, who had cursorily examined them some two days earlier in sickbay, clearly had done nothing to ease their anxiety.

They tended to venture into the mess only during off-peak times such as this; only a handful of Starfleet personnel were present, since the alpha-shift lunchtime rush wasn't due for another half hour or so.

At the moment, the quartet was taking a meal with varying degrees of evident nervousness, with the cattle-like pair of aboriginal Oghen appearing far more fearful than the rest of the group. Only the multipartite creature, evidently known as a Sturr, seemed more or less preoccupied with the meal before it, but that may have been either because he or she was utterly nonhumanoid, or because approximately half of the creature was seated and eating while the balance of its body parts had crawled over to the buffet table to obtain more food and drink. Although the Pandronians back in the Alpha Quadrant had evolved similar adaptations, Riker decided that the Sturr was easily the most fascinating sentient he had encountered in the past several years; he had to force himself not to stare, goggle-eyed.

The lone Neyel female, whom Frane had introduced earlier as Nozomi, sat vigil over a largely uneaten green salad, watching Riker and Frane with dark eyes that brimmed over with fear and suspicion. Riker couldn't really blame her for her apprehension; she and her fellows had been through a lot these past few days, and the Neyel military—to say nothing of the Romulans—had obviously given them all good reason to consider armed authority figures guilty until proven innocent.

"The sect devotes a great deal of its time and energy to study and meditation," Frane said in answer to Riker's observation, then deftly maneuvered his knight from a trap that Riker had assumed the younger man had overlooked. The move reminded Riker that it would be a mistake to underestimate Frane; despite his relative youth, the young

Neyel had clearly survived a great deal of adversity and knew how to think on his feet.

"Your sect also seems to have put a great deal of its time and energy into entreating your deity to wipe out your people," Riker said. "Not to mention a lot of innocent bystanders."

Once again worrying the bracelet on his wrist, Frane lapsed into what seemed to Riker an almost sullen silence. Riker felt a deep sense of disappointment, which only increased by the hour; during the nearly two days since *Titan* had set out for the beleaguered Neyel homeworld— her crew taking care all the while to avoid potentially lethal interactions between the starship's warp field and the Sleeper's increasingly frequent stirrings—Frane had once again become extraordinarily withdrawn. He continued to refuse Deanna's repeated requests that he sit for a counseling session, and he now seemed to endure even Riker's company only reluctantly.

And yet he finally started rooting for his homeworld's survival just the day before yesterday, Riker thought. *After years of literally praying for its destruction at the hands of a native Magellanic god.*

As among humans, old habits evidently died hard among the Neyel. Even, Riker realized now, among some of the younger ones.

Frane finally deigned to break the mess hall's deafening silence. "We sought only *atonement,* Captain. The atonement of the Neyel people for being slavers and heirs to slavers, and atonement for the indigenous races who allowed themselves to have been brought to such penury for so many generations."

"Seems like an overly harsh outlook to me," Riker said, using one of his rooks to seize one of Frane's bishops. "Does it leave any room for forgiveness?"

Frane shrugged. "Ask the Sleeper after He awakens," he said with audible irony, which he underscored by castling, thereby moving the red king to a place of relative safety.

Riker scanned the board again, hoping his next move would present itself in short order. He was disappointed. "Your Sleeper doesn't seem like the forgiving sort."

"The Neyel know the universe is not a forgiving place, Captain."

Riker considered the plight of the Neyel Coreworld of Oghen, and was forced to agree. He moved his rook to 6g, only two spaces from Frane's king, which had eluded him thus far.

Gotcha. "Nor is the chessboard, Mr. Frane. Check."

Frane wasted no time taking out Riker's rook with a bishop that seemed to have materialized from out of nowhere. "You're right, Captain. I'll have *you* in check in two more moves."

Riker's combadge chirped. *"Vale to Captain Riker,"* it said, relaying the rich, mid-register tones of *Titan's* executive officer.

Riker tapped the badge. "Go ahead, Christine."

"We're about five minutes from clearing the Oghen system's Oort cloud, sir."

"Any hails or challenges?"

"No, sir. The Neyel military evidently still have their hands full dealing with trouble on the homeworld. Long-range sensors are picking up multiple spatial disruptions and warp signatures in the inner system. As well as a number of antimatter detonations."

The Neyel ships are suffering warp core breaches, Riker thought, his belly quickening with horror. *My God, how much worse will this get?*

Two moves later, Riker was indeed in check. He

glanced back toward Nozomi, whose fearful stare silently accused him. He couldn't help but wonder how many of those doomed, vaporized ships had already been laden with Neyel and aboriginal Magellanic refugees, panicked men, women, and children seeking only to escape the devastation being brought their way by the progressive awakening of the Sleeper. . . .

"Sir?" Vale said. Riker turned away from Nozomi. He noticed that Frane, too, was staring at him.

Chess really isn't my game, Riker thought as he tipped over his king, resigning from the match. Then he stood. "I'm coming up to the bridge now. Riker out."

He excused himself, then walked past the Seekers After Penance and into the corridor. Moments later, the turbolift doors whisked open and admitted him. After he entered and turned back to face the corridor, he saw that he wasn't alone.

Frane had followed him, his bare, opposable-thumbed feet incongruously quiet against the deck.

Riker grinned at the impassive Neyel. "You're welcome to come along, Mr. Frane." As the door closed and the turbolift bore them both upward toward the bridge, Riker hoped that Frane's presence meant that he was once again pulling for his people rather than for an ancient, unforgiving deity.

Nearly twelve hundred kilometers above the surface of Oghen, *Titan* crossed the terminator into the harsh glare of the system's primary, a yellow-white F-type star.

"No response from Subdrech'tor Hiam," said Lieutenant Rager from the aft ops station. "Or anybody else in authority, for that matter."

"No wonder they haven't sent any ships to harass us,"

Riker said as the Neyel Coreworld displayed its many scars, most of which were apparently of very recent origin. The land masses on the planet's night side had been dominated by countless fires as panic spread and the cities emptied. Columns of smoke rose like soiled pillars in the spreading daylight, reminding Riker of photographs he had seen of Earth's Third World War.

Working at the aft tactical station, Tuvok pulled up enhanced images of the planet's surface, displaying them as insets in the viewscreen's corners, superimposing them over the view of the planet as seen from orbit. The Vulcan's efforts yielded a dispiriting pageant of burning cities, panicked, fleeing crowds that looked like swarms of soldier ants, massive vehicular traffic jams, funnel clouds, floods and other extreme weather phenomena, and hasty spacecraft launches—many of which ended quickly in horrific, explosive crashes.

But the strangest sights were the intermittent, multicolored flashes, the angry reds and bilious greens of energy discharges released by the relentless unraveling of ever larger volumes of local space. The effects would vanish as the surrounding space rushed in to fill the spatial voids, like a tear in a curtain being obscured temporarily by pleats wafted in a breeze. Some of these explosions appeared to originate in volumes of space ranging from the size of a human fist to a large house; they were all violent, some of them occurring in the atmosphere, and some in space hundreds of kilometers above Oghen. A new one would blossom at random every few seconds, and the frequency of the energy discharges was slowly but surely increasing. If the latest models created by Titan's science experts proved to be accurate—and Riker had no reason to doubt that they were—then those conflagrations would become a systemwide inferno that would burn itself out within two days' time, but not before replacing more than a cubic parsec of space with an expanding, apparently sentience-bearing protouniverse.

Once again, Riker wrestled with the knowledge that his actions—as well as Donatra's—might have greatly accelerated this growing catastrophe.

Titan rocked yet again beneath his boots. Grabbing the arms of his chair, Riker glanced to his left at Deanna, who seemed to be doing her best to appear composed. But he wasn't fooled in the least. He quietly reached toward her and took her hand, which she squeezed hard.

"Try to keep her steady, Ensign Lavena," said Vale, who was seated on Riker's other side. She was leaning forward in her chair, her wiry body fairly vibrating with tension.

"Sorry, Commander," Lavena said, scowling down at the conn panel before her. "But some of the waves of spatial distortion are taking us by surprise. The sensors are good, but they're not perfect."

"The world ends," intoned a voice directly behind Riker. He turned to face Frane, who stood behind the bridge's upper railing, his eyes fixed on the main viewscreen. Akaar and Shelley Hutchinson from security stood nearby, flanking him, though both were as intent as Frane was on the hellish vista unfolding down on Oghen. "Mechulak City. Founder's Landing. The Great Hall of Oghen. All gone."

Riker released Deanna's hand, rose from his chair, and approached the young Neyel. For his sake, and for the sake of everyone else on *Titan*'s bridge, he tried to impart confidence to his voice. "We're going to do everything we possibly can to save your people, Frane."

Frane responded with a wan smile that Riker could only regard as the equivalent of a polite pat on the head.

He's right not to believe me, Riker thought, growing more and more glum by the second. *Hell, I'm not sure I believe me. What the hell did I think I was going to accomplish here, anyway?*

Frane looked down, apparently studying his large, gray hands. Then Riker realized that the Neyel was actually looking at the bracelet on his right wrist.

"It belonged to my father," Frane said, raising his gray wrist so that Riker could clearly see the intricate weave of fabric, precious stones, beads, shells, and other less clearly identifiable objects. "And before that it belonged to his mother. Handed down through nine generations of Firstborn after leaving the hand of the revered Aidan Burgess herself."

Riker's eyes widened involuntarily. He gestured toward the bracelet, taking care not to touch it, since Frane had always seemed so disinclined even to show it; now the reason for the Neyel's caution was becoming apparent.

"This used to belong to Ambassador Burgess?"

Frane nodded. "Ever since Aidan Burgess first gave it to Gran Vil'ja, each generation has added something new to it. A story, represented by new stones, or by new weaves of titanium thread. I had expected to bring it home someday. But I never dreamed that it would outlive that home."

Glancing at Deanna, Riker saw that she was struggling not to weep as she regarded the increasingly despondent young Neyel. Frane seemed almost to deflate before his eyes, the hope the younger man had displayed earlier now fleeing in a great rush, like air escaping from a torn pressure suit.

Feeling fairly helpless himself, Riker resumed concentrating on the viewscreen and the carnage it revealed. The largest of Oghen's several ancient, cratered moons, visible only as a faint and distant crescent thanks to the relative position of the sun, was beginning to drop below the horizon. Another rocky satellite, evidently much smaller and closer, rose nearby in an eccentric, retrograde orbit, white sunlight gleaming off the limb of its irregularly cylindrical shape.

"The most we can hope to do here is to beam a few hundred people up from the surface more or less at random," Vale said. Riker saw only then that enormous tears stood in her eyes, though they seemed as motionless as boulders poised at a precipice. "Maybe we can save a couple of thousand, tops."

Riker nodded, then returned his gaze to Oghen's oddly shaped satellite as it continued to rise above the horizon. "If that's really all we can do, then that's what we'll do. It's better than nothing."

"We are assuming," Tuvok said, "that the spatial effects we are currently dodging will let us operate the transporters safely, and sufficiently often."

Lieutenant Eviku looked up from the main science console. "The transporters should be fine. At least for the next few hours. But after that . . ." He trailed off meaningfully.

"But *which* people do we rescue?" Deanna said, gazing forward. Her large, dark eyes appeared lost in the terror that was gripping the planet.

"I suppose it's going to be the way Christine described it," Riker said. "We grab as many Neyel as we can at random. Then we return to the spatial rift and try to get back home. Or at least somewhere clear of this Red King effect."

Riker fervently hoped that *someplace* would be clear of the phenomenon. What if it just continued to expand?

"But we're not just talking about the Neyel here, Will. According to *Excelsior*'s records, there ought to be at least small populations of native species on this planet as well. What about *them?*"

Riker rubbed his brow and scrunched his eyes shut. He could feel a truly brutal headache coming on. Opening his eyes, he turned toward Eviku. "Scan indiscriminately with regard to species. Coordinate with Lieutenant Radowski and begin transporting as soon as you and the security and medical teams are ready. Mr. Tuvok, Mr. Vale, please see to all the security arrangements, and alert Dr. Ree of incoming injured."

Tuvok and Vale chorused their acknowledgments while Eviku immediately got busy at his console.

"The refugees are going to be very distraught, Will. They'll need my help as well," Deanna said, her dark eyes wide, her tone urgent. It occurred to him that the fear radiating from the planet must have been close to crippling. She soldiered on anyway.

Riker nodded and Troi rose, striding toward the turbolift, which Vale and Tuvok had already reached.

The doors opened, and Jaza stepped out onto the bridge, followed by Ensign Norellis and Dr. Cethente. The Syrath astrophysicist's four baroquely jointed legs moved his tapered, tentacled, dome-headed body forward with surprising speed and grace.

"We may have finally found a workable solution to our Red King problem, Captain," Jaza said, sounding almost ebullient as he handed a padd over the railing down to Riker. "It will involve taking action in the immediate vicinity of the spatial rift. And it will have to be done soon."

Riker felt real delight at the genuine hope he perceived in the voice and manner of the science specialists. Nevertheless, he couldn't help but feel cautious just now about entire concept of hope. But as he glanced at the padd's table of contents hope began to seize him in spite of himself.

And he couldn't ignore the most immediate problem that faced *Titan* and her crew. "We're nearly two days away from the Red King's entry point at maximum warp, Mr. Jaza. Even if we were to head back there this minute—and that's assuming your plan will work—the people stuck on Oghen now wouldn't stand a chance of survival. Am I right?"

Jaza nodded, grim reality dialing down his earlier enthusiasm quite a bit. Norellis looked subdued as well.

"I agree," Cethente said, in a voice like rows of tiny crystalline bells. *"Our first priority remains rescuing as many people as possible from that planet below."*

Once again, Riker's eyes drifted to the viewscreen. The irregularly shaped, shadow-cloaked satellite continued to grow larger.

And more familiar.

Turning toward Frane, Riker pointed at the approaching chunk of rock and nickel-iron. "Do you recognize that object, Mr. Frane?"

Still staring at the apocalypse, the Neyel seemed to have drifted into an almost catatonic state. He roused himself a moment later, only after Riker had repeated his name.

"That is Holy Vangar, of course," Frane said in a near whisper. "The legacy of the Oh-Neyel People to all the Neyel who came after them."

Though the object in question remained mostly in darkness, Riker saw a look of recognition cross Akaar's features at that moment. Tuvok's eyebrows lofted higher than Riker had ever seen them go.

"Vanguard," both men said in perfect synchrony.

Of course, Riker thought. *They were both aboard* Excelsior *when Vanguard was found.*

He recalled from *Excelsior*'s reports that the lost O'Neill colony known as Vanguard—a self-contained terrestrial environment fashioned from a hollowed-out asteroid during the tumultuous first half of the twenty-first century—had been left parked in orbit about Oghen by the human ancestors of the Neyel. It was high enough so that its orbit had not yet been altered significantly by the long-term effects of upper atmospheric drag.

"Eviku. Tuvok. Scan that satellite. You'll find that it's hollow. I need to know if it's spaceworthy."

"It seems to be heavily shielded, Captain," Eviku said. "There's a lot of nickel-iron throughout the outer layers, as well as a fair percentage of other dense refractory metals, which make scanning difficult. But it appears to contain a significant internal atmosphere."

One of the millennia-old aphorisms of Sun Tzu, whose works Riker had read thoroughly during his second year at the Academy, returned to him unbidden: *"With whom lie the advantages derived from Heaven and Earth?"*

Tuvok crossed back to the tactical station, which was positioned only a few meters from the turbolift doors. "The Vanguard colony is approximately ten kilometers long," he said, his composure once again recovered and unassailable. "Its girth measures about three kilometers at its widest point."

"Life signs?" Riker asked.

"None discernible as yet, Captain. However, I am detecting rocky portions of the outer shell through which we can probably operate our transporters successfully." The Vulcan looked up from his scanner, meeting Riker's gaze. "The amount of space we can devote to refugees has just increased geometrically, Captain."

"Assuming that Dr. Ra-Havreii can give us enough power to keep the transporters and tractor beams going at full bore for a couple of days straight," Vale said, looking at Riker. "So the plan must be to fill that rock up with warm bodies, and then tow it as fast as possible toward the spatial rift."

Riker allowed a wry smile to turn his lips upward. Once again, there was no time for rehearsal; improvisation would have to suffice, and his crew knew their licks. "Looks to me like the best plan available under the circumstances."

Vale shrugged. "I have to admit I don't have any better ideas right now. I say let's try it."

"I must agree," Tuvok said, then resumed concentrating on his console.

Vale pointed toward the ancient husk of the still-approaching Vanguard colony. "I suppose it would be way, way too optimistic of me to hope that Vanguard can move under its own power."

"Vanguard had no functional motive propulsion of its own when we first encountered it eight decades ago," said Tuvok, stone-faced as he continued studying his sensor readouts. At the secondary science console beside him, Eviku was doing likewise. "Its drive units had evidently been cannibalized more than a century earlier," Tuvok continued, rising from his chair. "As yet I have found no reason to believe that the situation has changed."

"Of course. That figures. So we either tow it, or somebody's got to get out and push." Vale turned in Riker's direction. "I see another potential problem with this, Captain."

"Explain," Riker said.

"I've got to wonder: If converting that Neyel sacred relic into a rescue ark is really such a great idea, then why aren't the Neyel themselves trying to do it right now?"

Riker had to admit that his exec had raised an excellent

question. He had no definitive answer, of course—a quick glance at the ashen-faced Frane made it doubtful that one was forthcoming anytime soon—but he still had the capacity for, and the prerogative of, choosing optimism.

Gesturing toward the expanding assemblage of conflagrations raging across Oghen's land, sea, and sky, Riker said, "Look at the chaos down there. They're losing ships as fast as they can launch them, and they probably don't even know why yet. The crisis down there may have hit them so quickly that it just overwhelmed them."

They just got caught with their proverbial pants down, Riker thought. *Maybe in part because a Federation representative convinced them to stand down on their military readiness. Our fault, once again. Our responsibility.*

"Captain, I must point out that several other inhabited worlds also lay in the path of the spreading pattern of spatial disturbances," said Tuvok, who was walking back toward the turbolift to stand beside Vale. "With the Red King effect propagating superluminally through subspace, those systems will also be destroyed in a matter of weeks, if not days."

Deanna looked pale and mournful. "Then we can only help Oghen, because it's directly in harm's way now. We won't have time to do anything for the people on those outlying planets."

"Vanguard has only a finite amount of internal space," Tuvok pointed out. "Even if we had the time to mount other planetary evacuations."

"Perhaps we cannot aid other endangered worlds directly," Cethente said with a rhythmic jingling that reminded Riker of Christmas sleigh rides in Valdez. *"Unless we succeed in . . . lulling Mr. Frane's Sleeper back into a state of slumber."*

"How is that possible?" Vale asked. "We can't be talking about reading it a bedtime story."

Norellis grinned at Vale. "Actually, Commander, it's more like a sedative, for lack of a better term. We've got most of the theoretical work done already."

Riker decided he had nothing to lose by allowing himself to choose hope over reticence. If nothing else, it was a good way to keep despair at bay.

Raising Jaza's padd, he turned to face Vale and Tuvok. "Chris, Tuvok, get to the transporter room, or wherever else you need to be to coordinate a large-scale evacuation to *Titan* and Vanguard. And get Ra-Havreii and his people to work on making sure that big rock is habitable and ship-shape for towing. I'll bring you both up to speed later on how we're going to handle the Red King."

Riker glanced back at Frane, whose entire attention was still absorbed by the tragedy that continued to unfold on the viewscreen. He'd hoped that the horrors he was witnessing might galvanize the young Neyel to offer to assist in the rescue of his people. Instead, Frane merely seemed to have frozen in his tracks.

He's no good to anyone in that condition, Riker thought, imagining how much the presence of another Neyel might help calm the legions of the confused and panicked as they arrived. He briefly considered ordering Hutchinson to escort Frane down to sickbay, where Dr. Ree or Dr. Onnta could evaluate him for emotional trauma.

He decided that there would be time for that later. *That is, if there's any time left for* anything *later.*

Placing his focus squarely on Jaza, Riker gestured across the bridge toward his ready room doors. "Show me what your team has come up with, Mr. Jaza. And do it *fast.*"

• • •

"Can you really put this thing to sleep?" the captain said, seated behind the ready room's heavy Elaminite desk after having concluded a quick call down to Dr. Ra-Havreii in engineering.

Kent Norellis was surprised at how discombobulated the new Efrosian chief engineer had sounded when the captain had assigned him the task of prepping the ancient O'Neill colony for towing back to the Red King anomaly. Ordinarily, Norellis would have been relieved to learn that he wasn't the only one aboard whose nerves sometimes got the better of him. Under the current circumstances, however, he decided that he'd greatly prefer the company of unflappable, steel-nerved daredevils.

Now, as the impatient gazes of both the captain and Admiral Akaar buffeted him front and back, the astrobiologist felt as though he were caught in a crossfire between two such men.

"Putting it deeper into sleep is a pretty good metaphor for what we're proposing," Norellis said.

Responding to the confused expressions on the faces of both Riker and Akaar, Jaza stepped in, an apparent rescue maneuver that forced excessive heat and color into Norellis's cheeks.

"At least we believe there's a way to prevent the Sleeper from fully 'waking up,' " Jaza said.

Riker handed the padd up to Akaar to allow the admiral to review the science team's notes. "I think you may be straining the metaphor a bit here, Mr. Jaza. Unless I'm reading this wrong, your plan calls for artificially collapsing the spatial anomaly that brought us here in the first place."

Jaza nodded. "Well, it *is* the extradimensional conduit

through which our so-called Red King—which is nothing less than a rapidly expanding, sapienogenic protouniverse—is able to wreak destruction in *this* universe."

Riker made a sour face. "I wish you hadn't reminded me that some sort of intelligence seems to be guiding this thing."

"Why?" Norellis said. He almost physically kicked himself for blurting out the question, because the room went silent. Once again, every eye and sensory cluster in the room—Cethente stood motionless in the corner, where he resembled an antique Argelian lamp—was fixed on him.

"Because," Akaar said in a low, almost sepulchral rumble, "the issue of sentience raises certain unavoidable and perhaps irresolvable Prime Directive issues. As the ranking officer aboard *Titan,* I cannot simply ignore those issues."

"Nor can I," Riker said, looking frustrated, but also determined. "But that doesn't mean we shouldn't make every conceivable contingency plan." His icy blue eyes lit squarely on Jaza. "All right. Please explain for us lay people how you plan to go about this."

"It involves, in essence, 'jamming' the neuromagnetic signatures the anomaly is giving off," the Bajoran said. "Our computer simulations indicate that the simultaneous strategic detonation of about two dozen warp cores could essentially force the protouniverse—and the spatial rift that brought it here—back into de Sitter space, where it came from in the first place. The protouniverse would vanish, and the rift that let it into our universe would be sealed back up."

"Preferably the rift would seal up *behind* us," Norellis said. "*After* we retrace our steps through the anomaly's interspatial corridor back to Romulan space."

"Assuming that's possible," Riker said.

"Again, the simulations we've been running look good," Jaza said. "Of course, the only way to test them definitively is by actual experiment." He paused momentarily, allowing everyone to consider his words in silence. Then he continued, his tone as serious as the inscription on a granite tomb. "We have exactly one shot at this."

Riker sighed. "Of course. Okay, let's assume we get back home, with the spatial rift slamming shut right on our stern. Won't our Red King simply emerge again in some other universe?"

"Perhaps," Cethente said in a voice like a carillon. *"But it might lie dormant for billions of years first. It might even return here billions of years from now."*

Riker stroked his beard, a look of concern crumpling his brow. "So would we be arbitrarily killing off a universe full of sentience? Or just postponing the Sleeper's wake-up call for an eon or two?"

Or maybe we're just letting the Red King continue his dream for another billion or so years, Norellis thought. *So we don't all suddenly pop out of existence like soap bubbles. Or dreams.* He was glad that he seemed for once to be exhibiting the good sense not to babble his every errant thought out loud.

"We really can't say for certain that we'd actually be killing anything," Cethente said. *"We might simply be transplanting this nascent universe to some other universe. One that possesses no sapience to be wiped out by the, ah, Sleeper's full and final awakening."*

"Conversely, we can't prove that we're *not* slaughtering an entire universe full of sentience," Jaza said. "Of course, we all may well be doing that unwittingly every time we use the sonic shower. Or take an antibiotic."

"Don't get us started down that path, Mr. Jaza," Riker

said, allowing a small grin to escape. "We'll all end up as crazy as a Starfleet Academy exophilosophy instructor I once knew."

Still studying the padd, Akaar shook his head, then handed the device back to the captain. "My objection is less ethical than practical. The power requirements necessary for success are extraordinary."

Norellis couldn't argue with that. He could, however, imagine Ra-Havreii's head exploding like a supernova when he finally saw the equations on the padd.

"I'm afraid there's no getting around that, Admiral," said Jaza. "We would need the warp cores of several dozen Neyel vessels to generate sufficient power. But surely we can persuade the locals to help, given the seriousness of the current crisis."

Riker was shaking his head. "I've tried talking with the Neyel military officers we rescued. Several times. They still behave as though they're prisoners of war, even now. I'm afraid even Frane isn't very trusting, and he's the least paranoid of the bunch. I'm sorry, Mr. Jaza—I think you might have better luck trying to persuade Suran and Donatra to let us blow up *their* fleet inside the anomaly."

Akaar actually chuckled at that, a deep sound that made Norellis's spine feel as though someone had just dipped it into a beaker of liquid nitrogen.

"Actually, the subspace signatures of Romulan singularity drives might make them better suited for this purpose than Neyel warp cores," Cethente said without a trace of irony. *"In fact, we conceived the notion of using multiple vessels in tandem operation after reviewing how the Red King used Commander Donatra's fleet to destabilize that G-eight star three days ago."*

"Unfortunately, Romulan participation looks like a moot point right now," Riker replied, once again completely serious. "It looks like you and Dr. Ra-Havreii are going to have to find some other way to generate the power you'll need."

Norellis considered the spectacular explosions everyone had witnessed on the bridge viewscreen. He began to wonder if it might be possible to harness *that* energy somehow. *Too bad I'm not a dedicated physics guy,* he thought, turning the idea over and over in his mind.

"Are you really going to attempt this, Captain?" Akaar asked, interrupting Norellis's reverie.

Riker stood, though he still had to look up to meet the iron-haired admiral's stony gaze. "Until a better idea comes along, I want to have every contingency plan up and ready to execute. Do you have any objections, sir?"

Norellis wasn't sure, but he thought for a moment that he saw Akaar smiling, though very faintly. "None at all, Captain. Whenever possible, I like to extend Prime Directive protection to Starfleet captains by not interfering any more than absolutely necessary. Please keep me advised as to—"

The desk's comm unit spoke up then, issuing Lieutenant Rager's voice. *"Bridge to Captain Riker. We have incoming ships. Dozens of warp signatures. At least fifty vessels."*

Norellis felt another jolt of cold fear, though he was surprised that it had taken so long for the Neyel military to react to *Titan*'s presence over the catastrophe-besieged planet Oghen. Would the Neyel ships simply lash out, shooting first and asking questions later?

Riker touched his combadge. "Neyel vessels, Lieutenant?"

There was a pause, presumably while Rager checked her console readouts. Then: *"No, sir. They're Romulan."*

"I'll be damned," Riker said. "Hail Donatra and Suran,

Sariel, and pipe them in here." Shortly after Riker tapped the combadge channel closed, the computer atop his desk exchanged its neutral white-on-blue Federation seal for the anxious face of Commander Donatra.

"Do you require assistance, Captain Riker?"

Riker grinned broadly at the impassive Romulan. "Sometimes I think I've needed assistance every time we've ever seen one another, Commander. And yes, we can use all the help you can give us. How is your fleet at performing planetary evacuations and towing ten-kilometer-long hollow asteroids?"

"I believe we can manage," Donatra said, her lips curling upward slightly in a sly half-smile. *That looks downright creepy on someone who looks so much like a Vulcan,* Norellis thought.

A thoughtful expression crossed Riker's face. "I hope you don't mind my asking, Commander, but what changed your mind?"

Her smile didn't waver. *"Even Romulans may have a 'change of heart,' Captain. Please brief me in person after my fleet establishes orbit. Donatra out."*

Riker closed the channel, then grinned at Jaza and Akaar. "What do you suppose they'll say if I ask them to let me blow up their ships?"

Chapter Fifteen

In the eyes of Harn, the alien captain was nearly beside himself with both urgency and anger. *But he's maintaining control admirably,* the Neyel Hegemony Navy subaltern and helmrunner thought.

"Why should we cooperate with our jailers in any way?" Harn said to the leader of his captors, the man who identified himself as Captain William Riker.

It was the first time since the traitor Frane had had Harn and his subordinates brought aboard the alien ship that he had deigned to answer any of the alien captain's direct questions. Though Harn had consented to speak with his diplomatic representative—a surprisingly attractive, if soft, female—despite his men's whispers about her preternatural ability to see directly into the Neyel soul. . . .

Standing at the threshold of the surprisingly comfortable cell Harn had been issued, Captain Riker nodded to the pair of armed underlings who flanked him. They immediately withdrew and vanished from sight.

The one called Riker stepped into the room, alone, apparently unarmed, and showed no reticence whatsoever. Harn, who stood at least a full head taller than the alien and was considerably broader in the shoulders, was impressed by his captor's fearlessness.

"Because you are the ranking Neyel military officer on board," the alien commander said, suddenly looking both unhappy and unfriendly. "And we're not your 'jailers.' In fact, I'll be happy to set you and your troops down on Oghen right now—if you're really serious about wanting to face your planet's death unassisted."

Suspicious, Harn glared at Riker. "You say you want us to assist in your efforts to rescue my people," he said, pitching his voice low to make clear that he wasn't one to be trifled with. "Yet you have only a single, not-overly-large ship."

"That's not quite true. But we'd want to rescue as many of your people as our single, not-overly-large ship can accommodate, regardless," Riker said, scowling deeply. "And as many of the natives as possible."

"The alienborn *kaffirs*?"

Riker's restrained anger finally appeared to get the better of him. Moving so quickly that there was no time to react, the alien grasped Harn by the uniform lapels and spun him face-first into the nearest bulkhead. The impact nearly knocked the wind from him.

Harn regained his feet, his tail switching dangerously behind him as he turned to face Riker and prepared to grab him. At that moment he wanted nothing more than to tear him limb from limb.

But the alien captain stood his ground, either brave or foolish, his hands raised in some sort of martial-skills posture. Harn had no idea whether or not this Riker was a competent fighter; but it was beyond doubt that the alien captain was becoming enraged by Harn's responses to his overtures.

"I assume you're referring to the people whose ancestors lived on Oghen before the Neyel colonized it," Riker said.

Harn shrugged. "Call them what you will." Why did this creature care so much for those who were so clearly unimportant? It was no wonder that the late Drech'tor Gherran's wayward son had gravitated toward these soft-skinned weaklings.

"We're going to put as many people as we possibly can aboard Vanguard. The asteroid colony that orbits your Coreworld."

Harn's leathery brows rose involuntarily, and his tail tensed behind him. "Holy Vangar?" So this soft creature really did intend to bring far more to bear against this crisis than his lone vessel.

Riker nodded, though it was clear he was still angry. "Once Vanguard is filled with as many people as we can save, our rescue fleet will tow it someplace safe. We'll do our best to maintain order among the refugees inside the asteroid, Harn—with or without your arrogant presence. But we need the help of as many local people as possible if we're to succeed in saving anybody. Preferably people who've already been trained to deal with emergencies.

"We need you and your people, Mr. Harn."

Harn's desire to strike at the alien suddenly evaporated. He was speechless. He turned, crossed to the room's inadequately long bed and sat.

After gathering his thoughts, Harn looked up at Riker, who was obviously impatient to get his planned rescue under way. "You have a dedicated diplomatic officer on board," he said at length. "Why hasn't she approached the Coreworld's government with this request?"

Riker shook his head. "Your civil authorities have collapsed. Everyone is fleeing the catastrophe, even your military. Apparently it's every Neyel for himself."

Riker's blue eyes flashed concern, anger, desperation. "Your world needs you now. So you need to help *me* help *you!*"

The news chilled Harn to the marrow. He allowed his gaze to drop again to the deck for a measureless time. Then he looked straight into Riker's impatient, oddly hued eyes.

"What must I do?"

STARDATE 57037.2

Melora Pazlar felt apprehension twisting in the pit of her stomach as she and the others listened to Commander Tuvok. Fifty-three specialists had been hastily assembled in the launch bay, including among them every available security officer, most of the medical staff, those with piloting capabilities, several engineers, and various members of the exobiology department.

"What makes our shuttles any more resistant to the protouniverse's energy discharges than the Neyel vessels?" Lieutenant T'Lirin asked. Pazlar saw others nodding in agreement with the Vulcan security officer's entirely logical question.

"While the actual physical threat to our shuttles is as grave as that facing the Neyel craft, our technological capabilities are significantly more advanced than theirs," Tuvok said. "Our sensors will allow us to pinpoint in advance the likeliest sites of energetic interactions between the protouniverse and normal space. Even those few moments of forewarning should give us sufficient time to take appropriate evasive maneuvers and reinforce our shields as necessary."

Pazlar could only hope that Tuvok was right about that, though she already had her doubts as to how much protection any deflector shield system could provide. After all, space itself—including, very possibly, the space occupied by *Titan* and her eight shuttlecraft—was actually breaking down. She knew she was about to face a trial by fire.

Of course, today wouldn't be her first such experience. In addition to her skills as a stellar cartographer, Pazlar had maintained excellent pilot credentials over the years. She was used to evac missions, having flown in nine of them while stationed aboard the *Aegrippos* during the Dominion War. But in those days, her chief worries during her rescue assignments had been enemy ships and their firepower; here, today, she was going up against an entity more powerful than anything ever encountered by either side during the war.

Lieutenant Bowan Radowski moved forward in response to Tuvok's curt nod. "Coordination of the transporters from the shuttlecraft to the Vanguard habitat will be handled as much as possible from aboard *Titan,* aided by three of the Romulan ships that will be dedicated solely to this task," he said. "However, when you're in the thick of things down on Oghen, we will likely be unable to help you. The catastrophes that are occurring all over the planet will compound the problems for your rescue efforts. Because of the subspace interference being generated by the protouniverse, we're expecting to have a difficult time achieving transporter locks on targets entirely from orbit. That's where you shuttle teams come in, identifying en masse targets at close range and relaying the transporter locks to the orbiting rescue fleet ships. At the same time, you'll be using your shuttlecraft's own transporters to round up stray refugees; if the best you can do is to grab a few individuals at random, then that's what you'll have to do."

Pazlar felt yet another pang of anxiety, but didn't voice the question that gnawed at her. *How do we decide who to save and who to leave here to die?* She could see from the pained, somber expressions all around her that others were likely wrestling with the very same question.

It was a huge question, she realized, and answerable only in that it was patently unanswerable. She had to make a conscious decision not to listen to the small voice inside her that continued to ask it, and hoped everyone else could do likewise. *Otherwise, we'll be paralyzed with indecision. And if that happens, how can we rescue* anybody?

"Once your shuttles are full, break every speed record you can to return to the Vanguard habitat," Radowski said, his dark-skinned features looking strained and serious. "Since the transporters aboard your shuttlecraft may not be powerful enough to penetrate Vanguard's crust, we'll use *Titan*'s transporters and those of the Romulans to offload every survivor you have, so you can get back to the surface of Oghen as quickly as possible."

Ranul Keru stepped forward as Radowski finished. The security chief clearly wasn't operating at full bore—his skin still had an ashen tone, and Pazlar could see bulky bandages underneath his loose-fitting uniform tunic—but she had to admire his tenacious devotion to his duties.

"The main reason that we're having security aboard the shuttles—besides providing additional hands to carry out the rescue efforts—is that there will be no time to warn the Neyel or the other species down on Oghen of our efforts.

As far as many of them know, we could be invaders who are kidnapping them to enslave them, or we could even be the cause of the disasters they're facing."

Aren't we? Pazlar thought.

Keru continued: "Therefore a big part of your job will be to contain and calm the crowds as they're rescued, whether they trust you or not."

As Keru spoke, Pazlar saw Tuvok exchange a look with Mekrikuk, the Reman who had, until minutes ago, still been confined to sickbay. For some reason that she found unfathomable—and which hadn't yet been explained to anybody present—Tuvok had brought the Reman with him to the briefing.

Her gaze moved again, this time to Admiral Akaar, who stood to one side, apparently listening intently. Pazlar wasn't at all certain why he was present, since he hadn't opted to take direct control of any of the ground rescue missions. Perhaps he was the kind of man who could never be content to wait idly for the reports of subordinates, even when there was little he could actually contribute to the mission at hand.

The tall, gray-haired Capellan had been a paradox during the brief time she had known him so far; while she hadn't appreciated his commandeering of the stellar cartography labs in *Titan*'s pre-launch phase and the early days of their first mission, he had been nothing but charming and deferential to her and most of the officers with whom she had seen him interacting. The only friction she had witnessed at all seemed to be directed at Captain Riker and Commander Troi, and even that seemed to have lessened greatly over the last week or so. Pazlar assumed that Akaar was present now in order to ascertain that Starfleet protocols were being followed to the letter, since the admiral wouldn't be participating directly in the evac mission.

Keru finished speaking, and Tuvok began handing out specific shuttle assignments. All eight of the type-11 shuttles were being deployed. Pazlar was given the shuttlecraft *Gillespie* to pilot, along with a crew compliment of six: Lieutenant Pava Ek'Noor sh'Aqabaa, an elite member of the security force and an Andorian; Lieutenant Eviku, the Arkenite exobiologist; Ensign Vanda Kaplanczyk, a human conn officer who would act as Pazlar's second; Dr. Ree, *Titan*'s Pahkwa-thanh chief medical officer; and Cadet Torvig Bu-kar-nguv, a Choblik engineering trainee.

As her team assembled around her, Pazlar wondered how many of the doomed Neyel and other races they would actually be able to save.

STARDATE 57037.3

"When are you going to tell her, Will?"

Standing beside his command chair, Riker regarded Deanna with a slight scowl. He wasn't certain how best to break the news to Donatra that their plan to halt the advance of the protouniverse might involve the destruction of a good number of her fleet's ships.

"I'm not sure," he said. "When I think the time is right. For now, our immediate concern is making certain that the rescue operation goes well."

He knew he wouldn't be able to rely on his wife to help him identify that "right moment." She was going to be on the Vanguard habitat, along with Christine Vale, a dozen engineers and other crew, and the Neyel soldiers he had deputized as officers of the peace. The hope was that they would be able to get the habitat out of mothballs and spaceworthy enough to be towed back to the spatial rift without killing the hordes of refugees that were about to be crammed aboard her. Fortunately, Jaza had determined that Vanguard still contained an acceptably breathable, if stale, atmosphere.

So all we have to do is get her ready to move out of here, and all inside of a day or so, Riker thought, glancing at the image of the ancient, pockmarked asteroid colony that was displayed on the main viewscreen. *Before the interspatial energy flare-ups become too numerous and widespread to let us even try it.*

He briefly considered having Christine engrave the motto, *"How hard can it be?"* on *Titan's* dedication plaque, as a monument to his foolish optimism. *Or maybe I ought to have somebody etch it onto my tombstone,* he told himself. *Assuming any of us ever sees home again.*

Please try to think happier thoughts, Will, Deanna said without speaking aloud.

How can I, Deanna? came his wordless reply. *This is the biggest challenge I've ever faced. Suppose I'm not up to it? What if I'm not strong enough?*

He turned back toward where she sat, and she stared into his soul with eyes that radiated pure confidence and love. Then she stood, grabbing the padd that contained the Vanguard colony's internal schematics. *You have no idea just how strong you really are,* Imzadi, she told him, her thoughts as smooth as Tholian silk as they traveled along the mental-emotional link they shared. *This is going to work. We will save hundreds of thousands of lives. Maybe millions.*

Yes, he thought back to her. *But how many millions more will we be forced to leave behind?*

She leaned up and kissed him, taking him somewhat by

surprise. They had agreed that they would try not to show overt signs of affection on the bridge. Still, the kiss was far from unwelcome, and a quick glance around the room showed that everyone else was intent on their various tasks of the moment.

I'll see you soon, Imzadi, Deanna sent to him. He liked that she never told him good-bye anymore; it was yet another sign of her faith in him.

As he turned to watch her go, he saw Admiral Akaar in the back of the bridge near the turbolift, from which he had evidently just emerged. His expression told Riker that he *had* seen the kiss, but revealed nothing about whether he considered it appropriate or not. Riker suspected that the answer was "not."

But at the moment, he didn't particularly care.

SHUTTLECRAFT *BEIDERBECKE*, STARDATE 57037.7

Lieutenant Commander desYog banked the shuttlecraft *Beiderbecke* through great, columnar roils of smoke and the increasingly frequent bright energy discharges. Pitching the craft sharply upward, desYog narrowly avoided a spectacular airborne conflagration, then angled back downward toward one of the more populated areas of the coastal city.

"Scans show a relative safe landing area to the north side, four point two kilometers away," Lieutenant Commander Fo Hachesa said, mangling his gerunds and suffixes, as always.

"Got it," desYog said, his talons clicking on the interface controls of the shuttlecraft. "We'll be there in two minutes," he said loudly.

Behind him, he heard Lieutenant Gian Sortollo prep-

ping the other members of the team. Des Yog tried to tune
him out as he used the ship's sensors to navigate through
the ash-filled afternoon skies. It was hard enough keeping
the ship on track without worrying about how the others
were going to accomplish their mission.

They neared an open area, which was very near the
waterfront. Huge waves of purple-gray seawater crashed
against the docks, splintering them. Several Neyel space
vessels were docked on top of buildings, while sailing vessels bucked and listed in the suddenly turbulent waters of
the harbor. Through the forward window, des Yog could
see hundreds of beings scurrying to get to the spaceships,
even though none of them had begun to take off as yet.

"Scans show those ships are dead in the water, so to
speaking," Hachesa said, looking at the screens on the side
of the cabin. "Whoever's on them isn't get off the planet."

"Can we tow them?" Sortollo asked, peering over
Hachesa's shoulder.

"We can't spare the power," des Yog said glumly.

"Then we stick with our plan and get as many of them
out as possible."

As des Yog brought the shuttle in for a landing, the
Neyel and others among them on the surface spread out
just enough to allow the craft ingress.

"I don't think we'll having any trouble get them to
board, Lieutenant," Hachesa said.

Sortollo and the others prepared to open the hatch. The
terrified babble of the crowd was audible even through the
shuttle's duranium hull.

The moment the hatch began to open, hands and other
appendages began to claw at it. Even before it was a third
of the way open, a Neyel had scrambled aboard, his eyes
wide and his tail switching like a serpent about to strike.

Should have just used the transporter, des Yog thought.

Even if we do need to save all the power we can for the hazard-avoidance system. On the other hand, he knew he didn't want to end up tearing the shuttle to pieces just because he'd shortchanged the *Beiderbecke*'s ability to swerve clear of interspatial disturbances.

As others quickly followed the Neyel onboard, the Starfleet personnel tried to maintain some semblance of order. DesYog tried to ignore the terrified faces that were pressed against the forward window; he saw Neyel children struggling to stay upright among the larger adults, as well as representatives from at least four other races.

"Oh, *shit*," Hachesa said next to him, staring at a screen. The word meant "bride" in desYog's native Skorrian, but he knew that Fo had picked it up from humans, for whom the term had a far less pleasant definition.

Hachesa turned toward him, his olive-colored nose turning a vivid purple. "There's a tidal wave about to hitting."

Over the din of the crowd, Hachesa tried to get Sortollo's attention to warn him, even as desYog readied the shuttle to take off. Readings showed the swiftly gathering wall of ocean water to be two kilometers away, but closing fast. *Too fast.*

We have to leave now, he thought, but a quick glance aft told him that the ship was still not full to capacity. Still, they couldn't wait any longer.

DesYog punched the red alert button, and a warning klaxon went off, adding to the already cacophonous din inside the shuttle. "Lieutenant, we have to get up *now*," he yelled back toward Sortollo, though he couldn't even see the sallow-skinned Martian in the crowd.

The wave was getting close. DesYog sent a prayer to his goddess, teneYa-choFe; he was thankful, at least, that none of the Starfleet personnel had been pulled outside.

Then he tapped the control for the shuttle's hatch, pulling it closed.

Behind him, he heard screaming, but he couldn't tell if it was from those in the shuttle, someone caught in the hatch, or those outside.

As he pushed the shuttle upward, a tremendous clamor filled the air. He saw several Neyel and others clawing at the front of the shuttle as it rose, their fingers and tails catching at any crevice they could find, terror etched deeply onto their hard gray faces.

And then the wall of water struck the shuttle with immense force, and desYog felt himself—and the craft—tumbling over and over again, the lowering sun blocked out by brackish purple-gray seawater, all other sound crushed beneath a deafening roar.

Clutching the crash-straps that bound him tightly to his seat, desYog prayed to teneYa-choFe again, that the shields would hold, and that they would be able to save the scant handful of Oghen's populace they had brought aboard.

Not to mention themselves.

Chapter Sixteen

VANGUARD

K'chak'!'op felt completely at home within the Vanguard habitat. This discovery greatly surprised her. She had been among the first set of *Titan* crew members to be dispatched to the artificial world, alongside Deanna Troi, Christine Vale, Engineer Crandall, Counselor Huilan, Dr. Cethente, and about a dozen others.

Frane, *Titan*'s most prominent Neyel guest, had hand-picked a number of the Neyel military personnel who had accompanied them as well, and now everyone was busy trying to revive the sleeping world. The previously unco-operative Neyel commandos had apparently been much easier to convince to help once they had been shown the destruction taking place on Oghen, and the specific plans that *Titan* and the Romulans had formulated to save as many of its inhabitants as possible by transporting them to the Vanguard habitat.

K'chak'!'op worked steadily at the ancient computers, utilizing her foremost pair of legs, and all twelve of the tentacles that protruded from her head segment. The system was so archaic as to be laughable; it would be up to her and the team of engineers to retrofit the habitat's internal structure as quickly as possible to make certain it was up to the stresses of towing, warp travel, and passage through the spatial rift through which *Titan* had initially arrived here.

According to the chatter on the comm system, another huge wave of Neyel refugees had just been beamed in from *Titan* and Donatra's fleet, meaning that probably not many more mass transports would be necessary before the habitat teemed with a million or more sentients. The shuttle teams conducting their targeted rescues, and the transport engineers across the rescue flotilla, appeared to be doing their jobs very well indeed.

K'chak'!'op's attention was drawn to a cheer she heard coming over the comm system. This wasn't coming from inside the asteroid habitat, but rather from another source: it appeared that the shuttlecraft *Holliday,* the shuttlecraft *Marcellis,* and three Romulan craft had just arrived from the surface, carrying between them scores of Neyel and other natives who hadn't been reached by the last round of mass beam-ups. The exact information was too garbled for her translator/voder to accurately parse, but she gleaned enough good news from the transmission to buoy her spirits considerably.

She felt a tug against her mid-leg, and turned her head around to view whomever had interrupted her. She was surprised to see the multipartite member of the Seekers of Penance—Lofi, if she recalled the sentient's name correctly—and the almost bovine-looking companion of the independently-segmented creature.

"We wish to aid you," Lofi said. "However we can. I have some experience with Neyel computers, and Fasaryl was a *cro'loog'fin'shal* for his people before his *apprin-dining.*"

K'chak'!'op wasn't quite sure what Lofi had just said, but she assumed she should be grateful for the offer. "Whatever help you can offer will be received gladly," she said, her undulating tentacles signing her words, which her translator/voder dutifully rendered into what she hoped was passable Neyel.

And though the space around her had become slightly more cramped with the arrival of the two Seekers, K'chak'!'op felt comforted to be working alongside two others whose hearts and minds were sure to be as focused as hers was on the task at hand.

SHUTTLECRAFT *BEIDERBECKE*

To his credit, Hachesa had managed to activate the naviga-tional deflector and raise the shields just prior to the shuttle's inundation and submersion. The cockpit bulk-head had automatically sealed as well, protecting the forward cabin both from the elements and the frantic refu-gees.

Fortunately, the *Beiderbecke*'s shields had held, keep-ing the deluge outside at bay; the fact that everyone on the shuttle other than the pilots was also being kept out of the cockpit was a side benefit that gave desYog and Hachesa a few valuable moments to collect themselves.

DesYog scanned the instrument panels, ignoring the murk-filled forward windows in favor of the images on the monitor screens set into the panel below them. What the screens showed was hazy at best, however; all desYog could tell was that multiple indistinct objects were tum-bling through the brine toward the shuttlecraft.

"We're definite upside-down," Hachesa said, running his hands over the companels again. "That way is up," he added, pointing toward the deck.

The artificial gravity, which had kicked on automatically when the shuttle had rolled onto its back, was so comforting it almost disoriented him. But desYog knew that the feeling was illusory. He entered some commands into the computer, and felt the ship begin to move around him.

Suddenly, something large and dark smashed into the forward window. It appeared to be a piece of a building, but it was difficult to tell given the dim illumination in the water. Sparks shot out of one of the upper panels, alighting on desYog's wings, which were folded neatly behind him.

I can't worry about a few singed feathers, he thought, glad that his outer flocking lacked neural sensation. A quick glance at the console displays confirmed what the sparks had announced: The shields were failing.

"Shields are down to thirty-seven percent," Hachesa said. "We've got to get out of here. I think we can survive long enough to reach the habitat, but we can't take this water pressure much longer."

The companel crackled to life. *"DesYog, Hachesa, are you there?"* Sortollo's voice was nervous, rattled.

"We're fine, Lieutenant," desYog said. "We're attempting to get the *Beiderbecke* out of here now."

He pushed the controls and felt the craft shudder slightly as it rose through the crushing weight of water. Something dark came at them from ahead, and he pushed the shuttle even harder. They skimmed over the dark thing, narrowly avoiding it.

A bovine body slammed into the forward window with a sickening thud, then vanished into the receding murk.

DesYog tried not to think about all the dead and dying they were leaving behind. All the ones they had failed to rescue.

"Ten meters to the surface," Hachesa said. "Looks like we'll soon be in the clearly."

DesYog decided to allow his relief over the team's survival to distract him from the Kobliad's irritating abuse of Federation Standard.

The *Beiderbecke* broke the surface and pushed upward, into the dusky, smoke-clogged skies of a dying planet.

U.S.S. TITAN, STARDATE 57037.8

Akaar watched the monitors in the aft section of *Titan*'s bridge as the shuttlecraft *Handy* hovered near the Vanguard habitat, matching velocities with it. Tuvok's ship had returned from its third trip with another dozen survivors, after having assisted *Titan* and the Romulan fleet in locking onto and beaming up thousands more.

The Vulcan also related some surprising news.

"A refugee group we contacted has refused to listen to logic, Captain," Tuvok said from the main viewscreen at the front of the bridge. *"Apparently, their religion forbids them to use any sort of high technology. We were forced to go to another relatively undamaged settlement to rescue others instead."*

"Then there's nothing more we can do to help them," Captain Riker said, his voice grave. "Continue toward the next target. Your team has still been more successful than most, even with this setback."

Tuvok nodded, gesturing toward something behind him. *"I consider that due in part to the effect that*

*Mekrikuk appears to have on some of the more emotion-
ally volatile refugees, sir. He exerts an immensely calming
influence."*

Akaar gritted his teeth and finally stepped forward.
"Commander, what are the coordinates of the religious
compound?"

On the screen, Tuvok raised an eyebrow, his gaze moving to the side as he took in the Capellan admiral. *"Sending coordinates now, Admiral. However, atmospheric
ionization over that region of the planet makes transporter
use inadvisable. Would you like us to make another attempt to persuade them? I would have thought you would
be in agreement with Captain Riker."*

Akaar sensed in Tuvok's words something that was almost an accusation. Resentments now more than three decades old stirred again within him, but he tamped them
back down. "No. Find another target. If they are determined to die for their cause, we must respect their
wishes."

He turned his back quickly, as his lips began to tremble.
The rescue missions were becoming increasingly perilous
as the protouniverse's energy discharges became more
frequent; one Romulan ship, the *S'harien,* had been destroyed, hulled directly through the engine core by a pair
of simultaneous interspatial energy blasts that had appeared too quickly to be avoided. Another one of Donatra's
vessels was too damaged to continue, and would have to be
taken in tow. *Titan's* shuttlecraft had taken a beating as
well; the *Beiderbecke* had apparently just barely avoided
being crushed flat by a tsunami, and had just returned to the
main shuttlebay for a quick inspection.

Akaar crossed to an unoccupied bridge console and examined the data Tuvok had transmitted. The coordinates

for the religious compound were located in a remote desert area, a place that had so far remained mostly untouched by the ubiquitous calamities happening elsewhere on the planet. Apparently it had been relatively easy for these reclusive people to detach themselves from the dire necessity of taking action. Their decision to refuse assistance seemed ill-considered and selfish.

Was their decision the same one he had made back on Planetoid 437 all those years ago? The decision that Tuvok had thwarted, thereby effectively ending a friendship that had begun more than half a century earlier, aboard *Excelsior.*

His own rising anger answered the question for him. *How* dare *they refuse to help save themselves? Their race?* His blood burned. *We may be sacrificing everything by trying to save them, and yet they refuse to help themselves.*

He closed his eyes, made a decision, then opened them again and stalked toward the turbolift.

Once inside, he barked an order into his combadge. "Computer, locate Chief Axel Bolaji." He hated taking the new father on a mission that would place him directly in harm's way. But until *Titan* returned home, *everyone* was in danger.

And right now, he really needed a good pilot.

VANGUARD

Frane slumped exhausted against the wall of a public gallery. The gentle upward curvature of the floor, which conformed to the overall cylindrical shape of the asteroid in which Holy Vangar had been built, wasn't at all apparent at the moment. This might have been because of the growing, surprisingly orderly crowds of refugees. Or it could have been a result of his own fatigue. At the moment, he neither knew nor cared.

What he *did* know was that it had been around six hours since he had taken any nourishment, and his energy level was declining quickly. And yet he wondered how he could stop to replenish himself when so much depended on him.

Hundreds of thousands of Neyel and native Oghen refugees had now been ferried up to Holy Vangar, and he had worked tirelessly, right alongside Harn and his men, in greeting and feeding the newcomers, organizing and prioritizing their many needs, and even enlisting the help of those who weren't too badly shocked or injured to assist in those same efforts. Frane hadn't taken much time as yet to consider the irony of the situation, though he was certainly aware of it; he was now actively working against the cause he had supported for so much of his young life, the cause of the Sleeper and the self-flagellating Seekers After Penance.

After all, how could a just god allow the wholesale destruction that was happening now? He hadn't considered the ramifications of the punishment he had formerly wished upon his own people.

Until now. *I was naïve,* he told himself. The Sleeper was unworthy of both his worship and his respect if it could make no exceptions for those who were *anrorli,* innocent of the sin of slavery.

Even as his faith in his dread god crashed and burned around him, Frane knew that his faith in others was being restored. The humans from *Titan* and the countless Other Races of Men who also crewed that vessel were giving everything they had, risking their lives to save the Neyel and the natives alike. Even the Romulans, who had seemed so devious and treacherous when he had first encountered them, were not only assisting, but were providing most of the power required to make the evacuation of the Coreworld a success.

He felt his legs collapse beneath him, and spots began to appear across his vision.

A human appeared, a slender woman with dark hair and dusky features. He recognized her from the medical chambers aboard *Titan*. But whatever it was that she was saying was lost in the buzzing that had suddenly filled his ears.

She pointed one of her devices at him, her eyes alternately looking at him and the readout on the device. Then she removed another object from the bag that was slung over one of her shoulders. She pressed it up against his neck, and he felt a tiny sting.

Almost immediately, his vision began to clear and his hearing began to return to normal. He looked up at the woman, and into her large brown eyes.

"Feeling better?" she asked.

Frane nodded. "What happened?"

"Looks like your blood sugar crashed, and all this excitement didn't help," the woman said. "I gave you some glucose and tri-ox. That should keep you going for a while, but I'd suggest you get some food into you soon."

She reached down to pull him up. "I'm Nurse Ogawa, by the way."

Frane allowed her to help pull him back to a standing position, using his tail as leverage to help steady himself. "Yes, I remember seeing you in *Titan*'s sickbay. Thank you for your help."

She made an expansive gesture around them both. "We can't have one of the heroes of the Neyel miss the rescue of his people now, can we?"

Hero? The word was an explosion in Frane's mind, one he had never expected to hear in conjunction with himself or his actions.

He shook his head, unsure whether he was agreeing with her or trying to dislodge the very idea from his thoughts.

SHUTTLECRAFT *GILLESPIE*

Using the bionic hand at the end of his prehensile tail, Cadet Torvig Bu-kar-nguv reached out and tugged on the sleeve of Lieutenant Eviku, trying to capture the Arkenite scientist's attention quietly.

"Sir, have you noticed how many more Neyel we're rescuing than any of the other species?" Torvig asked.

Eviku pursed his lips, and looked around the shuttle. The aft section, visible through an open hatchway through which other Starfleet personnel were moving, was crammed full of refugees.

Torvig followed his gaze, mentally counting the many disparate species aboard. This was their fourth trip, and had proved to be the most dangerous one so far. The inter-spatial energy discharges and related natural disasters occurring on Oghen were making their rescue flights more and more dangerous by the second. It was a good thing that Pazlar's piloting skills were so strong, otherwise the shuttlecraft *Gillespie* might have gone down just like that Romulan warbird had.

"I'm not sure I see your point," Eviku said after a pause. "We seem to have a goodly number of the various local sentient races aboard."

"There are significantly *more* Neyel here than any other group," Torvig noted. "And they are human offshoots."

Eviku looked at him as if he had just grown a new eye. "What are you implying? That we're showing favoritism to the Neyel because they're genetically human?"

"I'm merely making an observation," Torvig said.

Eviku turned away momentarily, and Torvig's bionic eyes registered a look of disgust on his austere features when he turned back. The Arkenite opened his mouth as if to speak, then closed it again, apparently pondering the question further.

Finally, he said, "Let's say for the moment that the Neyel *are* getting preferential treatment. Could that be because they are more numerous than any of the other species?"

Torvig nodded, ready to concede that obvious fact. "But we could certainly try a little harder to find and rescue more of the indigenous peoples."

"I don't think we're ignoring anyone," Eviku said. "Have *you* ignored anyone? Has *any* member of this crew actively pushed aside an Oghen native in favor of a Neyel?"

Shaking his head, Torvig said, "No. Not that I've seen."

Eviku went quiet for a moment, apparently pondering again. Then, lowering his voice, he said, "I understand your misgivings, Cadet. I know that *Titan* has been lauded by many for its crew diversity. On the other hand, I also know that nobody can fail to notice that most of the chief decision makers for the ship are either humans or humanoids that I can't distinguish *from* humans without a tricorder. And that may indeed influence the way certain decisions aboard *Titan* get made. But I don't believe anyone involved in this rescue effort is practicing racial bias. It seems to me we're all working as hard as we can to save as many of these beings as possible, regardless of where their genes originated."

Torvig nodded, and surveyed the crowd once more,

facing forward again after the hatch had closed the aft section off from the cockpit once again. Upon further dissection of his perceptions, he was forced to agree with Eviku's conclusion. Still, he felt unsettled.

After all, the Neyel outnumbered the natives because they had enslaved, displaced, and slaughtered them centuries ago. Not because there had been more Neyel originally.

On Oghen and Vanguard, just as aboard *Titan*, the minority was ruling over the majority.

"You may be right, of course," he said to Eviku. "I was merely pursuing an interesting avenue of speculation."

Torvig wondered quietly how those speculations would play out in reality.

U.S.S. LA ROCCA, STARDATE 57037.9

Chief Axel Bolaji pushed the controls forward, sending the captain's skiff *La Rocca* deep into Oghen's distressed, highly ionized atmosphere. Mauve oceans and green-brown continents rose to meet the small craft. Towering columns of fire and smoke colored the dawn sky an angry orange, and quickly grew near enough to force the chief to weave the skiff carefully between them.

Akaar sat beside the chief and brooded on his own recent actions. He had informed Captain Riker only that he was personally joining the rescue efforts and that he was commandeering the skiff, the only *Titan* auxiliary vessel that hadn't been committed to the evacuation effort. Until now, the small craft had been held in reserve for use as an emergency lifeboat.

But the current mission met Akaar's definition of "emergency."

Accompanying Akaar aboard the *La Rocca* were Lieutenant Feren Denken, the now one-armed Matalinian who had received his injuries during the raid on Romulus's Vikr'l Prison, and Paolo and Koasa Rossini, the pair of Polynesian engineers. They were big and strong, which might help if they encountered any resistance.

From the report that Tuvok had made, the people of the town of Lfei-sor-Paric were intent on their own deaths—prepared to sacrifice themselves for their beliefs. And though it went counter to the spirit if not the letter of the Prime Directive, Akaar was determined to prevent them from making that entirely unnecessary sacrifice. The others on the skiff would help him. He didn't know, nor care whether they were doing it under duress because of his rank, or because they agreed with his line of reasoning.

Denken and the Rossinis had outfitted themselves in the black stealth isolation suits that the security teams had worn during the prison raid on Romulus, and Akaar began to don one as well, though the largest suit available was almost intolerably snug on him. They didn't need the stealth functions of the suits per se, but the standard environmental suits were all being used at the moment by the engineering crews working on the external retrofitting of the Vanguard habitat. And Akaar's group needed some kind of protection in order to execute the admiral's plan.

"Coming up on the enclave, Admiral," Bolaji said. "Two kilometers ahead."

Akaar watched the rapidly approaching desert plain, which was now being distorted by flashes of interspatial energy as well as intense heat. Watching the energetic flashes, the admiral thought, *Death is indeed coming for you. But so are we.*

"Scanning is difficult with all the atmospheric ionization," one of the Rossini twins said, looking up from a port-side console.

The other Rossini spoke up. "I'm guessing that most of the populace is inside the domed octagonal structure we've just picked up. I read at least fourteen life signs there, of various mixed species."

Akaar pointed toward Denken, who was standing ready at the transporter controls. "As soon as you have the coordinates, Mr. Denken, beam them in."

A few moments later, Akaar turned toward the aft section and watched the multiple dispersal canisters of anesthezine gas as they shimmered away from the transporter platforms. At such close range, beaming objects down wasn't difficult, atmospheric ionization notwithstanding. And soon, if all went according to plan, *Titan* would be able to lock onto and beam up every living thing in the desert compound.

"Hold position above the enclave," Akaar told Bolaji. "I will signal you when we have the pattern enhancers in place."

"Yes, sir," Bolaji said.

As Akaar and the others beamed into the spacious, cathedral-like enclave, they were astonished at the number of bodies they saw arrayed around them. There were a lot more than fourteen people here. Many were slumped over in chairs, while others lay prone on the floor or in the corridors. An attenuated residue of the anesthezine still lingered in the air.

Denken scanned several of the bodies, then looked over at Akaar. "Most of those in the chairs are dead, sir."

Akaar felt his hearts drop. Had these people been allergic to the anesthezine? Had he just killed an entire enclave of religious people by trying to save them?

One of the Rossinis spoke up, from an area that surrounded what may have been an altar of some sort, where a large number of people were slumped over haphazardly in several rows of pews.

"Sir, most of *these* people are still alive. It looks to me like the, ah, sacrament they came here to partake of has been *poisoned.*"

Akaar looked around him, more horrified now than he had been before. He saw children lying among the bodies, some Neyel, and others representing the many races that once had been enslaved by the Neyel. He didn't want to check to see whether they were all living or dead, but he knew it had to be done.

"Break out the pattern enhancers," he said. "Begin scanning and tagging anyone who remains alive, priority to the children. Direct *Titan* to begin beaming them aboard immediately, medical emergency."

As Denken and the Rossinis got busy, a small part of Akaar's mind seethed at the actions of the older believers. In spite of himself, he felt a pinprick of dark satisfaction at the knowledge that at least some of the adults here were not going to be rescued after all.

He heard the floor shift and creak in one of the church's upper galleries, and whirled to see someone moving swiftly away, blending into the shadows. He vaulted over several bodies, yelling into his combadge as he moved. "Someone else is here, Mr. Bolaji. I am pursuing."

He followed the running figure up a set of dark green, intricately carved wooden stairs, but he scarcely noticed the craftsmanship. He paused and set his phaser on heavy stun, unsure whether he was chasing down an adult Neyel or someone younger. Indeed, he didn't know whether his quarry would turn out to be friend or foe.

A step broke beneath his weight, causing his ankle to twist sharply. He ignored the pain. Moving forward, he soon reached the upper level, where he stopped again, pulled out his tricorder, and began scanning. He found a biosign ahead, apparently in the third antechamber that lay straight down the hallway.

Akaar crouched outside the doorway to the antechamber, his weapon at the ready, then scurried inside. A Neyel dressed in bright blue robes was crouched on the floor, its hands holding a book, its eyes closed.

He's some sort of cleric, Akaar thought. *He allowed this mass suicide. Probably* encouraged *it.* Rage swelled within him.

"Get up!" he shouted at the Neyel.

The creature stood and turned, its hands clasping the book. Akaar noticed only then that this was a female Neyel.

"Why have you invaded our sanctuary?" she asked, her gray eyelids shuttering closed, then open again.

"Why are *you* willing to kill your followers?"

"The Lfei-sor-Paric are believers. They go to the next level in peace, unsullied by the machines of Auld Aerth or elsewhere."

"This world is being destroyed," Akaar said. "There will be no more Oghen within the next day or so. And your religion will die with you unless you come with us."

The woman tilted her head in what Akaar interpreted as a gesture of incredulity. Or perhaps curiosity. "Our *world* may end, but *we* will not. And we are at peace with that."

Akaar shook his head. "The children down there didn't have the chance to make that decision for themselves."

The cleric looked at him—or perhaps through him— before responding. "You don't know *what* our children are capable of. Their sacrifice is as meaningful to them as the one you made many, many Oghencycles ago."

Akaar felt a chill go down his spine. *How could she possibly know?*

"What does that mean?" he asked.

"You made a sacrifice for someone who mattered to you then, but you were pulled back from the abyss. Your faith sustained you that your sacrifice was right and justified. And you hold on to the anger toward your savior even now." She paused and smiled at him. "Will you now take away from us *our* sacrifice?"

Akaar backed away, suspicious. "Did Tuvok tell you any of this?"

She tilted her head again. "I do not know *Two-vok*. What I know comes entirely from you. I am a *goquilav* of the Lfei-sor-Paric. I see many things that *were,* that *are.* Sometimes things that *will be.*"

She turned away. "Leave me here now. Take whomever you will take. They will decide later whether they wish to follow the Lfei-sor-Paric ways or not."

As Akaar carefully backed away another long pace, she turned her head once more to regard him. "But know always that *you* have made a decision to put your desires above our faith. How you will live with that is something I cannot foresee."

As he made his way down the stairs and to the enclave, Leonard James Akaar felt hot tears beginning to stream unbidden down his cheeks.

It was the first time such a thing had happened to him in over three decades.

CHAPTER SEVENTEEN

SHUTTLECRAFT *ELLINGTON*, STARDATE 57038.4

Moments ago, an enormous conflagration between normal space and the growing fabric of the protouniverse had destroyed most of the Oghen's largest moon. Fragmentary debris from the ancient, airless body's remains were even now raining down through the ionized, smoke-shrouded atmosphere of the swiftly dying planet. The majority of the rubble was arranging itself in a spectacular ring around the planet's equator.

Beautiful. But soon nobody will be around to see it.

Ranul Keru stared grimly through the forward window of the shuttlecraft *Ellington* as fiery streaks of moon debris plummeted through the atmosphere toward the planet's surface. He could see in the glass the reflection of the others in his rescue crew as they stood behind him. They were all exhausted and thoroughly beat up. He was trying to be a strong leader for them, but there were times when he felt he could barely even hold onto consciousness. The wounds in his chest hadn't fully healed, and he knew that he had coerced Dr. Ree into releasing him from sickbay a bit prematurely. Had Ree known that he had intended to participate directly in the evacuation runs over Oghen, he might have had been tempted to place Keru in a restraining field.

But I'm needed here, he told himself. Everybody *is needed.* There was scarcely a single member of *Titan's* crew, with the notable exception of new mother Olivia Bolaji, who wasn't taking part in the rescue missions in some capacity.

Ensign Reedesa Waen gave him a quick glance, her teeth gritted in concentration. The Bolian woman was a good pilot, even if that wasn't her primary assignment. He saw beads of sweat forming on the crest of the ridge that bisected her azure face.

"I hope this hailstorm of burning moon rock doesn't do us in," she said, keeping her voice steady, even if the calmness seemed a bit forced. "Dodging the spatial distortions is tough enough without also having to worry about boulders grinding us into powder."

"You'll do just fine," Keru said, patting her on the shoulder. He then turned toward the other members of his team: Kent Norellis, the human astrobiologist who seemed to have romantic designs on him, however unwanted; Nurse Kershu, an Edosian whose three arms and highly dexterous hands made her especially valuable during medical emergencies; and Lieutenant T'Lirin, the Vulcan security officer who'd proven herself to be quite tough, not only during the recent raid on Vikr'l Prison, but also over the course of the last three orbit-to-surface-and-back evacuation runs.

"This will have to be our last run," Keru said, though it

pained him to have to say it. "Local space is destabilizing too quickly. We've all done the best we can, but we won't make it home if we attempt any more evac runs."

Norellis turned to look at a monitor, on which a sensor alarm was flashing. His fingers tapped one of the touch-sensitive panels nearby. "We've found another small group of refugees, Commander. Only ten or twelve individuals. But it looks like they're not out in the open. They've taken refuge below ground, in a cavern. I'm having trouble getting a transporter lock."

"Head for their coordinates," Keru told Waen. "We're not leaving here empty-handed."

Moments later, the shuttlecraft was hovering about twenty meters over a settlement that had been built into a series of buttes. But a cursory glance at the rubble and smoke visible everywhere revealed that little of the village was left standing. To make matters worse, the ground itself was bucking and roiling, as cracks yawned wide and spewed plumes of molten magma and fountains of super-heated steam.

"The bedrock is completely destabilized," Norellis said, his tone edging almost toward panic. "We can't land. And the caves the survivors are hiding in are too kelbonite-rich to let us beam them out without pattern enhancers."

"We'll go in, then," Keru said. He turned toward T'Lirin. "You, me, and Kent. We'll each take a pattern enhancer. If we can persuade the survivors to stay in one place, we ought to be able to beam them out safely."

The shuttle veered to port, throwing them all toward that side of the craft. As they righted themselves and recovered their seats, Waen shouted an apology. "Sorry. A huge gout of magma was erupting right below us."

Keru felt as though his insides had been sliced open,

pain from his recent chest wound. "How do we get to the survivors?"

Norellis pointed through the forward window toward a cave opening on one of the buttes. The entrance was narrow, and the pathway leading to it had already crumbled away, no doubt because of all the recent seismic activity. "Line-of-sight transport. We beam ourselves just inside the opening, one at a time. Risky, but it's our best option."

Keru nodded, then looked quickly at T'Lirin. She nodded as well.

"I will go in first," she said. "I've traversed the volcanic plains of the Womb of Fire on Vulcan. I believe this will be easier."

Moments later, T'Lirin had successfully beamed over to the cave opening, followed quickly by Norellis. Keru was the last to go, feeling the beam engulf him in its disorienting shimmer.

The air outside the shuttle was oppressively hot and acrid-smelling, and Keru immediately began to cough as he made his way deeper into the caves. The situation reminded him briefly of the stand he and the other Guardians had made on Trill, when political terrorists had attacked the caves of Mak'ala.

He heard the echoes of footfalls coming from T'Lirin and Norellis up ahead, as well as a variety of screams and shouts beyond. He rounded a corner to find a broad chamber filled with a chaotic and frightened crowd of refugees. Most of them were members of the bovine native species that the Neyel had apparently enslaved long ago, along with representatives of a number of other sentient races, including Neyel, mixed among them.

As T'Lirin tried to explain to the refugees what would happen during the beam-out, Keru and Norellis arranged the tall, stanchion-style transporter pattern enhancers in a triangular formation that encompassed much of the wide chamber. They couldn't transport everyone out at once; they would have to do so in three groups.

Norellis took the first group, and while they seemed to flicker and linger a bit too long during their dematerialization, Keru was heartened to hear Kent's voice over his combadge a few moments later. They had reached the shuttle successfully.

The ground shook and groaned, as if the very bones of the planet ached.

"*You'd better get out of there quickly though, Ranul,*" Norellis said over Keru's combadge. "*These buttes are starting to collapse around us out here.*"

Keru looked to T'Lirin. "You go next."

The Vulcan woman shook her head. "Respectfully, sir, even though you are the leader of this mission, you must go next." She pointed at him.

Keru was about to disagree, when he saw that she wasn't pointing at him, but at his chest. He looked down to see blood seeping through his tunic. *His* blood. His wound had reopened.

"See you on the other side," he said, then joined a group of lowing, frightened Oghen natives within the triangle formed by the pattern enhancers. A moment later, a shimmering curtain of energy enfolded him, and he felt a momentary sensation of freefall.

Then he materialized in the shuttle, along with the refugees. Nurse Kershu turned toward him and her eyes widened when she saw the blood on his tunic.

"Get T'Lirin out *immediately*," he shouted. He'd be damned if he was going to leave any of his team behind.

Norellis yelled into the companel in front of him. "T'Lirin! Are you ready? T'Lirin?"

All that came back was static.

Waen turned back from the pilot seat. "Sir, sensors show there's been a cave-in. We've lost our transporter lock."

Keru's heart sank. *No. I can't lose her. I can't lose* any-one. He'd made that promise to himself when he'd agreed to take the job as *Titan*'s chief of security. Somewhere deep in the back of his mind, his coma visions of despair and bloodwine assailed him.

Waen shouted again from the cockpit, and Keru heard the sound of hope in her voice. "I'm showing life signs, Commander. And they're on the move."

"Is there any way to get them out?" Keru asked, push-ing the administering hands of Nurse Kershu aside and moving forward through the frightened crowd toward the cockpit's copilot seat.

"No, sir," Waen said. "But I think they're headed for an opening over there." She pointed to the forward window, toward another opening in the butte wall.

A moment later, movement was visible just inside the dark egress. Keru turned back toward Norellis.

"Kent, beam over anyone who exits the caves. Energize the moment you have a lock."

As he turned back toward the screens, Keru heard a ca-cophonous sound, louder than anything he'd yet heard. A moment later, something massive collided with the face of the butte, near the entrance the team had used previously. Rocks and dust scattered from the impact's epicenter, stone shrapnel banging against the shuttle's hull.

Waen turned toward him. "Commander, we're being hit by lunar debris, and it's only getting worse. We have to go *now!*"

"Not without T'Lirin," Keru said. He turned back to-ward the rear of the shuttle, just in time to watch another quartet of disoriented refugees materialize.

"There she is," Waen said, pointing. Through the dust-clotted air, Keru saw T'Lirin, her uniform torn and dirty. She was carrying a small Neyel child, and was standing near the lip of the cave.

"Lock onto them now!" Keru yelled back to Norellis.

"Transporter's down," Norellis shouted. "I can't get a lock!"

No! Eyes wide with horror, Keru looked at the screen, saw T'Lirin holding the Neyel child close to her chest, her image swimming in the heated air.

Keru was about to order Waen to take them in as close as possible to T'Lirin when something struck the shuttle, nearly hard enough to turn it over. Keru felt himself fly up out of the seat, and came crashing down against one of the consoles.

He heard screams, and saw flashes of light and showers of sparks and moving bodies, even as he rolled off the control panels and onto the shuttlecraft's unyielding deck.

A blue hand helped him up. "Sir," Waen yelled. "If we don't leave now, everyone we came to save will die."

Keru looked up at the screens, staring transfixed at the image of T'Lirin. Her face was a mask of utter calm, of acceptance. She raised one hand toward the *Ellington,* her fingers paired and parted into the shape of a V.

The shuttle shook again. "Sir!" Waen shouted.

"Raise shields," Keru snarled, his eyes brimming with tears. "Get us out of here, fast." But he forced himself to watch the consequences of his choice as T'Lirin and her charge dwindled from sight on the surface of the dying planet.

VANGUARD

Davin ran, and she knew she was running for her life.

Stay out of the lights, she told herself, avoiding the huge, mirrored structures that brought external sunlight into this place. She could hear crowds in the distance, could see some of them in the far distance on the opposite side of the place if she looked straight up.

But when she cried for help, no one came to her aid.

She had to assume they were still chasing her. There were four of them when she had last looked over her shoulder, but she was no longer sure there weren't more. All she knew was that she couldn't afford to turn to look again, lest they gain on her. Keeping her tail pointed straight behind her, she kept running, hoping she could find a way to elude her pursuers in this strange, curved place—*could this really be Holy Vangar, the moon placed in Oghen's sky by the original Oh-Neyel people?*—or at least ascend to the spincenter of the place, where the pull of gravity was said to be weakest.

She knew what would happen when they finally caught up with her. They would brutalize her as though she were a slave. They would have their way with her.

And then they would kill her.

Ignoring the pain in her side, Davin ran into a large shelter stacked at least three metriks high with crates, some sealed, some opened. Some of the opened crates, she saw, contained large sacks of grain and other bulk foods. Others were filled with machinery. Some of the food and other gear looked familiar, as though it had come from her home village on Oghen. The rest looked alien, unfamiliar.

She concluded that all of it had probably been stored

here by the strangers who claimed they had come to save the Neyel people from destruction.

No one seemed to be chasing her now. Had she lost them?

She decided she would risk pausing, at least for long enough to catch her breath. Sitting on the corner of one of the crates, she tore open a bag of food and quickly ate her fill, scattering crumbs far and wide. She knew she needed water as well, but didn't know at the moment where to find any.

This had to be some sort of storage depot. But where was everyone? *How can these strangers believe they can save an entire world when they can't even spare enough people to guard their storehouses properly?*

She heard a sharp, clattering noise, as though someone in a far corner had inadvertently kicked something over while blundering about in the darkness.

"You're at the end of your run, girl," called a sinister voice emanating from the deep shadows beyond the crates.

Adrenaline jolted her body off the crate where she had been sitting and onto her feet. She ran toward the entrance through which she had come.

Another angry figure stood in the portal, silhouetted in the external light, barring her way. She turned left, then right. Two more leering Neyel men approached from either side, both of them angrier now than they had been before, simply because she had run. Then she heard footfalls echoing behind her.

Surrounded. By men who believed that that all rules had been rescinded, now that the end of the world seemed imminent.

Sleeper take you all, she thought.

"Stop!"

Another voice, much more pleasant than the others. But with a quality that seemed to expect obedience. Heavy, determined footfalls approached, bringing that voice steadily closer with each stride.

"I said *stop!*" the voice repeated.

Davin looked around her. The four men surrounding her had gotten within five or six metriks of her. But they, too, had heard the voice, and all of them had turned toward it.

"Back away, friend, and we may let you live," said one of the men. *A primate chasing away a rival male,* Davin thought, feeling curiously detached from what she knew was about to happen next: combat and death, most likely including her own.

Davin finally saw the figure as it reached the fringes of the darkened sections of the storehouse.

"I doubt you are my friend. Why don't you leave this woman alone?"

"We won't warn you again, friend," said another of Davin's pursuers. Fear colored this one's voice.

The newcomer strode directly into the wash of ambient light that was streaming in through the main entrance. He was tall and broad in the shoulder, at least as large and powerful-looking as any Neyel male she had ever seen in her life.

But that was where the resemblance ended. He was chalk white, with rough, wrinkled skin, and large, severely pointed ears that brought to mind childhood horror stories of elves.

And fangs that seemed able to rip the throat out of even the toughest-skinned Neyel. *Like the Tuskers from the oldest tales of the Oh-Neyel People.*

The thugs somehow mastered their fear and drew their weapons, long blades. The white creature kept right on approaching.

"That would be a spectacularly bad idea," it said.

The men charged, their blades slashing at the air.

The fanged man closed his eyes, like a cleric in prayer.

The nearest of the attackers dropped his sword and fell to the ground screaming, at least two full metriks away from his prey. The white creature had never touched anyone.

He opened his eyes, which burned with barely contained rage. "Now, gentlemen: Are you willing to be reasonable?"

They dropped their knives and ran.

The horrible fanged creature continued moving forward, heading straight for Davin.

Gods, no. Now he's coming for me.

She ran again, panicked. Her foot connected with something on the floor, and she sprawled onto her face.

She rolled onto her back, and saw the creature looming over her. She heard other footfalls and saw a motley quartet of armed strangers running toward her as well. Were they also planning to rescue her, only to take her for themselves?

The four new arrivals, two of whom strongly resembled the elves from the old tales, came to a stop beside the fanged man. One of the other two opened a small container on her hip, and Davin could hear liquid sloshing inside it.

Water?

"Let us help you," the white creature said, extending a large, long-nailed hand down to her. For some reason she didn't understand, she felt reassured.

"My name is Mekrikuk," the creature said.

U.S.S. TITAN

"The fleet will be ready to move out in five of your minutes, Captain," Donatra said. *"Since* Titan *is taking the point, we will await your signal to begin. Donatra out."*

Riker sat behind his ready room desk, staring into the viewscreen that had displayed Commander Donatra's thoughtful visage only moments ago.

From the time of her initial change of heart about assisting with the evacuation of Oghen, Donatra had again proved herself to be an amenable ally. She and her staff had been nothing but cooperative during the several ad hoc meetings that had been convened so that the engineering specialists could determine the safest, most efficient way to tow the Vanguard habitat to the spatial rift—and then back to Romulan space through the aperture Donatra had called the Great Bloom.

Leaning back in the padded chair behind the heavy Elaminite wood desk, Riker wondered how she would react to the tentative plan that *Titan's* science and engineering people had devised: a scheme to seal the spatial rift up behind the towing convoy using improvised antimatter singularity bombs.

Improvised, Riker thought, *from the warp cores of about two dozen of Donatra's warbirds.*

Considering the plan's high cost, would Donatra take advantage of a one-time opportunity to put the Sleeper permanently to bed again? Riker could only hope that she would see the plan's merits. After all, she would lose only the warp cores in the bargain—not her ships or their crews, assuming that everything went to plan—in exchange for closing the spatial rift forever.

If she went for it, the door to the emerging protouniverse would be barred. The peril now facing entire sectors of Neyel space, and perhaps places far beyond it as well, would be neutralized.

Once Cethente finishes his final round of simulations, it'll be time, Riker thought. *I'll have to ask Donatra to help carry out the plan. And since I can't force her to sacrifice any of her warp cores, the decision will have to be up to her.*

Jaza had already finished working out the final details of the towing operation, aided by Ra-Havreii, Cethente, a quintet of Romulan astrophysicists and engineers, and a handful of other *Titan* officers and noncoms.

The plan was to have the entire fleet of Romulan warbirds network their tractor beams and warp fields, in order to tug the Vanguard colony along toward the spatial anomaly at high warp. The job would take approximately two and a half days, not to mention immense amounts of power, and would most likely be risky given the interspatial energy discharges that were popping up with such frequency throughout the expanse between the Oghen system and the rift. *Titan*'s job would be to keep its enhanced sensor nets alert for those, effectively taking the point and providing early warning to the rest of the convoy.

Only a few years prior, ten ships had performed a similar towing job, ferrying the Cardassian space station Empok Nor across a distance of three light-years. Now, they had to pull a much larger habitat across about twice that distance, though with far more ships and power to apply to the task. Jaza had argued that the Vanguard habitat's simple, blunt shape made it a far better candidate for warp-speed towing than Empok Nor, whose rococo Cardassian design had made it far more vulnerable to being sheared apart, either by tractor beam stresses or warp-field variances.

Though the science and engineering specialists had debated for some time, they had emerged from their meetings convinced that it could be accomplished.

Besides, this won't be the first time the old girl has been dragged across the universe at high warp, Riker kept telling himself. The asteroid colony had once served as an Earth-orbiting laboratory, and it had been ejected into deep space as a consequence of a failed twenty-first century warp-field experiment.

Riker had pointed out to Donatra that once the towing convoy was back on the Romulan side of the rift, her fleet wouldn't need to tow the Vanguard colony any further. At that point, other Starfleet or even Klingon vessels could be called in to take up the slack in towing Vanguard back to Federation space.

He resumed studying the padd that contained the Vanguard towing data for the next several minutes.

From his combadge, the voice of Ensign Aili Lavena interrupted him.

"Captain, your skiff has just docked onto Vanguard, apparently with minor damage. They managed to recover another twenty-two refugees, most of them children."

"Outstanding, Ensign."

Good for Akaar, Riker thought with a grim smile. He'd been wary of the Admiral's plan to use the skiff—which then constituted *Titan*'s only lifeboat, other than the emergency escape pods—to conduct a perilous rescue mission for which it wasn't designed. But the old man had apparently succeeded anyway. *Guess that's why he's still alive— and vital—after so many decades in Starfleet.*

Riker rose from behind his desk, exited his ready room, and stepped out onto the bridge. He stopped as he reached his command chair and faced the main viewscreen. It displayed the half-daylit planet Oghen. But instead of a pleasant, blue-green-brown M-Class world, it looked like one of Hieronymus Bosch's visions of Hell.

"How many ships are still down—"

Lavena turned toward him, interrupting. "Sir, we've just received word that the *Ellington* has been badly damaged." Her aquamarine eyes were wide behind her close-fitting, transparent hydration mask.

Riker frowned, feeling his pulse jump. "How badly?"

"She's accelerating from the surface toward orbit now, but she's losing power fast. I don't think she's going to be able to make Vanguard."

Riker considered his options. Within the next several minutes, they'd be towing the Vanguard habitat away from Oghen orbit. None of the Romulan ships in the towing fleet could be spared as the delicate preparations continued. That left rescuing the *Ellington* either up to *Titan* or one of her other auxiliary craft, all of which were now safely back aboard.

"Ensign Lavena, plot an intercept course toward the *Ellington*. Inform the Romulans that we will be ready to lead the convoy forward just as soon as we recover the last of our shuttlecraft."

"Aye, Captain," Lavena and Dakal chorused as they both went to work.

Riker's combadge chirped. *"Cethente to Captain Riker. I have news for you, sir."*

He touched the badge. "Go ahead."

"The latest simulations were successful, Captain. We can indeed seal the rift, as hypothesized. With Commander Donatra's cooperation, of course."

"Well done, Doctor."

"I trust that you will now, as you humans say, 'pop the question'?"

Cethente signed off, leaving Riker chuckling despite

his mood. On the main viewscreen, the *Ellington* hove into view, struggling its way clear of Oghen's gravity well.

"Mr. Dakal, open a channel to Commander Donatra."

As he waited for Donatra's image to appear before him again, he considered Cethente's peculiar choice of idiom. "Popping the question," of course, was a term reserved for a proposal of marriage. Such things were extremely serious.

It occurred to him then that to Donatra, the request he was about to make might seem *more* serious than even that.

VANGUARD

Dr. Ree and Dr. Venora were processing the latest group of refugees as they beamed in from the captain's skiff. As the group milled about, near panic, Tuvok saw Admiral Akaar leaning up against one of the habitat's walls, wincing.

Tuvok approached him warily, but respectfully. "Do you require assistance, Admiral?"

Akaar stared at him, his gaze inscrutable. It didn't appear to reflect pain from a physical wound, nor did it harbor the kind of simmering anger that Tuvok had seen in his erstwhile friend's eyes three decades ago—and over the course of the past week.

It was something else entirely.

"Yes. I do need your help," Akaar said, reaching toward Tuvok. "I twisted my ankle badly during the rescue."

Tuvok allowed the much larger man to put his arm around his shoulder, and helped him limp over to a recessed alcove amid several crates of relief provisions. Akaar sat down on top of one of them.

"I'll get one of the doctors," Tuvok said and turned to leave.

"Tuvok, wait," Akaar said.

The Vulcan turned back toward his Capellan superior. "Sir?"

Akaar hesitated for a moment, then spoke, his voice low. "I broke the Prime Directive down there, or at least its spirit. Not in a casual way or even an obvious one." He paused, then continued, his words spilling out as if the confession had to leave his mouth quickly. "The people I rescued were religious believers who abhor high technology. Rather than help themselves, or allow us to help them, they had chosen to commit suicide, and to kill their children, even as Oghen disintegrated around them."

He paused for another moment then, looking down. Tuvok remained silent.

"I did not *care* what they wanted," Akaar said. "I wanted to save them. I wanted their people to have a chance to survive and rebuild. I wanted their *children* to grow up with an opportunity to make their own decisions about their futures. So, essentially, I abducted them."

Tuvok nodded. "You made a command decision, Admiral. You did what you felt was right."

Akaar stared up at him, his eyes haunted, but said nothing.

Tuvok remained still. "Do you have something more to share?" he finally asked.

"There will undoubtedly be repercussions," Akaar said at length. "What would *you* have done?"

Tuvok squatted on his haunches, bringing his eyes to a level just below those of Akaar. "I would have done what I felt was right *as well*," Tuvok said. "Regardless of the repercussions."

Akaar shut his eyes for a moment and let out a long

breath, his shoulders deflating. When he opened his eyes again, they sparkled as tears played at the edges of his eye-lids.

"I am sorry, my old friend," Akaar said finally, his deep voice trembling. "I have wasted so much time in anger."

Tuvok put his hand forward and laid it gently on the Capellan's shoulder. Though it was a supremely un-Vulcan gesture, it seemed perfectly appropriate at the moment.

"That is why it is sometimes good to abolish emo-tions," Tuvok said very quietly. "Anger, and hurt, can be a cancer in one's heart."

Despite all his training and suppression of emotion, Tuvok felt regret and sorrow percolating into his own con-sciousness as well.

And one other emotion . . .

Hope.

U.S.S. TITAN

Olivia Bolaji looked over at Noah Powell as he watched the viewscreen with her in sickbay. He had come to be with her and her baby—to "keep them both safe," in his words—while almost everyone else aboard *Titan* was pre-occupied with the rescue mission over Oghen.

I shouldn't let him watch this, she thought, wondering if the boy had fibbed about his mother having given him permission to watch the events unfolding on the planet. Still, the ongoing disaster was only indistinctly visible from *Titan*'s current orbit, hundreds of kilometers above the surface. She made up her mind to deactivate the screen if Noah seemed to be becoming disturbed by anything he was seeing.

Bolaji was grateful to have learned several minutes ago that her husband had emerged from his sole foray down to the planet unscathed. The *Ellington*, silhouetted on the viewscreen against the raging fires of Oghen, hadn't been quite so lucky. Now, apparently, Captain Riker was in the midst of rescuing the shuttle's passengers and crew.

"So why didn't they save any of the animals?" Noah asked. "On the Vanguard?"

"I don't know," Olivia said. "Maybe they did. But I think they were trying to save as many of the sentient beings as possible."

Noah screwed up his nose in a thoughtful scowl. "Animals *are* sentient beings, too. They just think differently than we do. Why aren't *they* just as important?"

From out of the mouth of babes, Bolaji thought, unable for the moment to formulate an answer the young boy could accept.

"I mean, back in the olden days, when Noah built the ark, he took two of each animal, plus all of his family, so they'd have people and animals once the floods were over," Noah said. "He's where I got my name from."

"Really?"

"Well, kind of. Actually, my great-grandfather was named Noah, too, but I think he was named after the guy with the boat."

Bolaji nodded, and looked over at her own child, who was sleeping in his incubator. "Totyarguil was named after a star."

"Totyarguil is kind of hard to spell," Noah said guilelessly. He looked back at the screen. "My mom said that there never was a real Noah, that it's all just stories. I hope that's true. I don't think a god should destroy a world just because he's angry."

Bolaji smiled. "Neither do I," she told Noah. "But

there's more than one way to think about gods, if you believe in such things."

"I know," Noah said. "Like the Prophets of Bajor. But I heard they're just wormhole aliens." He thought for a moment, then wiggled his finger in the air. "Do you think that wormhole aliens look like worms?"

Suppressing a laugh, Bolaji said, "I don't know. Maybe. I've never seen one."

Noah pointed to the viewscreen. The image had switched, now showing the *Ellington* being tractored toward *Titan*'s main shuttlebay. The blue glow of an atmosphere-retention forcefield covered the bay's broad opening. "They're getting them back aboard *Titan*. Good. Uncle Ranul is on that ship. I was sort of worried about him. He wasn't even completely better yet from his coma."

"I'm sure he'll be fine."

"Me, too." Noah continued to watch the screen intently for a few moments, then looked back at Olivia. "So, do you think this thing that's trying to destroy their planet is *their* god getting mad at them?"

Bolaji wasn't quite sure how to answer that question either. She'd read some of the preliminary reports; Starfleet characterized the destructive force as an emerging protouniverse, while the local people and even some Neyel called it the Sleeper.

Some of the latter people certainly *did* consider it a vengeful god.

She was about to open her mouth to speak when the orange-tinged world on the screen seemed to collapse on itself, molten magma and rocky crust and mantle material jumbling, falling, flying, like a gigantic egg being beaten in some celestial mixing bowl.

She was about to deactivate the viewer for Noah's sake when the screen flared brightly, then abruptly went dark.

Oghen just died right in front of us. One of the interspatial energy discharges she'd read about, no doubt an enormous one, must have just ripped out the entire planet's guts. The thought was jarring, incredible, but also undeniable.

Bolaji heard the muted blare of the red alert klaxons and instinctively looked toward her sleeping baby. The tiny infant slept on, blissfully unaware of the sometimes violent universe into which he'd been born.

"Come sit up here with me," Olivia said to Noah, and scooted over to one side of her chair. The boy clambered up beside her quickly.

Her eyes fixed on Totyarguil, she held Noah tightly to her, saying a silent prayer to all the gods of her people, even though she, herself, had lost faith in all such things years ago.

VANGUARD

Ever since she had first come aboard Vanguard, Deanna Troi hadn't felt quite right. It was as though the great asteroid's hollow interior were somehow amplifying the emotional distress of the hundreds of thousands of people who had been hastily brought aboard the ancient Terran space habitat.

"You are dead on your feet, Commander Troi," Dr. Ree said, his sharp foreclaws clutching a handheld medical scanner that he ran quickly past her temples. The whirring sound it made was already giving her a headache. It was all she could do to keep from growling in irritation at the infuriatingly intrusive reptilian physician. Couldn't he see how busy she was?

"I'll be fine, Doctor. There's far too much to do here for

my condition to become anybody's priority. We still have industrial replicators to assemble, shelters to build, hordes of refugees to feed, medicine to distribute, childr—"

"None of which you can accomplish if you end up dead from psionic trauma," Ree said, shutting off the scanner. "I'd advise you to get back to *Titan* for some rest, Deanna. Now, preferably."

"Out of the question." She rose from her chair and walked toward the door of the prefab shelter. Through the window, she could see one of the Vanguard colony's broad, curving public spaces, which had already been dotted with many rows of other small, tent-like emergency shelters—as well as huge throngs of people numbering in the thousands, all of whom would soon need shelter desperately. Apparently, the interior of the asteroid was not only large enough to support more than a million people indefinitely, it also generated its own internal weather, making the tents a necessity until more permanent structures could be constructed.

But there are already more people crammed into this habitat than it ever supported before, Troi thought, growing increasingly worried. *I don't think more than a thousand or so people lived and worked here centuries ago when Vanguard was originally placed in Earth orbit. What happens when the sanitation gets out of hand in here? And what about clean water? And—*

"Counselor?"

It was Ree again, sounding insistent. How many times had he been forced to call her name to get her attention?

"Counselor, I'm sure you realize that I have the authority to simply *order* you back to *Titan.* Please don't force me to do that."

She scrunched her eyes closed and rubbed her temples. *Maybe he's right. Maybe the emotional intensity of so many people seeing their world end is too much, even for me.* Especially *for me.*

She opened her eyes and met Ree's concerned gaze. "Let's compromise. How about this: I'll go back aboard *Titan* before the Vanguard towing convoy goes to warp. That way, I won't be forced to stay here during the two days it will take to move Vanguard to the rift."

He sighed, a great sibilant rush of air. He was clearly willing to accept the compromise, but was just as plainly unhappy with it. "All right, Commander. Unless I see you taking a sudden turn for the worse in the meantime. But please remember, *Titan* needs you."

She nodded. *And Will needs me.*

But so does an entire society that's doing its damnedest right now not to die.

IMPERIAL WARBIRD *VALDORE*, STARDATE 57038.5

Even with the towing convoy now safely underway, albeit only at impulse speeds at the moment, the image still haunted her.

A planet on which billions lived had been cast, whole and screaming, into the afterworld of Erebus. The world the Neyel called Oghen was no more.

Scarcely a *verak* after having refused Riker's request, Donatra summoned him back to her ready room's comm screen.

"I have reconsidered, Captain," she said simply. "Can you guarantee that your plan will close the gate through which this ... protouniverse is leaking into normal space?"

"I believe so," Riker said, nodding. *"As much as I can guarantee anything."*

Donatra decided she was satisfied with that. Ambiguity, after all, was one of life's few constants, in her experience. "No more worlds should die this way, Riker. Least of all because *I* refused to act."

The human captain nodded solemnly. *"You are a person of honor, Commander."*

She thought of Suran, who had had no part in her decision, and wondered about that. Then she silently berated herself for allowing doubt to plague her. *I will do what I must,* she thought. *As I have always done.*

"I do have one caveat, however, Captain."

"All right."

"I am assuming that the Klingons will wish to accompany the convoy through the rift back into Romulan space."

Riker nodded. *"I've just spoken with Captain Tchev. He and I both agree that that's the safest way to proceed, given the condition of his ship. He's still keeping the* Dugh *at the station near the rift, awaiting our arrival."*

"It's too bad Tchev can't contribute substantively to the task of towing the asteroid colony to safety," Donatra said, stroking her chin thoughtfully. "Or even help keep our path free of spatial disturbances, as *Titan* is doing."

"We can't just leave the Klingons behind, Commander." Riker's eyes had narrowed ever so slightly.

"Oh, I agree. It should be a simple enough matter to enclose the *Dugh* inside the warp-field bubble of one of the other ships. Should one of my vessels do it, Captain? Or would you rather reserve that dubious honor for *Titan*?"

"We'll handle it here, thanks," the human said with a slight scowl. *"Now what's your caveat?"*

Donatra grinned in spite of herself. "How much does Tchev know about the plan to collapse the Great Bloom?"

"All of it, Commander. His crew are at risk as much as ours. He needs to be fully informed."

"Again, I agree. But Governor Khegh has no such need."

"Excuse me?"

"I don't wish to let the Klingon government know that more than half my fleet has been effectively crippled, if only temporarily. I do not like to advertise my disadvantages."

"I think that ship has already sailed, Commander. Khegh will know all about it when he reads Tchev's reports."

"I doubt it, Captain. Tchev will not wish it known that his vessel was rescued from the Great Bloom by Romulans. I believe I can trade my silence for his. My question to you is: can I rely upon *yours?"*

Riker paused, his deep blue eyes apparently trying to see into the depths of her motivations. At length, he said, *"I don't feel right about this, Commander."*

"Must I remind you that my participation in your plan to seal off the Bloom depends upon my willing cooperation?" Donatra allowed her right eyebrow to rise imperiously, a mannerism that she had often seen the false Praetor Tal'Aura use to great effect.

He seemed to sag backward into his chair. *"All right. I won't tell Khegh or the Klingon government about your warp-core maneuvers. At least, not until you get all of your ships repaired and operational again. Agreed?"*

Humans, she thought. *Haggling to the last, even when they have no leverage.*

But good enough was good enough. "Accepted," she said. "Donatra out."

The screen went dark, and Donatra rose from behind her desk and crossed to the ready room's door.

Stepping onto her bustling bridge, she decided that now

would be a good time to head down to the infirmary to look in on Suran.

I wouldn't want him to awaken at an inconvenient time.

U.S.S. TITAN

After the Romulan commander had signed off, Riker continued staring at the viewscreen on his ready room desk for several minutes while he considered the ramifications of the pact he had just made. He hoped he wouldn't come to regret it, but he could see no alternative. The stakes were simply too high to risk calling Donatra's bluff.

He got up and strode out onto the bridge. Glancing at the conn readouts, as well as the data scrolling up the port side of the main viewscreen, he quickly confirmed that the convoy was underway, but moving only at one quarter impulse so far. The fleet's networked warp bubble would surround Vanguard within the hour, once Jaza and Ra-Havreii finished double-checking the navigational hazard detection system. This system was based upon *Titan*'s enhanced sensor net, and depended upon virtually every bit of communications bandwidth possessed by *Titan* and the entire towing convoy.

And it *had* to function flawlessly at warp, or else the more than two million souls now aboard Vanguard—as well as the entire rescue fleet—would almost certainly end up the way the planet Oghen had.

Riker settled heavily into his command chair, suddenly hyperaware of the lateness of the hour. The responsibility that had landed on his shoulders had attained an almost crushing weight. He was glad that Deanna was due back aboard *Titan* before the convoy was to go to warp; though he expected he'd have precious little time to discuss his fears and misgivings with her immediately, they would certainly have time to thoroughly catch up with one another during the two-day voyage back to the rift, during which time he could finally unburden himself.

He wasn't certain at the moment which aspect of Deanna Troi he needed more: counselor, wife, lover, or senior adviser. He only knew that he needed her at his side.

CHAPTER EIGHTEEN

IMPERIAL WARBIRD *VALDORE,* STARDATE 57039.2

"Commander Suran?"

The voice seemed to be speaking from a great distance, as though Suran had fallen into a deep cavern while those left above searched for him in vain.

The darkness in the cavern lessened, even as Suran's sense of confusion increased. He could see now that he wasn't in a cavern after all; he was in a room, a place that looked familiar.

"You might not want to try to speak, Commander," said the possessor of the voice. "The drugs are only now beginning to wear off."

Suran focused on the voice's source: the bruised and swollen face of a young man dressed in a light orange infirmary gown. His arm was in a sling, which bore rank pins that revealed him to be an enlisted uhlan, a noncommissioned officer.

Suran struggled to sit up. Where was he? All at once he recognized the serene blue walls of the *Valdore*'s infirmary. The place was as quiet as the lowest underworld reaches of Erebus. "How . . . how did I get here?"

"Perhaps you were attacked," said the young enlisted man, who paused to cast a worried glance over his shoulder, even though the infirmary appeared to be empty. "I believe that Dr. Venora has been deliberately keeping you unconscious."

"Why do you say that?"

"I'm trained as a corpsman, Commander. I've been recuperating here ever since the *Valdore* got pulled into the Great Bloom. So I've had little to do but watch the medical staff minister to you. Before they got busy elsewhere with the rescue operations, that is."

Rescue? Suran swallowed, and found his throat to be as dry as the mines of Remus. "How long have I been unconscious, Uhlan?"

"Nearly four *eisae,* Commander."

It was a stunning blow. In essence, he'd been tossed almost four days into the future. And during that time, some sort of rescue had become necessary, an operation that had evidently greatly depleted the infirmary staff. *Why can't I remember anything?*

Something occurred to him then: amnemonic drugs, of the sort used as anesthetics during major surgeries. During his long decades of military service he had witnessed enough medical procedures to know that, say, a heart patient might be conscious during a delicate open-thoracic procedure, and yet remember absolutely nothing afterward because of such compounds.

But why would Venora do that to him? And why during a time of evident emergency?

Donatra.

With a pain-wracked grunt, Suran completed the laborious process of sitting up. A momentary bout of light-headedness seized him, along with a wave of nausea. He closed his eyes for several moments, allowing both unpleasant sensations to break over him and then recede like the tides of the Apnex Sea. Slowly, he allowed his eyes to open again and began taking in the entire room.

He noticed then that he, like the uhlan, was clad only in a loose-fitting patient's smock. He also confirmed that the infirmary was indeed empty except for himself and the junior crew member.

There was no way to know how long that situation might last.

"Uhlan, I want you to tell me everything that's happened since I was brought here."

"Yes, Commander. Though I'm sure I haven't been told everything."

"Just share whatever you know." Suran swung his legs over the edge of the bed, cautiously tested his weight against the deck, and then rose. "And help me find my uniform."

Alone in her ready room, Donatra leaned back in the chair, her booted feet up on her dark sherawood desk. Now that she had finally taken a few long-postponed moments to rest and gather her thoughts, she began to notice just how much pain her battle-scarred body had been suppressing over the past several *eisae*. Her side, festooned with old wounds that she charged to the account of the fraudulent praetor Tal'Aura, felt as though it had been plunged straight into a live volcano.

But at least the worst of this mission is finally over, she told herself, silently kneading her prominently ridged brow with the long fingers of both hands. *Soon the fleet will be at warp. Two days from now, my ships will be safely back in Romulan space, along with their crews.*

Of course, the passage home would not be without its costs, she reflected. But she was determined that no more of her vessels would share the fate of the Imperial warbird *S'harien,* which had already succumbed to the same forces that had erased the planet Oghen from existence.

"Commander Donatra!" The abrasive voice that issued from her desk's comm unit was half an octave higher than Donatra had ever heard it before. Nevertheless, she recognized it immediately. Her reverie blown apart like a dust cloud in a solar wind, she swung her feet onto the deck, leaned forward, and slapped a button on the comm.

"Go ahead, Venora."

"I've just beamed back aboard the Valdore *from the alien asteroid-habitat, Commander."*

Donatra knew that the transferal of hundreds of thousands of individuals from the planet's surface to the asteroid's vast interior space had strained the logistical and medical resources of the *Valdore, Titan,* and the entire fleet very nearly to the breaking point. She hadn't wanted to spare her chief medical officer during the intensive, lengthy evacuation mission, but had finally relented at Venora's vehement insistence.

"It's good to have you back with us," Donatra said. Whatever relaxation she had expected to experience abruptly fled. "What's wrong, Doctor?"

"Suran is gone, Donatra," Venora said, her voice colored a rare shade of panic.

"Did he regain consciousness somehow?" Donatra said, realizing at once just how stupid her question sounded; she had merely been thinking out loud.

"That may be a safe assumption, Commander, considering that he isn't in my infirmary any longer."

"All right, Doctor. I'll see what I can find out. In the meantime, watch your back, Venora. Suran must have henchmen among the crew acting directly on his behalf. Donatra out."

If only I could have placed guards around him, Donatra thought, closing the channel. *Or simply confined him in a holding cell.*

But she knew that such measures would have been overly provocative, as well as destructive to the already strained morale of the *Valdore*'s crew. She could not have afforded to undermine her personal authority—or risk enhancing Suran's—by making it appear that she felt in any way threatened by him. Especially now that Suran had confirmed that she did indeed have excellent reasons to perceive him as dangerous. He had, after all, just demonstrated that someone aboard the *Valdore* was willing and able to intercede on his behalf, most likely by working to interrupt or counteract the drugs Dr. Venora had relied upon to keep Suran out of action during the current crisis.

Donatra reached across her desktop again and activated another comm channel. "Computer, locate Commander Suran."

The door chime to the ready room sounded, startling her. Acting on instinct, she reached with her right hand for the small disruptor she kept in her tunic.

The computer responded in a flat, passionless male voice. *"Commander Suran is on the bridge."*

Of course, she thought as she used her left hand to enter a single command into the computer on her desk.

"Enter," she said a moment later.

The door hissed open, revealing Suran. His face was drawn and ashen. He moved into the room, unsteadily but relentlessly. After the door closed behind him, he raised a disruptor pistol. Donatra noticed that his hand was shaking slightly, as though Suran were fighting off the lingering effects of the drugs.

"I don't think you'll want to fire that in here, Suran. Security alarms, remember?" Donatra noticed that his eyes were sunken, the whites filigreed with tiny green blood vessels. Was he so unhinged by the drug residue in his system that he thought he could succeed with such a crude attack?

Keeping her gaze locked with Suran's, Donatra slowly moved her right hand away from the butt of her disruptor, allowing it to settle instead on the *jorreh*-handled haft of the short-bladed *ihl-sen* that she kept right next to it, tucked into a scabbard on her belt. The ready room's large desk concealed her careful manipulations.

Suran didn't lower his weapon. "The fleet should already be back in Romulan space by now, Donatra. Instead, you've opted to stay here and involve us in matters that are none of our concern. Why?"

She continued to meet his hard, bloodshot stare squarely. "Riker and his crew aided us in staving off a civil war, Suran."

"Riker and his crew are trying to save a population of refugees. *Human* refugees. It's not our problem. We have an empire to defend from the Klingons and the Remans."

"And the Reman attack against Romulus wasn't Riker's problem, either. Yet he acted on our behalf without any reservations. You and I, not to mention the empire we both revere, accrued a large debt to him that day, Suran. And I *always* pay my debts."

"Do you owe Riker more loyalty than you owe me?"

She chuckled. "Your notions of loyalty are peculiar, Suran. Right now, Riker isn't the one who has a weapon pointed at me." *Perhaps I should have followed my instincts and eliminated you long ago,* she thought. *If not for our mutual loyalty to Braeg, I very well might have already.*

Suran's weapon-hand showed no sign of lowering. "Your plan calls for jettisoning the warp cores of more than half the ships in our fleet, Donatra."

"Our ships won't be harmed."

"As the *S'harien* wasn't harmed?"

She ignored the comment. "The fleet will make it back through the anomaly and into Romulan space before their warp-field bubbles collapse. That's built into the plan, Suran."

"So you hope. But even if that's so, some two dozen of our *d'Deridex*- and *Mogai*-class warbirds will be hamstrung. We can't afford to let the Klingons who've set up camp inside our borders discover this. Or those savages on Remus and Ehrie'fvil."

Donatra shook her head. "We'll have all our vessels repaired and the fleet back to full strength by the time Colonel Xiomek or that idiot Khegh find out anything. I have already seen to it."

"Cut the human asteroid colony loose and take the fleet to warp *now,* Donatra," Suran said, an almost pleading expression crossing his pale features. "The crew need never know how close we came to crossing Honor Blades over this."

She regarded him in silence for at least a full *siure.* Though he looked no less depleted than he had when he'd first entered the room, he also appeared no less determined. But Venora's drugs were obviously still roiling within his blood, along with whatever counteragents Suran's unknown confederates had used to get him back on his feet only a few *dierhu* after she had last checked in on him.

This was indeed a formidable and highly dangerous man.

"All right," Donatra said, rising from behind her desk. Using her left hand, she made a show of preparing to open a comm channel.

With her right she threw the *ihl-sen* that she had placed inside her tunic cuff. Suran gasped and gurgled and immediately fell to his knees. Donatra rose and strode confidently around the desk, then approached him. She saw that Suran had dropped his weapon. Even if he had managed to hold onto it, she would have been in no real danger; she'd had the *Valdore*'s security system deactivate it while he'd still been standing on the bridge.

The matter was moot now, however; both of Suran's hands were presently clawing without effect at the wide, verdant wound that her serrated throwing knife had created. The short blade was lodged quite snugly in the man's windpipe.

Suran pitched forward onto his face and lay unmoving in front of the desk. His blood spread out in a swiftly expanding pool, dyeing the carpet a rich, beryl-emerald green.

Donatra regained her feet, approached Suran, and rolled him over onto his back. His flinty eyes stared back at her, as lifeless as polished *atlai* riverstones. Like Donatra, Suran had served under Admiral Braeg, and they had both pledged Braeg their loyalty. Donatra had become Braeg's lover, and both she and Suran had mourned him deeply after Braeg had fallen to Tal'Aura's treachery. Now, with Suran dead, her last living link with Braeg had passed from the world. For good or ill, her destiny was fully her own at long last.

There will be no more power struggles between us,

Suran, she thought, feeling unexpectedly wistful, but only for a moment. She knelt, picked up his weapon, then pulled her own free from the ghastly wound in his neck. She wiped the gore-spattered blade clean on Suran's sleeve, then returned it to concealment beneath her tunic as she rose to her feet.

All the while, she wondered why she felt so detached from the grisly reality of her longtime colleague's death. And from the fact that she had been its cause.

The comm unit on her desk chimed, startling her.

"Centurion Liravek to Commander Donatra. Titan is hailing us."

Donatra realized that she had been holding her breath. Recovering her composure with no small amount of effort, she touched the reply key.

"Acknowledged, Centurion. I'll take it here."

U.S.S. TITAN

From the moment the Romulan commander's face appeared on the bridge viewscreen, Deanna Troi was certain that Donatra was concealing something. Something terrible.

Will glanced toward Troi, who knew immediately that he had seen the look of alarm that had crossed her face. He had managed to keep his own "emotional tells" under control, however, like the master poker player he was.

"Commander Donatra, *Titan* and her crew are ready to go to warp. Our sensor networks are now fully tested and prepared to continue relaying real-time navigational hazard data to your fleet's computer network, at our highest warp speeds."

Donatra nodded, her face a mask of impassivity. But just below the surface, her emotions were in violent convection. *Why?* Troi wondered.

"Excellent, Captain. My crews stand ready to move at your signal. However, there is something I must tell you before we begin. Is this channel secure on your end?"

Troi watched as Will nodded toward Cadet Dakal, who entered a few swift commands, then nodded back at the captain.

"It is now, Commander," Will said.

Donatra bowed her head briefly, and Troi sensed a wave of gratitude rising from her. *"Captain Riker, what I'm about to tell you must be kept in the strictest confidence, at least until I am ready to announce it to my own people."*

"Of course."

"Commander Suran is dead."

Will's feelings of surprise briefly overwhelmed anything Troi was able to sense from Donatra, whose gaze was moving back and forth between Will and Troi. *She's considering how hard it will be for her to dissemble in front of me,* Troi thought as Will worked to tamp down his emotions.

"What happened?" Will said, breaking the lengthy, stunned silence that had followed Donatra's revelation.

"He attempted to abort our fleet's participation in this rescue operation. And because he did this by brandishing a weapon at me, I had no choice other than to respond in kind."

Troi looked toward Will, who was casting a gently interrogative glance in her direction. She nodded, wordlessly informing him that Donatra was essentially telling the truth. *Essentially,* she thought. *But not necessarily completely.*

Rising and facing Donatra again, Will said, "You say your crew hasn't been informed yet?"

"*Correct. And there's no reason to trouble them with the news just yet. At least not until* after *we conclude the current operation. The distraction and morale difficulties the revelation of Suran's death would cause now are in no one's interest.*" Donatra's dark eyes lit squarely upon Troi's. "*However, I didn't want to give* you *any reason to suspect that anything might be amiss aboard the* Valdore.*"

No doubt because you're justifiably wary around empaths and telepaths, Troi thought. *As are most people who like to keep deep, dark secrets.*

"I appreciate your candor, Commander," Riker said evenly.

"*Thank you, Captain. We shall await your 'go' signal. Donatra out.*"

The Romulan commander's face vanished, to be replaced by an image of the *Valdore*, which dominated the viewscreen. In the background lay the lumpen, rocky cylinder of the Vanguard colony and a swarm of sleek, single- and double-hulled Romulan warbirds. The vessels were arrayed around the asteroid habitat in precise formation, arranged into a pair of pyramids whose bases touched while bisecting Vanguard. The invisible tethers of tractor beams held the entire assemblage together.

Will touched his combadge, and it chirped gently in response. "Riker to Dr. Ra-Havreii."

"*Ra-Havreii here, Captain,*" the chief engineer replied, his words frosted noticeably with a broad-voweled Efrosian accent.

"Be ready to give us lots and lots of power, Commander. And then probably lots more on top of that."

"*Acknowledged, Captain. I will make you as close to*

omnipotent as the laws of physics will allow. We're as ready as it's possible to be down here."

Beneath Ra-Havreii's lightweight banter, Troi sensed a wave of sadness and regret that pushed against equally powerful crosscurrents of hope, trepidation, and confidence. She knew of the engine-room explosion aboard the *Luna* that had occurred under Ra-Havreii's watch, during the prototype vessel's maiden flight. She suspected he might be reliving that fateful incident right now.

"That's all I ever ask of a chief engineer, Doctor," Will said, grinning. "Riker out." He turned, facing Troi again and fixing her with an inquisitive gaze; she knew his mind was still on their exchange with Donatra.

"Donatra's not lying, Will. She *did* kill Suran. And under the circumstances she reported to us, at least in essence."

Will nodded, his expression serious. "I didn't think she'd try to lie right in front of you, especially about something as serious as killing Suran."

"Me neither. But she's definitely holding back *something*."

"About Suran?"

Troi shrugged. "Perhaps. But whatever it is she's concealing, I think it must be something quite important."

He sighed, apparently satisfied that there was no way to solve this mystery anytime soon. He turned toward Dakal, and quietly ordered him to send Donatra the "go" signal she was waiting for.

Troi stared straight ahead at the *Valdore*.

Just what is it you think you still have to hide from us, Donatra?

She had no answers. Only the hope that their ally's penchant for keeping secrets would get no one else killed.

CHAPTER NINETEEN

When *Titan* came out of warp, Riker could feel it right through the bridge deck plates. He stood restlessly just in front of the forward flight control console as Ensign Lavena brought the impulse engines on line, guiding the starship and the towing convoy toward the last leg of its journey back to Romulan space.

Remaining aboard his ship while key members of his crew—specifically Vale, Tuvok, Keru, and most of *Titan's* medical staff—were elsewhere, and quite possibly in danger, was an aspect of command that he doubted he'd ever get fully used to. Even when he knew that he'd deployed his people where they were needed most. After all, the Neyel soldiers Riker had deputized as Vanguard's peacekeepers needed some oversight to ensure that minority species, such as the cattle-like aboriginal Oghen, were treated well.

Besides, the away team would still be in danger, even here, he reminded himself for perhaps the hundredth time.

He thought of his wife, who had finally—if reluctantly—agreed to return to their quarters for a few hours of much-needed sleep. According to Dr. Ree, her time on Vanguard working among the refugees had left her emotionally exhausted, no doubt because of her powerful empathic sensitivities. *Deanna isn't any safer than the away team just because she's come back aboard* Titan. *None of us will be safe until after this mission is over. And maybe not even then.*

He turned toward Cadet Dakal, who was working the ops console situated at Lavena's right. "Aft view, please, Cadet."

"Aye, sir."

Dakal touched the panel before him, and the image on the viewscreen suddenly shifted to the starfield that lay astern of *Titan,* and the multitude of Romulan warbirds that followed her only a few hundred kilometers behind.

In another context, the sight of dozens of heavily armed Romulan vessels approaching from astern, and in apparent battle formation, would have thrown Riker's nervous system straight into fight-or-flight red alert status. Despite the close working relationship he had developed with Commander Donatra, his pulse quickened as he studied the swooping, aggressive lines of the phalanx of warships, several of which moved quickly out of position and back again from moment to moment as they responded to *Titan*'s navigational hazard data. Brief golden-orange and emerald flashes of light speared the empty space near the dodging warbirds as local space continued its violent process of unraveling. With the assistance of a fleetwide subspace radio-linked computer network, tractor beams and warp fields alike made near constant adjustments to the shifts in ship distances and spatial geometries.

"This had better work," he said, thinking out loud.

From behind him, a deep, sonorous voice answered. "Your staff has given it a strong vote of confidence, Captain."

Riker turned and found himself facing Akaar, who stood on the upper bridge, a position that made him look positively gigantic.

"And I agree with them, Admiral," Riker said, more for the sake of bridge morale than for Akaar's benefit. There really was no good alternative to optimism, under the circumstances.

But this stunt will either get us home or make us all very dead. We could still end up stuck here while Magellanic space finishes erasing itself.

Riker returned his attention to the main viewscreen. Focusing past the dozen or so ships that were visible in the foreground, he studied the bulbous, slowly spinning shape that Donatra's warbirds had so carefully shepherded here over the past two days.

The Vanguard habitat lay at the center of the escort formation, whose constituent vessels even now continued weaving and yawing to avoid the rips the Red King was constantly tearing into the fabric of local space, all the while maintaining tractor beam contact with Vanguard. A tactical overlay showed the elaborate cat's cradle of intersecting beams that linked each ship in the fleet—including *Titan*—with the ancient O'Neill colony in order to find safety for the two million or so anxious souls contained within. For a moment, Riker could imagine that the Romulan ships truly were the predatory birds they resembled; only rather than pursuing prey, they were guarding a precious egg whose hatching was imminent.

A little more than two million people, Riker thought. Though he was thankful that the numbers of Neyel settlers and Oghen aborigines that had been rescued would enable both species to survive, he couldn't stop thinking about the nearly two billion that the convoy had been forced to leave behind because of lack of time and resources.

Oghen, a world that had nurtured its own sapient life-forms for millennia—as well as a unique human society for centuries—was now gone forever. Utterly erased from existence by the continued encroachment of an expanding protouniverse.

But those cultures still have a chance to live on, Riker thought, doing his best to maintain a positive outlook. *And once we get this habitat someplace where those cultures can take root and flourish, we can finally get to know them better.*

As he continued watching the convoy's almost balletic motions, a flash of wan yellow light erupted momentarily on the asteroid's rocky exterior, sending a considerable volume of gray-black basaltic debris arcing into space. For an instant, the effect cast Vanguard's rough, cratered surface into sharp relief, and glinted off the silvery remnants of an ancient cluster of what appeared to be communications antennae. This was by no means the first time Riker had watched the asteroid suffer a direct hit from the Red King's ever-more-frequently occurring energy discharges; still, the sight made him wince.

"Asteroid status?" Riker asked Jaza, who was diligently monitoring *Titan*'s sensor web from his post on the starboard side of the upper bridge.

"No serious damage, Captain," the Bajoran science officer said. "Just some minor rearrangement of the surface rock layers."

Riker touched the combadge on his chest. "Riker to away team."

"Vale here, Captain."

Riker spared a quick glance at Jaza. The science officer

Eviku looked at him as if he had just grown a new eye. "What are you implying? That we're showing favoritism to the Neyel because they're genetically human?"

"I'm merely making an observation," Torvig said.

Eviku turned away momentarily, and Torvig's bionic eyes registered a look of disgust on his austere features when he turned back. The Arkenite opened his mouth as if to speak, then closed it again, apparently pondering the question further.

Finally, he said, "Let's say for the moment that the Neyel *are* getting preferential treatment. Could that be because they are more numerous than any of the other species?"

Torvig nodded, ready to concede that obvious fact. "But we could certainly try a little harder to find and rescue more of the indigenous peoples."

"I don't think we're ignoring anyone," Eviku said. "Have *you* ignored anyone? Has *any* member of this crew actively pushed aside an Oghen native in favor of a Neyel?"

Shaking his head, Torvig said, "No. Not that I've seen."

Eviku went quiet for a moment, apparently pondering again. Then, lowering his voice, he said, "I understand your misgivings, Cadet. I know that *Titan* has been lauded by many for its crew diversity. On the other hand, I also know that nobody can fail to notice that most of the chief decision makers for the ship are either humans or humanoids that I can't distinguish *from* humans without a tricorder. And that may indeed influence the way certain decisions aboard *Titan* get made. But I don't believe anyone involved in this rescue effort is practicing racial bias. It seems to me we're all working as hard as we can to save as many of these beings as possible, regardless of where their genes originated."

Torvig nodded, and surveyed the crowd once more,

was growing dangerously short. "We'll keep doing our best to avoid the worst of the bumps, Chris," he said. "How are the refugees doing psychologically?"

"I think we all have our hands full keeping passenger morale about as steady as you're keeping Vanguard. Fortunately, we've got some expert help."

"I thought Counselor Huilan and Counselor Haaj might come in handy over there."

"Oh, they have, Captain, believe me. But I was referring to somebody else: Mekrikuk. Granted, a few of the Neyel have reacted to him as though he's a monster straight out of a fairy tale. But he seems to have exerted a strong calming influence on a lot of the more agitated folks we've encountered here."

Riker was gratified to hear that. He was pleased to discover that such projective telepathy had an application other than wanton violence; he couldn't help but hope that the Federation authorities would look kindly on Mekrikuk's request for political asylum.

"You're doing great work, Chris. I need you to try to keep a lid on things just a little while longer," Riker said. "The convoy is approaching the periphery of the Red King now. We'll be making the passage through the rift in just a few minutes. We'll see you on the other side. *Titan* out."

He stepped back down to the bridge's center and took his seat. "Restore forward view, please, Cadet," he said. "Full magnification."

Dakal entered a short series of commands into his console. The viewscreen responded by replacing Donatra's fleet with a slowly swirling mass of glowing, multicolored clouds that might have been constructed out of the universe's entire stockpile of anger and violence.

The tendrils of energy that had seemed relatively benign some eight days earlier, when *Titan*, the *Valdore*, and the *Dugh* had first emerged from the center of the phenomenon, now seemed almost malevolent, bringing to mind the grasping fingers of some hungry carnivore. Their colors had shifted down toward the red and orange end of the spectrum, with the more peaceful blues and greens muted almost into oblivion. Explosive energy discharges appeared and vanished within the effect's apparently infinite depths, the interspatial equivalent of violent thunderstorms.

The Red King, preparing to snap out of the dream that keeps this corner of the universe running, Riker thought as he stared at the towering, ocher-and-crimson vista that filled the screen. *Or is it the Sleeper, getting ready to wake up and replace everything around him with a brand-new Creation?*

Even now, he still wasn't quite sure what he wanted to call this thing, or how it ought to be characterized. All he knew for certain was that the phenomenon was now far more than part of the cosmic cenotaph that marked the sacrifice of his late friend and colleague, Data. It was an emergent universe that threatened to displace a goodly portion of this one. It had already killed billions, and would wipe out countless more if left to expand unchecked.

Sleeper or sovereign, this thing had to be sent back to wherever it had come from, and as quickly as possible.

Lavena turned her chair to face Riker, her hydration suit gurgling almost inaudibly as she moved. He saw that she was smiling through the semitransparent breathing mask that covered most of her face. "Navigational sensors have just made contact with the *Dugh,* sir."

"Confirmed, Captain," Dakal said, his gaze riveted to the viewscreen, where the dark shape of a battered *Vor'cha*-class cruiser was swiftly differentiating itself from the energy tendrils that appeared to be trying to grasp it like some sea monster out of Earth's ancient maritime legends. "The Klingons seem to be right where we left them."

Riker wasn't surprised. He hadn't expected Tchev to cut and run prematurely.

"Hail them, Cadet."

The overflowing violence of the still-growing protouniverse disappeared a moment later, replaced by Captain Tchev's scowling visage. Lieutenant Dekri, Tchev's female second officer, was visible just beyond her superior's right shoulder.

"You're back, Riker," the Klingon commander said. *"At last."*

"QaleghmeH Qaq DaHjaj," Riker said with a small wry smile. "Nice to see you, too, Captain Tchev. Thanks for keeping the porch light burning for us, by the way."

Despite his good-humored banter, Riker found that he had to push back a small feeling of resentment; he reminded himself that Tchev's refusal to assist in the Oghen evacuation stemmed from the horrendously damaged condition of his ship rather than from cowardice. Donatra hadn't been wrong when she'd pointed out that the *Dugh* needed far more help in getting home than Tchev could contribute.

"We would not have waited for you much longer, Captain. The local spatial effects are becoming more intense by the hour."

Riker wondered whether the *Dugh* could have survived another crossing through the anomaly on its own, but declined to speculate on the matter aloud. If Tchev needed a tow, Riker would see to it without going out of his way to humiliate the Klingons.

"Then we won't waste any more time getting our ships under way," Riker said.

Tchev grunted just before he and Dekri vanished, their images supplanted by that of the roiling spatial rift. Riker supposed that the Klingon captain's surlier-than-usual mood had been inspired by the *Dugh*'s present vulnerability, and its unaccustomed reliance on outside aid. *My old friend Klag got used to having just one good arm,* Riker thought. *So I think you'll get over having your ship towed home, Tchev. Eventually.*

"Incoming hail, Captain," Dakal reported crisply. "It's the *Valdore*."

"On screen, Cadet."

A moment later, Riker's Romulan counterpart regarded him from the center of the viewscreen. *"Captain Riker. My apologies for not calling you in time to offer my regards to Captain Tchev."*

Though her face was impassive, something smoldered behind her dark eyes. At that moment he had never wanted Deanna at his side more badly. *Donatra was listening in on my conversation with Tchev,* he thought. *And she doesn't mind letting me know about it.*

He forced those dark thoughts aside; it was time to get down to business. *"Titan* is ready to move out. We'll take the *Dugh* in tow, since your fleet is already doing so much of the work of moving the Vanguard habitat."

Donatra slowly shook her head. *"I am concerned that* Titan *may stretch her resources too thin by towing the* Dugh, *Captain."*

"It's nothing my chief engineer can't handle."

"But the lives of my crews depend on your enhanced sensing equipment keeping us clear of spatial disruptions. As well as the lives of the millions aboard that asteroid colony."

Riker couldn't find fault with Donatra's logic. With so many dozens of powerful Romulan tractor beams drawing

Vanguard and the *Dugh* toward the spatial rift, the absence of *Titan*'s tractors wouldn't make much difference; the energy necessary to run them would indeed be better applied to warning the convoy of the potentially lethal spatial distortions and zero-point discharges that kept popping up from moment to moment.

"All right, Commander," Riker said. "I have no objection to your fleet towing the *Dugh*. Captain Tchev might not agree, though."

"He would appear to have few viable alternatives, Captain. Unless he is more eager than I think he is to fly straight into whatever afterworld his people believe in. At any rate, my fleet will be ready to enter the Great Bloom"—she turned away momentarily, apparently to consult with a subordinate—*"in five of your minutes. Valdore out."*

Donatra abruptly vanished. In her place on the viewscreen appeared the Red King's long energy tendrils, brilliant against the stygian blackness of Magellanic space. They seemed to beckon *Titan* forward, toward the phenomenon's dark central maw.

Or perhaps they were trying to warn her to stay away.

VANGUARD

"We're all going to die here, Frane," Nozomi said, her lovely, gray face shadowed and haunted in the habitat's dim interior illumination. With over two million people now dependent upon Holy Vangar for their survival—a far greater number than had ever before ridden aboard the Sacred Vessel—all resources were at a premium, including energy for the lights.

At that precise moment, Holy Vangar shuddered and

rocked like a gigantic bell struck by an equally colossal
clapper. The lights dimmed even further, and Frane could
feel the intense vibrations rising into his legs and hips
through his bare feet, which were splayed on the cold
stone floor. He reached out and grabbed Nozomi, prevent-
ing her from falling as his tail reached out to anchor his
body against one of the ancient public gallery's many
metal railings. Shouts and cries spread through the crowd
like a chill stormwind blowing through stalks of grain.

Somewhere, lost inside that increasingly agitated multitude, were Lofi, g'Ishea, and Fasaryl, the three non-Neyel
members of Frane's Seekers After Penance prayersect.
Hours after the chaotic mass motions of the crowd had separated Frane and Nozomi from their spiritual brethren,
Frane could only hope that they were still all right.

Watching the milling throng of confused and bedrag-
gled refugees—Frane supposed there were thousands of
Neyel of all ages present in this gallery alone, mixed with
what might have been dozens or perhaps even hundreds of
Oghen aboriginals—Frane was hard-pressed to tell Nozomi that she was wrong. *If these people succumb to
panic,* he thought, *then we'll all be just as doomed as if
Vangar had collided with a neutron star.*

Frane took both of Nozomi's hands between his own.
He spoke soothingly to her, as though by calming Nozomi
he might also comfort all two-million-plus of the lost,
homeless souls who now clung to life within the very
same habitat that had brought the First Neyel to the Coreworld of Oghen centuries ago.

"We didn't survive the destruction of the Coreworld
only to die in the Sleeper's shadow," he told her, hoping he
sounded more confident than he felt. "Riker will see us
safely beyond His reach."

"How can you be so certain of that?"

He *wasn't* certain, not in the slightest. But if he didn't cling to hope, then what did he have left? He considered mentioning a Starfleet mission report he had listened to shortly after he had first come aboard *Titan;* the translated audio recounted how a much smaller number of vessels had successfully tractored an enormous space station across an interstellar distance. There was no reason to doubt that *Titan* and the Romulan flotilla could accomplish the same feat with Holy Vangar.

As he gazed silently into her deep, dark eyes, a sudden inspiration seized him, prompting him to put aside the space station tale. Instead, he raised his right hand, allowing the sleeve to draw itself back in Vangar's gentle, spin-generated artificial gravity.

"I'm certain we're going to make it because I still have to take *this* back to where it belongs," Frane said, holding his story bracelet up and turning it into the dim light so she could see it clearly.

"Your father's wristlet?" Nozomi said, clearly puzzled. "But there's no way to bring it home, Frane. The Sleeper has swept the Coreworld away."

His answer was interrupted by a low rumble that he felt coming up from beneath the stone floor—"down" being the direction of Holy Vangar's outer crust—just before he actually heard it. Then came a roaring detonation whose report swiftly reached deafening proportions even as it rocked the Holy Vessel far more roughly than any previous blow the habitat had sustained.

An alarm klaxon, unused for ages and nearly inaudible beneath the rising din, echoed across the cavernous gallery.

Then darkness fell, and panicked screams drowned out everything else.

I.K.S. DUGH

"Captain!" Dekri shouted. Her voice strained to be heard over the violent thrumming of the *Dugh*'s overtaxed engines.

"Report, Lieutenant," Tchev said, turning his command chair toward his de facto first officer's station. His gauntleted hands gripped the arms of his chair as though he might be thrown loose from it at any moment.

"I am detecting variances in the tractor beams the Romulan fleet has attached to us," Dekri said, sending an illustrative graphic to the bridge's central viewscreen. It presented a wireframe rendering of the *Dugh*, tethered to perhaps a half-dozen straight lines attached to structurally strategic portions of the Klingon warship's compromised hull. Some of those energy tethers appeared to be pulling more tightly than others.

"Do you see what they're doing, Captain?" Dekri said, fear and anger coloring her words.

Tchev bared his teeth as he studied the torsions that threatened to pull the *Dugh*'s starboard impulse generator apart. "Lock whatever weapons we have upon the *Valdore*! Send all available hands to battle stations."

The hull moaned, making a sound like *Gre'thor*'s massed hordes of *Fek'lhr*.

"At once, sir," Dekri said, in tones that made it clear that she realized how hopeless the situation was. She knew as well as he did that the *Dugh* was in no shape for combat. But they would die in battle because of this order, at least technically. He prayed it would be enough to get him and his crew into *Sto-Vo-Kor*.

"Ensign Krodak! Get me *Titan*. Riker must be told what those cowardly Romulan *petaQ* are trying to—"

Tchev was interrupted by a sound as thunderous as an eruption of the Kri'stak Volcano on Qo'noS, followed by infinite darkness.

U.S.S. TITAN

"The Vanguard habitat has begun venting atmosphere, Captain," Jaza reported, his manner calm but intensely concerned. "I'm reading unprotected bodies in space. That last spatial disruption evidently disabled at least one of our emergency forcefield generators and tore all the way through into the asteroid's hollow interior."

Damn! Riker thought, gripping the armrests of his command chair nearly hard enough to snap them off entirely. "How bad is the damage?"

Jaza remained intent on his console and the readouts that were quickly scrolling there. "The good news is that the outgassing is falling off quickly. I'd estimate from the volume of atmosphere vented that only one pressurized section has been compromised. They were fortunate."

Except for the people who happened to be in that section, Riker thought. "Can the people in that section be beamed out?"

"Not without lowering our shields," Jaza said, sounding stricken. "We can't do that, and neither can any of the other ships in the convoy. Even if there were enough time, and if there weren't so much refractory metal in the asteroid's crust . . ." He trailed off, his meaning plain. Although there had been some documented cases of Neyel surviving for prolonged periods in a hard vacuum, everyone in the space-exposed section was sure to die.

Riker nodded slowly. "How many casualties?"

"It's hard to say for certain, sir," Dakal said, facing

Riker from the forward ops station. "Upwards of ten thousand, I would estimate."

Riker's shoulders sagged as though he'd been dealt a physical blow. He tried not to picture the faces of the children, the elderly, the helpless. Not to mention Vale, Keru, Tuvok, Mekrikuk, and the medical and security teams still working among the Vanguard refugees.

The bridge shook and rattled as though *Titan* had come under attack. Riker spun his chair back in Jaza's direction. "*Titan* has just crossed the phenomenon's event horizon, Captain," said Ensign Lavena, her gloved, webbed fingers entering commands into her console at a rapid clip.

"Shield status?" Riker asked.

"Shields at ninety-four percent and holding," said Dakal. He sounded intensely relieved that the passage home was so much smoother than *Titan*'s accidental arrival in the Small Magellanic Cloud had been. At least so far.

"Convoy status?"

Dakal touched one of the control surfaces before him, bringing a tactical diagram up on the main viewscreen. A congeries of blips dutifully appeared, representing Vanguard and the Romulan fleet. The convoy blips were towing the Vanguard blip through a wireframe representation of the Red King and the interspatial corridor that ran directly through its heart. A large white icon that represented *Titan* was taking the point, leading the way for the entire procession.

"Everything seems to be going according to plan, Captain," Lavena said unnecessarily.

"Sensor web remains fully operational," Dakal reported. "All navigational hazard telemetry links show green as well."

"At least the Vanguard habitat doesn't seem to be taking any further hits," Jaza said. "Probably because we're approaching the midpoint of the spatial rift."

The eye of the storm, Riker thought. He fervently hoped they wouldn't encounter still more trouble once they reached the other side, where Romulan space presumably awaited them.

"Crossing the midpoint . . . now," Lavena said.

"The *Valdore* is signaling, Captain," said Dakal. "Twenty-nine of her ships have just jettisoned their warp cores, per our simulations. The crippled vessels are riding their own collapsing warp bubbles to the other side."

Feeling a sensation of pins and needles in both his hands, Riker realized that he was once again gripping his chair arms far too hard. He released them with a conscious effort.

"Brace yourselves," Jaza said. "The subspace shock wave should reach us in thirty-one seconds."

Riker touched his combadge again. "Riker to Ra-Havreii."

"Engineering. Ra-Havreii here."

"This is the part where you earn your combat pay, Commander. The shields are your highest priority."

"We're ready for anything, Captain," said the chief engineer, though the tremulous undertone in his voice didn't inspire a great deal of confidence. *Don't fold up on me now, Doctor,* Riker thought.

"Something's wrong," Jaza said sharply.

Of course, Riker thought, rising from his chair and crossing to the railing that ran alongside the main science station. "What's the problem, Jaza?"

The Bajoran shook his head in confusion, his nasal wrinkles spreading upward and onto his forehead. "It's the *Dugh*, sir. I'm reading extreme stresses on her outer hull.

Maybe she isn't standing up to Donatra's tractor beams as well as we thought she would."

Oh, no. Riker paused to study Jaza's readouts momentarily before turning his attention back to the main viewscreen's tactical display. *Please let me be wrong.* "Cadet Dakal, hail Captain Tchev and try to warn him. And get me Donatra."

"Aye, Captain."

At that precise instant, the viewscreen blip that represented the Klingon vessel abruptly brightened, then vanished.

Ashen-faced, Dakal turned from his console to face Riker. "Captain, the *Dugh*'s hull has just collapsed. She was completely destroyed in the resulting reactor explosion."

Deanna told me you were hiding something, Donatra, Riker thought, a white-hot anger searing the inside of his chest as he returned to his seat. *And now I think I know what it was.* The chair's autorestraints gently snapped into place across his thighs as the final seconds before the shock wave's approach ticked away.

Titan rocked again, this time far more violently than before. The bridge seemed to invert completely before righting itself. The lights failed. Darkness enfolded Riker, as though he suddenly had been plunged beneath the frigid waters of Becharof Lake during an Alaskan winter.

He ceased thinking about the *Dugh,* the convoy, the Vanguard colony, the away team, the Red King, and everything else.

CHAPTER TWENTY

Ensign Crandall looked up from his engineering boards. If the warp core hadn't suffused the entire engine room with a deep, blue glow, the junior engineer's narrow, hairless face would surely have looked as white as a *mugato*.

"Dr. Ra-Havreii, the warp field is destabilizing!"

But Ra-Havreii didn't need to look at Crandall's readouts to understand that. The sudden, random syncopations and dissonances now thrumming up and down the length of the two-story-tall matter-antimatter dynamo that constituted *Titan*'s heart made the trouble obvious enough to him.

Ensigns Paolo and Koasa Rossini busied themselves rerouting a maze of EPS power taps in an effort to lower the warp core's steadily rising temperature. Nearby, crouched under the alarm-festooned master situation monitor, Cadet Torvig Bu-kar-nguv worked at the matte-black matter reactant injector controls, using both of his telescoping bionic appendages as well as the grasping hand situated at the terminus of his long, prehensile tail. Other trainees and technicians moved to and fro, comparing what was on their padds to the displays that appeared on various consoles.

Klaxons blared. *Titan* shook. The computer spoke, its manner irritatingly calm. *"Warning. Antimatter containment failure imminent. Warning."*

Sweat sluiced down Ra-Havreii's back, soaking into his uniform, turning his long white hair lank, and flattening his drooping, gray mustachios against his brown cheeks. He ignored this as best he could while grappling with his steadily rising fear.

He tried not to think about how his predecessor Commander Ledrah had died, roasted to death in this very engine room.

He tried not to recall the explosion that had torn through the engineering section of the *Luna*, the starship that had served as the prototype for *Titan* and all the other vessels of her class.

He tried not to imagine the treetop canopy of Efros Delta's forests accepting his dying essence into the eternal bliss of Endless Sky.

He tried not to visualize the soil of his homeworld tearing itself asunder beneath his feet, leaving him to tumble headlong into the much-feared volcanic fires of the Efrosian underworld.

The ship bucked and rocked again, harder this time. *"Warning. Antimatter containment failure in thirty seconds. Warning."*

Moving to the duty console that Crandall was using, Ra-Havreii gently pushed the young human aside. Closing his eyes, he concentrated on the sounds the warp core was making as it strained against the combined influences of interspace, subspace, de Sitter space, and perhaps even his own personal demons and unquiet old ghosts.

"Computer, manual override on antimatter intermix ratios," he ordered. "Authorization Ra-Havreii Delta Efros Delta Zeta."

He placed his left hand on the manual intermix vernier and closed his eyes. His hand and his ears became all that existed in the universe. He listened to the deep, increasingly discordant cry of the engine core with the same attentiveness he'd once devoted to learning the tribal lays of Efros Delta's ancient forest priests. His hand moved gently on the vernier in response to what his ears told him from moment to moment.

This time, he was determined not to fail. Even if success meant ending up as Ledrah had.

Riker was summoned back from the darkness by the shrill peal of klaxons. His eyes opened to the sight of *Titan*'s bridge, which was bathed in the subdued red tones of emergency lighting.

Until he glanced down at the chronometer's glowing readout on the left arm of his command chair, he had no clear sense of how long his interval of unconsciousness might have lasted. Counterintuitive though it seemed to him, only moments had passed since the universe had tumbled into oblivion all around him.

Seated behind the ops and flight control consoles set just forward of the captain's chair, Dakal and Lavena were moving groggily, as though both were recovering from a light phaser stun. His eyes drawn to his right by movement, Riker saw that a shaken-looking Admiral Akaar was helping Eviku up from the deck beside the secondary science station. At the console beside Eviku's, Jaza was al-

ready hard at work, a livid red cut on his forehead providing the only clue that he'd experienced anything the least
little bit out of the ordinary. Crewman Kay're crossed in
front of him, shedding feathers as he moved unsteadily toward the port-side ops station from which he had been
thrown during *Titan*'s passage into the rift.

Thoughts of the rift—along with the enigmatic hash of
random static now being displayed on the main
viewscreen—chased the last of the cobwebs from Riker's
mind.

"Cadet Dakal, kill those klaxons," he said. "And show
me what the hell is going on outside. Jaza, get me sensor
readings on our present position, asap." Until they had
some hard data to go on, there was no way to tell whether
Titan and the rest of the Oghen rescue convoy had made a
successful transit back to near–Beta Quadrant space, or
had instead taken a perhaps fatal interspatial detour.

The klaxons abruptly ceased and the bridge fell at once
into a subdued silence, which made the faint sloshing of
Lavena's hydration suit conspicuously audible. Moments
later the interference on the viewscreen began to clear, like
the fog over San Francisco Bay reluctantly retreating from
the wan summer sun.

There, dominating the screen, was the Red King in all
its multicolored glory. All angry ambers and blood reds,
its energetic tentacles seemed to reach directly toward
Titan even as its indistinct boundaries appeared to be expanding, slowly but inexorably, toward the screen's periphery, gradually painting over the underlying starfield.
Whatever this phenomenon had become, one thing
seemed clear: it was no longer in a peaceful slumber.

"Looks like our Sleeper may have woken up on the
wrong side of the bed," Riker said quietly.

"But at least *we* seem to be on the correct side of *it,*

Captain," said Dakal, turning toward Riker. In the dim, ruddy lighting, the young Cardassian's gray, almost scaly flesh looked like the patina of corrosion on one of the ancient copper statues in Golden Gate Park. "This is an aft view. We are now moving away from the phenomenon, at warp two point two."

"Then we've come out the other side?" Riker wanted to know.

"Position confirmed, sir," Jaza said, looking up from a semicircle of glowing displays. "Stellar positions are a match with those observable from our last recorded position in Romulan space prior to *Titan*'s initial passage through the spatial rift."

"Very good. Ensign Lavena, maintain our current heading," Riker said. Renewed hope surged within him, but he kept it firmly tamped down, at least until he knew what had become of the refugees, the convoy, and the people he had stationed aboard Vanguard.

"Aye, Captain," said the Pacifican conn officer. She turned her chair toward Riker and fixed him with an alarmed expression. "However, the phenomenon is expanding toward us quickly. It's propagating directly through subspace at high warp—and it will overtake our present position in approximately three minutes at our present speed."

"Noted, Ensign." Riker spun his chair toward Jaza. "How about it? What will happen to *Titan* when this thing gets close enough to give us a good-morning hug?" he asked, though he already felt certain that lingering here was far from his best option.

"Unpredictable, Captain," Jaza said, shaking his head. "But it's definitely not an experiment I'd advise anyone to try."

So I have slightly less than two minutes to decide

whether or not to cut and run, Riker thought, facing forward and once again staring into what might have been the very maw of Hell itself. "Maintain present speed for now, Mr. Lavena. Mr. Jaza, Convoy status?"

The Bajoran answered with another glum shake of the head. "There's no sign of them yet, Captain. There's been no response to our hails, even on the navigational hazard data channel we've been maintaining with them since our departure from the Oghen system."

The faces of friends and colleagues flashed unbidden before his mind's eye. Chris. Keru. Tuvok. Frane, his friends, and some two million of Frane's people and their former slaves.

Riker silently upbraided himself. Now wasn't the time for grief, personal or otherwise. Even if the worst had befallen both Vanguard and Donatra's escort fleet, there were still nearly three hundred others aboard *Titan* whose lives would depend on whatever he did, or failed to do, next.

He tapped his combadge. "Riker to engineering."

"Ra-Havreii here, sir," the designer-turned-chief-engineer said. He sounded utterly weary, but Riker couldn't spare the time to ask him why.

"Commander, please tell me your engines can still give me warp six or better at a moment's notice."

"It was touch and go there for a while during the passage through the rift, Captain. But at the moment my warp drive is, as you humans sometimes say, willing, ready, and able."

Riker heard a note of cheer enter Ra-Havreii's voice, and it buoyed him. "That's music to my ears, Commander. We may need to leave in a hurry, and *very* soon. Riker out."

He stared at the main viewscreen, gazing into the roiling, expanding depths of the inexorably approaching Red King.

" 'May' need to leave, Captain?" Akaar said, his voice a low, almost subterranean rumble.

Riker shot a hard glare at the admiral. "As Mr. Dakal just said, we don't know what will happen if and when the Red King reaches us. But we also don't know whether or not we'll have another chance to recover the convoy, or even to find out what the hell happened to them, if we leave now." Turning toward Dakal, he said, "Auxiliary power to the sensor web, Cadet. Mr. Jaza, keep searching every cubic meter of that energy cloud's interior."

"Understood, Captain."

"Two minutes until contact," Lavena said, sounding at least as nervous as she had on that long-ago evening in the embassy swimming pool on Pacifica. Riker realized then that he had to be more than a little overwrought himself, to be recalling that particular incident *now*, of all times.

The turbolift hissed open, drawing Riker's attention long enough to allow him to see a weary-looking Deanna Troi step out onto the bridge. She quickly crossed to the chair at Riker's left.

"You should be resting, Commander," Riker said quietly, noticing the dark circles under her eyes. "Dr. Ree's orders." Now that the fate of Vanguard and everyone aboard her lay in the lap of the gods, he felt acutely guilty about the sense of relief he'd experienced when Ree had persuaded her to return to *Titan*.

She smiled crookedly, crossing her arms across her chest. "I tried, Captain. I only came up to complain about all the noise. What did I miss?"

He tossed a curt frown her way and concentrated on the emotional-mental link they shared. *Let's hope you didn't get here just in time for the end,* Imzadi.

Don't mind me, then, Will, she thought back to him. *Get to work. And let's try to stay positive, shall we?*

She was right. Settling backward into his command chair, Riker stroked his beard, dismissed his doubts, and tried to project an aura of calm deliberation to everyone on the bridge.

"Anything yet, Mr. Jaza?"

"Negative, sir." Jaza's utterance was freighted with an uncharacteristic burden of despair. Riker considered all the times he had nearly lost Deanna forever, and wondered whether the science officer was having similar ruminations about Christine, who had remained on Vanguard. He was aware that the Bajoran had experienced a great deal of loss already, thanks to the decades-long Cardassian occupation of his homeworld. And he had noticed the way that Jaza sometimes studied Vale when he thought no one was looking.

"There's a great deal of interference inside the phenomenon," Jaza said. "Continuing scans, active and passive modes."

Several more eternities passed. Finally, Lavena interrupted one of them. "Forty-five seconds until contact."

Riker once again found himself gripping the arms of his command chair nearly hard enough to disrupt his circulation. In front of him, the boundaries of the Red King had reached those of the viewscreen. The background stars were no longer visible.

"Thirty seconds," Lavena said quietly.

"Will?" Deanna said, patient yet clearly concerned.

"Captain?" Akaar said, his tone sharp. "I cannot permit you to commit *Titan* to an act of *w'lash'nogot.*"

Riker tore his gaze away from the Red King. Though he wasn't certain he understood the reference the admiral had made, he gathered that Akaar thought he was contemplating suicide. *Doesn't he know me better than that by now?*

In a tone as sharp as Akaar's, he said, "We're not going anywhere until we absolutely have to, Admiral."

Riker glanced to starboard toward the main science station, where Jaza was frowning in apparent perplexity.

"What is it, Mr. Jaza?"

"The Sleeper is . . . *changing*, sir."

Riker rose and approached the railing that separated the lower bridge from the circle of duty stations that surrounded it. "Changing *how?*"

"It's thinning out, Captain. *Disintegrating.* And I think I'm finally picking up the subspace blast wave from the detonations of all those Romulan warp cores, though it's already become highly attenuated."

"I'm picking up a large-scale gravimetric flux along the phenomenon's event horizon," Eviku reported.

"Meaning?" Riker asked.

"Meaning the spatial rift itself is starting to collapse as the energy cloud continues to spread out and dissipate," Jaza said. "The protouniverse itself appears to be retreating into de Sitter space."

"It's withdrawing back to wherever it came from," Deanna said, tilting her head as though trying to listen to faint, faraway voices.

Fear clutched at Riker's heart in earnest then, though it wasn't for himself or even for his ship. *The door out there is slamming shut on the Red King's heels—and the convoy is still on the wrong side of it. There really* won't *be another chance to locate them if we can't do it* now.

"Fifteen seconds, sir," Lavena said, sounding more than a little apprehensive.

Riker glanced at Akaar, who continued to glare down at

him from the upper bridge. Before the admiral could say what was obviously on his mind, Riker touched his combadge as he crossed back to his command chair.

"Commander Ra-Havreii, stand by to warp out of here at my signal." Riker took his seat, staring resolutely forward as the Red King entered what appeared to be its death throes. He reached to his left and squeezed Deanna's hand.

Good-bye, Chris. Ranul. Tuvok. Damn!

"Ready, Captain," the Efrosian engineer said.

"Ten seconds," Lavena said.

"Captain!"

Jaza's unexpected cry braced Riker, like an adrenaline injection delivered directly to the heart. Still seated, he faced his senior science officer. "Jaza?"

The Bajoran's words came in rapid-fire succession. "Romulan warp signatures, just inside the cloud. Seventeen, no, eighteen of them, on roughly our heading—along with a large, rocky body."

Riker noticed that a handful of bright stars had become visible through the expanding, still-attenuating cloud. Dozens of other small, starlike shapes moved quickly in front of those distant suns, as warp-powered vessels towed a single larger one, along with the two dozen or more of their fellows that had crippled themselves in order to pull the rift closed while passing through interspace. The orderly procession moved as one in a graceful arc, like a descending swarm of meteors.

Even as the Red King effect grew ever larger and more transparent, revealing the indifferent stars that lay behind it, a hard realization struck Riker: there was absolutely nothing further that either he or *Titan* could do to help the convoy escape the Red King's final agonies.

Vanguard and her escorts would either survive now, or they wouldn't.

"Mr. Ra-Havreii, Mr. Lavena: Ahead, warp six."

IMPERIAL WARBIRD *VALDORE*, STARDATE 57097.6

It had been an extremely rough ride. Donatra thanked every god she could think of that the convoy had emerged from the waves of interspatial turbulence essentially intact.

"The Bloom is . . . *gone,* Commander," Liravek said, though it clearly wasn't necessary for him to say so aloud. But the centurion's aquiline features revealed such a study in astonishment that Donatra was inclined to overlook his lapse.

From her command chair, Donatra gazed back at the starfield being displayed across the front of the *Valdore*'s bridge. Except for a few wispy, vestigial remnants of what had once been the blazing, energetic ferocity of the Great Bloom—the enormous celestial maw that had swallowed the fleet she had once been so foolish as to hide within its fringes—space had resumed its familiar empty aspect. It now appeared black and infinite, intermittently bejeweled with local stars, distant galaxies, and ordinary nebula and dust clouds—just as it had for the billions of years preceding the detonation of Shinzon's thrice-cursed thalaron weapon.

Also discernible among those ancient stars were several dozen other small, steadily moving lights: her fleet, and the enormous life-bearing rock it continued to tow away from the now-vanished spatial rift.

Still another purposefully moving pinprick of light appeared, heading quickly toward the *Valdore*. Donatra intuited its identity immediately.

"Titan has just dropped out of warp, Commander," said Decurion Seketh, who was running the main operations console. "She's on an intercept course, five-hundred *k'vahru* distant, decelerating and closing. Captain Riker wishes to speak with you."

No doubt, Donatra thought as she rose from her chair. Her body felt heavy with fatigue, and her old wounds stung and burned her. "I will take it in my ready room, Decurion."

Once she was alone inside the small, private office adjacent to the bridge, she glanced down at the carpet. She noticed the tiny greenish-black spots spattered there. Suran's blood stared up at her in silent accusation.

Crossing to the desk, she activated the computer that sat atop it and dropped into her seat.

Riker's face appeared immediately. He was clearly furious.

"You blew up Captain Tchev's ship while the convoy was passing through the rift. Why?"

"Captain Riker. It's so good to see you again, too. Is your channel secure?"

"Of course, Commander. Nobody can hear our conversation but the two of us. Now: Why did you destroy the Dugh?"

Donatra schooled her face carefully until she felt certain it was free of any display of either guilt or innocence, anger or amusement. *A Vulcan would be proud,* she thought wryly.

"A great deal can happen inside a phenomenon like the Great Bloom, Captain."

"Are you denying *it, Commander? I trust I don't need to remind you that I have a Betazoid on board."*

She sidestepped his question, and his anger, lest her own be roused. "We have been allies, Captain. But I am a

Romulan, loyal to the Star Empire first and foremost. And the Klingons are our sworn enemies, the Dominion War alliance notwithstanding. You know this as well. So I ask you: Would you really believe *anything* I might tell you about the *Dugh*?"

"I'd believe the truth, Donatra. Governor Khegh is going to demand nothing less of me."

Donatra waved dismissively. "Governor Khegh won't want to admit in polite company that he sent a cloaked vessel to follow our ships into the Bloom in the first place. *Any* truth is therefore *more* truth than that fat, inept, Klingon *ryak'na* deserves."

"So you are *admitting it."* Riker looked disappointed, and Donatra found that this disturbed her even more than his outrage.

She retreated behind a shield of righteous anger. "I admit nothing, Captain. And as long as we are discussing truth, I must remind you of the promise you made to me."

"Promise?"

"Your pledge not to reveal that I was forced to cripple the majority of the ships in my fleet as part of our joint effort to neutralize the Bloom."

The human captain's brow creased into a perplexed scowl. *"What the hell does that have to do with the Dugh?"*

"Everything, Captain—that is, if I'm truly guilty of the charges you've leveled at me. If Khegh becomes as convinced of my treachery as you evidently are, he could very well figure out why I supposedly did this thing."

Riker paused, considering. *"Because Tchev would have reported that about half your ships jettisoned their cores inside the rift. And Khegh and the Klingon High Council might have seen that as an exploitable vulnerability."*

"Precisely. And Khegh would therefore decide that I would have had ample reason not to allow the *Dugh* to pass through the Bloom intact."

"So you're admitting you had a motive. You're making my case for me."

"Nonsense. Motive alone proves nothing."

"You also had means and opportunity, Commander."

In spite of herself, her anger began burning hotter than her wounds. "I'm not on trial, Riker, and you don't stand in judgment over me. *Take care* not to tread so heavily on our alliance. Don't forget, I control the Romulan fleet. That ought to make me someone you consider quite dangerous to trifle with."

Riker fumed in silence for a lengthy interval, clearly angered at having been so deftly outmaneuvered. *Federation humans,* she thought, her anger receding. *The best of them are so earnest and honorable. As well as naïve and tractable.*

"I won't lie for you, Donatra," he said.

"And I wouldn't dream of asking that of you, William. All I ask is . . . your discretion regarding the current vulnerable condition of my fleet. At least until a few weeks of repairs are behind us. We have deadly enemies on our doorstep, and the Empire's internal political stability remains in question, in spite of your noble efforts on our behalf. Surely you can appreciate the need to be . . . selective, at the very least, about what you decide to tell Khegh."

"Khegh's flagship is already on its way here, Donatra. His people will be scanning your ships. They'll know that half your fleet has been crippled."

Donatra allowed a tiny smile to escape onto her lips. Shaking her head, she said, "No, Captain. All they'll see are the false warp singularity-core readings being projected along our fleetwide internal subspace comm network from those of my ships that remain warp-capable. Khegh will learn only what I *wish* him to learn."

"Unless I decide differently, you mean."

"Consider your best interests, Captain. Your diplomatic mission to Romulus would be undone if anything were to add significantly to the antagonism the Klingons and their Reman clients already have for my people."

"True."

"And you still have to ferry the Neyel asteroid colony to the Neutral Zone so that Starfleet can tow it into Federation space. *Titan* cannot perform that task unaided. You need my cooperation and goodwill. Consider *that.*"

He glared at her, his blue eyes flashing like a pair of disruptor tubes. But she met his gaze without flinching.

"All right, Commander. You win this one. But you'd better understand something: Whatever 'honor debts' you might think I owe you, I hereby consider them all canceled. Titan out." He vanished from the screen without saying another word.

But his sour, disappointed expression seemed to leave a peculiar afterimage on the monitor screen. Focused, perhaps, through the lens of her conscience.

U.S.S. TITAN, STARDATE 57097.7

Vale woke up and immediately experienced a moment of extreme disorientation.

She began to remember where she was just as Jaza rolled toward her on the bed. She sat up, covering herself with a sheet as she rested her elbows on a heap of pillows, crumpled sheets, and bits and pieces of both of their uniforms. He smiled at her, apparently unfazed by their mutual nakedness.

They had ended up in Jaza's quarters, not hers, she recalled. It was the first place she had gone after reporting back to Captain Riker following her time aboard Vanguard.

"So. Hi there. Oh, boy," she said, stopping just short of addressing him as "Commander." She couldn't remember the last time she had felt so awkward. *What the hell have I just done?*

But she was also still intensely glad to see him, considering how close they both had come these past few days to never being able to see one another ever again.

"Are you all right, Christine?"

She laughed. "I'm good. Really good. Really."

Very gently, almost prayerfully, he took her hands between his own. Somehow, the sheet she had draped over herself remained in place; she suddenly felt embarrassed by her obvious attack of shyness.

"You seem uncomfortable," he said.

"Well, this does potentially change things between us, doesn't it?"

"How?"

"Well, for one thing, you aren't calling me 'Commander' anymore."

He chuckled. "Would you like me to?"

She answered with a laugh of her own, and the tension began to drain from her body. "Not at the moment. Maybe we can agree to leave Starfleet protocol on the bridge."

"Agreed. But seriously, do you have any regrets?" Jaza asked. "I don't. But I can certainly understand if you do. We're supposed to be officers, after all."

Vale nodded as she considered his question. Then she decided that her regrets would have been far worse had she not been honest with him about her feelings after her return from Vanguard. Who knew when some future emergency might separate them again, perhaps forever?

"If it's a problem—"

She placed a finger over his lips, interrupting him. "If it's not a problem for our captain and our chief diplomatic officer, then I suppose it doesn't have to be for us." Then she kissed him.

After they withdrew from the kiss, they remained reclining on his bed, regarding each other in expectant silence.

"Tell me what you're thinking," he said finally.

She grinned in response. "Are you sure you want to know?"

"Of course." Another one of his beatific smiles was slowly spreading across his face.

"All right. I was wondering what we're going to do for the next hour until we're both due on the bridge."

"I could make a suggestion or two," Jaza said. "Anything else?"

She grinned. "Yes. I was also thinking what a wonderful surprise it was to find that Bajoran men have ridges in places other than their noses."

She rose back onto her elbows and let the sheet drop away from her. Then she put her hands on his shoulders, and pushed him onto his back.

Standing just out of the sight lines of the comm system's visual pickup, Deanna Troi sensed her husband's barely contained frustration. It felt like a tightly coiled spring that might let loose at any moment, lashing out at everything in its path.

To his credit—or perhaps to his detriment, Troi

thought—not a trace of any such emotion was reaching Will Riker's face as the dour, gray-haired Klingon dressed him down from the computer screen sitting atop the ready room's Elaminite wood desk.

"I still don't think you've told me everything you know, Riker." Khegh, general in the Klingon Defense Force and governor-administrator of both the Romulan continent of Ehrief'vil and the newly brokered Klingon-Reman Protectorate, snarled from the small desktop monitor screen.

Will leaned forward across his desk, placing his elbows on either side of the ancient leather-bound book that lay open there. "Governor, all I can tell you is that the *Dugh* did indeed make it to the other side of the rift, in the Small Magellanic Cloud. She was heavily damaged during the transit, though, and apparently didn't survive the return trip. If you want more of the particulars, why don't you ask Commander Donatra?"

"Bah!" Khegh waved a large, gauntleted hand in front of the screen, momentarily throwing the picture out of focus. The plenitude of medals that crowded the front of the governor's ornate diplomatic vestments clattered noisily against one another. *"With all the trouble I've had these past few days dodging Rehaek's Tal Shiar assassins and trying to keep Praetor Tal'Aura from coming to blows with Colonel Xiomek and the rest of the Reman leadership, I have had a bellyful of ambitious Romulans. Let the diplomats deal with Donatra and her ilk from now on."*

Same old Khegh, Troi thought, shaking her head in silent amusement. *Never mind that he's the closest thing to a diplomat his government has in the entire Romulan Empire.*

"Governor, I regret the *Dugh*'s destruction nearly as much as you do," Will said, his manner suffused with a degree of empathy that would have done credit to an experienced ship's counselor. "Captain Tchev and his crew were fine officers."

According to Troi's recollections of the past several days, Tchev and his people had been anything but helpful during the Red King affair. But she also knew that there was no percentage in pointing that fact out to Khegh.

The hefty old warrior leaned back in a chair that looked nearly as heavily padded as he was. *"Nonsense, Riker. Tchev was an idiot. After all, he allowed those Romulan petaQ to kill him and destroy his vessel without a battle. None of the* Dugh*'s crew deserve a place in either the Hall of Heroes or* Sto-Vo-Kor. *Khegh out."*

As the governor's snarling face was replaced by the familiar starscape-and-laurel-leaf symbol of the Federation, Troi sensed that her husband's frustration had suddenly grown acute once again. *So that's what this is about. He not only regrets not being able to come clean about what Donatra did to the* Dugh, *he also wishes he could embellish the truth a bit so that Tchev and his crew would at least get a shot at the Klingon afterlife.*

She crossed to the chair where Will still sat, staring into the blank screen. Her hands reached out to the muscles of his neck and shoulders, which felt as hard as tempered duranium.

"Don't beat yourself up about the *Dugh* and Donatra, Will."

He looked utterly desolate. "Donatra played me. I trusted her, even became her ally. And she played me."

During the hours since the Vanguard convoy's return from Neyel space, Will had told her enough about the circumstances surrounding the destruction of the *Dugh* to convince her that he was being far too hard on himself.

"Donatra only did what she thought she had to do, Will. You have to remember that Romulans are still Romulans, our recent détente efforts notwithstanding. Sometimes our interests converge with theirs, and other times things go the other way."

He looked up at her, frowning. "Are you saying that Romulans can't be trusted as a species?"

"No, of course not. But I *am* saying that it takes time to build trust. And I'm also saying that you can't expect to win *every* battle."

Glancing up at her, he smiled gently. " 'Sometimes you get the bear, and sometimes the bear gets you.' Hey, I think I may have finally found our elusive dedication plaque motto."

She chuckled. "Keep on looking, Will. But there's a useful truth there, too. You may think Donatra 'played' you, but you've had your share of success recently doing the very same thing to the Romulans. In case you've forgotten, *you* maneuvered Praetor Tal'Aura into accepting a Klingon-Reman protectorate right in her proverbial backyard just last week. And you've just had an even *more* important success: Without you, the Neyel and who knows how many other species would probably have been entirely wiped out of existence."

"Because I persuaded Donatra to use her fleet to close the rift."

"Exactly." She was beginning to wonder if he was being deliberately obtuse, until his dark mood argued otherwise. Clearly, there were aspects of this mission she didn't yet completely understand.

"I just spoke with Dr. Cethente about that," he said, his words punctuated by a wave of sorrow that seemed almost capable of knocking her off her feet. "We really don't know for certain that closing the rift stopped the Red King from 'rebooting' all the matter and energy in the affected sectors of Neyel space."

Her jaw dropped. "I'm sorry. I didn't know."

He offered her a small, sad smile. "There wasn't any point in holding a senior officers' briefing about it. After all, it isn't as though we can do anything about the outcome, two hundred and ten thousand light-years away from Ground Zero."

"How soon will we know exactly what happened?" Troi asked.

"Cethente says that even with our most powerful subspace telescopes, it could take decades to find out exactly what that emergent protouniverse did after we entered the rift and sealed it after us. So there's no way to know if our Red King eventually woke up and annihilated the entire Neyel Hegemony, or if he settled back down for another harmless, billion-year nap."

She nodded. "So I guess there's no point in agonizing over it. Right?"

"Try sitting in the big chair for a while, Deanna. From that perspective, it's usually pretty tough to do anything *but* agonize. Take the away team on Vanguard, for example. I *finally* managed to find out that they were all safe only about ninety minutes ago. So what's a captain to do in the meantime? *Agonize.*"

She nodded again, caught in another gale-force wind of his sadness and self-recrimination. She almost felt she had to raise her voice to cut through it.

"Then I suggest you focus on your unambiguous successes, Will. For instance: There are over two million people aboard Vanguard right at this moment. You saw to it that they survived, regardless of whatever might or might not have happened to the rest of Neyel space."

He rose then and took her in his arms. His icy blue eyes were bright with unshed tears. "Thank you, Deanna," he said before pausing momentarily to recover his composure. Being an empath, she found the gesture endearing.

"Oh, by the way Counselor," he added. "I never gave you a formal 'welcome aboard' after Ree sent you back to *Titan*."

They separated then, though not enough to break the embrace. They regarded each other in silence, and she met his tired smile with a wry grin of her own.

"I'm glad you finally noticed that," she said. "But I know how busy you've been." *Everyone* had been busy.

"I'm sorry, *Imzadi*. I expect things to calm down by tonight, at least a little, once Ra-Havreii completes the damage inspections on Vanguard and we get back underway with her toward the Neutral Zone. Then I plan to execute a new plan."

Her grin widened. "Oh? Do tell."

"It's called Operation: Welcome Home, but as far as the rest of the crew is concerned the code name is Operation: Do Not Disturb. You are requested, and required, to participate. Captain's orders."

"I'm intrigued. Brief me."

His smile quickly glissaded from fatigued to playful. "Phase One involves my leaving the keys to the store in Chris's capable hands. During Phase Two, I'll go to our quarters and open that bottle of jakarine merlot that I've been saving. And Phase Three is actually a lot easier to demonstrate than it is to explain."

He moved in to kiss her and she turned her face toward his.

She was utterly unsurprised when his door chime sounded. *It never, ever fails,* she thought as the mood shattered. *Ever.*

He disengaged from her, his eyes tightly closed as he massaged his temples with both hands. The gesture made him look like a Vulcan attempting to perform a mind-meld on himself. "Come!" he said sharply.

The door whisked open. Frane entered, followed by Tuvok and Akaar, who had to duck slightly to avoid brushing his head against the top of the doorway.

"Have we come at a bad time?" Akaar said.

Will gestured toward the couch that was situated along the wall nearest the desk. "Not at all, Admiral. What can I do for you?"

Tuvok sat first. Moving with surprising grace, the big Capellan took a seat beside the Vulcan. This was the first time Troi had seen them both together since the evacuation of Oghen had begun. Though neither of them were displaying any more overt emotion than usual, Troi noticed immediately that something fundamental had changed between these two very reserved men. *Have they finally put aside their differences, whatever they were, after all these years?*

"I have been in touch with Starfleet Command, Captain," Akaar said. "A contingent of SCE vessels will rendezvous with *Titan* and Vanguard at the Federation side of the Neutral Zone. The Federation Council has granted Donatra's fleet permission to tow Vanguard that far. From there, Vanguard will be towed back to the Sol system, where I will confer with Starfleet Command and the Federation Council on the problem of finding the Neyel and the other species aboard Vanguard a permanent home."

"I hope we have the option of visiting Auld Aerth itself," said Frane, who had remained standing. "If not settling there."

Auld Aerth. In Troi's perception, the young Neyel's almost worshipful emotional state, coupled with his strange pronunciation of the name of Earth, conferred an almost mythic status on her father's homeworld. *Of course, to Frane—to all the Neyel refugees in the O'Neill habitat— Earth is mythic. A bedtime story told to children. The stuff of legend.*

"Lieutenant Pazlar is already searching the stellar cartographic records for a suitable permanent home for the refugees aboard Vanguard," Tuvok said.

Akaar nodded. "The search could take some time, however. Vanguard may serve indefinitely as a short-term home for the refugees while the council debates the matter, consults with the Neyel leadership, and takes its final decision."

"Mr. Frane has made an intriguing suggestion," Tuvok said. "At his request, Lieutenant Pazlar has widened her planet search to include K- and L-Class worlds that might be amenable to reasonably achievable terraforming efforts."

Will nodded, and Troi saw at once that he grasped Frane's reasoning even as she did. "To encourage the Neyel refugees to work cooperatively with their former slaves, rather than falling back into their old habits of exploiting them."

"Where in the Sol system does Starfleet Command intend to relocate Vanguard in the meantime?" Troi asked.

"Perhaps the asteroid colony can be placed in high Earth orbit in its original L-5 position," Akaar said. "The Neyel are humans, after all. Or it could be set in orbit around one of the Jovian or Saturnian moons."

Frane smiled broadly, though he still seemed unaccustomed to such facial gestures. "Saturn's moons intrigue me most, I think. Titan, for example, sounds like a nice place to get comfortable for a while."

Will smiled at that, and turned back to Akaar. "Speaking of *Titan*, Admiral," Will said. "When can we resume our original mission to explore the Gum Nebula?"

"Very soon, after you have stopped at Starbase 185 for repairs, and an inspection by Admiral de la Fuega. I caution you, Captain: she is tough."

Will's eyes widened in mock surprise. "Coming from you, Admiral, that's saying quite a bit." The huge Capellan responded with the subtlest of smiles.

Troi noticed then that Frane, his tail absently switching back and forth behind him, was looking with evident curiosity at the top of Will's desk. "What's this?" he said, pointing at the dog-eared book that lay open there.

"It's a journal, written by one of my ancestors," Will said, crossing back to his desk. "He was a soldier, and a survivor. I've carried his life story with me on every deep space assignment I've drawn since I graduated from Starfleet Academy. It has always served to remind me that no matter how far away from my homeworld I traveled, I had a commitment to survive."

Will closed the book carefully and carried it back to a broad wooden bookcase beneath a gold trombone and a bizarrely convoluted Pelagian wind instrument. He set the book gingerly on its display easel, right between a pair of U.S. Civil War–era Colt pistols. "At least long enough to get it back to the planet where Old Iron Boots Riker's bones are buried."

Frane continued staring at the book in wonder, and Troi sensed that he was all but overwhelmed by an emotion very akin to reverence.

Akaar rose from the sofa and approached Will, then beckoned Troi and Tuvok to approach as well. Lost in thought, Frane did not appear to have noticed.

"I have spoken with Dr. Cethente," Akaar said in hushed tones.

"So have I," Will said, nodding. "He says we can't know for certain whether or not we really saved Neyel space from nonexistence."

Akaar nodded, then trained his hard, dark gaze squarely upon Troi. "The question is: Should we tell Mr. Frane?"

"There's no need, Admiral," Frane said, still gazing in wonder at the book. He played absently with the elaborate bracelet on his wrist. Recalling what Will had told her of the bracelet's significance to Frane and his ancestors, she completely understood his fascination with Thaddius Riker's diary.

The Neyel turned to face them. "Auld Aerth existed as nothing more than a legend for centuries, as far as we Neyel were concerned. It was unreachable, unknowable, except in the realm of fables and stories.

"Oghen has been destroyed, and perhaps other key worlds of the Neyel Hegemony have died with it. Maybe *all* the Neyel places are gone. That is reality, and we must face that. We Neyel have been thoroughly punished for our past sins. Just *how* thoroughly is now a matter perhaps best left to fable and legend.

"But we endure. Enough of us, at least, to rebuild and create something worthier than fear and empire and conquest. And perhaps that is reality enough."

Troi sensed at once that everyone present agreed completely with Frane's sentiments. She could only hope that a majority of the people inside Vanguard were capable of seeing the universe the same way he did.

That, she thought, *would be victory enough.*

CHAPTER TWENTY-ONE

"It is good to see you, my husband," T'Pel said from the small monitor screen before Tuvok. *"At last."*

Seated behind the desk in his quarters—which was illuminated at the moment only by a pair of meditation candles, the light of the monitor screen, and the distant, glittering pinpoints visible through the window—Tuvok recognized the almost chiding tone that underlay his wife's otherwise calmly delivered words.

"I regret that I have not taken the opportunity to contact you before now," he said evenly. Even as he said the words, he found them inadequate; he silently reprimanded himself for not making more of an effort to call home sometime between his rescue from Vikr'l Prison and *Titan's* accidental detour to the Small Magellanic Cloud.

"I quite understand, my husband. My sources inside Starfleet informed me of your extended captivity on Romulus weeks ago. News of your subsequent . . . disappearance arrived only yesterday."

Tuvok couldn't help but wonder if Akaar had been among T'Pel's Starfleet "sources."

"I am gratified that your most recent absence was not nearly so protracted as the last one," she said.

"As am I, my wife," he said. Imprisonment and yet another accidental voyage to a remote region of space had made him more conscious than ever before of the brevity and fragility of life. "And I wish to take steps to ensure that we never again have to endure such a prolonged separation."

"Have you decided to leave Starfleet again?" she asked, regarding him expectantly.

He told her his idea.

Ranul Keru stared into the mirror, then winced as he touched the scar on his chest. The spanner had stabbed deeply into him; according to Dr. Ree, his injuries would have killed him instantly had his internal organs been arranged precisely identically to those of a human. Keru considered himself extraordinarily lucky that *Titan*'s first voyage had only left him with a nasty scar, three missing days because of his coma, and some very bittersweet memories.

Although Dr. Ree had offered to fix the scar tissue, Keru wanted to keep it. It was visible now when he was shirtless, but eventually the hair they'd shaved off his chest would grow back again and cover most of it. It was a wound that he had *earned,* and one that would remind him not only of his own mortality, but of the gains and losses inherent in his job. He considered it almost a badge of honor.

He'd been determined from the start never to lose or sacrifice a member of his security team—as Lieutenant Commander Worf had done years ago back on the

Enterprise—and thus he had trained his people hard, working them to the top of their potential and demanding still more beyond that. And yet, circumstances had led to his own injuries and coma, the loss of Feren Denken's arm after the prison rescue mission on Romulus, and more recently, the choice he had made on Oghen that had resulted in T'Lirin's death. He was aware of the curse of wearing security gold—their job was to put themselves in harm's way, after all—but he had never expected things to go so badly so quickly.

He closed his eyes and once again saw the bottomless stein of bloodwine that still haunted some of his dreams, frothing and bubbling malevolently. He recognized it now for what it was: not just his anger and resentment toward Worf for killing Hawk, but also his fears that he, Keru, would also turn into something he hated.

As he reached for his tunic, he came to a decision. *It's time to concentrate on looking forward. And maybe it's also time to start talking to someone about Worf.* But not Deanna. She had been too close to the situation; Keru recalled hearing her mention that she had once been romantically involved with the Klingon officer. On top of that, he didn't want to appear in any way weak or vulnerable in front of the captain's wife. He hadn't gotten a read on Counselor Haaj yet, and the tiny, blue-furred Counselor Huilan seemed a bit too cutely creepy to be taken entirely seriously as a therapist.

But there was one person aboard he knew he could start talking to immediately, someone who had also experienced the loss of a loved one, and who had also known the Klingon who had brought him so much pain. And he knew that he could trust Alyssa Ogawa to minister to his emotional health as a friend just as she had helped repair his body in her position as *Titan*'s head nurse.

Keru checked the chronometer mounted on one of the wall panels, tugged his tunic down one more time, then exited the room. The instant he entered the corridor, a body crashed into him, but the other, more slightly built figure took the brunt of the impact.

"Sorry, Commander Keru," the young man said. He held up a padd. "Wasn't paying attention."

Keru recognized the man as Lieutenant Bowan Radowski, the transporter chief, though he knew little else about him. "No harm done," Keru said, grinning. "But you might want to watch yourself in these corridors. You might trip over Chwolkk next time, and bumping into a Horta can be a head-over-heels experience."

"Understood, sir," Radowski said, then turned and walked away.

Keru took a few more steps, then turned to look at the retreating transporter chief. He saw Radowski turn back to do the same, then blush and turn away quickly.

Interesting, Keru thought.

He made his way to the turbolift, up to the bridge, then to the captain's ready room. Inside, Commander Vale was chatting with Captain Riker. Vale had a steaming cup of *raktajino* in one hand and a padd in the other as she sat in one of the chairs that fronted the starboard side of Riker's desk.

"Good morning, Mr. Keru," Riker said, standing and extending his hand in greeting across the desktop. Vale laid aside her padd and smiled up at Keru from where she sat.

"Captain, Commander Vale." He shook Riker's proffered hand, nodded to Vale, then assumed an at-ease stance immediately in front of the captain's desk.

"I have a ... modest proposal to make," Keru began.

• • •

Immediately after Keru left the ready room, Riker tapped his combadge and summoned two other members of his senior staff.

Tuvok was standing at attention in front of Riker's desk almost before his terse acknowledgment had ceased reverberating in the air.

"Commander Tuvok, reporting as ordered," he said as the ready room doors opened again, this time to admit Deanna, who stood beside Tuvok, looking equally businesslike.

Riker gestured toward the empty chairs beside the one Christine Vale occupied in front of his desk. "Please have a seat. You're both probably wondering why I've called you."

"I presume it has to do with the personnel rotations being planned for *Titan* after her arrival at Starbase 185," Tuvok said as he and Deanna sat.

"Right. I want to talk to you about the future."

Tuvok's left eyebrow lofted itself. "Indeed."

"I want you to stay aboard *Titan*, Mr. Tuvok. Permanently."

"Sir?"

Riker thought that Tuvok's face was registering about as much surprise as a Vulcan could handle. Deanna and Christine were both taking this in stride, of course; both were already in the know about his decision, particularly Vale.

"You heard me, Commander," Riker said, smiling. "In a very short time you have become an invaluable member of this ship's crew."

"Thank you, sir."

"Your experience in Starfleet as a teacher, an intelligence operative, and as *Voyager*'s second officer makes you too valuable an asset for us to lose. Unless, of course, you're determined to leave."

"Respectfully, sir, I have merely been filling in for Commander Keru during his convalescence. I am certain that Dr. Ree will soon pronounce him fit to resume a full duty schedule, if he hasn't done so already."

"I think you're misunderstanding us, Commander," Vale said. "Commander Keru is staying on."

"Captain Riker has merely decided to . . . reallocate his duties," Deanna said.

"Commander Keru was initially assigned to *Titan* in a dual role as security chief and tactical officer," said Riker. "Ranul himself suggested that we split those jobs up. He has agreed to stay on as chief of security—if we can count on you to serve as *Titan*'s permanent senior tactical officer."

"Of course, this posting would be very different from teaching at the Academy," Vale said, "or skulking around alien capitals for Starfleet Intelligence."

Tuvok nodded, and lapsed into a contemplative silence that lasted for several seconds.

"Were I to accept this position," he said at length, "I would have to make one request that might seem somewhat unorthodox."

Riker grinned. "You're aboard *Titan*, Commander. Unorthodox is what we do best."

Tuvok paused again, as though to gather his thoughts. "*Titan* appears to be more tolerant of shipboard family living arrangements than other vessels of comparable tonnage," he said finally.

Riker exchanged amused smiles with his wife. He noticed then that Christine seemed to be blushing, and saw that Deanna had noticed it as well.

"Well, I suppose there's no denying that, Commander," he said to Tuvok. "Just ask Nurse Ogawa, or the burgeoning Bolaji family. So what's your 'unorthodox request'?"

"When *Voyager* was lost in the Delta Quadrant, I was separated from my wife, my children, and my grandchildren for seven standard years. Over the past week, I narrowly avoided experiencing another protracted exile."

Vale looked alarmed. "This ship has a three-hundred-and-fifty-person complement, Mr. Tuvok. This isn't a *Galaxy*-class luxury hotel. We're not exactly set up to accommodate extended families."

"Of course not, Commander Vale. Nor would I make such an imposition. My children are grown, after all. However, my wife T'Pel and I have already discussed her joining me on my next posting, whatever that proved to be. I believe she may be amenable to living with me aboard *Titan*, subject to the captain's approval, of course."

"Done and done," Riker said. "As long you agree to one of *my* requests."

"Captain?"

"You have to accept the job of second officer as well," Vale said. "Third in command, right after yours truly in *Titan*'s cutthroat power hierarchy."

Tuvok's eyebrow rose. "I would be honored."

"As will we," Vale said.

"Congratulations, Commander," Troi said with a smile.

Addressing Riker, Tuvok said, "Then I suppose I should get started in my new position immediately."

"Dismissed, Mr. Tuvok," Riker said, smiling.

"Thank you, sir. All of you," Tuvok said, then turned and exited the ready room.

As the ready room doors hissed closed on Tuvok's retreating back, Riker realized he had finally, at long last, found that elusive perfect epigram for *Titan*'s bridge dedication plaque.

CHAPTER TWENTY-TWO

AULD AERTH, STARDATE 57071.0

Frane shivered under a fog-obscured late-afternoon sun that supplied distressingly little heat. He looked out across the blue-green bay toward a series of large rocks, upon which several large, wet, black creatures made an apparently vain effort to sun themselves; some of them made strange barking noises as they turned their broad bellies toward the waning rays. Above them, white-winged birds circled lazily in the sky, screeching and chattering.

The sight was unlike any he had ever seen before, and yet somehow exactly as he had imagined it would be. He felt the cool soil—so different in texture from the gritty, volcanic sands of Oghen or any of the other old M'jalla- nish worlds—beneath the toes of his bare feet. The vegeta- tion was green here, rather than bluish, though he had seen some flowering plants that looked almost exactly like the sweet-smelling portangeas of home.

"So what do you think of this place?"

Frane turned, reminded by the voice that he was not

alone, and that this was not merely some dream of Auld Aerth. He saw the large, gray-haired man walking toward him through the manicured grass, his shoulder-length locks set into gentle motion by the light breeze. Now that he had taken the time to get to know Admiral Leonard James Akaar, he didn't find him nearly so intimidating as he had initially.

"It's . . . cold," Frane said, shivering again. He drew his simple penitent's robe even more tightly about himself, though it did little to keep out the chill.

Akaar laughed, a deep, rhythmic sound that wouldn't have been out of place in an Neyel space vessel's Efti'el compartment. "You might be surprised how common that complaint is. According to local legend, an ancient human writer once said that the coldest winter he ever experienced occurred here during summertime. Welcome to San Francisco."

Frane recalled what he had been told all his life about the progression of Auld Aerth's seasons; it was currently the dead of the ancestral homeworld's northern winter, a month and several days past the solstice.

"Regardless of the weather, Admiral, this world is truly beyond my imaginings," Frane said to Akaar. He pointed out to the sea.

"I hope you and your people will get to know it well," Akaar said. "After all, it is more your birthright than mine."

Frane nodded, though this was a difficult concept for him to get his mind around. Being Neyel, Frane was genetically human, though his people resembled no terrestrial racial group owing to their many genengineered traits. Akaar, however, hailed from an entirely different world and heritage, despite his almost completely standard human appearance.

Frane's eyes were drawn back across the bay, to the strange, intermittently barking animals. "What are those noisy black things?" he said, pointing toward the rocks with the spade-shaped tip of his tail.

Akaar peered across the water and smiled. "Seals. They like to sun themselves out there."

Frane didn't understand. "But I saw them go below the water. They breathe both water and air?"

"They are marine mammals. I sometimes regard them as a kind of compromise between people and fish. In fact, according to some very old Earth legends, there used to be creatures known as mermaids that were half-woman and half-fish. When sailors observed the seals at a distance, they sometimes mistook them for mermaids."

Frane pulled his loose-fitting sleeve up and looked at the bracelet that had been handed down through nine Neyel generations, all the way down from the sainted Aidan Burgess to him through his multigreat grandmatron Vil'ja. He finally located one particular small metal charm.

He held it up so that the admiral could see it. "Is this a mermaid?"

Akaar peered closer. "That is indeed a mermaid."

"It was one of the original stories," Frane said. "Burgess brought it with her to Oghen." *Lost, beloved, dead Oghen,* he thought, briefly wondering whether the extinguished Neyel Coreworld would one day become the stuff of Neyel legend the way Auld Aerth had.

Akaar placed one of his large hands on the Neyel's shoulder. "Come with me. There is something here that I must show you before you return to your people."

As they walked, Frane stepped over and around the stone slabs that lay nestled in the ground, or rose from it. Each of them bore witness to someone from Auld Aerth, people who had been here once, but were no more.

After spending several minutes quietly looking at the stones and their inscrutable markings, Frane spoke. "I think we Neyel are like the seals."

"How so?" Akaar asked.

"We are half human and half something else. We are what we were made to become. Our Oh-Neyel fathers and mothers made us into something else."

"From what I know of your history, they had to alter the genetics of the people of the Vanguard colony in order to survive," Akaar said.

"They never expected that we would return," Frane said solemnly. He wrapped one of his hands around the bracelet, holding it in place on his arm as they walked slowly through the somber forest of inscribed stones.

Eventually, they reached a meter-high stone column, near a tree whose branches were laden with brown leaves, in bold defiance of the austere winter. Frane noticed other short columns as well, arrayed in concentric rings around the tree.

Akaar gestured toward some writing on the side of the nearest column. Frane could see the familiar chevron that the *Titan* crew wore on their chests, but he could not decipher any of the text.

"What does it say?"

Akaar crouched and pointed. "It says 'Aidan Burgess, Ambassador and Peacemaker.' "

Frane was confused again. "Why is this *here?* Burgess was assassinated on the Coreworld."

"This is an area where the Federation places markers commemorating those who have fallen in its service but are never recovered. Since Burgess's body was never brought back, they eventually placed this marker here in her stead."

Frane nodded solemnly. "She has a much bigger cenotaph on Oghen." He realized his slip, and quickly added, "Had."

Akaar gave a curious grin. "Well, she may have been more highly regarded by your people than by ours. She did not make a lot of friends toward the end of her career."

The notion astonished Frane, but he kept his thoughts to himself. He touched the cool stone, then wriggled the story bracelet off of his wrist.

"I have brought the stories back to Auld Aerth," he said to the column. "Where the oldest of them originated, with Burgess and her ancestors."

Akaar sat beside the column, his long legs folded beneath him. "Tell me about the bracelet," he said.

And Frane did. He spoke of Burgess's childhood, of her adventures exploring the world of her birth, and later, of the multiplicity of worlds that had surrounded her. He told of her coming to Oghen, of the life she had lived there, of the incremental yet necessary changes she had helped bring to Neyel society, and of the legacy she had left behind. With each story, he held up a tiny charm, until the skies had darkened to deep purples and his voice had grown tired and hoarse.

He stood and placed the bracelet atop the column, then slowly backed away. Akaar stood as well, a confused look in his eyes.

"You are leaving it here?"

Frane nodded. "I have returned it, full of memories. It belongs with Burgess."

Akaar shook his head, his iron-gray hair crowned in a nimbus of fog-shrouded city lights. "No, it belongs with someone who will tell its stories. It belongs with *you*, Frane. You should keep it, and pass it along to your children, and they to theirs."

Frane saw the man hesitate, then reach out to grasp the

bracelet. He brought it over to the Neyel and held it out to him.

It was probably the first time that someone other than a Neyel had touched the bracelet since the time of Burgess. And yet somehow it seemed right for Akaar to be handing it back to him. Akaar had *known* Burgess, had worked alongside her, and more recently, had helped to save the Neyel and the other M'jallanish native races from oblivion.

Frane took the bracelet and slipped it back onto his arm, then turned and began picking his pathway across the sprawling graveyard.

Akaar quickly caught up with him, but said nothing. They walked on in silence as the winter shadows lengthened farther.

"What will you do now that you are no longer aboard *Titan*?" Frane asked eventually.

"Oh, I was never formally assigned to *Titan*," Akaar said. "In fact, I have not had a permanent shipboard posting for many, many years. I sometimes think the fact that I am unwelcome on my homeworld keeps me from putting down roots of any sort elsewhere. Even on a starship."

"I gather that there were . . . complications regarding your actions on Oghen?" Frane asked. He wasn't certain how—or if—he should even bring up the subject.

Akaar stopped and looked skyward, into the gathering night. Frane also paused to look up, and saw that a smattering of unfamiliar stars, constellations he knew only from ancient drawings and photographs, was becoming steadily more visible. The gentle wind had intensified enough to send the fog into retreat, though enough of the haze remained to smear the lights of the city into a colorful wash across the southeastern sky.

" 'Complications' would be putting it mildly," Akaar said at length. "But I shall weather whatever storms may come. I have been doing this for far too long to do otherwise."

The admiral looked back over to Frane. "And what of you, Frane? What are *you* going to do next? You are considered something of a hero among the Oghen survivors now."

"When Starfleet secures a permanent home for my people, I may settle there," Frane said.

"That could take months. Perhaps years. What of the meantime?"

Frane sighed, and his tail switched back and forth in a classic Neyel expression of indecision. "I don't know."

Akaar's mien grew serious. "If I were you, I would not stay away from the Vanguard habitat for too long."

That piqued Frane's curiosity. "Why?"

"Because you could wield considerable influence over the people there. If you wanted to, that is."

"The people aboard Vanguard are safe from the Sleeper," Frane said, shaking his head. "That's the only influence I wish to wield over them."

"Is it? Once you wished divine retribution upon them."

Frane lowered his gaze to the carpet of greenery that blanketed the cemetery. He absently picked at it with the fingers of his right foot.

"Much has changed since then."

"Yes. And things will go on changing, whether you wish to pay attention to them or not. Whether you want it to happen or not."

Frane was quickly growing uncomfortable with the subject at hand. "What are you trying to tell me, sir?"

"Only that you have earned a certain degree of

celebrity among your countrymen. You could use it to lead your people."

Frane began to laugh then, and found it difficult to stop. "I am no leader. Just a seeker who has failed at just about everything he has ever tried."

Akaar shrugged. "Maybe you are. It does not matter. Your people perceive you as a savior right now, and *that* is all that matters."

"Leadership is something my father was good at, Admiral. But it is not a talent I share. I am no drech'tor. Perhaps such gifts skip a generation."

"Whether you understand it or not, you have already led your people this far. But I caution you: fame is a fickle mistress."

Frane shook his head, confused. "I do not understand."

"You have a narrow window of opportunity, Frane. If *you* miss it, I guarantee that others will *not*. And some of those might grasp the mantle of leadership with far less altruism and probity than you have demonstrated."

A queasy sensation settled deep in the pit of Frane's stomach. "You speak of Subaltern Harn."

"He is no longer a mere junior military officer, Frane. He was as visible as you during the evacuation of Oghen. Your people will listen to what he has to say. Perhaps even follow his leadership."

Gods, Frane thought with a shudder that had nothing to do with the chill winter evening. "Harn is a throwback to a much crueler age."

He recalled how contemptuously Harn had treated his aboriginal coreligionists and traveling companions. "Kaffirs," *he called them. They were just colonial wogs to him. Just like my father.*

Such men were indeed throwbacks to a horrible, formative period in Neyel history—paranoid, violent times that Aidan Burgess had spent her life working to help Frane's people outgrow. The influence of such men on frightened, dispossessed people could well undo all the progress toward peace that had been achieved since the bloody Devil Wars of the previous hundred cycle.

But maybe it really doesn't have to be that way.

Frane looked up and saw that Akaar was studying him carefully. He had no idea how long they had both been standing there in the glow of the nearly full moon that had just risen into the eastern sky.

Akaar chuckled gently. "Sometimes the best leaders are the most unwilling ones, Frane."

He felt the future coming down on him, giving him far too many things to think about at once.

"Do you recall Nozomi?" Frane asked.

Akaar nodded tentatively. "The female Neyel who was part of your religious sect?"

"Yes. I am considering formally asking her to become my partner."

Akaar clapped a hand on Frane's shoulder. "Good for you. Marry. Start your own family. You will build a future that you may even be willing to fight to protect.

"And you will have someone to tell your family's stories. Someone who will carry them forward."

Nozomi. One of the Starfleet audio texts he'd heard aboard *Titan* had explained that the name meant "hope" in the Terran language known as Japanese.

Frane raised his arm and looked again at the story bracelet. For the first time in years—perhaps since he was a child himself—he began to feel some genuine hope for the future. He still wasn't entirely sold on the idea of pursuing a leadership role in the rebuilding of his society. But he knew that the uncertain and tumultuous process of establishing a new life and a new home for himself and his people was a journey worth taking.

One of the rocks on the bracelet glinted as he turned his arm, and Frane lifted his gaze from that speck of brilliance into the evening sky, where billions of stars beckoned and promised the future.

CODA

Deanna Troi stood just inside the doorway and watched Mekrikuk. The huge Reman was dressed in the plain black Reman military jumpsuit that Nurse Ogawa had replicated for him, and he turned to face the transporter stage. He exchanged courteous nods with his escorts, Lieutenants sh'Aqabaa and Sortollo. The security officers—Andorian and Martian-human respectively—were already standing in at-ease positions on two of the rear transporter pads.

The fearsome-looking Reman turned back to face Will Riker, Tuvok, Ranul Keru, and transporter chief Bowan Radowski, all of whom stood behind the transporter console in front of Troi.

"So this is good-bye," Will said.

"Farewell," said the Reman. "I understand that in another three days you'll be getting under way on your original mission of exploration."

Will nodded. "We're bound for the Gum Nebula, in a

region of the galaxy beyond the space known to the Federation."

At long last, Troi thought, with no small amount of eagerness.

"I'll bet Starbase 185 won't be nearly as exciting as life aboard *Titan,*" Keru said.

The tall, chalk-white alien displayed his fangs in a smile, a facial gesture that Troi was gratified to discover no longer made her feel uneasy. Mekrikuk had more than proven that beneath his wide, battle-scarred chest beat a truly noble heart.

"After everything I have experienced since Vikr'l Prison, I would find a certain amount of boredom agreeable," Mekrikuk said in a pleasing tenor voice that didn't at all comport with his fierce countenance. "Besides, I do not believe my continued presence would be appropriate aboard a ship of exploration. I am certain that Starfleet would agree with that assessment."

"You have unique talents, Mekrikuk," Tuvok said. "Those talents saved countless lives on Vanguard, and will be sorely missed."

Mekrikuk nodded at the man the Romulans had once so brutally imprisoned with him. "Let us all hope then that your need for such talents remains infrequent, Commander Tuvok. Perhaps our paths will cross again one day. After my . . . immigration issues have been fully resolved, of course."

"Has Admiral de la Fuega scheduled a hearing yet on your request for political asylum?" Troi asked.

Mekrikuk shook his head. "I suspect that Starfleet Intelligence will wish to debrief me first."

"I'm sure they will," said the captain. "But only under Admiral de la Fuega's direct supervision."

Troi sensed some trepidation coming from Mekrikuk,

whose Romulan interrogators and jailers had doubtless more than justified such fears.

"Don't worry," Troi said. "Starfleet Intelligence is *not* the Tal Shiar." *At least, not most of the time.*

Will nodded. "And Alita de la Fuega is an honorable woman. I wouldn't want to trade places with any SI inter-rogator who tries to step out of bounds on *her* starbase."

He nodded, and Troi sensed that Mekrikuk was greatly reassured. Then he turned again and stepped up onto the transporter stage.

"Good-bye, Mekrikuk," Troi said.

"I am sure we will all see one another again," the Reman said. "Someday."

"Peace," Tuvok said. "And long life."

"Farewell, my friend," Will said.

"Farewell. Thank you all, and may Tenakruvek watch over you."

Will nodded toward Radowski, who slid his right hand forward across the top of the transporter control console. Mekrikuk and his escorts were instantly engulfed in a cur-tain of shimmering light, and then vanished entirely.

STARDATE 57080.6

Seated in her chair near the center of *Titan*'s bridge, Troi set down the padd she was reading and trained her eyes on the main viewscreen. She was rewarded with a vision of the beautiful blue world *Titan* was orbiting. But as lovely as the sight was, she felt more than ready to move on, as did everyone else on board. The buzz of eager anticipa-tion that energized the entire crew buoyed her, almost burying her traumatic memories of the death of the planet Oghen.

Almost.

Titan was quickly approaching the daylight terminator of Iota Leonis II, the aquamarine M-Class world upon which the sprawling Starbase 185 compound lay. The starbase's position in the Federation's Beta Quadrant frontier made it not only the closest starbase to *Titan* after her return to Romulan space, but also made it an ideal jumping-off point from which to access the rimward reaches of the Milky Way's vast, mostly uncharted Orion Arm.

The time had come to resume *Titan*'s original—and interrupted—mission of exploration; that mission had been the new starship's raison d'être prior to the emergence of almost simultaneous crises in the Romulan Empire and the Neyel Hegemony.

Now *Titan* was ready to get back to her real work. The last of her repairs, which had primarily involved the replacement of a number of compromised hull plates, EPS relays, and a few related circuits, had been completed hours ago. Every crew member who had taken shore leave at the starbase was now back on board. The repair technicians that Admiral de la Fuega had loaned to Dr. Ra-Havreii had all been returned to the planet's surface. *Titan* was ready, at long last, to cast off into the unexplored, as was her crew. Ahead lay the Gum Nebula, and the seductive beckoning of the Unknown.

But Troi knew that this ship wasn't going anywhere until Will tended to one final piece of unfinished business.

Glancing to her right, Troi noticed that Christine Vale seemed to be having similar thoughts.

"You're still staring at it," Troi said to Vale's back, obviously not referring to the planet that was turning majestically on the viewscreen, hundreds of kilometers below.

Vale chuckled as she turned the captain's chair back toward the front of the bridge. "Sorry to be so fidgety,

Deanna. But when Will took down my suggestion box, he left a huge, conspicuous bare spot on the bulkhead. I have to look right at it every time I use the turbolift. It's impossible to avoid, the way your tongue keeps going after a missing tooth."

"I wouldn't know about that, Chris. I still have all my teeth." Troi grinned broadly, displaying them.

Vale returned her smile with almost equal wattage. "I know, Deanna. Have I told you how much I hate you for that? You obviously never worked in security."

Troi stifled a guffaw behind the back of her hand as the turbolift whooshed open. She turned toward the sound and watched Bralik and Cethente moving out onto the bridge, the latter perambulating so smoothly on his four, outwardly splayed lower limbs that he almost could have been mounted on wheels.

Bralik stepped over to the bridge railing near where Jaza was working at the main science station. Troi noticed then that the Ferengi geologist had a bottle tucked under her arm. The bottle complemented the rack of delicately fluted champagne glasses that hung from one of Cethente's four tentacle-like upper appendages.

Bralik immediately fixed her gaze on the bare spot on the bulkhead that Vale had pointed out. "Good. They've finally taken the suggestion box down. Looks like the decision's been made. I just hope we haven't missed the ceremony yet. When do the festivities start?"

Personally, Troi had had more than enough of ceremonies of any sort, after the recent memorial services for Chief Engineer Ledrah and Lieutenant T'Lirin. The latter, who had been lost during the Oghen evacuation, had been memorialized in a very brief but dignified service, per the Vulcan security officer's own written directives.

But with T'Lirin's memorial still only five days in the

past, Troi could well understand the need that some of her colleagues might have for other, more life-affirming rites in the wake of so much recent sorrow.

Vale rose and crossed to the railing that ringed the bridge's central section, approaching Bralik. "Ceremony? We hadn't planned to make a huge production out of this, Bralik. It's really not a big deal."

Bralik's eyes grew large. "Not a big deal? *Not a big deal?*" She raised the bottle and produced a gleaming corkscrew with all the panache of a professional stage magician. "Any time a starship gets its official motto installed is a cause for celebration. It's like . . ." She paused, seeming to have to grope for an acceptable metaphor. ". . . like when a Ferengi business concern publicly unveils its mission statements."

" 'Statements'?" Troi asked, rising from her chair. "Why do they need more than one?"

Bralik regarded her as though she belonged to some newly discovered variety of idiot. "There's the one the company shows to the Ferengi Commerce Authority. And then there's the *real* one that management shows its employees."

Vale shook her head. "I still wouldn't make too much out of this, Bralik. It's just a dedication plaque, for crying out loud."

Bralik snickered as she opened the bottle, which made a loud "pop" but fortunately did not shower the deck with the bottle's contents. The Ferengi addressed Cethente as she accepted a glass from him. " 'Just a dedication plaque,' she says." To Vale, she added, "So why did you spend *weeks* agonizing over piles of quotes and epigrams from all over the galaxy?"

Vale hiked a thumb toward Troi. "My counselor says I work too hard. I needed a hobby."

Seated, respectively, at the forward conn and ops consoles, Ensign Aili Lavena and Cadet Zurin Dakal exchanged amused looks with Lieutenant Rager, who stood nearby.

Bralik let the vapors from the open bottle's neck drift toward her wrinkled nose. She made an approving face. "If you ask me, Commander, I think you're just trying to play down the competitive aspect of this situation."

"I wasn't aware of any competition," Vale said.

"Wasn't the captain's 'Help Select *Titan*'s Dedication Plaque Motto Suggestion Box' intended to be a competition?"

Vale shook her head. "I really don't think so, Bralik. The captain just wanted to give everyone's ideas a thorough hearing."

"You're only saying that because you want to soften the blow when you lose the contest," Bralik said.

Troi couldn't restrain herself from chuckling. "So you must think you have a much better chance of winning this 'competition' than Commander Vale does."

"Damned right I do, assuming all the entries get evaluated fairly. Of course, I probably don't stand as good a chance as *you* do, Counselor. After all, I'm not sleeping with—"

"Okay," Vale said, interrupting. Troi noticed that she and Jaza exchanged veiled, significant glances at that moment. "You don't want to go there, Bralik, trust me. And another thing: I've read all the entries in this 'competition,' and yours didn't exactly make our short list."

Troi couldn't get a reliable emotional "read" on Bralik, of course, because Ferengi brains were completely opaque to Betazoids. But she thought that the geologist looked genuinely wounded.

"Why?" Bralik asked.

Vale, too, was now having trouble holding back her laughter. "I'm sorry, Bralik. But 'tip your waiter' is not quite something I'd classify as a starship-worthy motto."

Bralik shrugged. "That's just because you Federation folk have a cashless economy. In the Ferengi Alliance, those are words to live by, believe you me."

The turbolift opened again, this time disgorging engineering trainee Torvig Bu-kar-nguv, astrobiology specialist Kent Norellis, and Lieutenant Eviku, the Arkenite xenobiologist.

"I hope we haven't missed the big unveiling," Norellis asked, beaming at Vale and Troi.

Torvig waved one of his biomechanical limbs toward the bare spot on the wall. "Obviously not."

"Then our wager is still on, Cadet?" said Eviku, tipping his long, swept-back cranium to the side as he regarded the Choblik engineering trainee.

"Our wager is still on," Torvig said.

"Wager?" Cethente asked in a tinkling voice that sounded almost as though his rack of champagne glasses might have just learned to speak. *"What have you and Mr. Eviku wagered on?"*

Eviku's eyes met Troi's, and he flushed baby-blanket pink with embarrassment. "I know it's not quite regulation, but I saw no harm in placing a small bet."

Vale frowned. "A bet on what?"

"On the outcome of Captain Riker's final decision regarding the dedication plaque motto," Eviku said. Then he turned his piercing gaze upon the ostrich-like Torvig.

"Cadet?" Troi said.

"May I speak freely?" Torvig asked.

Vale smirked. "All right. But just this once."

"I thought that Captain Riker might give preference to

a motto written by a human author. Sir. That is the thesis of my wager with Lieutenant Eviku."

"Because the captain is human?" Vale asked, nonplussed. "I don't think you're giving him enough credit, Cadet."

"I understand, sir," Torvig said. "However, your perspective is much the same as the captain's, Commander. Thus you may have similar exosociological 'blind spots.' You, too, are human, after all."

Vale nodded, a look of understanding crossing her face. "Ah. So you think *Titan*'s command hierarchy may have a built-in, systemic human bias."

The Choblik seemed delighted to have been so clearly understood so quickly. "Yes, sir. Precisely, sir. I could not have said it better myself, sir."

Eviku leaned forward, interposing himself between Torvig and Vale. "For whatever it's worth, Commander, I took the other side of the wager. My thesis in this debate was that the captain would choose a nonhuman aphorism."

Vale sighed. "That's great, Mr. Eviku." Under her breath, she added, "Remind me to put a special commendation in your service record for that."

The turbolift shushed open yet again. Ranul Keru, Dr. Ra-Havreii, and Melora Pazlar—the latter leaning carefully on her garlanic wood cane—tried to step out onto the bridge. They all looked surprised to see the room's aft portion so crowded.

"Whoa. What's going on?" Keru said, still standing in the turbolift's open doorway.

"The captain is evidently about to settle a bet for us," Vale said, deadpan. "In front of an audience."

"I think we still have room for a few more, Ranul," Bralik said with a smirk. "Step carefully, though; it's gonna be standing room only in here pretty soon. Start passing out those glasses, Cethente. I'll pour the drinkables."

"You know alcohol's not allowed on the bridge, Bralik," Vale said with a scowl, even as the Syrath got started distributing the glasses.

"Oh, snuff-beetle squeeze, Commander," Bralik said, raising the bottle as though for inspection. "This is syn-thale, not Klingon *warnog*." Cethente had frozen in mid-motion in a pose that made him look like some sort of garment rack—but not before he had placed glasses into the hands of Troi and Vale both. Troi looked toward the aft tactical station, to which Keru, Pazlar, and Ra-Havreii had retreated because there seemed to be so little room to stand anywhere else.

Troi sighed and shook her head as Bralik bulled ahead and began pouring the clear, sparkling liquid. *Somehow I don't think this is exactly what Will had in mind when he mentioned wanting a "quiet, dignified little dedication ceremony just for the bridge staff."*

The turbolift door opened once again. Dr. Ree stood in the threshold, his eyes nictitating rapidly in surprise at the crowd. "I think I'll come back later," he said. He took a single step backward and started to let the doors close in front of him. Bralik stepped into the aperture, which forced the doors back open. With her free hand, she grasped one of Ree's forelimbs and drew him insistently onto the bridge, forcing everyone to move forward in order to make room.

Releasing the doctor, Bralik then emptied the bottle in her other hand and left it perched precariously on one of the railings. Troi reached out and grabbed it before it could get elbowed onto the deck, but the Ferengi appeared not to have noticed.

"So when is this party supposed to get under way?"

Bralik said, consulting the small chronometer on her left wrist.

"Nobody planned a party!" Vale said. "This is the *bridge!*"

A door slid open, but this time the sound wasn't coming from the turbolift. Troi turned toward the bridge's forward section and saw Will and Tuvok stepping out of the captain's ready room, almost in lockstep. Will was carrying a large, cloth-covered oblong object under his left arm. Tuvok wore a golden medallion that hung from a chain around his neck.

Will's blue eyes twinkled with delight when he saw the crowd that had gathered. Turning to Vale, he said, "A party! Great idea, Chris."

Vale's mouth dropped open; it took a moment for her to gather her wits and muster a reply. "Thank you, Captain. Synthehol, sir. All part of the service. And we'll be moving this little soiree to the crew lounge. Just as soon as you're ready, of course."

A smiling Bralik approached Vale, snatched the untouched champagne glass from her hands, and handed it to Will.

The captain grinned, raised the glass in a salute, then drained the small amount it contained in a single swallow. He handed the empty glass back to Bralik. "Drink 'em if you've got 'em, people. Computer, activate audiophile program Riker Zeta Four."

The bridge suddenly came alive with the strains of Earth jazz. Troi recognized it as "Bessie's Blues," as performed by John Coltrane, one of Will's favorite stylists from the Terran jazz age.

She cast an eye at Torvig, who craned his head toward Eviku. "Earth music. Doesn't that tend to validate my bias hypothesis?"

"Don't count your extra holodeck time before you've won it," Eviku cautioned.

The crowd parted, allowing Will and Tuvok to approach the conspicuous bare spot that persisted on the aft bulkhead. Very carefully, Will set the plaque into its permanent place of honor on the wall, at just below eye level. The plaque's covering of gold cloth remained in place.

Will beckoned Tuvok closer. "Mr. Tuvok, do the honors, if you please."

Tuvok nodded, his face and emotional aura more somber than usual. "Thank you, Captain," he said.

Moving with the grace and reverence of a soldier folding a flag that had shrouded a fallen comrade's casket, Tuvok lifted and removed the cloth covering from the plaque, revealing the engraved bronze surface for all to see.

U.S.S. TITAN
LUNA CLASS
STARFLEET REGISTRY NCC-80102
UTOPIA PLANITIA FLEET YARDS, MARS
LAUNCHED STARDATE 56979.5
UNITED FEDERATION OF PLANETS

There followed the long list of Starfleet dignitaries and principals associated with *Titan*'s development and construction, which included Commander Xin Ra-Havreii. And below that, the revered words of Surak of Vulcan:

"INFINITE DIVERSITY IN INFINITE COMBINATIONS"

As Will had intended, Tuvok spoke the words aloud, his voice carrying across the bridge and piped through the comm system to every part of the ship. Coltrane played on, improvising his way nimbly through a small jazz combo's complex and frequent harmony changes.

"Do Vulcans count as humans?" Torvig whispered to Eviku, apparently seeking a way to save his wager from the jaws of defeat. Considering that Torvig was nonhumanoid, Troi thought his question a fair one.

Eviku grinned triumphantly at Torvig, then began slowly applauding Tuvok's presentation. The applause spread first to Bralik, then to Keru, Pazlar, Jaza, Vale, Lavena, Rager, Dakal, Will, and just about everyone else who wasn't presently holding one of the champagne flutes that Cethente had already begun conscientiously gathering up. Troi joined in the applause, which had all but drowned out Coltrane's tenor saxophone.

At first, Troi had wondered why her husband had delegated the reading of *Titan*'s motto. But as soon as Surak's words had left the Vulcan tactical officer's lips, she understood the reason.

It had not simply been a gesture on behalf of diversity, or the Vulcan IDIC philosophy that so eloquently articulated it, and had in turn found expression in the composition of *Titan*'s crew. It was all of those things, to be sure. But it had also been intended to help them honor a fallen comrade, and to mourn her passing.

It's for T'Lirin.

The crowd of appreciative crew members quickly scattered as Cethente and Bralik finished gathering up the glassware they had brought. Troi took her seat, realizing belatedly that she was still holding the empty synthale bottle.

After exchanging yet another brief but significant glance with Jaza, Vale resumed her customary seat at Will's right. Then the captain sat in his command chair, leaning forward enthusiastically, his eyes riveted to the main viewscreen. Troi knew from his eager gaze and the tenor of his emotions that he was looking past the limb of the cerulean planet displayed on the screen.

Will Riker was already soaring among stars that his kind had not yet traveled.

"Lay in our course for the Gum Nebula, Ensign Lavena," he said, refulgent with the hope of a man who had just been granted a chance to start over. "Break orbit on my mark."

"Course already laid in, Captain," Lavena said. *"Titan* is rested and ready, sir. Just give the word." The upbeat, wailing strains of John Coltrane's sax continued to reverberate through the bridge.

"From the top, Ensign," Will said, raising his index finger as though it were a conductor's baton.

"Take it away."

THE VOYAGES OF THE
STARSHIP TITAN

CONTINUE IN

ORION'S HOUNDS

About the Authors

ANDY MANGELS is the *USA Today* best-selling author and co-author of over a dozen novels—including *Star Trek* and *Roswell* books—all co-written with Michael A. Martin. Flying solo, he is the best-selling author of several nonfiction books, including *Star Wars: The Essential Guide to Characters* and *Animation on DVD: The Ultimate Guide,* as well as a significant number of entries in *The Superhero Book: The Ultimate Encyclopedia of Comic-Book Icons and Hollywood Heroes.*

In addition to writing several more upcoming novels and contributing to anthologies, he is currently directing and scripting a series of sixteen half-hour DVD documentaries for BCI Eclipse, to be featured in *He-Man and the Masters of the Universe* DVD box-sets.

Andy has written hundreds of articles for entertainment and lifestyle magazines and newspapers in the United States, England, and Italy. He has also written licensed material based on properties from many film studios and Microsoft, and his two decades of comic-book work has been published by DC Comics, Marvel Comics, Dark Horse, Image, Innovation, and many others. He was the editor of the award-winning *Gay Comics* anthology for eight years.

Andy is a national award-winning activist in the Gay community, and has raised thousands of dollars for charities over the years. He lives in Portland, Oregon, with his long-term partner, Don Hood, their dog Bela, and their chosen son, Paul Smalley.

Visit his website at www.andymangels.com.

MICHAEL A. MARTIN's solo short fiction has appeared in *The Magazine of Fantasy & Science Fiction.* He has also co-authored (with Andy Mangels) several *Star Trek* comics for Marvel and Wildstorm and numerous *Star Trek* novels and e-books, including this volume and the *USA Today* bestseller *Titan: Taking Wing;* the award-winning *Worlds of Star Trek: Deep Space Nine, Volume Two: Trill—Unjoined; Star Trek: The Lost Era 2298—The Sundered; Star Trek: Deep Space Nine, Mission: Gamma, Book Three—Cathedral; Star Trek: The Next Generation—Section 31: Rogue; Star Trek: Starfleet Corps of Engineers* #30 and #31 ("Ishtar Rising" Books 1 and 2); stories in the *Prophecy and Change* and *Tales of the Dominion War* anthologies, as well as in the recently-released *Tales from the Captain's Table* anthology; and three novels based on the *Roswell* television series. His work has also been published by Atlas Editions (in their *Star Trek Universe* subscription card series), *Star Trek Monthly, Dreamwatch,* Grolier Books, Visible Ink Press, *The Oregonian,* and Gareth Stevens, Inc., for whom he has penned several *World Almanac Library of the States* nonfiction books for young readers. He lives with his wife, Jenny, and their two sons in Portland, Oregon.

**Don't miss the next
epic adventure of**

STAR TREK
TITAN™

ORION'S HOUNDS

by Christopher L. Bennett

**Coming in January 2006
from Pocket Books**

Turn the page for a preview. . . .

Will Riker had known something was about to happen before it started.

It wasn't due to any great captain's intuition, though. He just knew Deanna Troi, knew her every nuance of expression better than he knew his own. So when she'd abruptly grown distracted as they engaged in light banter with the rest of the bridge crew (well, all except Tuvok—the middle-aged Vulcan tactical officer wasn't the bantering type), he'd realized that she was sensing something, and readied himself for what she might say or do next.

What he hadn't expected was that Tuvok would be the first to react. Hearing a strangled baritone cry from the tactical station, Riker whirled to see Tuvok gasping and clutching the console for support. His teeth were clenched and he was clearly struggling for control . . . but his eyes showed panic and dread. Glancing over at Deanna, Riker saw the same emotions in her eyes, though she seemed to be controlling it better. "Mr. Tuvok, report," Riker snapped, hoping the appeal to discipline would help him focus.

"I am . . . receiving telepathic impulses . . . raw emotion . . . terror! Pain! Aahh!" He wrenched his eyes shut, fighting the panic.

As Riker moved closer to Tuvok, Deanna came up behind him. "I sense the same things. Fear, agony, loss . . . also anger."

"Why is it hitting him harder?" Vale asked.

Deanna looked away for a moment. "I've . . . had reason to learn to strengthen my shields against mental intrusion."

Riker winced at the reminder of Shinzon, and of the other mental incursions Deanna had been subjected to over her career.

But this was a time for business. "Is this the same thing you sensed the other night? The nightmare?"

"I think so."

Tuvok was still struggling. If anything, he seemed embarrassed by Troi's superior control. "Bridge to sickbay," Riker said. "Dr. Ree, we could use you up here."

"*I was just about to call you,*" came Ree's growling tenor. "*Several crewmembers have just come down with severe panic attacks. Cadet Orilly, Lieutenant Chamish, even Ensign Savalek and the Lady T'Pel. All psi-sensitives, sir. I imagine Commanders Troi and Tuvok are reacting similarly, are they not?*"

"I'm managing it, Doctor," Deanna told him. "But Tuvok is having a harder time coping."

"*If you will have him brought to sickbay, I should be able to suppress his telepathic senses.*"

"No, Captain," Tuvok said, gathering himself with an effort. "The initial shock . . . has subsided. I am . . . in control."

"I still want the doctor to look at you," Riker said.

"No! I . . . believe this to be a distress call. If so, the insights I can provide may be needed. They are only emotions . . . I am their master."

Riker turned to Troi. "Do you agree? A distress call?"

"I do," she answered without hesitation. "Something out there is pleading desperately for help. Something with a very powerful mind."

And what could terrify something that powerful? Riker wondered. Whatever it was, they would need to be ready. He looked over Tuvok, gauging his mental state. The Vulcan's reputation as one of the fabled *Voyager* survivors had preceded him, but Riker still didn't know the man well enough to tell whether he was really in control or simply putting on a brave front. He decided to give him the benefit of the doubt. "All right. You're relieved from Tactical, Commander—" He cut off Tuvok's protest with a look. "But you can remain on the bridge to advise."

Tuvok nodded stiffly. "Acknowledged."

"Mr. Keru, take over Tactical." The big Trill worked his security station's controls, slaving the tactical console to it. Riker turned to the tan-skinned Bajoran at the science station. "Mr. Jaza, scan the area for life signs, psionic energy, any unusual phenomena. Let's see who's trying to spread around their bad mood."

Jaza replied promptly. "Stellar Cartography reports strong life signs at bearing 282 mark 20, range point one two light-years."

"Is there a star system there?"

"Negative, sir. They're in open space, moving at high impulse. Hold on. . . . I'm getting energy discharges."

"A battle?" Christine Vale asked.

"Hard to tell. The discharges seem bioelectric."

"Let's find out. Ensign Lavena—set an intercept course, warp eight, and engage."

"Aye, Captain. Estimate arrival in three minutes."

As the ship jumped to warp, Riker moved back to Deanna's side. "Do you still get the sense of familiarity?"

"Yes, sir," she said, maintaining proper discipline while they were on the bridge. "It's extremely alien, yet it's something I've been in contact with before . . . a long time ago, I think. I'm trying to remember."

"I believe I can get a visual on long-range sensors," Jaza reported. "Just a moment . . . There."

Riker turned to the screen. At first all he saw was a group of pearlescent blobs of light, little more than pinpoints at this range. They were moving quickly, on erratic, independent courses. As Jaza worked his console, a set of crosshairs targeted the nearest blob and the screen zoomed in, tracking it. It was a translucent, rounded shape, apparently lenticular, with one face turned nearly toward their vantage point. "It reads over a kilometer in diameter," Jaza said. It was illuminated from within by a bluish glow and by numerous points of reddish light arranged in concentric rings. Faint radial striations subdivided its surface into eight wedges. Riker felt the same sense of uncertain familiarity that Deanna described.

Then it angled sideways, and Riker recognized it instantly. The eight long, feathery tentacles that trailed behind it, giving it the aspect of a vast jellyfish swimming through the lightless depths of the ocean, made it instantly recognizable. "The Farpoint creatures!"

Vale turned to him. "Sir?"

"We encountered them on our very first mission on the *Enterprise,* Deanna and I," Riker explained. "Sixteen years ago, in the Deneb system. I think we ended up calling them 'star-jellies.' They're shapeshifters, and more than that. They could read thoughts and synthesize any object you could think of, like living replicators. They even have transporter capability."

"They sound more like ships than living beings," Jaza opined.

"They're definitely life-forms," Troi told him. "Immensely powerful telepaths and empaths. I've never felt such overwhelming emotions. That first time, whenever I lowered my mental shields, it was like I became a conduit for their emotions, feeling them as if they were my own, and unable to resist them."

"I can . . . verify that assessment, Commander," Tuvok said stiffly.

"That would explain what's happening to the crew," Vale observed. "But what is it they're so afraid of?"

"There's a smaller cluster of objects closing on the, umm, school," Jaza said. "They read similar to the jellies, but different." He switched the viewscreen to a wider view. Harpoons of purple light were flashing through the school, scattering the star-jellies still farther.

"Shields on standby," Riker ordered Keru.

"Shields, aye," the burly, bearded Trill acknowledged. "And weapons, sir?"

"Not yet," Riker said as the attackers came into view. He recognized them as well: gray, lenticular metallic shapes, firing destructive blasts of violet plasma from their central concavities. "They're another form of the star-jellies—apparently their attack mode."

Vale frowned. "Have we stumbled into some kind of civil war?"

"It could simply be competition for food or territory," Jaza suggested.

"Either way," Vale went on, "I don't think it's something we have any business interfering in."

Riker realized she was probably right, though it filled him with regret. There was something ethereally lovely about the star-jellies. He still remembered the sense of awe he'd felt when they'd revealed themselves at Deneb, when the one held captive by the Bandi had shed its imposed disguise as "Farpoint Station" and ascended into space, and reached out to caress its mate's tendrils in a gesture whose simple poignancy transcended species.

"Why don't they fight back?" Keru asked. Riker realized he was right; the attacks were entirely one-sided.

"Maybe they can fire only in the armored mode," Jaza said.

"There's more," Deanna said. "Somehow they just . . . can't. Or won't."

Just then, one of the jellies was struck a dead-on blow to its ventral side, between the tendrils. Two of the wispy appendages broke free and spun away. At the moment of impact, Deanna and Tuvok both convulsed in pain, and Tuvok let out a strangled scream. Vapor erupted from the wound, and the jelly's internal lights flared, flickered, and then fell dark, first the blue glow, then the rings.

"Counselor? Mr. Tuvok?"

"Apologies, Captain," Tuvok said. "Not just . . . the creature's death throes. The others . . ."

Deanna nodded. "The grief of the others, combined . . . it's extremely intense. Even with my shields up I felt it."

"Can you sense anything from the attackers?"

She shook her head. "But I can't really probe without lowering my defenses, and I'm hesitant to do that."

"Tuvok?"

"I . . . do not believe there is anything to sense, Captain. The creatures feel the attackers are . . . *wrong* . . . a corruption . . . there is a revulsion, as though toward a corpse."

Deanna nodded. "Yes. These are like dead things to them, and yet they're attacking, menacing. The jellies feel a sense of mortal dread, as though the attackers were . . . well, the closest analogies I can think of are the zombies from old Earth monster movies."

Vale frowned. "Jaza, scan the attackers more closely for bio-signs."

"If I remember right," Riker told her, "the *Enterprise*'s sensors couldn't penetrate them. There are substances in their hulls . . . or hides . . . that resist scans."

"We've learned a few new tricks in the past sixteen years, sir,"

Jaza replied. It was an understatement; the *Luna* class carried prototype sensors beyond anything else in Starfleet. "Uh-huh, those hulls are well-shielded, but just give me a moment to calibrate . . . There. The attackers show limited activity in some biosystems, including propulsion and defense . . . but no anabolic processes, and nothing that resembles cognitive activity. The walking dead, indeed. But I'm also reading numerous biosignatures inside them."

Riker looked up at him sharply. "What kind of biosignatures?"

"Just a moment, I'm refining resolution. . . . They seem to be endothermic bipeds, about our size."

Riker exchanged a look with Deanna, then turned to Dakal at Ops. "Cadet, try hailing them."

"Hailing . . . No response," the young Cardassian said.

"A crew?" Vale asked.

"I've been inside two of these creatures," Riker said. "In at least some of their forms, they contain passages that resemble corridors, with a habitable environment inside. They certainly could be adapted into ships."

"And we've encountered living ships before," Deanna said.

"Except these people don't seem to need them alive," Riker said coldly. "Dakal, keep hailing. Ensign Lavena, put *Titan* between the attackers and the star-jellies. Mr. Keru, shields at maximum." Vale threw him a look but kept her counsel for the moment.

There were too many ships for *Titan* to block standing still. But she was light, fast, and maneuverable, and her pilot had grown up slaloming through Pacifican coral forests and dodging serpent-rays. Lavena flitted the ship around almost playfully before the attackers' sights, keeping them from getting a clean shot and probably making them dizzy to boot.

"We're receiving a hail," Dakal finally reported. That was a good sign. "Hailing frequencies" were a standard first-contact handshake protocol, allowing two ships' computers to begin with universal physical and mathematical constants and build a translation matrix in seconds, if their databases didn't already have any languages in common. Any warp-capable species with any interest in talking to strangers eventually developed such protocols. The return hail meant that the attackers had at least the willingness to communicate, and that was a good start.

"On screen," said Riker, turning to confront the attackers. When the screen came on, his eyes widened. He hadn't expected them to be beautiful. The screen showed a number of delicate-looking bipeds, slim-boned and decked with downy, green-gold feathers. Hawklike eyes stared from above sharp-toothed, beak-tipped muzzles, and vivid-hued, feathery crests topped many of their heads. Their feathered coats gave them no need for clothing, but they wore protective gear on their joints and vital areas, plus various equipment belts or harnesses and assorted insignia or sigils. Behind them was a passageway of familiar design, triangular and round-cornered, its ribbed, cardboard-brown walls embossed with intricate patterns that seemed neither wholly organic nor wholly artificial.

"Flit off, for your own sake," the one nearest the camera said curtly. He (the translator gave the being a gruff, nasal baritone) was far from the largest of the group, his headcrest was threadbare and faded, and there seemed to be considerable scarring beneath his feathery coat; but he carried himself with a casual yet undeniable authority. *"Our quarry won't linger if they have time to gather their warp fields!"*

"I'm Captain William T. Riker of the starship *Titan,* representing the United Federation of Planets. I don't know the nature of your conflict, but my people aren't inclined to sit idly by when we see sentient beings dying. We don't intend to take sides, but we'd be glad to offer our services as a neutral mediator in your dispute." His voice carried more steel than his words; he only hoped their translators were good enough to render it.

"You talk against the wind," said the avian, his matter-of-fact tone clashing with his poetic phrasing. *"Toy with cosmic fire, and the Spirit's not to blame for your burns. The Hunt must be!"* His image faded, leaving stars.

"Captain, they're firing on the jellies," Keru reported.

"Block it, Lavena! All crew, brace for impact!"